A Month of Tomorrows
Chuck Walsh

Vinspire Publishing
Ladson, South Carolina
www.vinspirepublishing.com

Chuck Walsh

A Month of Tomorrows

ISBN: 978-0-9890632-6-5

PUBLISHED BY VINSPIRE PUBLISHING, LLC

Dedication

This book is dedicated to Rubin Stout, one of the finest men I've ever known. Rubin mixes the perfect blend of manhood and mischief to enrich the lives of those who know and love him.

This book is also dedicated to my family. To my wife, Sandy – this wouldn't be possible if not for your love and support. Your continual faith was my guiding light. To my children, Jessica, Brent, and Stephanie – thank you for providing eager ears to my far-fetched hopes and dreams. I love you all.

To Mom - thank you for teaching me kindness and compassion. I love you. To Dad – I miss you and wish you were here, but I feel your spirit every day.
Most importantly, thanks to God for teaching me that all good things happen in His time, not mine.

Chapter One

Porter Bennett's Oldsmobile rolled along the dirt road known to the locals as Vaught's Holler. The dry summer had hardened the narrow lane and a haze of yellow rose up behind the car. The dawn had softened night's ceiling of black so that storm clouds rolling in from the west were visible above the skyline of Jefferson Mountain. Porter spotted the light on Samuel Gable's porch, the same one that had cut shadows into the hollow for over sixty years. He wheeled his car into the driveway, and through the windshield the house looked peaceful, surrounded by pear trees and purple larkspurs. He turned off the engine, heavy in thought to the callousness of life.

Porter had been Samuel's best friend since childhood, war and marriage the only events able to separate them. They were a fraternity of two, joined at the proverbial hip by the rainbow trout that ran the fast waters of Birch Tree Creek. They were never mistaken as choirboys, taking great pleasure in igniting outhouses and chasing hogs through Sunday morning worship services. But the passage of time had slowly sapped the fire within them, flattening them in ways they'd never thought possible. As if battling old age wasn't enough, the circumstance at hand made life as gloomy as hell.

Gabby waited on the porch. She stood at the top of the eight crusty concrete steps that led to the front door, steps that marked the entrance to a home trying to hold at bay a harsh reality of the present while fighting to keep hold of its past. Gabby wore faded blue jeans and a gray sweatshirt with APPALACHIAN STATE printed in black.

Though she wore no makeup, her face looked soft and tender, evoking more the look of a college coed than a woman staring down the half-century mark. She slid her fingers through her shoulder-length brown hair, binding loose strands behind her ears. She always did this when she was worried.

"Thanks for comin', Dr. Bennett," she said. Porter guessed by her tired eyes that it had been a sleepless night. "Daddy's in the parlor."

"Mornin', Gabby." Porter placed his arm around her shoulders, and she touched her head to his chin. "Why the parlor?"

"Said he's looked out over the spring pond for most of his days. He decided it was the best place to spend his last ones. God, I hate it when he talks like that. Anyway, I moved his hospital bed in there two days ago."

The house was two stories, made of wood. The paint, chipped and faded to a pale tint of beige, told the story of a home that had survived three generations of hard life. Inside, the house was neat and tidy. Gabby saw to that. She led Porter through the living room, its walls covered in dark wood panels. A large hearth, laid in stones of slate, lay quiet and unused. Above the fireplace was an oak mantel with trinkets and collections from trips taken long ago. Above the mantel was a black-and-white photo of Rod and Eula Gable. The oval frame was made of ornate cherry. The picture of the handsome couple, taken over a century ago, appeared ghostlike, their dark eyes witness to ancient secrets. The outer edges of the picture were smoky gray, giving the couple the appearance they were peering out of clouds from some unknown world.

Gabby led Porter through the kitchen, the tile floor creaking as they walked past the wood stove. Porter set his black leather medicine bag on a doily-draped coffee table.

Blackie, Samuel's black Labrador, rose from the floor beside Samuel's bed. He moved alongside Porter's leg, and Porter knelt. He scratched under Blackie's ear, and the soft eyes of the strong dog looked about the room, his tongue hanging curved and wet. Porter forced a smile. "Mornin', Sam."

Samuel watched a pair of mallards glide across the pond outside his window and nodded to acknowledge the presence of his best friend. "Porter."

"Gabby tells me you ain't feelin' so hot."

"She worries more than she has a right to. Too much like her momma."

Porter rose, and Blackie resumed his position at the foot of the bed. "Well, since I took the time to drive over here, how 'bout you either feed me breakfast, or let me check your vital signs?"

"Gabby, fix the old fart somethin' to eat. You sure know how to root out free meals, don't you?"

"What's the point in making house calls if there's no food involved?" the good doctor asked. "I know I'm treating you for physical ailments. Didn't know I should be treating you for senility too."

"If I only had the strength," Samuel said, shaking his head, "I'd beat the tar out of you."

Gabby went to the kitchen, and soon the sounds of pots and pans clanged a subtle, soothing tune. Porter checked Samuel's blood pressure, heart rate, and placed a thermometer under Samuel's tongue. Samuel shook his head as he clamped down on the cold glass, murmuring some indiscernible words of unhappiness. Samuel's silver hair was tousled, and not quite as thick and wavy as it was when he was the heartthrob of the county a lifetime ago. His chocolate-brown eyes looked tired, though they still burned with valor.

When Porter removed the thermometer, Samuel said, "That thing tastes like it's been in a hog's ass. Don't you ever clean it?"

Porter let go a cackling laugh. "I clean it for everyone but you. I want you to taste what you're full of." He put his supplies in his bag. "Vitals are good. You're not quite as strong as Old Man Cason's mule anymore, but I'll be damned if you still ain't as stubborn. Gonna leave you an antibiotic since you're runnin' a bit of a fever."

Samuel had been diagnosed with lung cancer a year prior. He felt no ill effects, but went to see Porter just to stop Gabby from badgering him. Samuel had not had a physical in almost fifteen years. Porter notwithstanding, Samuel thought doctors were pill-pushing sorts who only looked to prolong sickness, not eliminate it. Except for his birth and a bout with malaria in the war, he'd made it eighty-six years just fine without medical assistance. He'd seen his visit with Porter that fateful day as a chance to set up a fishing trip. Unfortunately the visit led to something much more. X-rays detected a spot on Samuel's lung. Within a week, he was on his way to an oncologist to see what could be done.

Gabby walked in with two light blue plates filled with fried eggs and country ham still sizzling in its sweet juices. Porter retrieved a straight-back chair from the kitchen table and placed it beside Samuel's hospital bed. The two friends ate their food in silence, as just being in each other's company was all the communication they needed.

They watched the pond lighten as the sun made its first appearance above Shady Mountain. Thunder rumbled from the storm clouds to the west, invisible waves of sounds seeking the very corners of the hills and valleys before fading into silence. The sun winked, brilliant orange, as if it knew the clouds would soon hide it from view. Outside the house, two thick maples stood side by side on the backside of the pond. They cast shadows across half of the tiny lake, making the water appear as though it were a sparkling eye of green and yellow slowly opening its lid. Trout skimmed along the water's edge, adding movement to the otherwise still water.

"Want you to do somethin' for me," Samuel said, cutting a fat-laced piece of ham.

"Drivin' out here to visit your wrinkly tail was enough. I'm done for the day." Samuel smiled, though Porter felt certain it was forced.

"I want you to help me find somebody that might be interested in writin' somethin'."

"What do you mean?"

"I'd like for someone to write about my time spent in the war. I never told of what went on over there. After I'm cold and in the ground, I'd like to leave somethin' to Gabby, and to Caleb, if he ever has an interest, so they might know a little of what we went through."

"You mean to tell me after all these years, you finally want to talk about what went on over there? I thought you were taking that to your grave."

"I will if we don't find somebody soon. I've made my mind up. I want to get it out while I'm still able."

"Well, let's see." He worked with his tongue at a piece of ham caught between his teeth. "How 'bout the Swift boy? He writes for magazines, newspapers, and the like. Abigail Swift's young'un. Want me to call her and see if she'll talk to him?"

"Would you? See if he's got an interest. He'll probably think it'd be a big waste of time."

***

The phone rang three times before Pete realized it. He tapped away at his keyboard, aggravated that someone was interrupting his train of thought. *Let the answering machine pick up.* Surely it was another telemarketer promising free steak knives or unheard-of low prices on aluminum siding. When Pete heard his mother's soft voice on the machine, he jumped from his chair. "Mom?" he mumbled into the cordless phone. "Sorry. Couldn't find where I'd set the phone."

"Honey, I hate to interrupt your work, so I won't keep you long." She always tried to refrain from calling during daylight hours even though Pete did not technically work in an office.

"It's okay, Mom. What is it?"

"Porter Bennett, from my Sunday school class, asked me to call you. He wants to know if you'd be interested in interviewing Samuel Gable."

"Who?"

"Sammy Gable. He lives near Jefferson Mountain. Your father knew him."

"Yeah, I think I remember the name. Why does he want to be interviewed? Is he looking to have something written for a local magazine, or the Tomahawk newspaper?"

"No, nothing like that. He's battling cancer, and the doctors say he's only got a few months at best to live. So he wants someone to record his days fighting in the war, for his children."

"I can't, Mom. I've got two articles due this week, and that's after I finish the Karen Landry story. Besides, I've got a truckload of query letters to mail to agents for my book."

"I know you're busy. But I don't think he's asking for you to give him a lot of time. Maybe you could find an hour or so. Remember what I said, he doesn't have much time left. Besides, I think you'd really like meeting him. He's a special man."

Pete drew in a deep breath and looked out into a thick group of pines outside his window. He always had trouble telling his mother no. "Well, maybe I could make it over to see him sometime later this week. I couldn't stay long, though."

Pete wrote Samuel's number on a notepad and promised he'd call. He returned to his computer, struggling to recapture his train of thought. He tapped his fingers on the keyboard, trying to perfect the closing paragraph. He'd spent six weeks on Karen's story, a twenty-four-year-old fighter pilot from Crystal Creek whose chopper was shot down in Iraq. Pete had met Karen's parents through an acquaintance. He'd read about her death in the paper, but had no idea how true a hero she was until he talked with her parents one morning in their living room. It was a gut-wrenching meeting, and he fought back tears as they shared the heartache of losing their only child. Pete kept thinking of Kate during the interview, wondering how he could survive if his only child were taken away from him. He kept a picture of Karen on the desk beside his computer as a reminder that she would never dance with her father at her wedding, never get to see her child's first steps, never hold the hand of her grandchild. In the picture she stood smiling, in the arms of her mother and father, the day she graduated flight school. A smile that knew not the dismal fate that lay ahead.

***

Pete hadn't noticed darkness had fallen until he heard the front door open. He stretched his arms, deciding to reread Karen's story just one more time before he submitted it. "Hey, baby," Sarah said as she entered the kitchen. Pete pulled the latest copy from his printer. "You finished Karen's story yet?"

"Maybe. I think I need to go over it one more time."

"You'll 'one more time' it a hundred times. Let me read it. I'll let you know if it's worthy."

Pete rose from his chair and yawned. "Not yet. Don't know if I'm ready for anyone to read it." There were two things in life, outside of family, that drove Pete to strive for perfection. The first was baseball, and since he'd hung up his cleats after college, the sport played no part in his daily life. The second was writing, and in a way it provided a chance to compete again, on paper instead of the baseball diamond.

"I got a call from Mom this morning. She said some man named Samuel Gable wants me to write about something he did, or went through, in World War II. I promised her I'd call him, maybe spend an hour or so with him." He glanced over the intro paragraph of Karen Landry's article. "I really don't have the time to do it, though. Should have told her no. I've got to learn to say no."

"You can't say no to your mother. Then again, you can't say no to anybody. You're just a pushover."

"Well, that's about to change. I've got my sights set on something big here, and I can't keep letting others get in the way."

"But that's a part of life. Do you want to live on a deserted island where no one can bother you? To leave you alone so you can write without any interruption? Ain't gonna happen."

"It's not a bad idea, though." He laughed.

"You'll turn into a lonely hermit."

"Yes, but a successful one."

"All depends on how you measure success."

Pete shook his head and began to pore over his article again.

"So what's the story with this Gable person?" Sarah asked. She looked at the back of Pete's head as he read, rolling her eyes as if perhaps to suggest he'd become too absorbed in his work for her liking. "I mean, what was he, a prisoner of war or something?"

"Don't have a clue. All I know is he's dying, and I don't have the time to listen to someone who won't be paying me for my time."

"Look at it as a chance to hear about things you've never known or experienced before. I'll bet he has some interesting things to say."

"Interesting or not, he better not plan on talking long, because I don't plan on staying long."

Chuck Walsh

Chapter Two

Pete placed three AA batteries in the pocket of his black leather jacket. He set a small brown spiral notebook on the passenger seat, along with his digital recorder. The notebook was more of a backup system, or a security blanket. Whenever Pete conducted interviews, he always had some strange fear that his recorder would malfunction, even though it was a top-of-the-line piece of electronics. He'd imagine himself sitting at his computer listening to dead air, thus having to call the person again to ask for a do-over. And so he'd write furiously during every interview, in some hieroglyphic style that he could barely make heads or tails of. Thank God for the person who invented the digital recorder.

The clock on the dash read 7:40. The car was cold and quiet. Turning the key, Pete bounced the name of Samuel Gable in his head. It seemed like he remembered hearing his father talk about Samuel when he was a boy. He couldn't remember the nature of the conversation, or why Samuel's name had come up. He didn't give it much thought.

It was early October, and the morning air was thin and crisp. The winds contained a sharpness to them, the kind that whispered the change of season in the high country. The sun, surrounded in baby blue, sat above Shady Mountain, casting shades of purple on both Shady and Jefferson Mountains. Along Watauga Valley, which split the mountain ranges, grassy hillsides rose in waves of hunter green. Wheat fields rustled in the breeze, soon to be cut and harvested. As Pete drove along the winding valley highway of State Road 84, known to locals as Elizabethton Highway, he looked out at the farmhouses that stood timeless, a link to the hard, simple past of the Appalachians. Along the valley Sinking Creek carved out a snaky path, running like the vein of a lightning bolt on a hot summer's evening. Roby Nichol's cattle and saddle horses grazed along the highway in no particular hurry. The seven-mile ride to the Gable house was a soothing one for Peter Swift, freelance writer.

When Gabby opened the door, her delicate smile caught Pete off guard, as did the bold look of her smooth, brown eyes. He'd expected Mrs. Gable to answer, or perhaps a housekeeper of some sort. When Gabby extended her hand, the soft warmth of it wasn't lost on Pete.

"Good morning," she said. "You must be Pete."

"Yes, I am. And you are?"

"Gabby. The daughter. Please come in."

She led him through the kitchen, and he looked at the clock above the stove as he followed her. Exactly eight o'clock. Pete wanted to be on time, as always, but he reckoned Samuel, being a military man, was not one to be kept waiting.

"Mornin', Mr. Gable," Pete said as he entered the parlor. Samuel was looking at a black-and-white photo. Blackie rose, barked once, and when Samuel snapped his fingers, the dog returned to its lying position.

"Beautiful dog."

"Let me show you somethin'," Samuel said. He was not interested in introductions. Gabby brought Pete a chair from the den. "This here's four of my army buddies. Two of 'em died in the Battle of Leyte. That's me right there."

His finger trembled slightly as he pointed. "The fella kneelin' beside me was Bryson Steele. I pulled that boy off the battlefield after the Japs tossed grenades in his foxhole. That was a hell of a day. A *hell* of a day."

Samuel handed Pete the grainy picture. The men stood alongside a banyan tree with massive limbs extending above their heads like gnarly fingers of pale wood. Long, fan-like limbs of nipa palms grew thick from the ground behind them, forming an interwoven wall in front of sky-reaching fig trees covered with vines. Pete looked closely and noticed Samuel squatting low, his elbows resting on his knees. His right hand held a floppy khaki hat. His face wore no expression. Behind him, a slender soldier stood, shirtless, the outline of his ribs visible. A cigarette hung from his lips. Beside them sat a man on a cot, turned and looking over his shoulder as if the camera had sneaked up on him like an enemy soldier. Behind him another stood, looking down at a pocketknife he appeared to be folding. Of the three men whose eyes faced the camera, Pete noticed a hollowness in them all. It wasn't sadness they showed, but a lack of emotion entirely.

"That's a powerful picture," Pete said, looking one last time before handing it to Samuel. Pete sat. "How are you feeling?"

"You a doctor?"

"No, sir."

"Well, unless you are, don't ask me how I'm feelin'." Samuel waved his finger toward Pete. "I want no sympathy. If you're interested in hearin' what I got to say about the war, let's get started. Otherwise you may as well go home."

Pete raised his eyebrows slightly, and for a brief second was tempted to call the whole thing off. Instead, he removed his recorder from his coat pocket, opened his notebook, and removed the pen clipped to the front of it. "Well, since I have no idea what it is you want me to do, can you clue me in?" Pete's statement was purposely tinted with sarcasm.

"I want you to write somethin' about my days in the war," Samuel said as if he thought Pete was clueless. "Especially in the Philippines. I'd like for Gabby to know a little bit about what we went through overseas. Somethin' I can leave for her after I'm gone." He rubbed his chin. "For Caleb too, I guess. I don't know."

"Who?"

"Never mind. Anyways, what do you say we stop the fiddle-fartin' and get to work."

Work? Wasn't this supposed to be an informal chat about the war? "I need to let you know I don't have a lot of time to devote to you."

"What's the notebook for?"

"In case the recorder doesn't work."

"Why wouldn't it work? Don't you have good batteries? Did you buy a cheap brand?"

"No, I didn't buy a cheap brand, and yes, the batteries are good. I just feel safer having a backup in case the recorder malfunctions."

"Well, put the pen and pad away. I'll feel at ease if I can just talk without havin' to worry whether you're keepin' up with me or not."

Pete shook his head, smirked, and turned on the recorder. "It's all yours." Pete checked the volume and set it on the bed beside Samuel's arm.

Samuel looked toward the bottom corner of the room, as though he were a man looking to remove himself from his sickbed and into another time. He glanced out at the pond as if he were searching for the ducks. "You know, I was born right here in this house," he began. "Course that was three hun'ert years ago. I still remember Momma sittin' by the kitchen window when I left home to join the service. Maybe I should start there."

***

April, 1942

Samuel packed the last of the T-shirts sitting on his bed into his green duffel bag. He closed the canvas bag and looked out the bedroom window into his mother's flower garden. Red, pink, yellow, and white blooms covered the tall lattice fence. Plump bumblebees moved about them as though they were the last food source on Jefferson Mountain. Looking in the yard, he smiled as he thought of the day when he had run a polecat through the garden. He couldn't have been more than nine or ten. His cousin Vita had sat on the ground that day, her legs curled inside her pastel, flowing dress. She read a book of poetry by E.E. Cummings, and looked a little too prim for Samuel's liking. The polecat had provided a necessary antidote to stifle her high-society musings.

He tossed the bag over his shoulder and glanced back at his room a final time. On into and through the kitchen to the living room he went. He looked at the picture of Mom and Dad above the fireplace, noticing the youthfulness in their eyes. He made it to the front door, hoping that Momma wouldn't be there. He didn't want to

19

see her cry, and knew it would only make leaving harder. Besides, they had exchanged their good-byes in the kitchen the night before. His brother Bert stood on the front porch, holding his black fedora nervously in his hand.

"You ready?" Bert asked.

Samuel only nodded, though he felt certain he didn't look convincing. They stepped off the porch and onto the dirt driveway. As Samuel opened the car door and tossed his duffel bag inside, he saw Mom standing at the living-room window. Tears rolled down her face, and Samuel tried to smile away her worries. He lowered his head and slid into the front seat of the clunky Ford.

The Tennessee dust rolled behind them as the brothers drove down Vaught's Holler to the gray gravel of State Road 84. The men rode in silence, and Samuel studied the twists and turns of the winding road as if burying them in his mind. On they drove, both wanting to talk, both wanting to say what weighed heavy on their hearts. The ride toward town, a small mountain hamlet called Carter Springs, seemed way too short.

"How long's the trip to Fort Jackson?" Bert finally asked, breaking the silence.

"Don't know. Think we have to make a few stops along the way." Samuel looked at the papers on his lap. "All I know is we're supposed to be on the bus at the courthouse by nine."

"You nervous?"

"Nah. It's what I've been wantin'. That's why I enlisted."

"I'm worried about Momma."

"Make sure you take good care of her while I'm gone. You're all she's got now, so don't screw it up."

"Quit your belly achin'. I'll take care of her."

"If I find out you're not doin' your job, you'll receive a whippin' of major proportions when I come home."

"I ain't scared." Bert tried to smile.

Bert looked across the hillsides and tapped his fingers on the steering wheel. He loved driving the winding stretch of highway that bridged Jefferson Mountain with Carter Springs. But not on that morning. "You know, I figured I'd be carryin' Momma to watch you play ball, not totin' you to town to hop on an army bus."

"Plans change."

"But that was a plan you'd mapped out since you were a kid."

"True. But I can't do anything about it now."

"It just ain't right. There ain't a better ballplayer in the state. You know it. I know it."

"That's in the past. I've thrown my last pitch."

Bert shook his head. "Momma sure loved to watch you play. When you were on that pitcher's mound, she swole up with pride like a sow's belly. I ain't never seen nobody so born to play the game as you. How many no-hitters did you throw in high school? Six?"

"I don't know. It's best not to keep up with those things. I just wanted to play ball. Loved the game. That's all that mattered."

"And then that witch of a girl ruined it all. I can't believe what she did to you."

"What's done is done. Can't change it."

"It just ain't right."

21

"I know. But all that matters now is I'm headin' to the US Army. I'll be competin' against Japs instead of ballplayers."

When they pulled in front of the one-story, vanilla-brick courthouse, they found the small parking lot nearly full. Family and friends hugged the young men who had come to be taken away from their quiet town. A nondescript bus waited in the parking lot, two soldiers standing erect at the door to usher on recruits. Bert pulled into the lot and started to get out of the car.

"No," Samuel said. "Just let me get out by myself. Don't want to make it harder than it is."

Bert reached over and hugged Samuel, and they embraced for several seconds. "Make sure you come back home."

Samuel nodded and removed the duffel bag from the backseat. He got out, turned, and held up his hand to his younger brother, and neither hid their tears. Samuel stepped across two puddles in the unpaved parking lot, verified his name with one of the soldiers outside the bus door, tossed his duffel bag in the storage door, and climbed aboard.

The others filed on the bus, many with teary eyes. They waved good-bye as the bus pulled onto Main Street on its way to Boone. Samuel looked at the small buildings of the town as the little village came to life. Tom Benson, whose son Billy Joe was a schoolmate of Samuel's, wheeled two sacks of grain on a metal cart. Across the street, Virgil Ames extended the awning above the window to his clothing store. As the bus passed Murle Stuppe's one-pump gas station, Samuel glanced west to

Jefferson Mountain, the place he had called home for nineteen years.

Earl Grayson sat across the aisle from Samuel, and he wiped the tears from his eyes with his sleeves. Fourteen young men, all under the age of twenty, knew their lives were about to change forever. Some had enlisted, but most were drafted. Carter Springs always had a high number of its youth in the armed services. Their fathers had fought in World War I, and they were all schooled on the patriotic responsibilities that came with serving their country.

Passing through Boone, one of the soldiers sent to escort the recruits to Columbia talked about a girl he met at the Daniel Boone Resort one summer. He wondered aloud if she still lived in the area. As he told anyone in earshot of how he took full advantage, slipping off into the Blue Ridge Mountain evening with the blond-haired, blue-eyed mountain gal, the bus worked its way south through small towns like Hickory and Hendersonville. By midday it crossed the South Carolina line on its way to Columbia.

Most of the young men slept. Talk was minimal at best. Samuel removed his charcoal-gray wool coat, and as he placed it on the seat beside him, he noticed a folded piece of paper in the side pocket. He removed it, seeing *Samuel* written at the crease. He unfolded it, and a silver cross necklace dropped onto his lap. He looked at the necklace, placed it in one hand, and read:

My dearest Samuel,

I just wanted to let you know that I am so proud of you. And though I'll worry each and every moment until you return, I know you will serve your country proudly. Represent your family, your town, and your state with pride. You were born to lead, so be prepared when you are called to do so. I hope you will write as often as you can, and I will send you letters as well. Don't worry about me. You just take care of yourself and do everything in your power to return home. The necklace was your father's. Think of it as a circle of love and protection. Wear it and nothing can hurt you. I love you more than words can ever say, and you have taken my heart with you.

With all my love,
Mom

Samuel folded the letter and placed it back in his coat pocket. He looked out at a grassy hillside and rubbed his eyes.

Chapter Three

Pete set his recorder beside his computer and played a message on his cell from *Appalachian Trail.* Kristen Matthews, editor of the regional periodical, had called, assigning Pete a story for the winter issue. He was to interview Charlie Coleman, curator of the Daniel Boone Museum. The deadline was twelve days away, a fifteen-hundred-word story, so he knew he'd better secure an interview soon. Pete dialed the number to the museum but then flipped his cell phone closed and placed it beside the computer. He couldn't let go of his time spent with Samuel Gable.

He looked at the recorder, rubbing his fingers along the sides of the slender device. So much work to do. *Call Charlie Coleman*, he thought to himself. He looked beside his computer, where the latest copy of the Karen Landry story sat, and he wanted to read over the intro paragraph one last time. He picked up his phone, flipping it shut again as he popped it against his chin. He read the first sentence of the Landry article. He stopped, and glanced at his recorder. *Maybe for a minute*, he thought as he turned the recorder to play mode.

As Pete listened to Samuel recount the day he'd left for the Army, Pete detected something in Samuel's voice that he hadn't heard during the interview. Maybe it was because he was agitated by Samuel's gruffness, or perhaps it was Samuel's indifference to the fact that Pete was taking the time to listen to someone when the end result would not be a paycheck. Samuel's voice came through sure and steady, unlike a voice that gave an indication that death was knocking on his door.

As Samuel spoke, his crotchety tone disappeared. Pete clicked on the Microsoft Office Word icon, and as Samuel's voice continued, he created a document and began to tap away on the keyboard. As Samuel talked, Pete's fingers tried to keep up. In between pushing the Rewind button and the Play button, he put Samuel's story down in sporadic fashion. Pete couldn't help but think of the look in Samuel's eyes when he spoke of the day he left to join the Army. When he spoke of seeing his mother standing at the picture window the day he left for Columbia, a slight quiver was noticeable in Samuel's otherwise commanding voice.

***

The afternoon skies turned a darker shade of blue, and a thin blanket of clouds cloaked the western sky in deep red. Pete thought it was the kind of day that inspired painters to create masterpieces, poets to pen sonnets, writers to capture the perfect scene with words. He thought about walking outside just to feel the fresh air against his face, but he glanced at the clock on his computer. He had told Sarah he'd have dinner waiting when she arrived home from work. He spotted Charlie Coleman's number on his notepad, and for a moment thought of calling to set up an interview, yet he couldn't bring himself to stop writing. He thought of the letter Samuel had found in his coat pocket, the necklace, and his mother's words proclaiming it would keep him safe. He pictured Samuel walking to the bus while his brother watched from the car.

"What a day," Sarah said as she walked in the door. "Hand me a glass of wine and toss me a juicy slab of meat." She set her purse on the kitchen table and removed the sunglasses that sat atop her head like a headband.

"The wine is in the fridge, and your slab of meat is sitting here working."

Sarah walked up behind Pete, placing her hands on his shoulders. "What are you working on?"

"I'm putting down some of the things Mr. Gable told me this morning. He's a cranky old guy, but there's something about him…I don't know. Anyway, enough of that. I've got to call Charlie Coleman at the Daniel Boone Museum. I need to work on something that actually results in an exchange of legal tender."

"What do you want to do about dinner?"

"I don't care. I think there's some leftover pizza in the fridge. Why don't you eat that? I'm not really hungry anyway."

"What about our plan to spend the evening together? Mom has Kate for the night, and we haven't had an evening, just the two of us, in almost a month." Sarah sat on Pete's lap, placing her arms around his neck. "Let me take your mind off Daniel Coleman, Charlie Boone, or whatever that guy's name is." She placed her lips gently to his neck, her soft lips working their way slowly upward until she nibbled on the lobe of his ear.

"Let me call this guy and set something up. Then I'm all yours." Pete kissed Sarah on the forehead and helped her to her feet. "Why don't you open the wine? I'll have a glass when I'm finished with Mr. Coleman."

***

Sarah slipped into a hot bath and held her glass of Chardonnay in front of her, watching the wine capture the light from the ceiling. She debated on what to wear for the evening, and after some thought, decided on a black low-cut sweater tucked away somewhere in the back of the closet. She thought the short black skirt she'd recently bought would complete the look. There was something about the color of black that made her feel alluring. And she knew Pete loved that color on her. She smiled at the possibilities of the evening but wasn't quite ready to leave the warmth of her bath water, so she sipped her wine, closed her eyes, and wrapped herself in quiet solitude. She heard Pete's soothing voice in the Florida room, the room where he wrote everything from sports stories to his novel. He was a soft-spoken man, and it was one of the things she loved most about him.

Emerging from the bedroom, smelling sweetly of Pete's favorite perfume, Sarah took him a glass of wine. He wore dark jeans, and his white T-shirt clung tightly to his chest and shoulders. To her, he looked like a college student taking an exam, focused, concentrating hard to make an A. He looked like a student in need of distraction.

"Time to clock out, Bub," she said as she placed the wine on the desk.

He continued to bang on the keyboard, seemingly unaware of anything other than the computer. She slipped quietly through the French doors and into the living room. She lit three multitiered white candles on the coffee table located in front of a black leather couch. She tossed the throw pillows from the couch to the love seat and dimmed the lights. Glancing at herself in the living-room mirror, she was pleased with the way she looked. She wanted Pete to feel like he was the luckiest man on earth.

Sarah walked to his chair and kissed the back of his neck while his fingers furiously stroked the keyboard. He leaned forward as if her lips were a nuisance. She moved beside him, kissing his cheek.

"You don't play fair, do you?" he said as she ran her hands through his hair.

"No, I don't," she said with a precocious grin. She could tell he wanted to keep writing, as though he were on a mission to prove he was the greatest writer ever. She, however, wanted to show him she was much more interesting than compiling words. With her fingers, she guided his lips to hers by turning his chin. She lightly pressed her warm mouth against his, touching his face while she looked into his eyes. Kissing him was something she loved. She saw a spark in his eyes when her warm breath gently brushed his skin.

She took the glass of wine with one hand, and with the other, led him to the couch. He sat, and she placed the glass in his hand, watching him take a sip. She turned on the stereo located on the bottom shelf of the bookcase. The light of the stereo cast a blue-neon glow as Etta James's haunting voice carried softly across the room. Sarah sat beside him and stared into his eyes, a deep gaze that told him nothing existed outside of the world where they sat. Her brown eyes softened in the darkness, and she smiled playfully. She touched her hand along his forehead, gently brushing his hair.

"Dance with me," she said.

With her cheek touching his shoulder, and her hand inside his, she sighed. There in the dark, two silhouettes moved in unison to the music.

"God, you smell good," he said.

She rubbed her finger along his lips, her eyes an open door to her heart. "I love you," she whispered.

"I love you too." He gently pressed her head closer to his chest.

The dance continued, and she kissed him again, and the whites of her eyes sparkled in the dim light. "Do you know how lucky we are?" she asked while rubbing her fingers along his shoulders.

"Yes."

She placed her hands at the back of his neck and whispered into his ear, and he pulled her mouth to his. Love and desire all in one. Passion laced with a tender touch.

***

Her head rested on his shoulder while they lay on the couch. She touched his chest and felt his heartbeat. A teardrop rolled off her cheek. In that moment she felt their hearts were one. "That was incredible," she said. "This is when I feel closest to you."

Pete kissed her head and nodded. After a moment she felt his head turn toward the Florida room.

"Don't even think about it," she whispered. "You're done for the night."

"I *really* need to work on Mr. Gable's interview. And I better get some thoughts down about Mr. Coleman's article while it's fresh in my head. Why don't you slip on off to bed and I'll join you in a bit?"

"Why don't you pick it back up in the morning and come to bed with me now? I promise to keep you warm."

"Just give me an hour and it's a date."

"Promise?"

"Promise."

***

Sarah rolled over and looked at the bedside clock. It was two-thirty, and she glanced at the pillow beside her. Empty. She saw the light from the Florida room and heard the faint sounds of the keyboard, a steady pecking. She lay in the dark, thinking about life, and about Pete. For thirteen years they'd been married, dating for two years before that.

When they first dated, she was touched by Pete's attention and affection. He sent her roses on what seemed like a weekly basis. He left romantic cards on her windshield in the parking lot where she worked. She thought his display of affection was a phase where he simply wanted to win her over. But as time went on, his attention to her only grew. He cooked for her, trying to fix exotic dishes that he thought she'd like. He took her to concerts in Boone and Knoxville. Many times it was for artists Pete could barely stomach. But as long as she enjoyed it, that was all that mattered to him.

Sarah was a dark-haired beauty with eyes so bold and dark they held a shade of black. She had smooth olive skin, a result of her father's Spanish bloodline. Her petite body curved in all the right places. Pete knew she was quite the catch, and she drew the attention of many young men in and around Carter Springs.

As much as Sarah received attention from other guys, she truly felt lucky married to Pete. It was clearly known to her family, and her friends, that she thought Pete was as fine-looking a man as she had ever known. She thought his ice-blue eyes were Hollywood worthy. His cheekbones, his smile, his kiss — especially his kiss — made her certain she'd hit the jackpot. She was in love with him heart and soul. But she sensed a strange shift of importance, as if satisfying her had become more duty than desire for Pete. His attentiveness had become wayward. A new passion seemed to stir his heart, his emotions, directing his affections elsewhere.

***

As he drove to the Gable house, a pickup truck forty yards in front sprayed water from the wet road, coating Pete's windshield. The wipers moved in harmonic rhythm and Pete tapped his index finger on the steering wheel.

Gabby waited at the front door, opening it as Pete walked up the steps. "Morning." Her voice was soft, a gracious tone to it. "Thank you for coming, but Daddy's having a tough morning. I'm not sure if he's going to be able to spend time with you today."

Pete shook his head and smirked. "I wish you would have called before I drove out here. I have a ton of things I need to work on today." He instantly wished he could take back those words.

"I'm sorry," Gabby said, taken aback by Pete's rudeness. From the hallway Samuel's cough rattled. Gabby turned to see Samuel leaning against the wall. "Daddy, what are you doin' out of bed?"

"Let that boy in the house."

"You okay, Mr. Gable?" Pete followed Gabby inside.

"You a doctor?"

"I know, I know. No questions about how you're feeling."

"That's right." Samuel pulled his hand to his mouth, gagging as though he had swallowed a sponge. For several moments Samuel struggled, and Gabby placed his chair behind him.

"Sit, Daddy."

"Take me to the parlor," said Samuel. "I got a lot to talk about."

Samuel looked at the pond while Gabby brought him a glass of water. His face had reddened from the coughing attack, and he rubbed sweat from his forehead with his wrist.

"This dyin' nonsense ain't all it's cracked up to be." Samuel wiped the corner of his mouth with a beige handkerchief monogrammed with a gothic-style G. "If I had my druthers, I'd be trout fishin'."

Pete smiled, intended more to soothe than to show acknowledgment of the old man's sarcastic wit.

"Sit down, son. Let's get at it."

Pete turned on his recorder and sat back in his chair. He'd known not to bring the notebook.

Sunlight warmed the parlor, casting the hardwood floor in shades of orange. Pete looked about the room, sensing a peace within the house, as though souls of previous generations had returned to listen to Samuel talk and comfort him along the way.

Samuel looked down toward his stomach, scratched above his right eye, and nibbled on his lower lip with his top two teeth. "Let's see. Where was I wantin' to start?"

"Yesterday you left off as the bus was pulling into Columbia."

"I know that. I *know* that. But that ain't what I want to talk about today. I had somethin' on my mind when I woke up this mornin', and I'll be a suck egg mule if I ain't already forgot it. I'm certifiable."

Samuel looked at the pond in frustration. He rubbed his chin a bit and shook his head. He slipped his hand along the part in his hair, as if he suspected some strands had moved out of place. "The first battle. That's it. That's what I want to talk about." Samuel pointed to the recorder. "Turn that machine on."

January, 1944

Rain rolled off Samuel's helmet in small beads as he glanced across the river. The water was wide and smooth, straight and powerful. On either side of the river were steep, rising mountains thick with klinki pines and maples draped with clinging vines. The thick forest of the mountains made the jungle floor impossible to see from the river. It was the northern coast of New Guinea, and in Samuel's eyes, made the Appalachians seem like nothing more than rolling hills.

The Japanese Army sought to take control of the entire South Pacific. Worldwide, Japan's reputation was one of invincibility, and she bore an army that was more than prepared to die for her. The Japanese Army had firm hold of the Philippines and New Guinea, and New Zealand and Australia were now in their sights. With a legion of snipers — hidden pillboxes strategically placed to cover all of the field of fire — the Japanese front was considered impregnable.

Samuel wiped his hand inside his shirt along his chest, hoping to dry it enough so he could hold the barrel of his wet rifle. The clouds hovered thick and low, as if heaven had lost its desire to border the sky. Random gunfire tapped across the mountainside, undistinguishable as to the source. Samuel was with the 32nd Division, 126th Regiment, Company L. They were known as the Red Arrowmen, a label laid upon them because they had never found an enemy line that they couldn't pierce. They were a collection of brash young men who had no clue of the brutal reality that war was about to rain on them. Their knowledge of the jungle was slim, and they were a unit dependent on resolve and instinct.

Sporadic gunfire popped through the hillsides, and Samuel guessed it was the result of skirmishes in the jungle. Samuel looked at Earl, and his eyes showed a combination of fear and anticipation. Samuel nodded as if to say that everything was going to be okay. Earl was a simple boy who looked to others for guidance, though he was loyal to those he trusted.

The men knelt on one knee, their rifles pointing forward. Behind them the master sergeant conferred with the lieutenant.

"Lieutenant, we're hemmed in," Sergeant Herbert Swanson said. "Scouts confirm Japs are closing in on both sides."

"We've got to cross the river," Lieutenant Baskins replied, "but there ain't no spot narrow enough. Get the men hunkered down in the foxholes. We got no choice."

"Sir," Samuel said as he rose to his feet. "Let me cross it. Strap a rope to me and I'll secure it on the other side."

"Negative, soldier. We don't know how strong the currents are."

"We're boxed in like a turtle's pecker. We got no choice, sir. I know I can make it."

Samuel ran along the edge of the river, the rain blowing in sheets across the water. He'd left his rifle with Earl, carrying only his black-handled trench knife and a spool of fishing cord. The cord was tied to the end of a thick piece of rope that Bryson Steele secured to a thick pine. The route Samuel ran skirted a cliff twelve feet above the river, where limbs of nipa palms branched out from the forest floor like green fans brushing against his legs and arms. He pulled the fishing line, loosening it from scrubby sago palms and mulberry bushes as he ran. Gunfire tapped about him, thumping into the trees and the dense jungle floor. Almost a hundred yards upstream, he placed the blade of his knife in his teeth, securing the line to his belt. The rain beat against his face like pellets of ice, and the sweat he'd developed while climbing the humidity-laced mountainside cooled his body under his jacket.

The river's chill enveloped Samuel as he pushed off into the water at the base of the cliff. Since he'd spent his boyhood years swimming the icy mountain creeks and streams along Carter Springs, he shrugged off the river's chill as no more than a minor inconvenience. When he swam the streams back home, more times than not it was on a dare or a bet, especially when the Adams sisters came down to the creek to cool their toes.

The river was the color of auburn, and the rains bubbled up the river bottom's silty soil. Samuel pushed hard across the water, and he felt no fear swimming the fast waters. His strokes were long and smooth, freestyle in appearance. The river's width was seventy-five yards at its most-narrow point, and Samuel stroked away to touch down at that spot.

Sporadic pops of gunfire came from along the bank, splashing water about him in quick, geyser-like form, something the raindrops were unable to do. His strong arms pushed on to keep him at the top of the water, though the undercurrents tugged at his knees and midsection. He was within thirty feet, and the water felt as deep as it did midstream. He aimed for a fallen coconut tree that hung from the bank, its top extended into the water's edge. As he grabbed hold of the upper trunk of the calloused tree, he kicked his feet so he could pull his body out of the water.

Bullets ripped into the bank, and when one hit the tree trunk in front of him, it only served to piss him off. He scurried ten feet up the bank and began pulling the line. Quickly his hands pulled, right, left, over and over, his forearms tight. The rope was let out from the other side, and when it made it to him, Samuel secured it around a klinki pine. The taut rope ran ten feet above the water.

Within minutes, the battalion, at just over one hundred men, took to shimmying across the rope. Their weight lowered the height of the rope, causing their bodies to dangle inches above the stream. Again, gunfire zipped about them and they quickened their pace. Earl was first across, and when he tossed Samuel his gun, Samuel opened fire in the general direction of the gunshots in an attempt to provide interference.

Most of the men had cleared the stream, and as the last few soldiers grabbed hold of the rope, Abe Rentz, a stocky soldier from Ohio, panicked. Abe wasn't the fleetest of foot or hand, and wanted to come across last. Baskins, bringing up the rear, ordered Rentz onto the rope, and Rentz grabbed hold with uncertainty. Seven men dangled on the rope behind him, and when Abe stopped, they cursed and yelled.

Samuel jumped on the rope and headed to the logjam of soldiers. Shots rang from a nearby hillside and one of the men dropped off. His body rolled across the top of the water as blood rose to the muddy top. "Move your ass, Rentz," Samuel shouted, "before you get us all killed."

"I can't make it any farther," Rentz cried. "Let me drop. Let me go."

Samuel's wet backhand knocked Rentz on his forehead and he closed his eyes to absorb the pain. "I'll beat you all the way downstream if you don't climb to the other side."

Rentz looked down at the fast-moving stream below him. Samuel reached around Rentz, almost falling as he took hold of the rope behind Rentz. "If you can't move your fat ass, then I'll move it for you." Samuel placed his boot firmly against Rentz's backside. "Move!"

Rentz frantically slid across the rope to the other side, and the rest of the men followed close behind. The platoon on the bank returned fire across the river as the Japanese troops slipped through the jungle to the water's edge.

"Good work, soldier," the sergeant said to Samuel. Samuel cut the rope from the tree and flung it into the river.

***

The troops moved north by northwest toward Aitape. Word spread that the Japanese were prepared for an all-out assault, amassing close to fifty thousand soldiers. Samuel's battalion was to move through the jungle, away from the coast. With U.S. troops set to attack from the water, the Red Arrowmen planned to fall in behind the Japanese and cut off their supplies, their food, and their ability to get reinforcements.

The days were long, and the oppressive heat and humidity took its toll. Earl tried to keep up with the days of the week, using a small calendar Vernon Peeples had given him from Peeples Feed & Seed back home. The rains began to take its toll on the calendar, which Earl kept in his knapsack. The writing faded so that he was unable to tell which day was which, though he refused to throw it away. It was a piece of home and he wasn't about to part with it.

The skirmishes the Red Arrowmen had encountered so far had been light, but that was about to change.

Chapter Four

Pete glanced at the clock on his computer. It was almost one in the morning. His eyes were weary, and his mind as soft as Aunt Reba's gelatin mold. Still, he couldn't pull himself away from his desk. His face glowed in a bluish hue, the house darkened so as not to awaken Sarah. His fingers had described the bullets buzzing through the jungles while his mind searched for the fear, the adrenaline rush, and all the emotions that were going through the men of L Company in the jungle. He was amazed at how Samuel eased the tension of the story with an almost innocent approach, as though no one clued him in that the war was something to be taken seriously. Surely Samuel felt the fear. As far as Pete could tell, Samuel treated the war as something along the lines of a hunting trip where his prey had taken the shape and form of the human variety. It was as if the enemy was a wolf circling the fields in search of sacrificial sheep, with Samuel shepherd of the flock.

When the morning alarm sounded, it was seven and Sarah was already in the shower. Pete wandered to the kitchen for a glass of orange juice. The skies were soft purple, the winds calm, the sun not yet clearing the eastern horizon. When he turned on his cell phone, he noticed he had missed a call. His voice mail had one unplayed message, and he listened as Gabby explained how Samuel wasn't feeling well, asking if they could postpone Pete's visit.

***

Pete used Samuel's postponement as a chance to interview Charlie Coleman. Under a blue sky stretching endlessly in all directions, stopped only by the steep horizon of the Appalachians, Pete drove north to the museum. The sun, high in the eastern sky, with not a cloud to compete with, sparked the reds and oranges along the hillsides and the peaks in the distance. Frost held to the shadows and the winds were silent, the creeks in the valley running fast and hard as if in search of new worlds abound with endless mystery.

Pete interviewed Charlie at a small desk in the back of the museum. The tiny room served as both office and kitchen. The strong smell of coffee floated through the air as Charlie talked of Daniel Boone's travels through eastern Tennessee and his days living in western North Carolina. Charlie had spearheaded the campaign to build the Daniel Boone addition to the county museum. He lived across the North Carolina line on the back side of Snake Mountain in a secluded town called Trade, making the forty-five-minute drive to the museum six days a week.

Though Charlie, in his midsixties, was very personable, Pete couldn't help but think how he'd rather be sitting in Samuel's parlor listening to more about battles in the jungles of the Philippines.

Within an hour the interview was complete, and Pete shook Charlie's hand in the parking lot. Charlie told Pete he'd stir up pictures he could use for the article, and in a day or so would have them available for Pete to pick up. Pete went home to put some of Charlie's quotes onto the computer.

When Gabby called that night to tell Pete that Samuel wanted to give it another try the following morning, she could sense the excitement in Pete's voice. Pete spent no more than an hour on the Daniel Boone story, and instead began reading over what he'd written of Samuel's tales.

Morning couldn't come soon enough for Pete, and he was out the door by seven-thirty. He didn't want to show up too early, so he stopped at Mike's Quick Stop for a diet soda. Mike's had a short order grill where breakfast and lunch were served. A group of elderly men, farmers by the looks of them, sat around a table eating and passing the morning. The smell of fried bacon and sausage gravy wafted through the air.

"Mornin', young man," came from the table when Pete passed by. Pete looked at the group, trying to find the person who'd spoken. A portly man in green overalls with a beige thermal shirt removed his cap and rubbed his hands along his sparse smattering of silver hair. "Ain't you Abigail Swift's boy?"

Pete stopped, and with a puzzled look, tried to place the man's face. "Yes, sir, I am."

"I'm Leland Akins. I grew up with your ma. We went to school together. She brought my wife and me one of your articles a while back and I recognized you from your picture."

"It's a pleasure to meet you." Pete shook Leland's wrinkled hand and noticed that Leland was missing most of his teeth.

"Us old farts gather 'round here ever' mornin'," Leland said.

A diminutive man, his faded County Co-op hat angled so high on his head that the bill arched across his crown, said, "Who you callin' old?"

"He don't care if you call him a fart," said Leland. "Just don't call him old." The men broke into strong laughter. Leland shook his head and smiled. "So, what brings you out this side of Shady Mountain?"

"I'm going to Samuel Gable's house. I'm writing a little something about his time in the war."

"Samuel Gable is a man's man," another man at the table said. "We grew up in the same holler. I've seen him whip three men at a time, though he weren't never one to initiate trouble. It looks like he's met his match with the cancer, though. You tell him Archie Spence sends his regards."

"Yes, sir. I certainly will."

***

Blackie ran to meet Pete's car when he pulled into the drive, running alongside, barking, wagging his tail. Blackie was rock-solid, and though he was over ten years old, he had spitfire in his eyes just like his master. Samuel sat on the porch in his wheelchair. Blackie waited outside Pete's car door, assumed a sitting position, and Pete rubbed his hands along the smooth fur on the dog's back.

"Mornin', Mr. Gable." Pete climbed the six steps that led to the porch. "You must be feelin' better." Pete watched Gabby come through the front door, and she smiled briefly as she stood beside her father. In a white long-sleeve T-shirt, faded jeans, and argyle socks, she placed her hand on his shoulder. *Cute as cute could be*, he thought.

"Hi, Gabby," Pete said. She nodded.

"We're goin' on a field trip," Samuel said.

"We are?"

43

"Yep. So I need you to ease me down the steps. Then you can sling my rump in the pickup and we'll take off like a bat out of hell to the countryside." If Vaught's Holler wasn't considered countryside, Pete couldn't wait to see what was.

Pete worked the wheelchair carefully down step by step and crossed the grassy yard to the gravel driveway beside the house. Samuel wore a pair of blue jeans and a green coat with a high collar that hid the bottom of his chin. Pete pulled the chair alongside the passenger door of the blue Ford.

"How are we going to do this?"

"Just let me lean my arm agin' you and slide me in the seat like a greased pig." Samuel shakily pulled himself onto the seat and Pete pushed against Samuel's slender leg and arm until he was securely on the vinyl seat. Samuel removed the keys from his coat pocket, looked at Gabby, and smiled. She leaned against the porch rail, her arm crossing in front as she took hold of her elbow, her eyes full of compassion for the man who was as much hero as father.

"You boys behave yourself," she said.

"Can't make any promises." Pete smiled. He looked above the tin porch, a shutter hanging on by a thread outside a window. Looking upward, he said, "I think you're falling apart."

Stunned, she replied, "This hasn't been easy."

Pete smiled. "Not you. The shutter." Gabby walked into the yard and looked at the window.

"Great. Everything's coming apart at the seams."

"Come, Blackie," Samuel yelled and the dog leaped in through the driver's side door. Blackie positioned himself on Samuel's lap. Pete, taking his cue, waved to Gabby and got in the truck. Blackie lowered his head, resting it on his paws, his dark eyes looking downward. Samuel rubbed the dog's head.

"Where are we going?" Pete asked. "By the way, Archie Spence says hello."

"Spence? He's a good man. Family was a little tetched though. When they moved here from Kentucky, they came in a flatbed truck with chickens in wire baskets. A goat sat in the backseat with Spence's ma. She once told me the goat was the smartest of the bunch, and she relied on him to tell her who to vote for come election time."

Pete chuckled as he pulled onto Vaught's Holler, easing down the eighty yards of dirt road that stopped at State Road 84. "Okay, let's turn east," said Samuel. "Gonna ride the mountains. See if we can't stir up some trouble. You got a taste for moonshine? Maybe share a little eye opener?"

"No, thanks. But if you feel the need…"

"I'm just jerkin' you around. Let's ride."

Soon they were on a gray, gravelly road which ran alongside Spear Branch Creek. The road snaked its way along a tight hollow of small wooden houses, the hills climbing high on both sides. They passed the Doe Valley Baptist Church, and the lane began to climb a steep slope. All was quiet, with little sense of activity; old barns, falling apart, some hidden by vines and tall weeds. To Pete it looked like a place time had forgotten, left behind to fade into the past as had been done for hundreds of years. Along hills and hollows where generations of people once lived, only faded grave markers along hilltops acknowledged their existence. To Samuel, it held a world of memories that defined who he was. It was a world that he'd slip back into in a heartbeat if God would allow him that favor.

"Pull over," Samuel said, pointing to the side of the road. "Slide up on the shoulder."

Across the road from where the truck sat was a wood building. Ivy and weeds enveloped most of the structure, and what wood was visible was the color of slate. "That's where I went to school. Started back in '29. It had two rooms. Younger chaps and those with minds of the simple variety were on the left. High school kids had their own room on the right."

"You're telling me that that building held classes for elementary on up through high school?"

"Had two teachers. One principal. The principal was a hard-ass who used a leather strap to whip us."

"You sayin' he used it on you a time or two?"

"It was a weekly ritual. Course, I deserved it." Samuel let go a laugh. Pete followed suit.

"What did you do that'd give him cause to whip you?"

"Basically, he had no sense of humor."

"What do you mean?"

"Well, he didn't appreciate my attempts to bring levity into the classroom. I was prone to bring varmints to class. The normal kind: possums, pole cats, snakes."

"Well, that's not exactly like bringing a bowl of goldfish."

"I remember one day, I was about thirteen. Mr. Poston was his name. Anyway, he had wore me out good with the belt on account of me throwing a garter snake into a group of gals at lunchtime. We ate outdoors if the weather was nice, and as you can see, the crick runs along the edge of the schoolyard. So it was pretty easy findin' slimy creatures. Anyways, Poston laid into me pretty good, and I got a little pissed off. That day after school I ran up the holler and got Jim Mason to loan me his daddy's hammer and a wrench.

"Back in those days, most folks moved around by buggy. Mr. Poston was born into some wealth, and he liked to show it off. He had this buggy with a leather seat and a fancy pearl-handled brake. I liked to climb on it from time to time. He'd always chase me off it. Anyways, I took the hammer and wrench and loosened the bolts to the wheels. Not all the way, but just enough. Me, Jimmy, and his brother hid in the woods across the crick. Not long after, old Poston brought out the horse he kept in a barn next to the school, hooked him up, and took off. He made it about thirty yards and the wheels took to wobblin'. He tightened up on the reins and seemed to think the horse was unsteady. After a few more rotations, the right front wheel came off, followed by the back right, and the buggy fell over into Spear Branch."

Pete laughed aloud at the visual of the buggy coming apart at the wheels. "He probably tried to bury you under the school for that."

"He knew right away it was me who did it. I never confessed, but I let him strap my backside just for the fellowship aspect of it."

"Sounds like you had an interesting school career."

"Well, most memories are good. Some, not so much." Samuel looked off through the passenger window at a meadow at the base of Jefferson Mountain.

***

May, 1934

When Mr. Poston rang the red iron bell beside the front steps, Samuel placed his notebook and pencil inside his wooden desk. He reached underneath the desk and grabbed a small brown vinyl suitcase by its black handle. There was chatter about the classroom from the children as they headed out the dingy high-ceilinged room.

"Are you excited, Samuel?" Mrs. Fields asked when he walked in front of her desk. Mrs. Fields had taught at Persimmon Hill for sixteen years, including Samuel all four years of his elementary days.

"Yes, ma'am," Samuel said with a huge grin. "We're going to a baseball game tomorrow. The Kingsport Blue Sox are playing the Butler Yankees. I ain't never been to a ball game before."

"You do love baseball, don't you?"

"Yes'm. Gonna play in the big leagues one day."

"Don't forget I was your teacher when you're rich and famous."

Rod, Samuel's father, was a bean trader. He owned the Burley Gap Trading Company, and traveled throughout eastern Tennessee and western North Carolina to oversee twelve warehouses. He'd been on the road for two weeks and was passing through Carter Springs on his way for the Saturday morning auction of a tobacco warehouse that had gone under. He decided to take Samuel with him for a weekend getaway.

"We're stayin' at a hotel in Kingsport," Samuel continued as he stood in front of the teacher's desk. "Mom even let me bring the good suitcase." He raised the suitcase with both hands.

"It sure is a fine one. I'm sure you'll have a great time."

He walked down the wide wooden steps into the schoolyard, the suitcase lightly rubbing against his leg as he walked. When he made it to the flagpole next to the road, he placed the suitcase on the dusty ground and straddled it. He removed a three-by-five black-and-white photo from his pocket and rubbed his tiny finger across it as if trying to smooth the bent corners.

Dressed in gray wool pants and plaid short-sleeved shirt of various shades of green and brown, Samuel looked down and rubbed his black canvas sneakers together. His white socks bunched slightly at his ankles.

The other children scattered about as they made their way home. Two Model Ts disappeared over the horizon as Potter's Hill swallowed them up. The sun slipped behind a low line of soft clouds, cooling the mountain air. Samuel didn't notice or care. He just looked impatiently toward the dusty road, his hands on his lap, clutching the picture tightly.

Thirty minutes later, dust kicked up on the road as a car came into view. Samuel rose, his back arched, as the dark-colored car rolled forward. A silhouette of a man, broad-shouldered, sat high on the seat as it closed the gap to the school to within seventy yards. Samuel stood and took his suitcase by the hand, anxious to climb aboard. As the car came upon Samuel, he looked into a pair of unfamiliar eyes. The stranger nodded at Samuel and continued on.

Mrs. Fields walked out of the school, seeing Samuel searching anxiously up the road. "Not here yet?" she called out.

"No, ma'am. But he'll be here any minute."

Mrs. Fields lived in a quaint wooden home, painted white, a quarter mile from school, and would walk to and from school in the warm months. As she took to the road for home, she turned and saw Samuel's excitement slowly fading. "Mind if I wait with you till your dad comes?" she asked as she walked toward him.

"Yes'm. Did I tell you he's taking me to a ball game?"

"Yes, sweetie, you did."

"I bet we get popcorn and hotdogs. Daddy said he might buy me a glove."

A gleam rose in his eyes as he spoke of the day his father had brought home his first bat and ball. His dad would toss the ball to Samuel, and watch Samuel run a make-believe base path when he hit the ball toward the barn.

Mrs. Fields glanced at her watch, as four o'clock was just minutes away. Samuel rubbed the picture again and looked toward the road. She tried to occupy his mind with talk of baseball, and games he liked to play at recess, but she could tell he was preoccupied. Close to an hour later, shadows stretched across the parking lot. Samuel looked down at the picture again, rubbing his father's face. The picture was taken at Samuel's birthday party when he was six. In the picture, Samuel stood beside his dad holding the new bat.

"Samuel, it's almost dark. How about if I get Mr. Fields to come take you home? Maybe your dad's waiting for you there."

Samuel shook his head. "No, ma'am. He said he was picking me up here."

Mrs. Fields rubbed her hands along the back of his head. His thick, dark brown hair ruffled gently as the spring breeze blew across the school grounds. He looked toward the road once more, tears welling in his tender eyes.

The sun was on the verge of slipping behind Jefferson Mountain. "Sammy, here comes Mr. Fields. Let us take you on home now."

Samuel shook his head. "I think I'll just walk."

"Please let us take you. It's getting late."

"No, ma'am. Thanks anyway." Samuel stood, lifting the suitcase by the handle. Head lowered, he walked toward home. He wiped his eyes with one hand while he held the suitcase tightly with the other. Mrs. Fields dabbed the tears from her eyes with tissue as she watched him walk down the dirt road into the shadows of the valley, on his way toward home.

Chapter Five

Kate slipped into the room. Her baby doll, made of cloth, dangled in her hand. The legs of the doll surrounded her tiny fingers as she leaned her elbow on her father's lap. "Miss Emily wants to give you a hug," she said as she lifted the doll to her father's face. Pete disregarded Kate's comments, and slipped his arm up slightly to block the intended hug.

"Not now, Kate. Daddy's working." Pete glared at the computer screen, and he scratched his forehead.

"She just wants to hug you." Kate again lifted the doll toward her daddy's face. Her eyes sparkled with bits of green and yellow. The soft ringlets of her blond hair hung close to her forehead. Her smile, which was known to melt Pete's heart in an instant, went unnoticed.

"I told you I'm working." Pete pushed the doll away. A more painful dagger he couldn't have thrown. As Kate walked to the den, head down, Pete looked at her. He began to speak, but didn't. She sat in a red-and-yellow chair constructed of giant pencils.

"It's okay, Miss Emily." With tears in her eyes, she kissed the doll on its soft chin. "Daddy's really busy."

Sarah walked in carrying two bags of groceries. Kate sat on the chair singing to her doll. "Why are you crying?" Sarah asked, noticing Kate's red eyes. Kate continued to sing, cradling her doll to her chest. "What's wrong, sweetie?"

"Be very quiet," Kate said. "Daddy's busy. We don't need to 'sturb him."

Sarah put the groceries on the kitchen counter and walked into the room where Pete worked on the computer. "Why's Kate crying?" Pete mumbled something and continued tapping at the keyboard. "Will you leave that computer alone and look at me? All I see is the back of your head anymore. It's like trying to carry on a conversation with someone on a bus."

"I've got to finish this article by tonight. Hear me? *Tonight.* Plus, the time I'm spending with Mr. Gable is cutting into the time I should be spending on finding a publisher." He shook his head, but his fingers stroked the keyboard. "I should have told Mom that I didn't have the time, because I don't."

"Publisher or not, that's no excuse for treating us like we're a nuisance."

"I'm not treating you like you're a nuisance. I'm just really busy right now. I feel a lot of pressure."

"You're the only one putting pressure on yourself."

"I'm mailing queries out to agents and publishers, but with no offers or book deals, by the way. Plus, all the articles I'm working on are coming due."

"Well, Kate and I are going to the park. We'll get out of your hair. We don't want to interrupt your train of thought."

Pete shrugged his shoulders and continued working. He heard Kate say as she walked out the door, "Bye, Daddy. I love you."

Pete didn't respond.

***

The phone was ringing as Sarah walked into the house. "Pete? Are you getting that?" The phone rang twice more by the time Sarah placed her Bible on the kitchen table.

"Daddy, we brought you something to eat," Kate said as she carefully carried the Styrofoam container to her father. "Look. I got you the cookie that's got paper on the inside." She placed the fortune cookie on Pete's lap.

"Just put it in the refrigerator, Kate. I don't have time to eat right now."

Kate looked curiously at the plastic wrapper that held the cookie. "Open it. Mommy says it will tell you your foo-cher."

"Not now, I said. Put it in the fridge with the food."

Sarah, while talking on the phone, took the container from Kate and placed it on the top shelf of the refrigerator. Kate pushed her hair away from her face and went to her room to find her doll.

"Hold on, Gabby. I'll put him on the phone for you." She handed the cordless phone to Pete. "Here. It's for you."

"Who is it?"

"It's Mr. Gable's daughter."

"What does she want?"

"I'm guessing if you talk to her you'll find out."

"Hello," Pete said abruptly into the phone.

"Pete, this is Gabby. I'm sorry to bother you on a Sunday."

"It's okay. What can I do for you?"

"Dad wanted me to call you. He wants to know if you could come over. He's feeling pretty good today. Said he feels like talking. Wants to know if you feel like listening."

Pete shook his head. "Can't do it. I've got a deadline to meet tonight."

"No problem. I hated to interrupt your Sunday, but when Daddy has his sights set on something, he wants to see it through."

Hearing Samuel talking in the background, Pete hesitantly asked, "How about in the morning? Can't give him more than an hour, and I'd have to do it early. Will eight work?"

After conferring with Samuel, Gabby said, "Eight would be great. Thanks so much."

***

Pete showed up at the Gable doorstep a little after eight. Recorder in hand, he followed Gabby to the parlor.

"Sit down, Pete," Samuel said. "My mind's thinkin' clearly today, so let's take advantage of it. You know, they say on a man, his memory is the second thing to go."

Pete shook his head but managed a smile. He turned the recorder on.

***

June, 1944

Samuel lay on his elbows along the edge of his foxhole. The bayonet of his rifle pointed into the darkness. It was a darkness with no depth, a canvas so heavy with nothingness that it appeared as though only open space lay in front of him. He saw no land and he saw no sky. Two feet behind him lay Bryson Steele, on his back, breathing slowly and steadily as he took advantage of his two-hour sleep shift. Samuel had tossed and turned earlier when it was his turn to sleep. He couldn't remember the last time he'd slept soundly, perhaps in Australia where he was stationed before being shipped off to New Guinea.

The sounds of the night were all around him. Creatures of unknown variety moved about the jungle floor, calling out that the night belonged to them. He heard whooshing, flapping sounds in the trees as fruit bats moved about. It was a moonless night, and Samuel could almost feel the clouds hanging thick and low above him.

Samuel was in search of sounds as well as smells. The Japanese had a strong odor about them, and though they moved in relative silence through the night, the smell gave advance notice of their arrival. And so his ears and nose became his eyes. The fear of being pierced by the enemy's bayonet shook off any sleepiness he might have battled.

Dawn was still hours away, though Samuel saw no reason to switch places with Steele. Might as well let Steele get a full night's sleep, was the way Samuel saw it. And so, when dawn began to lighten the darkness, Samuel was glad that they'd survived to see the light of day.

It was late June, and the men had marched through the jungles for two months. Their destination was Leyte, where ten thousand Japanese soldiers waited. In Leyte were strategic airfields that were crucial for supplying the Japanese army. The journey was slow and tedious. Trade winds had changed, and the rainy season was under way. The troops trudged through the dense jungles, advancing hill by hill. By day they fought, small skirmishes, as the enemy tried to wear down the Allies before they could make it to Leyte. Malaria and Dengue Fever had worked its way through the battalion, and the daily onslaught of rain made it impossible for the men to dry out. At night, the foxholes would fill with water, and the men would sleep with their bodies submerged except for their faces.

It was morning, no different from the rest, and the men prepared for a long march. They tied canvas between two coconut trees in an attempt to eat food not soaked with rain. Breakfast was small rations of beans and chipped beef. Suffocating clouds hung heavy, and the treetops became hazy, lifeless bones of gray.

Samuel and Bryson Steele moved out, the first pair, and the rest of the scout squad, eighty men in all, fell in close behind. They moved in small groups, staying low, slipping through the muddy jungles in silence. They were on a trail two miles shy of the Daguitan River. As Samuel and Steele slipped into a ravine, they heard whooshing sounds and crouched in cover. Looking closely, they saw vultures jockeying for position as they ate the remains of lifeless Japanese soldiers, tearing through their uniforms to pick the meat off their bones. The bodies, sprawled across in random fashion, indicated a surprise attack.

As Samuel and Steele led the way through the scattering of the dead, Samuel noticed movement in the bushes. He signaled Steele and crouched with his rifle raised. He stepped slowly toward the ground-covering nipa palms. As he parted the long limbs with his gun, a Japanese soldier, just a boy, held his hands up in the air as he lay on his back. His bloodstained jacket covered the wound to his midsection, and the canvas-like material of his shirt adhered to the opening in his stomach. Samuel removed his canteen, stooped beside the young soldier, and held his head up to give him a drink. The rest of the battalion came upon the scene.

"Let that Jap die, Gable," Samuel's commanding officer said. Samuel ignored the order, and the Japanese soldier grasped hold of Samuel's sleeve as he struggled to drink. "Did you hear me, soldier?"

Samuel shrugged off the order. "Just easin' his sufferin' if I can." He nodded toward the soldier's midsection. "He won't last much longer. His belly's done turned to green." The putrid smell of infection loomed heavy, and the young man's eyes told of one who knew death was just a few heartbeats away. The soldier struggled, speaking softly, looking at no one, and Samuel wondered if the boy was calling the names of loved ones. His breathing became labored, coming in short bursts, and his eyes rolled back as blood began to trickle from his mouth. He looked at Samuel one last time, and his grip on Samuel's sleeve began to ease. His head fell lifeless against Samuel's forearm, his last breath dissipating silently into the heavy air.

The men continued toward the river, and word spread of enemy troops amassing along the eastern bank. The jungles were busy with sounds. A small band of long-tail macaque monkeys moved about in the treetops, their high-pitched chattering echoing through the dense forest. Swifts darted low around the palms, the killing jungle their playground. As the Red Arrowmen moved on, the sounds of the jungles were replaced by gunfire coming from the hills above them. They came upon a small band of the 77th Infantry, dug in a perimeter. The Japanese were hidden in bunkers and foxholes on the side of the thick jungle hillside, and they seemed to have hemmed in the soldiers from the front and both sides.

Samuel spotted a medic tending to a wounded soldier. The young soldier writhed in pain, his midsection heaving as the medic attempted to stop extensive bleeding in his chest. As the medic worked frantically to stop the bleeding, a bullet ripped through the medic's neck. His body crumpled across the injured soldier, suffocating him. The two became silent as Samuel's regiment took cover, bullets raining down from the hills above. Several of Samuel's men were hit. Samuel took cover behind a fallen tree, looking at the hill in front of him. The wounded cried out as panic began to overtake some of the men.

The field medics began to organize the removal of the wounded as the troops shot into the jungle. It took four men to carry each wounded soldier, and as they jostled the men out, many screamed in pain. The battalion returned fire and the volley of bullets rang through the air. Steele tossed a grenade toward a pair of Japanese soldiers who slipped in from a thicket. The explosion sent their lifeless bodies into the trees. As Steele knelt next to Samuel, he glanced over his shoulder. Samuel watched as a medic knelt beside a soldier who had taken a bullet to his thigh, which was ripped to shreds, blood pouring out so that there was no visible appearance of skin. The medic injected him with morphine, and four soldiers placed him on a canvas gurney. As he was carried away, his exposed femur bone bobbed like a buoy.

The rains roared and the winds blew, and the troops saw that hell was not confined to hot pits and roaring furnaces. They retreated quickly, one hundred and twenty yards from the base of the hill. Three more men were struck as they retreated. While the men pulled away under a cloud of fear and frustration, Samuel felt anger that he was unable to help the men.

The men dug foxholes as the last traces of day disappeared. They whispered quietly in the pitch blackness, eating rations of jerky in tag-team fashion as the rotation began manning watch from the bunkers. They tried to ease the worries of what awaited at daybreak, knowing an attack might come in the darkness.

Before dawn, Jackson, the commanding officer, instructed Samuel, Steele, and Joseph Amato to work their way to the base of what was called Tanqray Hill. Jackson concluded that the amount of rapid fire coming from the hill had to be from a machine gun. As the men planned their strategy, a hooded pitohui cried out from a tree branch above them. Its black-and-orange wings flapped harshly as it chased the eastern sky.

The sun was still an hour shy of making its appearance above the massive mountain range, but it had begun to soften the night sky into soft shades of orange and purple. It had been weeks since they had seen a sunrise that wasn't gray or lifeless. New hope, perhaps. As the three men made their way through the underbrush, they neared the bottom of the steep-sloped hillside. They sneaked into a foxhole that had been dug for some previous battle, and Steele scoured the hill with binoculars. Samuel saw no movement in the jungle, but smelled the pungent odor of the Japanese soldiers nearby. As Amato pointed to a clump of bamboo leaves sixty yards in front, gunfire erupted. The men dived into the foxhole, bullets zipping around them.

The fire from the gunner had Samuel, Steele, and Amato hemmed in. They were caught in crossfire, and could not advance or retreat. Their only chance was to survive until dark and then retreat. The men were weary, and when the last traces of the day faded, they moved along the jungle floor back to their platoon.

The next day was rainy and bleak. Steele, Samuel, and two other soldiers again advanced to the bottom of the hill amid sporadic gunfire, just below the sight line of the machine gunner. The men were pinned in as the gunner opened fire whenever they tried to rise up or move away from the foxhole. Since the machine gun was set in a permanent bunker, it could only depress so far, which kept Samuel and the others safe so long as they stayed in the foxhole.

Two soldiers lay in front of Samuel, their bodies decaying in the heat and humidity. Samuel tried twice to get to them, the thought of them lying dead and exposed like animals making him seethe. The men deserved proper burial, and he promised them silently he would take care of that. First, the machine gunner had to be taken out.

As they crouched in the foxhole plotting their strategy, a grenade tumbled into the shallow bunker behind them. Shrapnel from the explosion ripped open the right side of Steele's body, wounding him in the arm, hip, and leg. The impact knocked him to the top of the foxhole, and the gunner opened fire. Steele's flesh burned, and the smell made him roll to his side, the pain so intense that he vomited. Samuel leaped beside Steele's bloodied body.

"Help me, Sammy."

"I got you."

"Don't let me die."

"No chance of that."

Steele writhed in pain as bullets buzzed a foot above him. Amato spotted the grenade thrower and took him down with a single shot.

"Hold it together, Steele," Samuel replied as he hovered above him, so close that Steele felt the warmth of

Samuel's breath against his face. Samuel, who had taken shrapnel in his forearm, knew he had precious little time to move Steele out of harm's way if he had any hopes for survival. When Samuel noticed the bloody shirt around Steele's midsection, he assumed he had been hit in the stomach. A shot to the gut was fatal in those days.

Gunfire surrounded Samuel as the gunner tried to make a hit. Steele was going into shock, and a medic had scampered to the scene. He injected Steele with morphine, and bullets roared in from the hillside. Samuel rolled to his knees, looking down over Steele, bullets zipping inches above his head and shoulders. He took hold of Steele's sleeves at the shoulders. "Hold on, I'm gettin' you out of here. Cover me," he yelled to Amato, as Amato began shooting toward the hill.

With adrenaline pouring through his veins, Samuel dragged Steele, who weighed nearly two hundred pounds, from the edge of the foxhole and into low-lying bushes and ground cover. Bullets ripped the trees and bamboo as Samuel pulled Steele across the muddy terrain. He made it a hundred and twenty feet, disappearing into the thick jungle. Two medics met the pair as Amato was gunned down trying to escape the bunker.

"If you don't survive this, I'm gonna kill you," Samuel said as Steele was carried away by stretcher.

"I'm too stubborn to die," Steele said. As the medic's truck drove off, Samuel prayed he was right.

***

Samuel looked out across the pond and scratched his forehead. "You know, I thought that old boy was dyin' that day. But he made it. He died last Christmas in Atlanta.

You know, there ain't but a few of us left from my company. Soon, there'll be one less."

The men sat in silence for a moment. Pete wanted to say something to console Samuel, but was at a loss. "That's all I got for today," Samuel whispered. He held the side bars as he let go a vicious cough that seemed to originate from deep in his lungs. Pete contemplated placing his hand on Samuel's shoulder, but simply turned and walked out of the room.

Gabby sat on a rocker on the porch, crying quietly. Pete's first thought was that she looked utterly alone and helpless. He touched her shoulder, more of a pat than anything else, and then headed down the steps. He wanted to speak, but what could he say that would help? A writer he was, but the spoken word escaped him when it pertained to the matter of death.

He opened his car door and looked back at the porch. Gabby had pulled her feet onto the rocker, her face pressed up against her knees. Pete looked skyward for a moment, reluctantly closed the door, and returned to the porch. "Are you okay?" he asked quietly and with no pretense of looking to intrude. "Is there anything I can do?"

She rubbed her eyes with the inside of her long sweatshirt. She shook her head and took a deep breath. "You're already doing it. He's finally telling his story, and I can't thank you enough."

"I'm not doing anything special. Just listening, allowing him to speak what's on his mind, in his heart. Your father is quite a man." Pete sat on the top step of the porch, at the foot of the rocker.

Gabby raised her head, wiped her eyes with her sleeve, and looked out over the hollow. "He's the toughest, most stubborn man I've ever known. I was never afraid when I was with Daddy. Inside his arms was the safest place in the world." She sighed. "But now his arms are growing weaker by the day. Soon he'll be gone and I'll never feel the safety of those arms again."

"Gabby, I wish I knew what to say." He looked out toward the open sky. "I hate that you're going through this. It's obvious he loves you very much, and what you have is something many people go a lifetime without experiencing. So, in that regard, you should feel lucky."

She nodded, a look of numbness in her eyes. "I know," she whispered.

Pete felt surprised in a way that he was actually saying words which seemed to comfort. He turned, rising to one knee so he was kneeling in front of the rocker. He saw the look of hopelessness, and he touched her shin, rubbing gently against her jeans. He smiled, and she simply nodded. "It's great that you love him so much. I can only hope that my daughter feels the same toward me some day."

She took the hand that was touching her leg, and she stood, guiding him up until he was standing in front of her. She turned her head and placed it against his chest, slipped her arms around him, and wept. He slowly put his arms around her, and though the hug caught him off guard, she felt good in his arms. He tenderly moved his hand along her spine, and she spoke no words, as if content just feeling the beating of his heart. Though she wore no perfume, she smelled delicately sweet. Maybe it was her shampoo, her deodorant, or the fabric softener in her soft shirt. Whatever it was, Pete loved the aroma.

She pulled away from him ever so slightly, rubbing her hair away from her forehead. She looked into his eyes, and he could see the pain deep within her. She reached up and kissed him on the cheek. "Thanks for being here. Thanks for helping Daddy."

"I truly wish there was something more I could do. You're shouldering this all on your own. I slip in, listen to his tales, slip out, and you are left all by yourself to deal with the situation."

Gabby touched his face softly with her fingers. "You are doing more than I could ever expect."

As they stared into each other's eyes, their arms still wrapped around each other, Pete felt her vulnerability, her casting emotions unashamedly onto his heart. He saw the beauty within her, deep within her, and his heart softened. The sound of Samuel coughing broke the gaze their eyes held.

"I need to check on Daddy."

"Sure thing." He watched her walk to the door, and she turned to him and smiled faintly.

The ride home was filled with clouded thoughts.

Chapter Six

Pete lay in his bed, staring quietly at the ceiling. He couldn't help thinking about the tender kiss he had received from Gabby. It felt so innocent, and surely was just a spur-of-the-moment show of gratitude. To him it was understandable that Gabby was simply showing her appreciation to Pete for easing her father's pain, even if he was simply listening to Samuel share his stories. And with no one else to turn to, it was only normal she turned to him for consolation.

Sarah finished brushing her teeth and crawled in beside him. She reached to turn off the lamp on the nightstand when she noticed Pete staring at the ceiling. "You okay?" she asked.

"I'm just running some ideas through my head about the Daniel Boone story." The soft fragrance of Gabby drifted delicately about in his memory.

"How did it go at Mr. Gable's today?"

"What?"

"You sure look deep in thought. I asked how it went at Samuel Gable's today."

"Good. Pretty good, I guess." He noticed her looking at him as he continued to look at the ceiling, as though she was hoping for a little more input.

"Well, is that it? What did he talk about? Still wishing you hadn't committed to interviewing him?"

"No," he said, trying to hide his guilt for feeling that something new, or rather someone new, had presented itself as a reason to visit Samuel. "I'm realizing how amazing he is. I see in his eyes a man who represents everything good. I hear him speak and it makes me feel inadequate in so many ways. I think of his life, his ability to face death for so long, and his ability to leave that horrible time on the battlefield as an accountant might leave his ledger books on his desk when the five-o'clock whistle blows. His body is weakening, but there's a fire in him that I can only imagine. And I see Gabby's heart breaking each day."

"It's got to be hard on her watching him die. I'm glad you're taking the time to listen to him. Are you going to write an article about him and pitch it to a magazine?"

"Haven't decided yet. He sure has a lot to talk about. And it is amazingly interesting. At the least I'm going to accumulate the stories and write something up to give to Gabby. He said the name Caleb. Don't know who that is. His son, maybe."

"What did he say about him?"

"He just mentioned his name and said something about wondering if he might want to read whatever I write. When I asked who he was, he brushed me off, saying he was ready to get started. He definitely wasn't in the mood to discuss it."

"When do you plan on seeing him again?"

"I don't know. Don't know how much more he wants to tell me. Maybe he's about through."

"Can you imagine being at the end of your life and you're trying to describe it? If it were me, I'd want to talk about how much I loved my family, not some time spent in a war."

"You should hear some of what he's been through. I think that would change your perspective."

"I think he's very lucky to have someone who can put into words what he's leaving behind for his family."

"I've got some good material to work with, that's for sure. It's mind-boggling how vivid his memory of the war is."

"What about his wife? Does he talk about her?"

"No. I think she died years ago. Mom said something about it the other day. I remember her saying how sad it was,. Her passing, I mean. I didn't ask about it."

"Wonder if he'll tell you about her."

"I'm hoping he sticks to the war. I've got so much work to do. Anyway, he seems pretty private when it comes to family matters. Besides, if I don't find a publisher for my book, I'm going to start losing my mind. I can't pass on any magazine opportunities. I'm tired of you carrying the load. I've put years into this, and I'm so close to getting published that I can't set that aside for Mr. Gable. No matter that he's dying."

***

Pete lifted his head slightly and glanced at the caller ID. He saw the Gable name, and his heart jumped. Was Gabby calling to apologize? Was she wanting to invite him back out to see her father? To see *her*? Pete felt a sense of guilt and decided to let the machine pick up. From the kitchen he heard a scratchy voice say, "Hey, Pete, this is Samuel Gable. I was hopin' you could stop by today. I've thought of more to tell you about. Maybe you could make it for dinner. I'll get Gabby to throw another chicken leg in the pot." After a series of coughs: "Sorry about that. Anyway, hope to hear from you."

Pete tried to write but his mind couldn't focus. What to do? Dinner with Mr. Gable; dinner with Gabby? What if he became an easy crutch for Gabby? That could get dangerous. He thought about how good she felt in his arms, and hesitantly turned on his recorder to listen to Charlie Coleman's comments about the museum.

Nightfall came, and Sarah and Kate walked in the front door. Pete had spent the day at his desk, his shoulders slumped slightly in front of his computer. As Kate came in for a hug, Sarah played the message on the machine. "Mr. Gable called. Did you already go see him?"

"I didn't go. Don't have the time."

"Did you call him back and reschedule?"

"Nope."

"You should at least call him."

"I will."

***

It was Wednesday morning when Pete dropped the handful of letters in the mailbox outside the post office. He was sending query letters and sample chapters to agents in New York. He had sent at least thirty already and knew it was a numbers game. He wanted a book deal more than anything he'd ever wanted. His cell phone rang as he cranked the car. "Hi, Mom."

"Hello, Pete. Did you hear about Samuel Gable?"

"No, ma'am. Is he okay?"

"They had to take him to Boone Medical Center last night. His blood pressure dropped and they're worried he might have suffered a stroke."

Pete headed down Jefferson Highway toward home. He had two more days to finish his Daniel Boone story. As he approached the rolling lane that climbed the hill to his home, he made a U-turn and headed for Boone.

***

The nurse at the desk outside ICU, looking over some color-coded chart, removed the phone from its base when Pete walked up.

"Excuse me, but can you give me an update on Samuel Gable?"

The nurse placed the phone on her shoulder, turned, and looked as a second nurse walked up. "What's the latest on Mr. Gable?"

"Are you family?" the second nurse asked.

"A friend of the family." Pete looked down the hall and noticed Gabby stepping into the corridor. "There's his daughter. Can I walk down and see her for a minute?"

The nurse nodded and began dialing the phone.

Gabby leaned against the wall, dressed in dark jeans and black North Face jacket. Her arms were folded across her chest. She stared at the black-and-white tile floor. Her shoulder-length hair hung down around her face, and Pete couldn't see her eyes. To Pete, her despair only seemed to make her look more endearing.

He walked up beside her, his hands in his jacket pockets. "Hi, Gabby. How's he doing?"

Gabby slowly shook her head and bit her bottom lip. "I found him on the floor beside his bed. His body was shaking, and he was just coherent enough to try and pull himself up. He looked like a frightened child who didn't know where he was. He was gasping for breath, his eyes wild and unfocused."

Pete placed his hand on her shoulder and his fingers touched her soft hair. "What did the doctor say?"

Gabby brushed the hair away from her face. "They're running tests to see if he suffered a mild stroke. Daddy hates hospitals, so he's not going to be happy. Daddy said no matter what, he wasn't going to die in a hospital."

"Can I do anything? Can I get you something to eat or drink?" He longed to soothe her sadness.

"No, thanks. Would you like to see him?"

"I really shouldn't. It's just…"

"Just for a minute. I know he'd like to see you."

Pete followed her through the door. Samuel lay with his eyes closed. A thin tube ran along his face, just under his nose. He had needles in his hand and his chest. Gabby walked to the side of the bed and rubbed her hand along his forearm. "Daddy, you have a visitor."

Samuel slowly opened his eyes and glanced about the room. He looked at Gabby, and saw Pete standing behind her.

"Caleb?"

Pete looked at Gabby, and slowly looked back at Samuel. "No, sir. It's Pete."

"This place don't look familiar." His eyes looked cloudy. He looked at the needles attached to his body. "This ain't the Carter County Hospital."

"No, sir," Gabby said. "This is Boone. They thought you might have had a stroke and so they brought you here."

"Get me out of this place. Take me home." He looked at Pete. "What are you doin' drivin' here to Boone?"

"I was just worried, sir. Wanted to see if you were okay. To let Gabby know I was here if she needed me."

"I appreciate the gesture, but it's a waste of time 'cause I'm headin' home."

"Daddy, you can't leave. They're running tests on you in the morning. They've got fluids pumping through your

71

veins. You think they're gonna just let you walk out of here and go home?"

"Pete, while you're here, how 'bout you remind my daughter that I ain't dyin' in a hospital. That's all a hospital is, a place to die."

"Well, you might not be able to take on the Japs in the jungle right now," Pete said, "so maybe you oughtta hang out here a little longer."

"Ah," he waved his hand, "what do you know?" Pete looked at his feet like a scolded pup. "Did you bring your recorder?"

"Sir?"

"Your recorder. Do you have it?"

"It's in the car. Why?"

"Do you have time for a story?"

"Daddy, you need your rest," Gabby said. "Besides, Pete has more important things to do than sit around here and listen to you talk while you're hooked in and strapped up."

"Hog testicles. I don't need rest. Restin's all I do anyway. How 'bout it, Pete?" Samuel raised his right hand to his mouth, the one with no needles attached, his cough rattling from deep in his throat.

"Are you sure you're up to it? Would you rather wait till you feel better?"

"When your days are down to your last, you best take advantage of them while you can. So just shut up and get your recorder."

"Yes, sir. I'll be right back."

"That's nice of you to offer, Pete," said Gabby. "But you don't have to stay."

"It's not a problem," said Pete as he turned toward the door. His to-do list was long, but he just couldn't say no to Samuel. How many days did Samuel have left to tell his story? Pete didn't want to waste one he couldn't get back.

When Pete slipped up beside Samuel's bed, sitting in a metal chair Gabby had found in the closet, Samuel excused Gabby to the cafeteria. She hadn't eaten since breakfast, and he wanted her fed. A nurse, stocky in nature with a flowery top of blue and mauve, brought two pills in a tiny cup which she placed on Samuel's tray. "Mr. Gable, you need to take these pills." She looked at Pete's recorder, frowned, obviously not happy. "You really need to get some rest."

"Don't you have a bed pan to change?" Samuel asked. "Go. Git." The nurse lowered her eyebrows at Samuel, shook her head, and left the room without speaking. "Afflicted. We're smack dab in Psychoville. And I'm the mayor."

Pete couldn't help but laugh as he turned on the recorder. "Fire away."

Samuel again looked to gather his thoughts, which Pete thought would be impossible given the needles and beeping and whirring sounds of the machines around him.

"Well, I witnessed many things in the war. Some things I saw I wouldn't wish on the devil himself. Fightin, killin'. Takin' lives of young men. Men who were probably like us in many ways. They were fightin' for their country. Whether or not they were forced into it or chose it, I'll never know. But that wasn't for us to decide, to worry about. We did what we had to do. We were a close-knit bunch. War will do that. When you're countin' on the man beside you to save you, you better be ready to do the same. With regard to my men, I woulda done anything for 'em. And they'd have done the same for me. As bad as we had it, there were those worse off than us. And so I don't want this storytellin' to be made out like I was the only guy over there livin' in harm's way."

"I understand. What I write will just be for your family. Surely they'd want to know what you went through, what kind of soldier you were. I'd want to know that about my dad."

"Well, there was something I did for the cause that I will say I'm proud of, and don't mind you writin' about it in such a manner."

"What is it?"

"The Villa Verde Monument in Luzon. We lost nine hundred and sixteen men in that battle. We had to climb the Villa Verde trail in order to capture Luzon and Yamashita's men. It was our final battle. We sealed the deal with that one and the Japs surrendered. The island was ours at that point."

Samuel coughed and his face turned red. Pete gave Samuel water that sat in a plastic cup, a small straw bent to the side. Pete took the cup from Samuel when he'd finished and set it back where he'd found it.

"So, you want me to mention something about the monument?"

"Well, yes, but specifically about restorin' it. It had been tore all to hell and we had it restored in 1987." Samuel coughed again, took a deep breath, collected his thoughts, trying to block the pain raging through his body. Pete wondered if he could ever have the willpower Samuel possessed.

"Can you give me background on the battle before we talk about the monument?" asked Pete.

"Well, I can. Don't you want to hear about the monument now?"

"After the battle. And I want all the details."

"You're a sneaky little weasel, ain't ya?"

"You got that right."

"After that you'll listen to me talk about the monument?"

"Absolutely. You're a sneaky weasel yourself, ain't you?"

"You got that right."

***

February, 1945

The men of the 32nd arrived at Luzon weak and weary. Samuel, meanwhile, was in a makeshift hospital outside of Tacloban City in Leyte. On a narrow cot he lay, flushed with fever. Sweat soaked his body, and the blanket underneath him had soured. For two weeks, night and day held no meaning as he drifted through a foggy revolving door that bridged consciousness and delirium. His eyes held no focus. His mind became a black-and-white reel of horrid dreams. Were the muffled voices around him the sick and indigent of the hospital, or were they the voices of men dying on the battlefield?

Blaney Sims was a nurse from Columbus, Georgia, who'd worked the MASH unit for nine months. She tended to Samuel, trying to lower his temperature, which hovered around one hundred five degrees. She washed his face, his neck, his arms, and dampened his chest. She could feel his heart beating heavily.

Though she tended to many of the wounded, she felt drawn to Samuel. Several times she thought he was not going to survive. Samuel would call her Callie, and he would reach for her hand and squeeze tightly. She knew he was delirious, but the way he called her that name, the way he touched her hand, she began to think that Callie was a loved woman. A woman who was lucky enough to have the heart of this soldier.

When Samuel's fever finally broke, and he regained his ability to think clearly, Blaney sat by his bed, talking to him, asking him questions about his hometown. She wanted to ask who Callie was, but couldn't bring herself to do it. She wanted him healed, but in some way didn't want him to leave. On the twelfth day, he was antsy and told the doctors he was ready to be rejoined with his men. A young doctor named Mahaffey, from Richmond, asked him if he realized how close to death he was. Samuel replied that he didn't care, that he was healed and that was all that mattered. It mattered not that twice the chaplain had given last rites. Samuel declared his last rites were to be determined at a much later date. For now, it was time to return to the fight.

Traveling by ship, Samuel was on his way to rejoin his company. Military transport carried him from the ship to shore by way of an amphibious tank-looking vehicle called "the Duck." As he rode along the dusty dirt highway to join the troops, he glanced across the skyline that lay before him. The mountain rose in waves of barren hillsides to a peak that faded into the haze of the late-morning sky. The burnt-red canyons reminded him of the time he was taken by train to California before shipping off to Southeast Asia. Growing up in the lush Appalachians, the red granite mountains of Luzon made him wonder if he'd been driven to Mars.

Luzon was the last Japanese stronghold. If it was lost, there was nothing standing in the way of the US troops and the coast of Japan. General Yamashita had little support left from his naval and air forces, and had assembled three militia groups to protect this northernmost island of the Philippines. For the men of the 32nd, the task was to ascend the rugged mountains and take control. What stood between them and Yamashita's men was a twenty-four-mile path called the Villa Verde Trail.

Conquering the Japanese in such an intense theater of war, a place described as hell on earth, was hard enough. Adding to the misery starvation and disease, reducing the men to a zombie-like state, had them believing they would die in the foreign land they had grown to despise. Still they pressed on, hoping that the battle of Luzon would either bring an end to the war or quicken their date with destiny. Ascending the Villa Verde would be their final stand.

At the base of the mountain were tents and lean-tos that housed the men of the 32nd. Samuel walked to the captain's tent, where he was instructed how to find his men. What he found was a depleted group of soldiers. They had lost over one hundred men from the original outfit of two hundred and eight, and replacements had not yet arrived. Samuel spotted Jack Stern outside his tent, eating from a can of beans.

"You're one ugly soldier," Samuel said as he walked up.

Stern looked slowly skyward and pushed his helmet away from his forehead. "You old snake. We thought you was dead. But here you stand, looking pissed off and ready to take on the Japs all by yourself."

"I ain't takin' on the Japs by myself. I'm sending you instead." Samuel sat on his duffel bag and Stern listed the names of the men who'd died in Leyte. Many more were injured, and Samuel wondered about their fate.

"Lieutenant says if we take Luzon, we're goin' home," Stern said. "I been here so long, I don't know if I even care about goin' home. At least here I know what my purpose is. Back home I don't know what I'll do. I ain't heard from Angelina in six months. Who knows, maybe she done run off with somebody else."

"Ain't none of us heard any word from our loved ones, so stop your belly-achin'," said Samuel. "You might be ugly, but you ain't stupid. Everything will be fine once we finish our job here and make it back home."

Luzon was well-defended, and protecting the Villa Verde trail was paramount for the Japanese. Every step of the trail was protected by heavy artillery and mortars, soldiers hunkered down in pillboxes all along the winding path that was not much wider than a hog trail. Destiny awaited the Red Arrowmen, as it was either time to die or seal the victory and go home.

Juan Villa Verde was a Spanish priest who'd devoted his life to educating the hill people of Luzon in the 1800s. The trail was originally created in almost vertical fashion, and Father Villa Verde led the way in creating a more tolerable path that snaked more subtly across the mountain. He was dead and buried long before it was to become a part of the biggest theater of war in the history of the United States.

Within a week, more men had arrived to shore up the troops, and orders were given to climb the trail. Samuel was ready to lead his team. He spoke with his men the night before they were to begin the climb. Where they had spent the previous eighteen months forging ahead in the jungles, the barren mountainside would call for a completely different strategy.

It was before daybreak, though the skies had begun to lighten. A steady drizzle fell, tapping Samuel's tent in a soothing melody that strangely reminded him of lazy, rainy mornings back home. The men of the 32nd, tired and weary, were ready to ascend the mountain in what would culminate into a four-month epic battle.

***

Gabby sat in the cafeteria. An hour had passed since she'd left Pete and Samuel to talk. She held a cold cup of coffee in her hand, and though her stomach growled, she had little appetite. Sitting alone in front of a window that looked out over the library of Appalachian State University, she watched students walk underneath the yellow streetlamps and she longed for the simpler days when she'd walked the same path, worrying only about going to class and lining up her social calendar.

***

Samuel began coughing and Pete refilled his paper cup from the plastic jug sitting on the food tray. Samuel sipped slowly.

"Mr. Gable, let's finish the part about the battle when you're feeling better," Pete said. "You need your rest."

"I won't hear of it, so stay where you are," Samuel said. "It ain't the battle I want to tell you about now. It's the monument."

"I don't understand."

"When we finished the battle of Luzon, and the war was decided, we got sent back home. We had been there the longest, so they had fresh troops come in and finish up. Well, for the next forty years I went without knowin' that a monument had been erected by the troops after we came home. I found out about it from a soldier I ran into on a trip to St. Louis. Anyway, I wanted to go back and see the monument. We lost so many men on that trail and I wanted to pay my respects. So I flew military standby back to the Philippines. It took nearly a week to get there. I found some local guy to drive me from the base to the monument. And what I found made me sick."

"What was it?"

"The monument still stood, but it was in terrible shape. The plaque that had been placed on the monument had been removed, or stolen. Don't know which. The base of the monument was black as soot. My driver said floods from typhoons had caused the damage, and none of the locals did anything about it. So I returned home intent on restoring it."

Samuel told of how he found out the men of the 32nd had formed a veterans association. He flew to a meeting in Michigan to tell them the situation of the monument, and that he needed assistance. He talked about the need for raising money to re-create a plaque. A plaque that he would, two years later, carry on his lap by plane to the Philippines. The money they raised paid for two local men to paint the monument and restore the plaque.

"Of all the things I've done in my life related to the military, restoring that monument gives me the most satisfaction. I sure couldn't bring back the soldiers who died on that trail, but at least I could keep their memory alive. They deserved that."

***

After the story was told, Samuel tired and began to doze off. Pete slipped out of the room and walked to the cafeteria. Gabby sat, staring at her cup of coffee, digging her nail into the side of the cup as if carving hieroglyphics for the janitor to decipher. She looked up when she saw Pete approach, and she was glad he'd found her. "How's he doing?"

"He's asleep. Seems to be resting pretty comfortably."

"Thanks for taking the time to come here. I realize you really went out of your way."

"Not a problem. I'm growing quite fond of the old guy."

"He can be a little gruff, especially to other men. But he's softhearted."

"Is that where you get it?"

"I don't know if I *got* it, but I think I did get a good dosage of both Mom and Daddy."

"Let me buy you something to eat."

"No, thanks, I'm good."

"How you gonna keep your strength up if you don't take care of yourself?" Pete looked at the menu on the wall behind the counter. "Let's see, they got sandwiches, salads, fruit." He pointed to the counter. "They've got cookies the size of tractor tires. How about one of those chocolate ones?"

81

Gabby laughed briefly. "Really, I'm okay." She was embarrassed at the attention.

"If you don't pick something, I'll do it for you, and there's no telling what I might choose. I'm inclined to get you the bison burger."

"Okay, okay. But no buffalo." She looked at the menu. "Do they really have that here?"

"Sure, right next to the haggis and ostrich." He laughed. "No, no bison." He shook his head in mock disappointment and she laughed. She liked how he made her laugh.

She looked at the menu. "Well, the chicken salad sounds good."

"Done." Pete walked to the counter, and Gabby smiled as she watched him talk with the elderly lady who prepared the sandwich, noticing how quickly he brought a smile to the woman's face. Gabby noticed Pete was able to make those around him feel at ease. For the first time, she noticed his broad shoulders; his athletic build. Something inside her churned. She wondered how she had not noticed before. She wasn't sure, but she knew she liked the way he looked in his black leather jacket.

"Here you go," he said as he placed the paper plate in front of her. He put a bottle of water beside the plate. "Thought you might need water to choke down the food. I'm not really up to speed on the Heimlich, so I prefer you handle the dislodging of any food yourself."

Gabby smiled and took a small bite, though she had no appetite.

"What do you do for a living?" asked Pete.

"I was an insurance agent before I quit to take care of Daddy."

"Insurance, huh?"

"Riveting stuff, isn't it? I can see the envy in your eyes."

"Well, somebody's got to sell it, right?"

"I guess. Actually, I'd been thinking of changing careers before I quit." She sighed.

"So you plan on doing something different down the road?"

"God, I hope so. Can I tell you a secret?"

Pete leaned forward in his chair. "Sure."

"I've always had a desire to write."

"Really? Well, why don't you?"

"I wouldn't know where to start."

"What kind of writing interests you most?"

"I'm a sucker for epic love stories. And I like a little murder mystery thrown in for good measure."

"Sounds like you have a good place to start."

"There are a few ideas stored in my head that I think might make for a good story, although I'm sure everyone feels they have the perfect novel inside their head just waiting to be written."

"I think a lot of people want to write but either don't take the time, or have the time, to do it."

"You're writing a book, aren't you?"

"It's already written. I'm looking for an agent. And let me tell you, it's a long, hard process."

"Tell me about the book."

Few things sparked Pete's emotions like talking about his novel. A four-year project, the book changed his path in life. Working nights and weekends, glued to his computer, Pete found a part of his being come to life he never knew existed. An awakening had occurred, and he quit his full-time job to take the plunge of his life. He convinced a small magazine to let him write a small piece, and from there it grew to writing for ten different publications. But it was his book that defined everything he was, not just as a writer, but as a man. He wanted nothing more than to find an agent and pen novels till the day he died.

"Have you ever wanted to go back in time?"

"Back in time?" Gabby asked. "You mean like Roman Empire, Biblical times, kind of stuff?"

"No, not that. I'm talking about your past. Haven't you ever thought how cool it would be to relive a part of your life, totally aware of how your life had already unfolded in the future?"

"Of course. Who wouldn't?"

"I'd jump at the chance to go back. To be with my family, and with my childhood friends, playing baseball when nothing else mattered but what happened on the field. To be a kid again, knowing all the things I know now."

"So, in this book, you go back in time? What age are you? Do you relive your whole life?"

"I'm twelve years old again. But just for a few weeks."

"Do you tell your family that you've gone back in time?"

"I tell my mother at the very end. The purpose of the book is to take people back, to a time when we didn't have to worry about parents dying. No bills, no budgets. Just a second chance to be young again. In the book, I spend time with my family, as well as try to right the wrongs I made the first time."

"Sign me up."

"What kind of books do you like to read? Who is your favorite author?"

"I like many, but my favorite is Cormac McCarthy."

She smiled and shook her head. "I love McCarthy."

Pete was stunned. "You're jerking me around, aren't you?"

"No, why would I?"

"Women aren't suppose to like McCarthy. He writes 'manly' books."

She laughed. "Manly or not, I love his work. Wasn't *Blood Meridian* unbelievable?"

Pete had never, ever found any female who liked McCarthy's work, as they always claimed it was too cold-blooded and depressing.

"*Blood Meridian* is phenomenal." He rubbed his hands through his hair. "I can't believe you like him. He's the best writer in the world. No one else comes close." He shook his head. "You have just made it to the top of the list of people I'm most impressed with."

"That's good to know. What does that get me?"

"Name it."

She batted her eyes and smiled. "How about an autographed copy of your book when it's published?"

"You got it. I'll hand deliver it to you." Pete watched her run her fingers through her hair.

It was getting late, and Pete needed to head home, though he was in no hurry to leave. Gabby took another bite of her sandwich, and a small crumb hung at the edge of her lower lip. "Um, you have a little something on the side of your mouth."

"Oh, do I?" She rubbed her napkin along the corners of her mouth. "I was saving it for later."

"It's still there." She moved the paper napkin across her lips but missed it again. Pete reached across and brushed the crumb away, his finger gently touching her lip. "Got it." She stared at him, eyes soft, and for a moment there were no words spoken.

"Well," she said, blushing, "guess I better head upstairs and check on Daddy."

Pete nodded, wondering how someone so pretty and sweet could be single. She *was* single, wasn't she? She wore no ring.

Pete walked her to the elevator, and their arms touched slightly as they walked. "Thanks again for coming tonight. I know Daddy appreciates it too. Oh, and thanks for the food." She smiled and touched the lapel of his jacket. "The conversation wasn't too bad either."

"I'm glad I was able to be here." Pete shuffled his feet, glancing toward the floor, looking a bit nervous, as if he was about to take hold of her hand. "Nice to find someone who knows good writing when they read it."

There was a brief silence as the elevator door opened. "Well, good night," Gabby said as she placed her arm around Pete's back, laying her head softly against his shoulder. He placed his arm on her shoulder. A soft aroma of perfume wafted from along her neck. Her hair was soft against his chin.

He watched her get on the elevator, and she waved to him as the door closed.

Chapter Seven

Gabby was on her knees, a pail of soapy water and a rag in front of her. The red-checked bandana she wore was doing a poor job of keeping her hair away from her eyes. The bathroom floor had taken on a dim shine, and, as if she didn't have enough things to occupy her day, she knew it wasn't the self-cleaning kind. And so she scrubbed, using circular motions, the smell of ammonia clearing her sinuses.

At first she didn't hear the tapping sounds, but after a few moments she stopped, turning her ear toward the door. No sounds came from the parlor. Samuel had just fallen asleep and was usually out for a good hour in his morning naps. She returned to scrubbing the floor, and again the banging returned, repeated taps vibrating through the woodwork. She dropped the rag in the pail and walked toward the kitchen, tracing the source. Out the kitchen window she noticed Pete's car parked in the dirt driveway. When she opened the front door, she saw a ladder leaning against the tin porch roof.

Down the steps she walked, and looked at Pete shakily standing on the porch roof. He was holding on to the windowsill with one hand while he smacked away at the hinge of the broken shutter with a thin hammer. "Oh my Lord, a Peeping Tom," she said with fake disgust. He continued to drive a nail into the screw hole of the hinge. "You are so busted."

Pete was too unsure of his footing to look anywhere but straight ahead, so he shrugged his shoulders and continued with his work. "Aw, girl, you caught me. I knew I should do my peeping after dark."

"I'll ask the judge to show mercy on you."

"I'm not worried about the judge. I just want to make it off this roof in one piece." He popped the final nail twice and then gripped the hammer with his teeth. Squatting, he placed his hands on the roof, looking like some strange jungle native biting on a hammer instead of a spear. The tin buckled and popped as he slid nervously down the steep roof.

"Easy, now," she said. "We only have one hospital bed in the house."

Though he wore jeans and a simple white T-shirt, she thought he cut a dashing figure in the soft morning sunlight. The ladder began to shift when he began his descent. Gabby grabbed hold for support. "I've gotcha," she said. As he stepped down, she tried not to look at his backside but couldn't help herself. She retreated two steps as he stepped on solid ground.

"Good as new. " He placed the hammer in his back pocket. "Well, almost."

"You shouldn't have gone to the trouble, but I really do appreciate it."

"As you can see, I'm fairly dangerous with a hammer. By the way, that's one sharp-looking bandana."

She quickly slid it off her head and ran her fingers through her hair, trying to hide her embarrassment. "Sorry. Doing some housecleaning."

"Don't take it off on my account. Though I'll admit, it is nice to see that pretty head of hair of yours."

"Oh, please." She looked at him with surprise. "It's a raggedy mop."

Pete shook his head. "I'm guessing most women would kill to have that raggedy mop."

"Stop it." She touched him on his sleeve.

"How is Mr. Gable today?"

"He's had a pretty good morning. Ate a decent breakfast. Read a little. He's taking a nap right now. He'll be appreciative of your work on the shutter, even though you used nails instead of screws."

"What?" He looked up at the shutter and rubbed his temple. "Screws? Are you sure?"

"Positive. But it looks like the nails are doing the trick."

"I suck."

Gabby smiled and reached her hand to his forehead. "Hold still." She brushed at his hair, removing a paint chip that had fallen from the shutter. "There." She ran the back of her fingers along his cheek. "You're so sweet to help us." Her smile was replaced with a pensive look, her eyes taking on a solemn look; the reality of life was impossible to forget.

Pete softly touched her forearm. "I sure wish I could make this all go away."

"Me too."

"Is there anything else that's in need of repair?" He removed the hammer from his pocket and tapped it against the palm of his hand. He looked about the yard, and she suddenly wanted to request that he repair her heart.

"Well, there is one thing you can do if you don't mind."

"As long as it doesn't involve electricity, I'm ready. Don't feel like blowing myself up today."

They walked around the side of the house. Gabby's arms were folded, her right hand cupping the elbow of her left arm. At that moment she wished she looked more presentable, as Pete's visit was a surprise one. She opened the thick door of a wooden shed thirty feet behind the house. She pulled on a string above her head, and a yellow bulb cast a pale light about the shed. Kneeling, she carefully removed a wool army blanket from atop a small rocker.

"Daddy made this when I was three. I used to pull it up beside his recliner and sing to him. God, I sang what few songs I knew, and some I made up as I went along. And he didn't seem to mind a bit." She gently ran her hand across the faded wood. "I was trying to polish it the other day and the seat came loose. I don't want Daddy to see it in this condition, so I brought it out here. Was going to fix it, but I just haven't found the time."

Pete picked up the chair and turned it upside down, examining it closely. "Even *I* can fix this. You head back inside and tend to whatever needs tending. I'll take care of the chair."

She pointed out the toolbox in the corner. "See you in a bit," she said. She walked to the house, the weight of the world on her shoulders, returning to the dread reality inside.

Samuel was looking out at the pond when she entered the parlor. "Hey, Daddy. How you feeling?"

Samuel gave a short nod of acknowledgment. "Stop worryin' about me. You need to slow down. You're workin' yourself to death."

She fluffed his pillow. "I'm fine, Daddy."

He took her hand and looked through the window to the pond. The sunlight carved the grayness from the room. The love between a father and his daughter was palpable — a more special love there could not be.

Samuel took a breath. "I remember walking you to the pond when you were just a tiny little thing. You'd hold my hand, much like the way you're holdin' it now. You'd cackle when the ducks would land. 'Duckies, Daddy, duckies.' I'd lift you up and you'd spread your arms like imaginary wings, and I'd hold you just above the water's edge so you could pretend you had come in to light with those ducks."

Gabby smiled and breathed a delicate sigh. "You made me feel like a princess."

"You were a princess. My princess." He kissed her hand. "I really never knew complete love until the first time I ever held you."

"Luckiest girl in the world to be held by you."

Gabby sat on the edge of her father's bed. Still clutching hands, looking out the window of time, they returned in their minds to those days long passed. To days that knew no heartache and no pain. Pure joy. Blessings from God. A father and young child, a lifetime ahead of them, with minutes and hours and days saved up. Those minutes were now small in number.

Gabby was in the kitchen pouring Samuel a glass of lemonade when she looked out the window. Pete stood on the porch, pointing at the front door. He smiled and waved before heading to his car. After she gave Samuel his drink, her curiosity led her to the front door. The chair was on the porch, looking almost brand new, and it was freshly polished. She rubbed her fingers across the seat and tears welled up in the corners of her eyes.

***

Pete noticed the letter when he opened his mailbox. His heart raced. He tried to remain calm as he walked in and tossed the rest of the mail on the kitchen table. The letter was from a literary agency, but there was no return address. He recognized his own handwriting, as it was standard to include a self-addressed, stamped envelope when querying agents so they could respond. Maybe this was the one. When he opened it, however, he realized it was the actual query he'd sent the agency. Penned at the bottom were the words: *Thanks for the query, but it is not a fit for us.*

Pete crumpled the letter into a ball and threw it across the room. He looked out the kitchen window and spotted two hummingbirds battling each other for position at the feeder. He had grown weary of the rejection letters, especially after going through the heart-pounding process of opening them, thinking that each one might contain the offer he'd been waiting for.

He set the recorder beside his computer and struggled to find the desire to look at the Charlie Coleman article. This is just *great*, he thought. He decided he should have never quit his job. He should have never thought he had what it took to have a novel published. Small time, that's what he was destined to be. He shook his head, biting his lower lip, his dreams of becoming a novelist seemingly a million miles from reality. He wondered if the four years spent creating his fiction work was nothing more than wasted time.

Pete laced his running shoes tight and headed out the door. It was time to take out his frustration on the pavement. He'd been a workout enthusiast since his high school days. The way he figured it, lifting weights in the morning got him jump-started for the day, and running in the afternoon served two purposes: it kept him in shape, and it cleared his mind so he could create ideas for his book, to play out in his mind the characters, the plots. His goal was to be the consummate storyteller, to take readers by the hand, so to speak, to be their eyes and ears. Even when writing articles for magazines, he refused the journalistic, news-informing variety. He sought people or places that had a true depth about them, forming a connection with the subject so he could write the story the way it deserved to be written.

Sarah unfolded the balled up paper that Pete left by the kitchen sink. She read the words scribbled on the bottom of the page. When Pete entered the front door, she stood holding the letter as though it was evidence in some trial. "This agent doesn't know what she's missing. When your book sells she's going to kick herself for passing on you. Besides, you deserve an agent who shares your passion for the book."

Pete said nothing and headed to the shower.

As hot water rolled down his back, Sarah sat on the bathroom counter.

"You can't let this get you down," she said.

"It's too late for that. I'm tired of these letters coming back with a line or two scribbled saying that my work is not worthy."

"That's not what they are saying. All they say is that your book is not what they are looking for."

"Translation: it sucks, so leave us alone."

"That's not true."

"Yes, it is. Let's face it. I'm not good enough."

"Yes, you are. You're an awesome writer."

"You're supposed to say that. You're my wife."

"And a smart one at that." She laughed.

"I appreciate what you're trying to do, but I'd just rather you not patronize me. I'm a big boy. I can handle it."

"Obviously you can't." She hopped down from the counter and shut the door behind her.

As Pete slipped on a pair of jeans, Sarah walked into the bedroom. "I'm going off for a while. I don't want to hang around all this self-pity."

"Good. If you need me I'll be working on an article about a little old lady who saves stray cats. Or maybe I can find a story to write about the bag boy at Big Country who takes out the groceries for old farts."

"I hate your sarcasm."

The front door slammed.

***

The phone seemed to rattle on the receiver when Pete turned on the bedside lamp. "Hello?"

"Pete?"

"Yes?"

"Samuel Gable. Did I wake you?"

"Well, as a matter of fact..."

"Well, son, it's time to get your no count self out of bed. Sun'll be up soon. Meet me at my house in thirty minutes. I feel stronger now that the hospital refilled my diesel tank. I want you to take me somewhere."

"Mr. Gable, I'm not sure I can make it there in a half hour. Can't we do this around eight?"

"You're talkin' to a man whose warranty is about up. Now, you comin', or do I have to come over there and drag you out of bed?"

Pete's stomach growled as he drove up to Samuel's house. Smoke billowed from the chimney, and the first traces of the sun reflected off the upstairs bedroom window. Samuel waited at the door in his wheelchair. "Crank up the truck," he shouted through the doorway as Gabby walked outside with the keys.

"I'm so sorry," she whispered. "I tried to talk him out of calling you so early, but he wouldn't listen."

"It's all right."

She smiled and all was right with the world as far as Pete was concerned. "You doing okay this morning?"

"Not bad. It's good to see you again."

"You too. Thanks so much for fixing the rocker."

"It was nothing."

As Pete warmed the truck, Gabby fetched two fishing poles and a can of worms from the shed. "I guess you've figured out what he has in mind," she said as she handed it to Pete, who placed the fishing gear in the rear of the truck. Gabby walked to the foot of the porch steps to push Samuel to the truck. Pete stood by the passenger door, wearing a gentle smile, ready to help put Samuel in the seat. She carefully rolled her father to the truck. After they helped him onto the seat, Pete folded the chair and placed it in the truck bed.

"Got your recorder?"

"Yes, sir. You wantin' me to get some quotes from the trout?"

"Somethin' like that."

The pair drove along the dirt road in front of the house. They headed west as if they were riding the sun's rays. There was a touch of frost along the bank of Birch Tree Creek. Samuel instructed Pete to pull the truck off the road where a patch of wild phlox grew along the edge of the water. Tall reeds mixed with cattails gathered along the edge on the far side, dancing in the soft breeze. The creek at that point was thirty feet wide, and the brisk, clear water moved in swift surges, thanks to gray and brown rocks that rose up from the creek in a manner as if they had been cast sporadically by God's own hands.

Pete stood beside Samuel, propped high in his chair, at the water's edge. Samuel placed a worm on Pete's hook and lifted it away from the chair as if he were afraid Pete would snag it on his chair, or worse, his leg. He then placed bait on his own hook. "Set this can on the ground beside me. Make sure not to turn it over." Pete nodded. "Done much trout fishin'?

"No, sir, not really. My dad took me a few times when I was a boy. I don't have the time to fish nowadays."

"That's your own choosin'. You could set aside time if you wanted to. You got a daughter, right?"

"Yes, sir."

"What do you do with her? You know, for fun?"

"You called me out at sunrise to ask me that?"

"Just answer the question."

Pete cast into the water, the bait almost reaching the reeds on the far side of the creek. "Well, she's only four. So, I don't know, push her around on her tricycle, maybe go to the park sometimes. Sarah usually does that kind of stuff with her."

"If she were a boy, would you do more?"

"Yeah, sure. It's easier with a boy."

"Don't be so sure." Within minutes Samuel's rod bent, and a fish crashed through the water's surface. "Walk down to the edge and take hold of the fish. I'll lead him right to you." Samuel guided the fish to where Pete stood, and it flapped out of Pete's hands three times before he could grip it. Samuel shook his head in frustration. "Just put your finger through the gills. He'll become still as a steamrolled possum."

"That's a nice fish." The rainbow trout, speckled brown with a touch of blue running along its side, was close to a foot in length. "Want me to put him in the bucket?"

"Well, first you might want to grab your pole before it gets too far downstream."

Pete tossed the fish in the empty bucket and ran along the edge of the bank. The fish that had taken Pete's bait was moving quickly downstream. Pete could barely hear Samuel's laughs as he chased the pole. He stepped in the icy water to grab hold, but the fish seemed bent on reaching the spillway underneath Lawson's Bridge. Pete made it to an open field that bordered the creek, running at full speed, slowly making his way ahead of the fish. As the trout neared the bridge, Pete jumped in, the icy water knee high, and grabbed hold of the slick rod. As he did the fish leapt from the water, snapping the fishing line in two.

Pete walked back holding the pole, the line waving in the air behind him like a broken spider web. "Looks like I'll watch you fish the rest of the morning," Pete said, his brown Timberlands soaked, his jeans wet to his calves.

"Guess I should have told you to bring rubber boots." Samuel removed a plastic case from his coat. "My eyesight's not what it used to be, and my hand's not as steady, so you'll have to tie the hook." He handed Pete a black, one-inch hook from the case.

Pete kicked his legs to shake off the water from his jeans. He shook his head, tied on the new fishhook, and cast his line.

I got up for this? Pete thought. "So, we talking war stories today, or are we just here to freeze our toes off?"

"Take off those boots, son. Ain't no way your feet are gonna dry with them on."

"You mind holding my pole this time? I don't care to go swimming again."

"Hand it to me." Pete struggled to remove his boots. "Tell me about your family."

"My family? What do you want to know?" His socks were bunched and soggy.

"You have a wife and just the one child, right?"

Pete took the rod, and then spent several minutes explaining how long he'd been married, and how much life changed when Kate was born. Samuel questioned Pete for a bit, intent of getting a gauge of his family relationship.

"Enough about me. We're supposed to be talking about your story."

"That's why I called you this mornin'. It ain't exactly a war story, but I think the kids might want to have somethin' written about it. You up for it?"

"Yes, sir. Hang on a second." Samuel sent him to the truck for an empty bucket, and Pete placed it upside down beside Samuel. He set the recorder on top of the bucket.

"I had a four day furlough before I was to be shipped out to California and on to Australia. I wanted to come back home one more time to see Mom, Bert. See Porter. I thought it might be the last chance to see them, what with heading off to fight the Japs. Think that recorder can pick up my voice with the noise of the crick in the background?"

"Yes, sir, so fire away."

***

October, 1942

The Greyhound bus dropped Samuel and Earl Grayson a block away from the courthouse, the spot where they'd boarded the bus that carted them off to Fort Jackson six months prior. After boot camp, the men were sent to Fort Benning, Georgia. Earl looked at Fort Benning as a step toward getting further from home, a way to ease the process of going halfway around the world. Samuel looked at it as a nuisance to some degree. The way he figured it, he was an excellent marksman, he wasn't afraid of the Japanese, and he was ready to go. Scrubbing barrack floors and preparing foot lockers for inspection had nothing to do with helping defeat those who'd declared war on the good ol' USA.

It was Thursday, and the ride from Fort Benning had taken almost nine hours. The young soldiers were anxious to see family, yet decided to keep their homecoming a surprise. The sun had dropped behind Shady Mountain, softening the town in a blanket of sapphire. Samuel let the peace of it all surround him as he slowly inhaled the cool mountain air. The hot, humid days of South Georgia could be suffocating, and the mountain air seemed to release a claustrophobic cape surrounding Samuel's lungs.

"How you plan on gettin' home?" Earl asked as he tossed his duffel bag on his shoulder.

"Let's walk down to the Dairy Bar," Samuel answered. "There's bound to be somebody there who can take us home."

"It's only two miles to my house. I think I'm gonna double-time it. After them months of cross-country runs the army put us through, this should be a Sunday stroll."

"You go right ahead. I don't feel like runnin' seven miles, so I'll take a chance on findin' a ride." He bid Earl good-bye.

His broad shoulders carved an imposing silhouette as he walked along the edge of the graveled road. In dark green khaki dress uniform, his wide brim hat high upon his head, cocked slightly to the left, Samuel moved on through the quiet streets. Darkness had chased the shopkeepers home. The streets were silent, the yellow lampposts on the street corners providing the only light. The Dairy Bar was two blocks from where the men had been dropped off. Carter Springs was a small town, so one would only need to walk a couple of blocks in any direction before finding himself on the outskirts of town.

The Dairy Bar was the only business open after dark, and one of three restaurants. Jimmy's, a six-table diner across from the courthouse, served breakfast and lunch. The Clear View Hotel had a small dining area, and was also the only hotel in town. The Dairy Bar was the popular hangout for the high school crowd, as well as those who were high school age but didn't attend school. Though it was open after dark, it wasn't exactly a place with a late night drive-thru. Eight o'clock was the shutoff time, except on weekends where it would stay open to the late, witching hour of nine.

The Dairy Bar was part drive-in, part picnic area. It had one wing to the left of the restaurant that housed eight slots for automobiles. There wasn't an indoor dining area, just a large A-frame roof that covered six picnic-style tables located in front of the walk-up window where food was ordered. Two late-model Fords sat in the drive-in when Samuel walked up, and he recognized one of them as Glenn Jordan's, the town pharmacist. Samuel placed his bag on one of the tables and walked to the window.

He tapped the sliding glass, purposely staying to the side so as not to be recognized.

"What'll ya have?" the raspy-voiced woman behind the counter said as she slid the glass open. The smell of hamburgers sizzling on the grill reminded Samuel how hungry he was.

"Possum burger with a side of hog jowls."

"What the...?" she said as she leaned forward. "Sammy Gable. Oh my Lord. It's great to see your face."

"Evenin', Mary Lynn. Thought I'd never say it, but it's nice to see your face too."

Mary Lynn, short and stocky with a large gap between her front teeth, leaned both elbows on the counter so that she could inch closer to Samuel. "Ain't no good lookin' fellers 'round here since you left. You done broke the hearts of half the county when you up and left us."

"Well, I'm only here for a few days, so you gals better take advantage of the situation." He noticed a burger cooking on the metal grill. "Say, could I get one of those? I could use a break from army chow."

"You can have anything ol' Arthur can throw on the grill."

Arthur, donned in a white apron dabbed with grease spots, slid his paper hat up with the back of his hand. "Hello there, Samuel. Good to see you. This burger's on me."

"Nope. I got money. You know if you give away the profits, Miz Annalee will set you out by the roadside like a sack of rotten taters."

"She don't got to know about it," Arthur replied. "Now, have a seat, and I'll bring it to you when it's ready."

"Much obliged," Samuel said as he winked at Mary Lynn. She slid him a bottle of soda, and he walked to the table where he'd placed his bag. He looked about the street, the silence of it all, and he realized how much he'd missed his hometown. Though the place was dark and quiet, it warmed him like the soft porch light on cool evenings at home. Speaking of home, he was anxious to get there, but two things he needed first: food and a ride.

Mary Lynn brought Samuel his burger, and as he ate, three girls walked toward the window. Two of them he knew, but the third, the one he had his eyes on, was either a visitor or a new addition to town.

Vera Patterson noticed the familiar smile and began running toward Samuel. "Oh, my God," she yelled as her arms surrounded him from behind. "Lord, I have missed you. When did you get to town? How have you been?"

"Just arrived ten minutes ago. It feels good bein' back." Samuel stood as Helen Hicks walked into his arms. "Hello, Helen, good to see you. How's Ben?"

"He's fine. He comes home from Elizabethton every now and then. He's workin' at the bean warehouse, and I know he'd love to see you." She rubbed her arms along his shoulders, inspecting his physique. "You look great. All grown up."

Samuel looked at the new girl, and for a brief moment his usually calm demeanor disappeared.

"This is Callie Butler," said Helen. "She's from Bristol."

Samuel removed his cap and nodded. "Pleased to meet you," he stammered. He stared briefly into her coffee-brown eyes that were encased in long, curled lashes. Her eyebrows were soft and curved. Her thick brunette hair, shoulder length, was pulled away from her forehead with a white bow, and her deep red lipstick enhanced the white of her teeth as she smiled. Her dress was the color of tapioca, knee-length, with a white sweater buttoned around her neck but draped across her shoulders. Her eyes looked deeply into his, and he glanced at his feet for a second to regroup. Helen spoke, and when Callie looked at her, Samuel glanced at Callie, hoping she didn't notice. She was more beautiful than any girl he'd ever seen.

The foursome talked briefly before the girls walked to the window to order. Callie turned and smiled at Samuel as he sat down to finish his burger. A car pulled into the drive-in and took the first spot. Mary Lynn's younger sister, Lucy, notepad in hand, walked to the car to take the order. Samuel sneaked behind Lucy, sliding around to the open passenger window while Lucy walked to the driver's side. Inside the car were Bobby and Abel Jenkins. Bobby was a childhood friend of Samuel, and Abel two years younger than Bobby.

"You boys get out of the car," Samuel shouted as he grabbed Abel by the elbow. Abel flinched, completely caught off guard by Samuel's surprise attack.

"Hey, man," Bobby said when Samuel leaned in the car. "Where in the world did you come from? The Japs attackin' Carter Springs?"

"If they are, I'm heading back to Georgia," he said with a carefree laugh. "Actually, I just got dropped off on the street corner like a stack of newspapers."

"How long you in town for? Want to go out tonight and stir up some trouble?"

"I can't. Got to get home and see the family. Momma'd have a fit if I went out the first night back. Speakin' of home, I'm lookin' for a ride. Can you boys help me out?"

"Sure thing," Bobby answered.

As the young men caught up on the previous six months, another car pulled in two spots down from Bobby's car. Two boys emerged from the car, both wearing navy slacks. They wore T-shirts with thick grease stains that dimmed the white of their cotton shirts.

"You boys ain't gotta get out of your car," Lucy said as she walked up. "I'll take your order and bring it to you."

"We ain't eatin' in the car, dummy," one of them said. He was tall, lanky, and his dark hair was slicked against his head.

Lucy, a bit miffed, mumbled "Suit yourself" and returned to the screen door that led inside the grill.

Samuel talked with Bobby and Abel, but the loud voices of the two strangers turned his attention toward the counter. The boys were laughing loudly, making comments about Mary Lynn's stocky stature.

A walnut Wurlitzer jukebox was located to the left of the counter, facing the drive-in wing. Callie walked to the music box and Samuel watched her. Her dress seemed to sway as she walked, and she moved with graceful steps. As she tapped the glass lightly with her dime, trying to decide which song she wanted to hear, Samuel stepped beside her.

"Anything worth listenin' to on this box?" he asked, looking at the jukebox without making eye contact.

"Depends on what you like," she said nonchalantly. "Got any requests?"

"Well, I am considered the musical expert in town."

"Really?" She smiled at him, with a slow turn of her chin his way. Her smile took his breath away, just for a moment. "Let's see," she said, placing her hand on her hip, "I'm guessing you to be a tuba player. Maybe the cymbal."

"Wrong. The triangle. I was asked to record an album but I lost the metal beater. I tried using a fireplace poker but it didn't sound quite the same. Plus it made for a sooty mess in the living room."

She dropped her change in the slot and made her three selections. As Dick Haymes sang the soft ballad "You'll Never Know," she turned toward Samuel. "Where are you stationed?"

"Fort Benning. I'm home for four days, and then I ship off to California and on to Southeast Asia."

"Are you scared?"

"Of what?"

"Of everything. The unknown. Getting shot. A foreign country."

"Haven't given it much thought. I reckon I will know when I get there."

She smiled, and her eyes sparkled. Her soft cheeks looked pink and warm. "Samuel. I like that name. Did you grow up here?"

"Well, my house is at the base of Jefferson Mountain, about seven or eight miles west of here."

"Do you like being so far away from Carter Springs? What's it like in Georgia? I've been to Fort Oglethorpe once, but that's closer to Chattanooga."

"It ain't like home. Land's a might too flat for my likin'. Too many bugs, clothes stick to you when you're outdoors. Course, the jungle will be worse than that so I guess it's a way of gettin' used to it."

"So you base happiness on the slope of the land you're standing on?" Their elbows gently touched, and she looked down at the song selections. He wasn't the only one with a spunky attitude.

"Well, I like where I'm standin' right now."

Abel, his head poked out the window, watched from his car as though he were jealous of the time Callie was stealing from Samuel. "Looks like your friends are getting lonesome." Callie smiled. "And I guess I better go back and run my mouth with Helen and Vera. It was nice talking to you, Samuel." She liked saying his name.

"My pleasure," he said, backpedaling.

"What was goin' on at the music box?" Bobby asked Samuel when he returned to the car.

"Just passin' the time."

"She is one sweet-lookin' thing."

"Yes, she is."

Samuel noticed the two guys in the greasy T-shirts had moved from the table where they'd been sitting over to Callie's table. One of the boys put his foot on the bench on which she sat. He placed his arm around Callie's shoulder, and she immediately pulled away. He then sat beside her, his legs straddling the bench so he faced her. Callie nudged Helen so she could get some distance between her and the stranger.

"Whatsa matter, doll?" the boy said. "Afraid of me?" He placed his hand on her wrist.

"Get your hands off me," she said as she pulled away.

"Get out of here, Dobie," Helen said.

"Shut up, Helen. This don't concern you. Come on, honey. I'm a lot of fun once you get to know me."

"Thanks for the invitation, but I think I'll pass." She slid closer to Helen.

"Don't be so quick to turn me down. Is there somethin' you want? I'd be happy to give it to you." Dobie's buddy laughed loudly as Samuel moved toward them. Dobie took hold of Callie's wrist again, and she slapped him across his face. Dobie flashed an evil grin. "That ain't the way to get in my pants, darlin'."

As she tried to pull away, Samuel took hold of Dobie's wrist. "Leave her be," he said. Dobie's friend stepped behind Samuel.

"Boy, you best let go of me before I give you a beatin' you ain't never gonna forget," Dobie said.

"I said leave her be," Samuel said, his jaw taut. "Why don't you and your *girlfriend* skip on outta here?"

Arthur reached under the counter and emerged with a baseball bat. "Don't make me use this bat," he yelled. "Dobie, you and Stevie Ray move along now. Git."

Dobie pulled his wrist free and stood nose to nose with Samuel. "You don't know who you're messin' with."

"Time to go, Junior."

Dobie turned from Samuel as if to walk away, and then quickly turned with his fist coming toward the left side of Samuel's head. Samuel dipped as the fist found only air, and he drove his left fist into Dobie's midsection. Dobie bent, clutching his stomach. Samuel caught him across the chin with a right uppercut, knocking him over the bench and onto the gravel lot. Stevie Ray grabbed Samuel around the neck, and Samuel bent forward, tossing Stevie on top of Dobie. As Samuel stood over them, fists clenched, Arthur walked up.

"I ain't gonna tell you again," Arthur said. "Go home, Dobie." Arthur tapped the bat in his hand. Dobie and Stevie slowly rose to their feet, and Dobie rubbed his hand through his greasy hair.

"This ain't over, boy." Dobie wiped the blood from his lip.

"I ain't your boy," Samuel said as Dobie slowly stepped toward his car.

Dobie turned and stared at Callie. "You ain't seen the last of me either."

"Sorry about that, Arthur," Samuel said as he picked up a bottle of soda that had fallen from the bench. "But I couldn't sit still while he disrespected this lady."

"You ain't got to explain yourself," said Arthur. "I know what you were doin'. That boy's nothin' but trouble."

"Who is he?"

"He moved to town a couple months ago," said Helen. "He tried to cut Billy Reynolds last Saturday in the parking lot of Food Country."

Samuel looked at Callie. "Are you okay?"

"I'm fine," she replied. "Thanks for coming to my rescue."

"Anytime." Vera handed Samuel his hat that he'd placed on the table. "Well, I best be leavin'. Time to head to Vaught's Holler." He placed his hat on his head, and he towered over Callie. Shaking her hand, and then tipping his hat, Samuel took hold of his duffel bag and walked to Bobby's car.

***

Eula Gable scrubbed the black skillet with lye soap, the water in the wash pail splashing gray waves about the wide bucket. She stopped when she saw the pebble bounce beside her leg. She looked to her left, to her right, and returned to scrubbing. Again a pebble skipped beside her. Though the sun had set behind Shady Mountain, the skies contained a purple tint, and there was still light enough to distinguish the shadows from the trees. Eula looked behind her, still on her knees, soaked to her elbows, when she saw the silhouette of Samuel standing in the road.

Without bothering to dry off, she ran to him, wrapped her arms around him, and tears immediately started to flow. "Look at me, gettin' your uniform soakin' wet." She raised her apron to dry his shirt.

"Don't worry about that, Momma," he said as he took hold of her hands. He wiped a tear that was slipping down her cheek.

"Why didn't you tell me you was a-comin' home?" she asked. "We could have brought in half the county to welcome you."

"I wanted to surprise you. Looks like it worked."

"I'll say. How long do you get to stay?"

"I have to take the bus back on Sunday." She hugged him again, squeezing him tightly around the chest.

"Lord, I have missed you. Come inside and let me fix you somethin' to eat. You got to be starvin'."

He knew better than to 'fess up about the burger. She would have scolded him with a mighty force. He also knew better than to turn down any meal she prepared. Duffel bag in hand, he followed behind as she carried the pot to the house.

"Leave the pail be," she said as she walked to the porch. "I'll be a-needin' it again after I dirty the pots for you."

Samuel stood at the doorway and soaked in the smell of burning embers in the wood stove. The hickory grandfather clock beside the couch clicked loudly, the seconds ticking in pops that echoed across the room. He went to his bedroom and lay on the bed. A soothing quiet enveloped him, a familiar darkness broken only by light slipping across the hall from the bathroom. Arms folded across his waist, he closed his eyes, surrounded by the familiar feel of the mattress. The old house held a warm presence, and Samuel heard food sizzling in skillets on the stove.

Eula walked with extra pep in her step when Samuel entered the kitchen. She had already rolled out the flour and buttermilk mixture on the counter, and Samuel knew he would soon taste her batter bread.

Supper was eaten at the kitchen table, looking out over the pond. The waning gibbous moon cast a dim light along the roads and the fields. Samuel talked of the daily rigors of the army, all the while making sure she understood that while he was being adequately fed, it was nothing compared to her cooking.

"What time is Bert coming home?" he asked, after taking a swallow of sweet milk.

"He's off coon hunting in Doraville. I'm sure he headed there straight from work at the lumberyard. He'll be home in the mornin'." She could see how Samuel had filled out, solid as a tree trunk, and smiled. "You make a fine soldier. Your father would have been so proud," she said as she refilled his glass. "So proud."

"Yes'm. I think he would."

Chapter Eight

The morning sun slipped through the bedroom window, cutting shadows into elongated patterns of light across Samuel's bed. He rose, leaning on his elbow, and looked about the quiet room. Pots and pans rattled in the kitchen, and Samuel walked to his window to reunite with the world he'd left behind. Memories down a forgotten path to younger days flooded him. He saw the sun emblazoning the hillsides along the hollow in gold, and decided Heaven could never be quite so beautiful.

"Mornin', Momma," he said when he stepped into the kitchen. She was busy at the stove, and he placed his arm around her, kissing her on the cheek. She patted his arm, leaning her head against it, and smiled. Her boy was home again, and though it was only for a short while, Samuel could see the joy in her green eyes. Her long hair, silver-laced along the temples, was pulled tightly into a bun at the back of her head. She wore a pastel dress of blue and yellow.

"Sweetie, did you sleep well?" She removed a glass from the cupboard and placed it in his hand.

"Can't remember when I've slept so good."

"Milk's on the table. Coffee's on the stove. Grab what you want and find yourself a seat at the table. Breakfast is almost ready."

"Momma, you shouldn't have gone to all this trouble." Fried eggs bubbled in the skillet. A cotton cloth soaked up grease from sausage patties. Grits simmered in a pan, and the biscuits had just been pulled from the tiny wood stove oven.

"Nonsense. No tellin' how long before you get to eat another home-cooked meal. I don't think the South Pacific is much on grits and gravy and biscuits."

Bert walked through the front door, past the living room, and into the kitchen. "Mornin'. Lord a mercy, somethin' smells good in this kitchen." He walked past the kitchen table, unaware his brother sat smiling at him. Something made him stop and turn toward the table, and at first he was too stunned to speak.

"'Bout time you came home," Samuel said nonchalantly.

"Well, I'll be danged." Bert moved quickly around the chairs at the table and Samuel rose. They embraced, hugging for several seconds without speaking.

"You sleep with the coon dogs?" asked Samuel as he placed his hand on Bert's shoulder. "Must have been a good night for huntin'."

"It was. Shot seven myself. Just finished skinnin' 'em. On my way in I saw Ernie Mallard workin' on his tractor. I thought he could use my help. That man needs a new tractor in the worst way, but the old boy won't cough up the money."

"Alice has been on him for years to get a new one," said Eula. "But he knows there ain't no need to plop down money for a new one when Bert'll fix it for free."

"I don't mind," said Bert. "Besides, he pays me, just not with money." He pulled a small knife from the pocket of his blue-denim jacket. "He gave me this. Ain't sharp enough to cut melted cheese, but it makes for a good toothpick."

"You are a sweet young'un," Eula said. It didn't matter that Bert was approaching his twenty-fifth birthday. He'd always be a young'un to Momma.

"What kind of lies was the old boy tellin' today?" asked Samuel.

"Now, Samuel," Eula said with a look that fell short of showing sternness.

"Momma, you know he's a better storyteller than Mark Twain. Only thing is, Twain knew his stories were made up."

"You got that right," Bert added.

"I didn't raise you boys to talk about folks that way."

"No, we came about it our own selves," Samuel said. "Took years to develop." Samuel grabbed a biscuit from a wooden bowl lined with a soft dish towel. "So, what was his story?"

Eula waved her hand to the ceiling, shook her head, and poured a cup of coffee from a tin pot sitting on top of the wood stove. Her children—how they loved to be contrary.

"Well, Ernie said that when he was a boy, fishin' in Birch Tree, Tom Dooley passed by."

"Is that a fact?"

"Yep. Said Tom traded him a Confederate coin for a bologna sandwich and a pickle Ernie kept in his burlap pouch. Tom sat on the bank with Ernie, exchanging fishin' tips. Said all that talk about him killin' that gal in Wilkes County was hogwash."

"Don't suppose you asked to see the coin, did you?"

"He told me he kept it in a pillbox in his closet. Said he'd hunt it down for me sometime."

"Don't hold your breath."

***

After breakfast Bert and Samuel took to the dirt roads and graveled highways around Carter Springs. They traveled to town, stopping off at Stuppe's Esso station to talk with Murle and the Niven brothers. The three men were known to sit in straight-back vinyl chairs positioned beneath the shade of a sturdy oak. Each morning they solved the world's problems while waiting for customers.

On that morning, Murle's uncle, a crusty old fellow with little to no sense of humor, stopped by for an oil change. Woody was his name, and he sat next to Ollie Nivens on a cinder block turned sideways. Murle performed the oil change in the one-bay garage, stopping to participate in the conversation when he had something to add.

Bert and Samuel chatted with the men for a bit. Samuel fielded questions about military life from Virgil Nivens. Murle wanted to know if Samuel had plans to single-handedly kill the entire Japanese army. Bert removed two bottles of soda from the slender red drink machine to the left of the bay, handing one to Samuel. Woody was feeling bitter and nasty, a typical day for him, and spouted off about what an idiot General Macarthur was. He told of how he would retaliate for Pearl Harbor and wipe the Asian enemy off the map. As he spoke, Freddie Brayburn, a nine-year-old boy who lived with his mother and two sisters in a tiny shack behind the gas station, carried a bucket of blueberries across a grassy path. He alternated holding the bucket with his left hand, then his right, before trying to lug it with both. He smiled at Samuel as he walked the narrow path that led from the road to his house.

The men sitting had their backs to him and were oblivious that Freddie walked behind them. As he walked closer, Woody still carrying on, Freddie noticed Samuel motioning to him with his hand. Puzzled, Freddie set his bucket on the ground and watched Samuel lift his arm as if pouring something from an imaginary glass. For a moment Freddie watched in silence before Samuel's request took hold. He walked up behind Woody, raised the bucket shakily above his head, and in one swift move, poured the blueberries on top of Woody's head.

His head covered in purple syrup, Woody began to curse. Samuel flipped a silver dollar to the boy and he took off running with his empty bucket.

***

Saturday came, the minutes flying by like seconds, and twenty-four hours stood between Samuel's stay and the bus ride back to Fort Benning. Samuel truly loved the folks along Carter Springs and especially those around Jefferson Mountain. The feeling was mutual. His friendships weren't confined to age limits, as he was just as likely to fish Spear Branch with Spence Akins, all ninety-two years of him, or carry twelve-year-old Charlie Slidell to chase foxes along Boone's Holler.

Word spread that Samuel was home, and the girls around Carter Springs were primped and ready in the event he stopped by to visit. But there would only be one girl so lucky, and for now, she would have to wait.

Samuel and Porter Bennett had made plans to fish Saturday morning. Porter and Samuel were almost inseparable in their teen years. They had fished every stream within a ten-mile radius of Jefferson Mountain. And many a squirrel and gopher had met their fates at the hands of the young men during hunting season. They even shared a secret identity when they traveled to West Virginia and Kentucky to watch rooster fighting. They raised a few chickens of their own, fighting in local bouts throughout the northeastern corner of the state.

***

"Hello there, Sammy," Bertie Bennett said at the door. She wrapped her arms around Samuel's broad shoulders. "Sweet Jesus, it's so good to see you." After a few strong pats on the back, she released her grip and they stepped inside. He shut the door and she spoke as she led him to the living room. "Porter ain't been the same since you left. Mopin' 'round here like some mutt what done been sprayed by a polecat."

"Well," Samuel said, "we'll have to do something to change his disposition."

"Come on in and set a spell. I want to know all about your days in the Army. Porter says you have to leave tomorrow. Is that right?"

"Yes'm." Samuel followed Bertie into the small living room, its vinyl floor colored in pastel swirls of blue, pink, and yellow. A tiny wood stove still held the smell of embers from the previous night. A porcelain plate, white with a scene of a mountain stream painted in light blue, hung on the wall over the exhaust pipe of the stove. A picture window, a light coating of dust along the edges, revealed the peaceful serenity of Shady Valley. Porter sat in a hickory rocking chair, holding the cork handle of his fly rod.

"'Bout time you showed up," said Porter. "The trout are so anxious to be caught, they started jumpin' on the bank this mornin'. I tossed 'em back in and told them to wait till you got here."

"Well, here I am. I assume you took good care of the Bandit."

Porter opened a small closet door where he removed an ash pole. "I've protected it with my life." He handed the brown pole to Samuel. "Can we go now?"

"Wait a doggone minute," Bertie said. "I ain't had time to visit with Sammy. You boys best just cool your jets. The fish can wait."

Porter headed for the back door. "Bye, Momma. Hug Sammy and tell him you love him. The fish are calling." He opened the door and held his hand to his ear. "Hear 'em?"

Bertie grabbed hold of Samuel and squeezed tightly. "Love you, Sammy. Come back for lunch and I'll have a pot of dumplins ready for you."

***

The pair walked the dirt road, and the sun warmed their shoulders. Their rods pointed in front of them, jousters in need of horse and armor. The cloudless morning revealed dew glistening along the bank of the stream, blanketing the grass in an endless array of sparkling light. The creek ran fast and hard, the sound of the water, old as time itself, a continual roar that could not be turned off. The stream carved a winding path across its floor of rock, clear water racing and rising up in waves of white as it flowed on an endless path.

Talk was small. It usually was when the boys were together, even though it had been six months since they'd seen each other. Their thoughts were on the water, the fish. It was all about the game, conquering the slender brown trout that were as much a part of the mountains as the hills themselves.

"Want to go to the Bean Queen pageant tonight?" Porter asked. He whipped his line back and forth through the air. He guided the fly onto a soft spot twenty feet downstream. "Supposed to be some lookers in it this year."

"Lookers, or hookers? Just want to know how friendly these ladyfolk are."

"You'd stand a better chance with the hookers. You know these gals 'round here want nothin' to do with you." Though Porter spoke in jest, he couldn't hide the envy he had for Samuel's hold on the ladies of the county.

"Not sure if I can make it. I have to leave tomorrow. Don't leave me much time to spend with Momma. She's been right emotional these last three days. And besides, it's gonna be a long time before I come back." Under his breath he whispered to himself, "If I make it back."

"I heard that. Say that again and I'll make you my personal hand puppet. You're a Tennessean, by God. So you will be comin' back."

They moved along the banks, dragonflies skittering above them like kamikaze bandits. Thin fishing wire whipped through the air as the young men sought out fertile bedding holes. Their split-cane rods would bend, setting the fishermen into motion, backpedaling, guiding the fish to the bank before placing them in their burlap sack prison. Again and again they would guide their flies to the water, their fingers waiting for the familiar tug, their eyes watching the bend of the rod as their boots moved along the stony, icy creek floor.

It was a perfect blend of man and nature: two men with childlike hearts, in like heartbeat with the Creator of the mountain, a part of the world surrounding them.

***

"They were runnin' good this mornin'," Porter said as they began the walk back. Samuel carried the sack, savoring the chaotic movement of fish flopping about in it. This was a ritual they'd shared for fourteen years, and on this day the path to childhood was revisited in perfect harmony.

"Ain't nothin' like it, is there?" Samuel asked. "I didn't realize how much I missed this. The creek, the mountain. Momma, Bert. You."

"Cut out the sappy story, son. Go on home, visit with the family, and I'll come get your squirrely ass later. We'll check out the lineup at the pageant. And I ain't takin' no for an answer."

"You want me to sacrifice precious hours with the family just so we can get into some trouble?"

"I just have your best interest at heart."

"I'm sure you do."

"I'll pick you up around six," Porter said. "That'll give us time to piss off Marvin Maness. What a crazy one he is. A hun'ert years old and he still comes, hopin' to marry one of the contestants."

The Bean Queen pageant was held for several years in the late thirties and midforties when the area enjoyed extreme success as the leading bean producer in the country. The pageant was the culmination of a day of celebrating and giving thanks for the crop that helped sustain the town. The folks of the county were not the kind to flaunt any financial success they might have, as they knew life was hard and money was no more a guarantee than summer rain. So the aim of the celebration was in the spirit of thanksgiving, and it gave the county an opportunity to come together in fellowship. The day had various contests, from pies to pickles to roping hogs. But the highlight was the beauty pageant, where young ladies would come from as far away as Johnson City to enter. Many of the finest were represented, with a few thrown in who were either too shallow to realize they weren't beauty-queen quality, or ones whose parents couldn't see that fact.

When Samuel and Porter arrived, Marvin Maness was eyeing the contestants while sitting on the front row of metal chairs that lined the floor of the Civitan Club. There were enough chairs to accommodate one hundred and fifty people, while dozens would line the back wall just to get a glimpse of the contestants. Samuel spotted Joe Long, an eight-year-old boy who wasn't the sharpest knife in the drawer. Samuel walked up to him, whispered in his ear, and placed some change in his hand. Joe walked up behind Marvin and smacked his ears. Marvin yelled and Joe took off out the back door.

As the crowd shuffled in, they couldn't help but notice Samuel, a dashing figure in his dress uniform. Many wished him well, and soon Vera and Helen snatched him away from three teenaged girls, leading him to the second row. "You'll want a good view tonight, Sammy," Vera said. She giggled and looked at Helen, wearing a giddy smile.

"Why is that?" Samuel could tell something was amiss. "Too much mischief in the eyes of the innocent."

The girls pretended Samuel had not spoken and looked around to see who had shown up. The seats were filling fast, and some folks milled around the back wall. Samuel never took the pageant seriously, treating the event as simply justification for leaving the house on a Saturday night. The after-pageant fun was what he looked forward to, stirring trouble up in the valley before daybreak.

The lights flickered, and a makeshift purple curtain was pulled to the side of the stage by Ada Thompson, the event organizer. Unveiled to the audience were a dozen females in evening attire, standing side by side. The crowd began to clap and the dull murmur of voices carried across the room. Some pointed at the contestants, lobbying their thoughts on who looked to be the winner. Samuel nudged Porter with his elbow as he spotted pudgy Geraldine Carter, the mayor's daughter, but then his attention soon turned to the girl in a hunter-green gown with white gloves. She flashed her radiant smile at him, and at first he was too caught off guard to smile back.

Vera leaned and whispered in Samuel's ear, "See anyone you know?"

Callie glanced briefly again at Samuel as she walked to the front of the stage, a wooden platform constructed by the Carter County Lumberyard. The stage was T-shaped with three steps to the left where the young ladies and the emcee could enter and exit. One by one, the ladies walked down the center walkway, twenty feet long, looked at the four judges at a table next to the walkway, smiled at the crowd, and turned to resume their spot in line. Samuel stared at Callie, unable to even send a passing glance to the other contestants. Her eyes sparkled under the four floodlights hanging above the stage from the ceiling. Her gown clung tightly to her shapely figure. Her olive skin looked smooth and firm, her shoulders and arms exposed. The crowd reacted to her beauty in muted whispers, and soon even Geraldine knew she was no match for the visitor from Bristol.

There were no questions asked of the contestants. There was no talent portion. No piano-playing, no tap-dancing, and no singing. It was, pure and simple, a contest about looks. As demeaning as that might have seemed, no one seemed to care, although surely Callie wondered at the true purpose of it all.

Marvin clapped the loudest when Callie was named Bean Queen, looking at her as if he had found his next bride. The other contestants gathered around Callie to congratulate her, and for a moment Samuel lost sight of her. When she reemerged, she seemed embarrassed by the attention. Dottie Edwards lined the ladies up for a picture for the Carter County Gazette.

The crowd began to thin, and Vera and Helen waited on Callie as she changed clothes in the office of the Civitan Club with the other contestants. Porter tried to convince Samuel there was tomfoolery waiting to be doled out along the countryside, but Samuel was in no hurry to leave. Soon Callie walked from beside the stage, her gown folded over her forearm.

"Congratulations," Helen said as she hugged the new queen. "The whole place knew you were the winner as soon as they raised the curtain."

"I can't believe I let you talk me into doing this," Callie said, blushing as she hugged Helen. Callie hugged

Vera and then smiled at Samuel. "Hi, Samuel," she said softly.

"Hi, Callie. So, this is why you came to town."

"Against my wishes. I just wanted to come visit."

"Well, you look about as pretty as anything I believe I've ever seen."

"Oh, stop it. You're making me blush. I felt like a girl with two left feet up there. I don't know anything about pageants and contests. I was just trying not to trip or faint."

"Hey, why don't you boys come on over to the house?" Vera suggested, touching Samuel on his sleeve. "Momma's fixed food. She's made carrot cake. Daddy's gonna build a bonfire."

"Well, that sounds real nice and all, but we have to—" Porter began.

"We'll be there," Samuel interrupted.

"Great," said Vera. "See you in a bit."

***

Porter pissed and moaned the entire way up Laurel Holler, a snaky dirt road that led to Vera's house.

"We'll still have time to tip an outhouse or two," Samuel said. "But right now, I ain't passin' up the opportunity to see that gal from Bristol."

"Sammy Gable, fallin' in love. Never thought I'd see this."

"I didn't say nothin' about fallin' in love. I just think she's about the prettiest thing I've ever laid eyes on."

"Well, lot of good that'll do you when she heads back to Bristol and you ship out to New Guinea or wherever it is you're a-goin'. She'll just cloud your mind and probably cause you to get your head shot off in some foxhole."

Samuel looked at Porter, and Porter knew he had gone too far. "I didn't mean that," Porter said. "I'm just sayin' you don't need any distractions."

The old Model T pulled under a hickory tree and the boyhood pals quietly got out. Inside, the girls sat in a small parlor where a phonograph played Benny Goodman songs. Vera's parents chatted with Helen's mother and her aunt from Boone who had driven up for the pageant. Soon the girls took Samuel and Porter out back, where a fire crackled and blazed in a pit thirty feet from the back porch. Chairs encircled the fire, three rockers and three straight-backs fetched from the kitchen. Porter and Samuel took the straight-backs, while the girls sat in the rockers.

The fire danced upon Callie's face, her chocolate eyes mirroring the flames that rose and dissipated into the night air. She smiled at Samuel, and he could not turn away. He pretended to look interested as Porter talked of a cockfight that was taking place on Iron Mountain. Vera and Helen were carrying on and laughing, lost in the conversation common to young ladies. Samuel sensed Callie's disinterest in her friends' topic of conversation and moved his chair beside hers. He reached over and picked up a maple stick beside the stack of firewood, poking the fire as he likewise hoped to stoke a flame within her heart.

He asked about her home, how life was growing up in Bristol. She lived on a small tract of land with her parents and younger brother. Samuel wondered why her family hadn't come to see her in the pageant, though he didn't feel at liberty to broach the subject. Callie wore a knee-length, navy-blue dress, and her legs crossed at her shins. Her smooth skin took a darker tone against the firelight, and the flickering flames chased the shadows that crept across her face. She liked the cutting figure Samuel made by the fire, sitting arrow-straight in his chair. He removed his hat and placed it on his lap. The evening was bringing on cooler air, but the heat of the fire warmed them.

Porter grew bored quickly, attempting to pass the time listening to Vera and Helen. There was no one there that piqued his romantic interests, and the only one he cared to talk with was being mesmerized by the Bean Queen herself. Vera nudged Helen, nodding in Samuel and Callie's direction. Their matchmaking scheme appeared to be working as planned. Neither Callie nor Samuel noticed they were being watched as they talked. When Vera's mother spoke from the porch, letting them know that the time was approaching when all good girls should send male suitors home for the night, Samuel wanted to tell her to go back inside and mind her own business.

Callie looked at Samuel. "I wish you didn't have to leave."

"I don't want to. I could sit by this fire all night with you."

They returned to the house, and Vera's father thanked the boys for coming. Vera hugged Samuel. "Will we see you tomorrow before you leave?" her father asked.

"No, sir. I'll eat breakfast with Momma and Bert, and then Bert will take me to the bus stop. So I guess this is it until next time." When Helen hugged him, she squeezed tight and fought back tears.

"Good luck and God bless," added Vera's mother, reaching for a hug as Helen stepped away. "You'll be in our prayers." Samuel nodded in appreciation.

Samuel smiled at Callie and extended his hand. "It was a pleasure meeting you. Congratulations on being the queen of beans." They laughed, all except Callie. She could not hide her sadness. They turned to the door, quietly walking to Porter's car. When Samuel shut his door, he looked back at the house, wishing there were some way he could return to the fire with Callie. Porter put the car in reverse, the brake lights turning the dust into a cloud of red. As he pulled onto the road, Samuel noticed someone running toward the car.

"Hold on a second," Samuel said, and Porter pressed the brake.

Callie ran to the passenger side and Samuel lowered his window. "Meet me outside Vera's bedroom window at midnight." With that, she turned and ran back toward the house.

"What's goin' on here?" asked Porter. "Looks like she's all hot and bothered for you."

"It's not like that. We just ain't finished our conversation is all. Nothin' more."

"You just make sure you don't send her home to Bristol with Sammy Junior."

Samuel cut his eyes at Porter. "Don't talk about her like that."

Porter turned the car onto the dirt road toward home. "Sorry. I didn't mean anything by it."

The young men rambled down the valley. The moon, approaching its final quarter just above the dark skyline of Jefferson Mountain, cast a milky blanket across the hollow. Cattle, their shadows flat beneath them in the fields alongside the road, slept like frozen beasts. No porch lights or lanterns were visible as families bedded down in preparation for the new morning. As the young men came upon Vance Whiteside's farm, Samuel had Porter pull off the side of the road. Vance owned a handful of goats, and a stocky billy slept in a field near Whiteside's brown barn.

"You got any rope?" Samuel asked.

"Always." Porter reached back in the floorboard of his 1927 Model T and lifted a small rope from beside a tiny toolbox. The car was old, but Porter kept it in great working condition. "Are you thinkin' what I think you're thinkin'?"

"Old Vance needs some excitement when he takes a piss in the mornin'."

The boys walked slowly to the barbed wire fence on the far side of the road. The air was still, the cicadas busy in noisy chorus. They leaped the fence in one bound, and the billy goat lay motionless. Samuel made a noose and slowly draped it over the horns of the animal. The goat began to shake its head as it awakened. It charged at Samuel and he moved to the side of the mad animal, trying to hang on to the rope. He began running toward the outhouse that was forty yards across the grassy field. The goat rammed into Samuel's leg as Porter muffled his laughter with his hands. Samuel and the goat looked as though they were performing a psychotic version of the Tennessee Waltz, twirling about as the goat homed in on Samuel's thighs.

Samuel swung the outhouse door open and tried to coax the goat inside. The goat would have none of it and pulled away. The billy circled left of the tiny latrine, and then right. Finally, Samuel stepped into the outhouse and yanked the goat toward him, jumping on the wooden toilet seat. He leaped over the goat and quickly shut the door behind him.

The pair laughed heartily as they made their way to the car, so much so that they didn't see Mack Gibson, the Carter County deputy, his left foot resting against Porter's bumper. "Evenin', boys," Mack said, removing his foot so he could stand squarely, face-to-face, with the two pranksters. "So, ain't been home hardly forty-eight hours and you're already up to your old tricks."

"See, the thing is, I won't be back for at least two years," Samuel said, his hands on his hips. "So if I don't do it now, when?"

"I see you boys have graduated from tippin' outhouses to hidin' livestock. And Gable, here you are carryin' on while in uniform." Mack was only twenty-four and had been a deputy for two years. He had served long enough to know that Samuel and Porter had always had an inclination for waywardness on a Saturday night. "Let's go."

They walked to Mack's black Chrysler. "You boys are a-gonna have to stand on the runnin' bars 'cause my seats are filled with feed."

"Usin' your police car for personal business, huh, Mack?" asked Samuel.

"Get on the side board and keep your mouth shut."

"What about my car?" asked Porter.

"Leave it be. The goat can drive it for all I care."

Mack hopped in and cranked the car while Porter stepped on the running board on the passenger side.

Samuel hopped on the driver's side, and under the pale light of the moon, the boys and the car cut a silhouette along the likes of a horned traveler, silent except for the rumble of the wheels. After a few minutes of sucking on dust from the road, Samuel reached across the roof of the car. "Give me your hands."

"What?" Porter shouted above the purr of the engine.

"Take hold of my hands." Porter reached across and took hold. "Let's piss off our escort some." The pair took to rocking back and forth in unison, and the car started to veer left and right. Mack was having trouble keeping the vehicle from running into the ditch on either side. He yelled out the window at the pair to cease and desist, reaching his arm out the window in hopes of stopping the nonsense and lack of respect from his prisoners. The boys paid no mind, swerving the car all the way to Sheriff Pendleton's modest home on the outskirts of town.

It took Freda Pendleton several minutes to put on her robe and open the front door. She turned on the porch light and secured her robe. "Mack, what in the world is a-goin' on?"

"I caught these boys tamperin' with livestock."

"Couldn't this have waited till mornin'?"

"I just thought Sheriff Pendleton would want to deal with them immediately."

"Well, follow me to the bedroom, cause he ain't gettin' out of bed if he don't have to."

The men followed Freda to the bedroom, where the sheriff sat up and rubbed the mangled strands of his hair in a failed attempt to cover his bald crown. "Mack," he mumbled as he grabbed his glasses from the nightstand, "this better be good."

Mack told of how he'd caught Samuel placing the goat in an outhouse and insisted the meanness had to stop. When he had finished, the sheriff looked at Samuel and Porter in mild disgust. His sleep, interrupted by two young hell-raisers loved by the entire county, and a deputy gone overboard in maintaining justice in the sleepy mountain borough, was too much to digest at such a late hour.

As his mind pondered the situation, and how to settle the matter in time to get back to sleep, Mack chose to sit in the chair next to Freda's dresser. When he did, his right cheek sat on Freda's false teeth, where she had mistakenly placed them before turning in for the night. The choppers clamped tightly onto Mack's bony backside, and he let fly a high-pitched scream. He jumped to his feet and yanked the teeth from the firm grip they held on his behind.

Samuel found the situation extremely funny and began laughing. He got so tickled that his body began to shake, his laughter increasing in pitch, making it impossible to stay quiet long enough for the sheriff to dole out punishment.

"Son, you don't seem to understand the seriousness of the situation," the sheriff said. Samuel paid him no mind, bent at the waist, his hands on his knees, while his body continued to shake as Mack shook his backside. The sheriff had seen enough of the sideshow taking place in his bedroom and pointed to the door. "Get out of my house. All of you."

Samuel convinced Mack to drive them back to get Porter's car, though it took some persuading. Midnight was approaching, and Samuel wasn't about to let Mack cost him his chance to see Callie. After Mack dropped them off, Porter drove home. As soon as his car pulled up to the house, Samuel hopped from the passenger side door, crossed in front of the headlights, and opened Porter's door. "I'll bring the car back to you in the mornin'."

In less than ten minutes he approached Vera's house. He pulled into a small ravine around the bend from the modest brick house and turned off the engine. The night's chill grew stronger, and he put his black peacoat on. He took to running in the dark, his feet landing in the shadow cast by his body. He had just passed a large oak located by the dirt driveway that led to Vera's house when a hand reached out and grabbed his sleeve. He flinched briefly before noticing the familiar shape.

"Gotcha." Callie laughed.

Samuel took hold of her hand, and her smile disappeared as he pulled her close to him. In the moonlight, surrounded by the silence of the mountain, Samuel placed his lips to hers. Delicately, slowly, their young hearts opened. He touched her face with his fingers, feeling the warmth of her soft skin. The moon's light ran pale across Callie's face, an angelic glow that made her dark eyes appear like soft stones. Eyes that stared into Samuel's. His lips found the corners of hers, and he explored her mouth gently with his tongue when she parted her lips. When she allowed her tongue to meet his, he felt her tremble.

He pulled her close to his chest, and her face fell into the shadows. His fingers traced the contours of her face as if he were committing it to memory. Her hair smelled of jasmine, and he rubbed his hands through it as he pulled away, the moonlight finding its way back to reignite the sparkle in her eyes.

They walked hand in hand down the quiet road, away from the house. They soon heard the steady rush of water along the rocks at Samson's Creek, and at once Callie loved its melody. Samuel led her to a soft bank beside the stream. She wore a sweater and dungarees though he removed his coat and placed it over her shoulders. They sat side by side, Samuel to her left, his right arm steadying him on the bank. He kissed her again, and she turned her head so that her lips fit perfectly against his. Samuel had kissed his share of girls in the county, but they had never sent sparks through his body like when he kissed Callie's tender lips. On this night, he sensed Momma's proclamation that one day God would send an angel to him had at last come true.

The waters of Samson's Creek wove a smoky trail in front of them as the moonlight captured each and every sense of movement within the stream. Callie moved in front of Samuel, his legs steadying her on both sides as she faced the water in front of him. She leaned back into his chest, and his arms surrounded her. His chin rested on her shoulder, and her cheek rested on his arm.

"I can't imagine a more incredible setting than this," she said softly. "I've lain in bed and wondered if a night like this was possible, though I never really thought it was. Now that I know it's true, I can't imagine being anywhere else but here with you."

Samuel turned his head so his cheek touched her soft hair. His eyes looked over the creek, and he knew he had never been a part of anything so magical. How he could fall so hard, so fast, for Callie was beyond his comprehension. Everything about her excited him, not sexually, but emotionally, spiritually. The touch of her skin, the smell of her hair, the taste of her lips, all touched him in the furthest depths of his being.

"There's so much I don't know about you, but all I know is I want to know everything about you," Samuel said, lightly squeezing her waist. "To think two days ago I had no idea you existed, and now I'm holding you in my arms…it's more than this simple mind can handle."

Callie removed Samuel's arms, turned on her knees, and leaned into Samuel until his back rested on the soft grass. She hovered above him, on her elbows, staring into his eyes. Her breath brushed his cheek, and tears formed along the corners of her eyes. "I don't know what to make of all this," she whispered. She kissed him softly, with such innocence. "I'm falling in love with a boy I barely know. A boy I may never see again. I suppose I should just treat this as a night where I shared kisses under the stars with the most gorgeous thing I've ever laid eyes on, but I can't. You've touched me in a way I don't think I can shake loose."

Samuel pulled her to him, and felt her tears on his face as they kissed.

"I'm sorry I can't stay." He brushed away her tears.

"Please don't go. Come away with me. I'll hide you in my spring house."

Samuel smiled. "If only I could. You're the only gal who could make me think those kinds of thoughts."

She kissed his hand and placed it against her cheek. "Do you know how long it will be before you come back?"

"I'll be overseas for at least two years."

"Two years," she repeated as though she hated saying it. "That's such a long time."

"I know," he whispered almost apologetically.

She placed her cheek to his. "God, I can't believe how quickly I've fallen for you. Vera told me you were special, but I had no clue. I'm glad they talked me into entering the pageant."

"This beats anything I've ever seen. I've never really been close to any girl, and that was by design. I kept my feelings for them at a distance. But with you, it's not that way at all."

The moon dropped behind the skyline of Jefferson Mountain. The Big Dipper had crawled above the shoulder of the North Star, glowing in dim sparkles as the slightest trace of gray appeared in the eastern sky. As if trying to fight off the morning, the young couple lay on the ground, his jacket underneath them, with her in his arms. Samuel told her how the military had long been a fascination of his. He spoke nothing of his dreams of playing baseball. That was a chapter closed forever, and it would be too painful to discuss. He talked of his uncle who fought in World War I. He spoke of his admiration for military leaders like Julius Caesar and Alexander the Great. He told her how he loved his country, ready to defend it.

But now, with Callie snuggled gently in his arms, he wondered, for the first time ever, how he could leave home and the mountain land where he was raised. His veins flowed with icy Tennessee waters, and he intended to live out the rest of his days in Carter Springs. Callie made him want to begin doing that right then and there.

Callie told Samuel how she was the only one in her family to go to college, and she felt as if she was representing them all. She talked of traveling. In some ways she felt, as did Samuel, that the world was an endless open road, though no matter how far she might wander, she couldn't see herself staying away from Tennessee for long. Though she attended classes at the local community college in Bristol, she said she couldn't imagine going to class on Monday and resuming normal day-to-day life knowing Samuel was being sent so far from home. He had changed her world in almost an instant. Life had been very safe, very normal in Bristol. Now, it seemed unimportant.

As the sun began to slip above the rim of Shady Mountain, the pair walked hand in hand to Vera's house. Callie was taking a big chance coming in at sunrise, but she really didn't care. All she knew was she had spent the last six hours with the man who completely melted her heart. His handsome face, his wavy hair, and his broad shoulders were nice extras. But to her, his warm smile, gentle touch, and youthful playfulness were what made her wonder when she would be in his arms again.

"Tell me how I can get letters to you," she said.

"Tell Vera to stop by my house and Momma can give her the information. Put your return address on your letters so I can write you back. I have no idea how hard it will be for me to get letters to you, but I'll do my best."

Callie began to cry softly as Samuel held her, next to the oak tree where she had waited for him earlier. He removed the cross necklace from his neck and placed it around hers. "No, I can't accept this," she said. She took hold of his hand in an attempt to stop him.

"I won't leave unless you take it."

"Good, because if I don't take it, you'll have to stay with me forever." She smiled briefly before lowering her head to hide her tears.

"This way I'll be close to your heart," he said as he placed it around her neck. She rubbed the cross as it touched her chest, and she kissed him, firmly pressing her lips against his while he held her tightly in his arms.

"Promise you'll come back for me," she said as tears streamed down her face.

"I promise. No matter what happens, I swear I'll come back for you." He kissed her softly one last time. "I *will* come back." He pulled slowly away, their hands last to part.

In an instant, the desperate feeling of loneliness overcame them. A barrier had been laid between them that could not be torn down until he returned. She walked backwards for a few steps so she could look at him one last time. And then he was gone.

Chapter Nine

Three days had passed since Pete and Samuel fished Birch Tree Creek. Samuel's appetite had waned, and he spent most of those days confined to his bed. His fever returned, and his body ached so that even his bedsheets felt painful to touch. The serenity of the pond, the mallards moving across it like tiny boats with erratic rudders, were a sight wasted from the parlor window. Blackie slept at Samuel's bedside, raising his head whenever Samuel moved or moaned. The dog whimpered slightly when Samuel winced, the dog's compassion not lost on his master.

Porter stopped by on the second day, visiting with Gabby in the living room while Samuel slept. He brought food his wife Earline had prepared. Gabby was running herself ragged, and Earline thought a hot meal might bring some comfort. Food was a form of consoling in Carter Springs, as much as hugs or comforting words. Before he left, Porter walked into the parlor. He held Samuel's hand in silence, and for the first time since the cancer had taken residence in Samuel's body, Porter cried.

***

Gabby hoped the prospect of talking with Pete about stories of his past would keep driving her daddy to push on, to show the toughness in him that he had displayed his entire life. She thought briefly about asking Pete to come over, and that maybe Samuel might awaken to see him sitting there, recorder ready for another story. She watched him sleep, rubbing his hair. She looked at the wrinkles of his face and neck, the age spots on his hands.

To her they were simply markers and monuments designed to document a journey well spent. Each wrinkle was a victory line that hid the tales of someone who touched the hearts of countless people.

It was breakfast time, and Gabby was barely able to awaken Samuel. He was in obvious pain, but he uttered not the first complaint. He nibbled on a piece of toast laced lightly with strawberry and fig preserves. He was constantly thirsty, drinking glass after glass of water. In the afternoon the county nurse stopped by, checking vitals and tending to bed sores which had grown on Samuel's hamstring and calf. Normally Samuel would have fussed and cussed at her to leave him alone, but he was too weak to even mumble. By early evening Gabby finished cleaning the kitchen and bathroom, and she lay on the couch in the den for a short break. She tossed and turned and soon began to dream.

In her dream she was young, around six or seven. She rode in a truck with her father, and they had set out to visit some of the folks of the valley. Samuel was younger too, strong and healthy. They stopped by Minnie and Tita Morgan's house. The elderly sisters had lived alone for as long as Gabby could remember, and Samuel stopped by as often as he could to check on them and do odd chores around the house if the need arose. Of course the Morgan sisters loved the attention and would always set to baking and carrying on in the kitchen to feed their favorite visitor. The food they prepared was old school: kraut and gizzards, field onions, and rutabaga pies. Gabby felt the joy her father brought to the lonely spinsters.

The next stop they made was to Gabby's grandparents' house, which had been torn down some twenty years ago. In the dream the tall, two-story wooden house again stood, thick grape vines hanging from lattice along the porch ceiling. Gabby followed Samuel through the door and felt a sense of warmth like that of a girl in the embrace of her mother's arms. Her childhood days were filled with wonderful memories of Grandpa and Grandma Butler's house.

Walking into the familiar kitchen, the smell of biscuits baking in the oven wafted across the room. Gabby noticed someone in a long pastel dress, sitting in a chair next to the kitchen table, but Samuel's body hid her from view. Scooting around her father's side, she began to cry as she spotted her grandmother smiling back. Grandma had passed away in her sleep when Gabby was in the fifth grade, so memories of her were limited to her early years. Grandma spoke not a word, but only smiled at Gabby.

It seemed like only seconds that Gabby and Samuel were there, and in an instant the pair stood on the front steps. As they walked down the porch steps, Gabby looked back inside the house and saw her grandmother smile one last time. She wanted to run back inside to her grandmother, to hold her hand, to ask her a lifetime of questions. But the dream had other ideas. In an instant she stood by the roadside, looking out across a lake that seemed to stretch all the way to the base of Jefferson Mountain many miles away. The water was soft and still, the look of pink chiffon. When Gabby turned to look back at the house, it was gone, only the porch steps remaining. When she awakened, her tears had stained the throw pillow on the couch.

Gabby walked into the parlor and gently stroked her father's hair. His shoulders, once broad and powerful, were sunken and bony. She cried quietly and glided her fingers across his cheek, and she wished with everything inside her that he would be healed in an instant and leap out of bed. She lifted his frail hand, which leaned over the rail, and placed it across his lap. She smiled at Blackie, and he watched her walk to the kitchen and retrieve a chair from the table. Putting it beside Samuel's bed, she sat close to him, taking his hand in hers. If he couldn't look at the pond, she would do it for the both of them.

***

Pete had barely an hour to finish writing and arrive at Kate's birthday party. He was amazed that five years had passed since the day she was born. He'd thought he knew what life was about when he'd married Sarah. But when he first looked in Kate's eyes at the hospital the night she was born, he realized he hadn't had a clue. He saw in those eyes how precious love was, how at that moment all that mattered was the soft grip she placed around his pinky. It opened a door for him to a world where love existed in its purest form. She made him want to be a better man.

Pete loved to listen to Kate's voice when she played in her crib in the early hours. He bathed and fed her each morning. He rocked her to sleep each night. They listened to James Taylor records, Pete rocking her as her soft hair tickled his chin, her head always at his chest, looking inward, his heartbeat echoing off the sound of hers. When Kate turned three, too old to rock, Pete began lying beside her in bed, telling wild stories of the Three Little Pigs living in double-wide trailers, and how Goldilocks's taste buds called for anything but porridge. After Kate's laughter would subside, she'd turn, facing the wall, as Pete rubbed her hair until she fell asleep. Somehow Pete's recent obsession with writing had clouded those memories.

After showering, Pete put on dark blue jeans and a blue short-sleeved polo shirt. He looked on the dining room table to make sure Sarah had not taken the gift he'd picked out for Kate's birthday. Sarah and Kate had left home almost two hours prior, picking up items for the party that was to take place on the playground at the Carter County Park. The girls were going to stop by to visit Sarah's father to receive Kate's present early. No one was allowed to give presents to his only grandchild until Papa did.

With twenty minutes to spare, Pete grabbed a diet soda and picked up the gift bag that held Kate's present: two tickets for the Veggie Tales Rockin' Tour in Boone. As he started for the door, the phone rang. He looked at the caller ID and noticed the area code was from West Tennessee. He thought about letting the answering machine do its thing, but turned instead and picked up the cordless phone. "Hello."

"May I speak to Peter Swift, please?" the pleasant voice inquired.

"Speaking."

"Hello, Peter, this is Paul Douglas with *Southern Life* magazine. How are you doing today?"

"Good," he said, a bit puzzled. "How are you?"

"Doing well. Listen, I got hold of the article you wrote about Billy Troutwig in *Faces of the Appalachians* magazine. I thought it was a fantastic piece, and was hoping you'd be interested in writing something for us." Pete knew *Southern Life* had a large and wide distribution list of readers. Bigger than any magazine he'd written for.

"Sure. Have you got something picked out, or do you want me to come up with an idea?"

"Well, I've got some ideas, but I'd love to hear yours also if you've got a few moments."

As the conversation carried on, in Pete's excitement Kate's party slipped his mind completely. Pete went to his computer and e-mailed Paul a few articles he'd written that he'd not yet submitted to any publications. He was pumped to hear such positive comments about his writing ability. By the time the conversation was over, it was five-thirty. Pete raced to the car, present in hand. He sped to the park, and when he arrived Kate had just blown out the candles. The gathering of friends and family sang to her, and Sarah cut a mean look at Pete as he ran down the hill.

"Daddy!" Kate yelled, a multicolored festive hat on her head.

"Sorry I'm late, sweetie. Daddy had an important phone call."

"That's okay. Look. Papa got me a shiny necklace." The red cubed plastic stones covered most of Kate's neck. She loved big shiny jewelry. Sarah's dad was smart enough to ask Sarah about Kate's likes as far as gifts were concerned. He was on the mark with this gift.

"Would you like to open the present I got you?" Pete asked as he scooted beside Kate on the park bench. Kate didn't respond, but she climbed on her knees to look inside the green-and-white gift bag. Kate removed the colored tissue paper and took hold of the tickets. "We're going to see the Veggie Tales."

"Yay!" she yelled. "Veggie Tales, Mommy!"

Sarah smiled, but Pete sensed the smile was mere pretense for Kate's sake. Her body language told him she wasn't happy, and he felt certain a lecture would soon follow so she could piss and moan about how he placed the family on the back burner while he pursued his writing career.

Chapter Ten

The clouds thickened, expanding across the sky like a celestial life form stealing light from the once-blue sky. The dimness cast upon the land faded the bold colors of the hardwoods along Jefferson Mountain. The morning chill, combined with the dreary clouds, gave Pete a feeling of isolation.

Pete received a call from Gabby letting him know her father was feeling stronger, had eaten breakfast, and had things on his mind. Pete quickly left his house. He had spent the last five days working on Samuel's story, and though he knew his deadline for the Boone Museum was quickly approaching, he couldn't stop putting Samuel's tales on his computer. Samuel's stories had become habit-forming, and Pete was not only intrigued by them, he was anxious to fill in the gaps. He had questions aplenty, but wasn't sure which ones to ask or how they might be received.

When he arrived at the Gable house, it was just past nine. Gabby had Samuel dressed and waiting on the porch when Pete arrived. Samuel's face was pale and drawn, and he was looking out at the fog that draped along the base of Shady Mountain. He was weak, but he at least retained a bit of spark in his eyes, a look Pete guessed was more determination to finish his story than anything else.

"Mornin'," Pete said as he walked to the front steps.

"Mornin', Pete," Gabby said. Samuel simply nodded, but in a manner that Pete felt was sincere and warm. Blackie lay at Samuel's feet, lifting his head for Pete to pat.

"Daddy wants to sit by the pond today. There's a nice spot above it with a swing and some bird feeders. Been a lot of blue jays and cardinals of late."

"Pete, if you'll hold me by the arm, I think I want to try walkin'."

"I'll lead you anywhere you want to go."

Gabby smiled at Pete's enthusiasm and his genuine sense of wanting to please her father. Though Samuel looked better on that dreary morning than he had in the past couple of weeks, Pete tried not to get a false sense of comfort that Samuel was somehow winning a losing battle against the one enemy he could not defeat. Pete had watched the ups and downs of cancer with his own father and had false hopes ripped from his heart. But for now, it was a day to be thankful for, and he was ready to make the most of it.

Though it was slow going, Pete and Samuel walked down the steps, moving their way alongside the house in front of the kitchen and around the side of the house to the parlor. They had to climb a small, steep slope that led them above the pond. Twice they stopped so Samuel could regain his balance. Blackie circled the pair, and halted to a sitting position when Pete steadied the swing. Samuel gripped the metal chain, lowering himself onto the faded blue wood. The pond was no more than fifteen feet in front of them, down a steep bank so it seemed as if they were on a platform above it. Though the clouds darkened the water, the men saw the black shapes of trout swimming near the edge of the bank. Blackie watched the fish with his ears perked, a sense of curiosity in his eyes.

"Tell me, Pete, how long has it been since your father passed?" The question caught Pete off guard. "It's been a couple of years now, right?"

"It will be two years next month."

"I heard it was cancer that got him," said Samuel. "Which kind?"

"Lung."

"Damn. How long did he make it after he was diagnosed?"

Pete kicked at the grass below his feet. "'Bout a year and a half. When he first went through chemo and radiation, the tumor shrunk to a few centimeters. It disappeared from his lymph nodes and he did well for a year." Pete rubbed the edges of his thumbs together, trying to fight back the reemergence of sad memories. "Then it came back with a vengeance, and three months later it took him. Funny thing is, in the final weeks he thought he had pulled a muscle in his back. Thought that's why he was in pain. I don't know if he said that to us so we wouldn't worry, but we figured the cancer had spread into his spine. The only good part about it was he didn't suffer long. I remember eating breakfast with him on a Wednesday morning at his kitchen table, and we talked about going fishing over the weekend. On Thursday he lost his ability to stand. By Saturday he was in a coma, and Monday he died."

"That's the best way to go out, son. I hate wiltin' away, havin' people take care of me like I'm a child. I see the look of pity in their eyes, like they're thankin' God right then and there that it's me and not them."

"His passing shocked my mom like you wouldn't believe. It was hard on us all, but she was such a prayer warrior, and she held tremendous faith that Dad would be healed."

"Let me tell you what I think about prayer, and God's desire to take care of us. I think prayer is very important, and we should trust Him to provide for us. But I believe that only pertains to the goings-on of day-to-day life. It has nothing to do with death. God knows when He is going to take us away from this world, and because of that, prayer matters not to Him in such matters other than bein' pleased in our faith. We can't live forever, and when our time is at hand, God's agenda has nothing to do with prayers. It's His plan, not ours, and we have no say in the matter. It can't be altered."

"I'm not so sure about that."

"Then we'll just have to differ in opinion. But let me say this: I've lived a long time. I've watched people die. I've held their hands while they prayed for God to save them in their final moments. Prayers that God didn't answer. And on the level of a most personal kind, I've laid witness to my own unanswered prayers with regard to the timeline of death."

Pete looked at Samuel with sudden curiosity. "With regard to whom?"

He waved his hand in the air as if to dismiss the question. "That's for another day."

Pete looked across the pond. "Can I ask you something?"

"All right."

"Speaking of fathers, why didn't yours pick you up from school that day when you were a boy? The day you waited out front with your suitcase?"

Samuel looked down at the soft grass underneath his feet, and then glanced off toward Shady Mountain as though a debate were taking place within him. He took a deep breath. "With regard to this particular timeline of death, I'll talk about it. Where's that recorder?"

"Got it right here." Pete pulled the gray and black recorder from his jacket pocket.

***

May, 1934

When Samuel walked through the front door, suitcase in hand, his mother saw the disappointment in her son's eyes. Though he was merely a boy, he could quickly tell by the look in hers that something was wrong. Eula led him into the living room where Bert and his sister Anna sat on the couch. Anna was the oldest, three years older than Bert. She was the mother hen of the family and tried to watch over her brothers whether they wanted it or not. Eula spoke no words as she sat in the oak rocker, waiting until Samuel sat beside his siblings.

"What's wrong, Momma?" Anna asked.

"Somethin's happened to Daddy," Samuel said. "That's why he didn't pick me up today, isn't it?"

Their mother looked down at her hands, her fingers interlocked. "Children, I don't know how to say this any other way," she said as she looked briefly at the ceiling, sighing. "Your father died this morning."

Anna jumped up from the couch and ran from the room crying, slamming the bedroom door behind her. Bert looked at Samuel, unable to speak. Eula Gable looked stoically out the window as if the words that just came

149

from her mouth were comments about dinner plans or what the evening chores would be. Samuel knew it was her attempt to stay strong for them.

"What happened?" asked Bert, saying it as if he wished he hadn't.

"He had an aneurysm. He had just finished up his work in Damascus, and Ernie Greenway saw him collapse as he was walkin' to the car. Ernie said he was gone by the time he hit the ground. Said it didn't seem like he suffered at all."

She then looked at both boys sternly. "We are going to be strong through all of this. You can miss him, but you can't get caught up in self-pity. There's a household to run, and you boys are going to have to assume some of the duties your father had."

***

Pete watched a mockingbird skirt the tail of a cardinal at the feeder which stood at the corner of the pond, as Blackie gave chase. His barks echoed across the pond. Pete glanced at Samuel, who removed a picture from his coat pocket. It was the picture he'd held in his hand the day he waited for his father to pick him up from school. The day his father died.

"I was determined not to let my children go through life without their father," Samuel said. "I wanted them to feel safe, to know they had someone taking care of them and looking out for them."

"And you did that, from the way it sounds."

"I think so. I hope so. Though there were times when I wondered if I would make it home alive from the war. If I'd ever see Callie again. Ever see Momma. Bert and Anna.

As the war continued, it began to look like those things were never going to happen."

"It must have been hard enough just surviving the extreme conditions over there. But to have to endure that while dodging bullets must have been a nightmare."

"More times than not, the Japs were hunkered down waitin' on us. We were on the move, on the offensive."

"Were there any battles worse than the others? I'd guess there weren't any easy ones, but was there any particular battle or time where you truly felt you were going to die? Where you thought 'this is it'?"

"Leyte. That's the one where I didn't see any chance we'd make it out alive."

"What happened in Leyte?"

***

April, 1944

The rain poured from the low, dark ceiling of clouds that hovered at treetop level, falling as though God had unleashed His fury from heaven. The truck that carried injured Bryson Steele away from enemy fire had disappeared into the thick palms and coconut trees, and the rains washed away any trace that the truck had passed. Samuel took refuge with his outfit two hundred yards from deadly Tanqray Hill. The machine gunner lay hidden and silent.

The company commander, Captain Carl Finebaum, had been quickly promoted due to the heavy casualties. His first assignment was sending word, by way of a runner, that the hill was to be attacked at dusk, and L Company was to lead the charge. He reasoned that a full-scale attack at night would allow the troops to penetrate the hill and take out the bunker which held the fifty-caliber machine gun. His plans weren't well-received.

"Tell Cap'n we won't attack the hill," Samuel told the young runner, "until he attacks it with us. Side by side."

The runner shimmied out of sight, unsure as how to present Samuel's response to the captain. Within an hour Finebaum slipped into Samuel's foxhole with the aid of one of the sharpshooters in the platoon.

"Sergeant, I passed along instructions for you to lead your men at dusk and overtake this hill," Finebaum said sternly.

"Yes, sir, you did," said Samuel. "But we're not goin' unless you join the festivities."

"You want to be court-martialed for insubordination?"

"If it means saving the lives of my men, you go ahead and toss me in the brig. But if you insist on sendin' us off to die, it's only fair you die with us."

"Sergeant, for the last time, I gave you an order. Now execute it."

Samuel climbed outside the foxhole. Mired in mud, his wet clothes clinging to his tired body, he fired three shots into the jungle. At once gunfire erupted from the hill, and the rapid cracks from the machine gun screamed through the trees. Samuel squatted, his rifle lying across his legs. "Like I said, you want us to die, you die with us."

Finebaum looked up at Samuel from the foxhole. Samuel's eyes looked like dark stones, the whites of his eyes showing in sharp contrast to the mud-encased thick whiskers which had not met a razor in almost a week.

"If you want to take this hill, here's how we're gonna do it. Sir."

Plans were made, and an hour before dawn the men assembled for final instructions. The rains fell steadily, beating against the maple leaves and the long wands of palm limbs so that they bobbed in constant movement. Fog had settled in, a smoky mist which carved shadows from the trees and provided a depth to the darkness, something not seen by them since a moonlit night two months ago. The jungle floor was a mire of cold mud as they moved off toward the hill. The men stepped carefully, crouched low, through a band of shoulder-high kunai grass, and there were no sounds except the echoes of the raindrops on the thick foliage. In front of them were walls of jungle undergrowth that snaked up the trees, making it hard to determine the true depths of their surroundings.

The sky began to lighten as daylight slipped in from the east. Using hand signals, Samuel led fifty men to the west side of the hill, after sending forty-two to the right. Thirty minutes passed before the rest of the platoon, almost one hundred in number, began firing at the hill from straight in front. As the enemy returned fire, the men on both flanks began to ascend the hill from either side.

Samuel and his men crossed a stream that branched out in winding, interweaving veins. The countless days of rain had turned the water khaki in color, and when the men stepped through the slow-moving rivulet they were a seamless fit of uniform and water. Leeches took hold of their boots and pants, and they swatted them away with wet fingers. As they slipped back on dry land, now facing the slope of the steep hill, they could hear Japanese soldiers communicating in short bursts of chatter. They climbed a steep slope of five hundred feet on what looked like a hog trail, and Samuel began positioning his men in pairs fifty feet apart as he continued to the top.

His days on the baseball diamond had trained him well, and he was deadly accurate as a grenade thrower. He slipped around from the top of the hill and tossed a grenade in each of three foxholes that were no more than ten feet apart. He heard the frantic voices of the enemy before the explosions sent dirt and bodies flying. The Japanese soldiers who survived the blasts emerged from the foxholes with rifles aimed. Samuel's men cut them down, ripping their bodies with bullets from the side of the hill where they waited. Samuel continued to move down the hill, throwing grenades in each foxhole like a crazed exterminator. The soldiers from the opposite side of the hill had joined in the battle, and the Japanese had no chance.

By the time Samuel worked his way to the machine gunner, Ben Thompson had buried a trench knife into the gunner's back. The hill was conquered.

The battle was a sign of things to come, as the battles intensified throughout Leyte. Victories were achieved one foxhole and one hill at a time. The Japanese were bedded down all around the thick jungles, waiting for the Americans in hidden silence. Skirmishes by day became standard, and by night the men shared foxholes, trading watch in the darkness.

In a six-month march they moved north near the coast, and they received instructions to make their way to Ormac Highway, the primary supply line in the region. U.S. troops had cut off the Japanese as they tried to backtrack along the trail, and the commander of the 126th spread word that friendly troops should be the only ones on the trail.

It was late afternoon, and Samuel and a slender private named Terry Bradley, a new addition to the company, dug a foxhole a hundred yards from Ormac Highway. Samuel closed his eyes briefly, the sounds of the jungle indicating a place of paradise as macaws and parrots sang their noisy tunes. Within minutes, reality returned as Samuel spotted a group of Japanese soldiers, eighty to one hundred strong, coming up the muddy highway. Samuel quietly alerted the others to lie low. The Japanese were tired, weary, and hungry. Their weakened state, combined with the element of surprise, was their downfall.

After the ambush, Samuel had his men remove hand grenades off the dead Japanese soldiers. Japanese grenades were different from the ones used by the U.S. military. To activate the grenades required firm taps that were distinct in sound. As Samuel's platoon lay still that night, they heard more Japanese soldiers making their way up the trail. Samuel took hold of one of the foreign grenades, crouched, and tapped it on his helmet that lay at his feet. The Japanese heard the familiar sound and called out to soldiers they thought were their own. Two other soldiers joined Samuel, and the screams of the enemy were drowned out only by the explosions that rained down upon them. As they lay dying, the Japanese shouted into the darkness for their comrades to stop.

The platoon inched its way to what would later be called Starvation Ridge. The Red Arrowmen had gone five days without food. The soldiers were so desperate they risked their own safety in order to eat. Samuel was holed up with a soldier named Martinez in a battle that lasted for three days. A dead Japanese soldier lay just a few feet from their foxhole. Martinez spotted two sweet potatoes in the dead man's pack, but each time he tried to leave the bunker, gunfire erupted.

The lack of food and water took its toll, and the platoon knew they couldn't survive much longer. The rains eased, and water became a scarcity. Two of the men lost their lives when they bolted for a stream during a gun battle.

And so it went, day after day. Combat was oftentimes hand-to-hand, and many soldiers met their fate by way of the bayonet and knife.

Along with the loss of life, the jungle warfare took its toll mentally. Samuel became weary of having to choose which men would be lead scouts, knowing that at any minute they could—and would—draw fire from the enemy. To him, it was a much harder task than finding snipers or defeating the enemy, but he knew it had to be done to accomplish victory.

One day, mid-morning, the sun broke through the clouds, and the humidity hung thick in the air. Corporal Dex Jackson spotted yellow wires pulled across tree limbs like some jungle clothesline. The Japanese used the wires to communicate, and Jackson was able to pull on the wires with the working end of his military issue rifle. Samuel removed his trench knife to cut the line. As he did, a bullet hit Jackson in the chest. Samuel dragged the young soldier behind some sago palms as the jungle fell silent. The others aimed their rifles at the deep-green treetops, ready for the next shot so they could return fire. A medic tended to Jackson while the men branched out, hiding in strings of ivy that raced to the treetops. Samuel held Jackson's hand as he breathed his last.

The platoon began to move forward slowly, and within minutes Paulie Damon, a 2nd Lieutenant, was shot in the neck. Blood sprang from his jugular as he took hold of his neck with his hand. Again the jungle fell silent as the troops lay low, looking for the source of the bullet. Slowly the assassin picked off another, and another, and they could not pass. Captain Finebaum, in an act of desperation, devised a plan to reveal the sniper's hiding place. Samuel and his men were told that at daybreak two men were to walk around the area until the sniper fired.

Sleep was hard to come by that night. Many offered up goodbyes should they be selected to walk into the sniper's firing line. At dawn, the men woke to the sounds of three shots. Vinny Sturgeon, a new soldier to the unit, had found and killed the sniper.

The monsoon season was in full swing and couldn't have come at a worse time. Weak, hungry, already battling the heat, and now the rains came hard and steady. At one point, the men had gone over thirty days without being able to remove their boots and dry their feet. Dengue fever hit, striking down soldiers in domino fashion. Those not stricken carried the load, digging foxholes and scouting the landscape for enemy soldiers.

Strong and bull-headed, Samuel was determined that they would not fall to what he considered a weaker people. When the opportunity for hand-to-hand combat arose, the Red Arrowmen took full advantage. To Samuel, the enemy was capable, but they weren't Americans. Specifically, they weren't *Tennesseans*, where men grew up tough as nails and true to their country.

Rations were thin, and at one point the platoon was down to two cans of beans. Samuel taught the men how to catch and eat Draco lizards, which had flounder-shaped bodies and long tails. As the men marched on to Luzon, and what they were told would be the final stand, Samuel became feverish. He battled extreme chills, and his body ached to the touch. Still he pushed on, leading his men through the brutal conditions. For five days his fever raged, and Doc Parker, a medic from Milwaukee, took notice.

"Sam, we've got to get you outta here," Doc said as the pair sat on a fallen log. "I believe malaria has gotten hold of you."

"We're almost to Luzon," Samuel said. "I can make it." Samuel wiped his forehead with his sleeve, and the wet fabric only served the purpose of spreading the drops that had formed under his helmet into an oily film above his eyes.

"You're not going to make it one more day, much less to Luzon. I'm taking you out of here. There's a mobile hospital unit near Tacliban. I'm sending you there."

"You're out of your flippin' mind. Just give me a shot or somethin'."

"You need more than a shot. And you can't argue or fight your way out of this one."

When Samuel arrived at the tiny mobile military hospital, he was dehydrated and unclear of his surroundings. There were many soldiers who came and went while Samuel was there, though he never knew it. The men shared cots in what amounted to an overgrown circus tent. It was difficult to sleep, as the moans and cries from the wounded were loud. Samuel remembered vaguely hearing last rites being given to soldiers, and anguished pleas from them to pass their love on to their families.

It was at the end of the twelfth day when a nurse came to Samuel's cot. His color had returned, and he asked that he be sent back to his unit.

"I believe they're about to release you," the nurse said. "Maybe one more day, is what the doctor said."

"Good. I ain't doin' nobody any good here."

"I got a letter for you from the States. It's the first time they knew where you were. Apparently they've been trying to deliver it for a while."

Samuel looked at the return address and immediately noticed Callie's name. He quickly rose on his elbows and opened the letter.

Dear Samuel,
I don't know if or when this letter will get to you.

Samuel looked at the handwritten date on the top corner of the letter. It had taken over six months to reach him.

I keep in touch with Vera and she knows to contact me should any sad news come back home about you. Though I've heard nothing, I will only think the best and know that you are okay. The reports we get in the news here tell us that we are winning the war. I pray each night that it will end soon so you and all of our soldiers can come back home.

Though it's been well over a year since that night we spent at the bank beside Samson's Creek, it doesn't diminish or lessen the feelings I have for you. I think about you all the time. I've never met anyone like you, and I'll be waiting for you when you return.

I am taking classes at the community college and will finish my degree next spring. I've been working summers at Daddy's office. My brother James has given Daddy grief about letting me work with him. James says I'm Daddy's favorite, and though I would never admit it to them, somehow I feel maybe he's right. I've always felt so close to my father, and up until I met you, never thought anyone could ever be like him.

If there is any way possible to write, please do so. I would love to hear from you. Maybe you could tell me where you are and I can find it on a map so I can look at it and know exactly where you are. If you know when you will be returning, please let me know that too. I will be patiently waiting.

With deepest affection,
Callie

Samuel read the letter a second time, and he touched the letters of the dried black ink. After folding it carefully, he placed it in his shirt pocket. He vowed to keep it on him, to be buried with him if necessary.

Moments later a doctor entered the tent to check the soldiers.

"Doc, I'm ready to go back and join my men."

Chapter Eleven

War has been around since the beginning of time. Battles have been waged in the four corners of the world; some in the name of God, others in the name of greed, hatred, and glory. Young men set off for war, fighting foes known and sometimes unknown, many never to return. For all the hope the world holds for peace, for love, there is an innate power that runs through its underbelly pitting man against man, nation against nation. As if some primitive desire for blood sport was placed within the deepest depths of men's hearts, held by chains that can't be unshackled, the world stands at odds against itself. It's a battle for survival, a quest for power. And though the conquest of others comes at the expense of the sons and fathers of the homeland, it's deemed a vicious, but necessary, sacrifice.

Though the battlefield has been witness to armed conflicts with numbers larger than the human mind can fathom, there are also wars that take place on the simplest of levels: wars that occur in the evil hearts of those who wage war with the mere control of one's mind; the ability to instill fear; the desire to take what one thinks he is rightfully due.

***

September, 1944

While Samuel's world revolved around the fight for survival, the will to make it home to Callie never left him. His thoughts of her were relegated to times when the war seemed to sleep. Lying in a foxhole, he'd imagine meeting Callie by the stream again. When it was his turn to stand guard, staring out into the blackness, he'd wonder what she was doing, how her life was going without him in it.

Though he knew focusing his efforts on the war around him was paramount to survival, Samuel couldn't fight the odd feeling that life back home contained battles of its own.

***

Vera waited on the front steps, surrounded by the songs of crickets and cicadas welcoming dusk's blanket of darkness. She heard the rumble in the distance, and soon saw the dim headlights approaching. When the green Ford sedan pulled in front of the house, Vera ran to the roadside.

"I've been waiting an hour for you to get here," Vera said as she opened the car door. Callie removed the key from the ignition and slid out off the seat.

"Sorry I'm late," Callie said as she hugged Vera. "Mom wouldn't let me leave until I helped her can the pole beans."

"Don't worry about it. I've just been so anxious to see you. Helen's coming over after dinner." Vera removed Callie's brown turtle-shell suitcase from the backseat. Callie carefully grabbed clothes draped across a hanger, wrapped in vinyl, from the floor of the trunk. Darkness was coming on fast, and they cut silhouettes from the grayness of the evening as they made their way to the porch.

"Well, well," said Vera's mother as they entered the kitchen. "Callie, you're even prettier than the last time I saw you." Callie blushed and smiled while the diminutive woman wiped her hands on her smock.

"Hello, Mrs. Patterson. It's good to see you again." When they hugged, Callie could smell the light, buttery aroma of biscuits baking. "Is that what I think it is?"

"Yes, dear, and I hope you're hungry. I've got enough food here to choke a horse."

"I've been dreaming of those biscuits for weeks."

Mrs. Patterson removed a drinking glass from a white wooden cabinet with glass windows. "Here, sweetie. Pour yourself some lemonade and you gals scoot. I gotta get the rest of dinner fixed afore it burns."

The young girls retreated to Vera's bedroom.

"I can't believe I let you talk me into coming here this weekend," Callie said while sitting on Vera's bed. A handcrafted quilt of pink, blue, and yellow covered the bed, and Callie held tightly to her glass of lemonade.

"Well, they're making such a big deal of it around here. With you coming, they'll have the last six winners of the bean pageant together to priss around the stage before the pageant tomorrow night."

"That's what I mean. I don't want to priss around. It was hard enough standing up there when you entered me in that stupid contest two years ago. Standing up there like a side of beef at Stace's Meat Market. I just don't feel comfortable doing that."

"Well, this will be so much easier. You take a short walk, smile for the crowd and Marvin Maness, then leave the stage and you're done."

"I guess."

Callie took a sip and became quiet for a moment.

163

"Have you heard any word about Samuel?" Callie asked. "I haven't received a letter, or any contact at all."

"I talked with Bert a few days ago. He said they've not received any mail from Samuel in over a year. Mrs. Gable tries to stay away from reading the paper. She doesn't want to worry any more than she has to. She just waits on word in the mail from him."

"I worry about him all the time. I've sent him letters, but I haven't heard back from him since he first landed in New Guinea. If he's okay then why won't he write back?"

"Daddy says that those jungles are so deep and thick they can't get mail in and out of there. He says they are there to fight a war, not to work on their penmanship."

"I just wish I could know he's okay."

"I'm sure he is. Otherwise, his family would have known by now. Besides, it looks like the war's going well, according to news reports."

"I guess. I just miss him so much. I can't believe how hard I fell for him. I've never met anyone like him."

"I told you. He's every girl's dream."

"That night of the pageant was the best night of my life. I wanted to freeze time, so he'd never have to leave."

"Don't worry. You'll get your chance again. There's no way Samuel won't make it home. I'd bet the farm on it."

"When he does, I guarantee you I'll never let go of him again."

***

Eula Gable sat in the kitchen, turning the wooden handle on the butter churn. Her days were filled with tending to her garden, making butter, preserving vegetables and jams for the spring house so that the winter would find them with ample supplies of food. The headlights from Bert's car skimmed across the top of the kitchen window. Eula drained the leakage of the churn into a silver jug, liquid that would provide buttermilk for the evening dinner.

Bert parked the car at the right corner of the porch. He looked tired from the day's work. He reached into the back of the car and removed a metal cooler. His large hands grabbed the handles at each end, and he walked around the back of the house to the scaling table. Rafe Mobley had fished Timothy Branch that morning and caught his limit of trout in less than two hours. He and Bert were fishing buddies from way back, and they had shared their catches for years. When Bert was a young boy, he'd walk the two and a half mile stretch of dirt road to Rafe's house just so he could follow Rafe to his hidden fishing holes.

The mouthwatering aroma of fish cooking in the skillet soon filled the air, slender pieces of meat lightly dusted in flour. They ate at the kitchen table, as Eula had also prepared creamed corn and pole beans. Plump yeast rolls were served with the trout.

"Rafe sure knows where to find the best tastin' trout," Bert said as he pulled a strip of meat away from the spine of the nine-inch fish on his plate.

"They say he sings to 'em from the bank," his mother replied.

"He does. I've seen him do it."

"I'd give anything to have Samuel here eatin' with us. I've seen him eat a dozen of these trout in one sittin'."

"Don't worry, Momma. He'll be sittin' at this table again soon."

"Why won't he write? Surely they've got a way to carry the mail out and send it home."

"Jack Grayson says he ain't heard from Earl in over a year. I guess there ain't many mail drops in the jungles. Besides, I think they're a little preoccupied with whippin' those Japs."

"Still, it don't seem right to keep family in the dark."

"You know if there was a way, Sammy would have found it. Trust me. As long as we don't see anybody in uniform knockin' on our door, Sam's okay."

Bert had a way of soothing others' fears, and he felt a calling that led him to think that he should consider the ministry. Tall, handsome, with light brown, wavy hair, Bert was the spitting image of his father in looks, and temperament. Until Samuel returned, he felt it best to stay close to home and tend to his mother. It was his way of sharing the load of the worries of war.

***

It was Saturday night, and the townspeople began to fill up the Civitan Club. Marvin Maness took his spot on the first row, thinking maybe this was the year he could win the heart of a young maiden forty years his junior. Callie was dressed in a cream-colored skirt with matching jacket. Though her clothing was not flashy or showy, she stood out amongst the other five young women who had come back to be honored as former queens. Talk was small, though the other girls knew beyond a shadow of a doubt that Callie was the prettiest one. They seemed to look at her for signs of flaws, to see if she wore her beauty front and center, conceited perhaps in some ways, as she would have a right to be. But they could not deny the innocence and elegance of a young woman who seemed completely unaware of it.

The former winners were brought out on stage at the beginning of the pageant, and after hefty rounds of applause, were shown their way to the back where they were free to venture out and watch the pageant. Callie found a spot along the back wall, and Vera and Helen joined her.

"Let's get out of here," Helen whispered. "Let's go to the Dairy Bar."

"No," Callie said. "Not till the pageant's over. We can't be rude."

"We really don't know any of the contestants this year," Vera added.

"Doesn't matter," Callie responded. "It shows a lack of respect."

***

The sun hovered in the western sky above the crest of Holston Mountain, and shadows stretched long and deep across the valley as if trying to bridge Holston with Shady Mountain. The sky was still a bold sea of blue, and the temperature was beginning to fall as Sunday evening came calling. Callie said her good-byes to Vera and Helen, promising to return again soon. She eased her way down the dusty road toward Samson's Creek, the car kicking up dust behind it in some strange gray mist that melted into the evening air.

Two miles down State Road 84, Callie heard a thumping sound and her steering wheel began to shake. She looked at her side mirror, and eased off the highway on a flat stretch of shoulder. She shook her head. "No way." She checked the tires on the driver's side. Both looked normal. As she walked around the back to the passenger side, she noticed the front passenger tire was flat.

She opened the trunk, and carefully removed the outfit she'd worn the night before at the pageant. She placed the clothes carefully on top of the car and changed into a blouse and jeans from her suitcase. She also removed a rope and tackle box of her father's and set it on the ground so she could gain access to the spare. She'd watched her father change flat tires on several occasions, and she was familiar with the routine. She took hold of the cold jack and the black tire iron. In workmanlike fashion, she placed the jack under the car, on her hands and knees making sure it had secure footing to lift the car. As she began loosening the lug nuts with the tire iron, she heard the slight squeal of brakes as a car pulled up behind her on the shoulder.

The car door opened and closed, and she could hear footsteps on the gravelly ground. She was on all fours, loosening the last of the four nuts.

"So," the raspy voice began, "looks like you got trouble on your hands."

Wiping hair away from her eyes with the back of her forearm, Callie placed the nuts in the hubcap sitting upside down on the ground. "Nothing I can't handle," she said with a smile, her head down. She pulled up on one knee, preparing to take hold of the tire iron.

"We'll see about that."

Callie looked up at the stranger. The sun, close to setting, cast a horizontal light as if it were a giant flashlight, surrounding the stranger in a gray silhouette. She stood, grease smeared on her cheek. "Excuse me?"

Dobie leaned against Callie's car, his arms folded. He flashed a wicked grin and moved the toothpick from the left side of his mouth to the right with his tongue. "I told you you hadn't seen the last of me."

Callie placed the tire iron in a slot on the jack and began to turn it. The car began to lift as the jack rose. She did a poor job of acting as though she was not bothered by the situation. "I'll change the tire and be on my way." She slid the flat tire off the wheel and walked to the trunk. She looked down at the tire as she walked, but she could see the grin on Dobie's greasy face.

"So," he said, turning his body so his back pressed against the passenger window, facing the green meadows which led up to Shady Mountain, "looks like you ain't got none of your friends around to rescue you."

She placed the flat in the trunk and began to roll the spare along the shoulder beside the car. "I don't need any help. I can do this all on my own."

"Can you?" He took hold of her elbow as she passed in front of him. She stopped, cutting her eyes at the wild-eyed man.

"Take your hands off me."

She pulled away and he released her. She knelt and carefully placed the spare on the wheel. Dobie glanced west up the highway, turned his head and checked the east side as well. He pulled the toothpick from his mouth and flicked it to the ground. Callie placed the lug nuts on and tightened them gently. She then lowered the jack until it was free from the car. As she tightened the nuts with the tire iron, Dobie slid up behind her.

"Fine-lookin' caboose ya got there." His hand rubbed across the left cheek of her deep blue denim pants. She quickly slapped it away.

"Don't you touch me." She stood face-to-face to him, trying to show no fear. He grabbed hold of her wrists, and she could smell the stench of his breath against her face.

"You ain't in no position to tell me what not to do. Not today. Not when it's just you and me." Callie shook loose her right hand from Dobie's grip and slapped his face. He closed one eye, flinching for a brief second, before flashing a sly grin. "You're gonna pay for that." He pulled her by the wrist and opened the passenger door. He shoved the passenger seat forward. "Get in."

Callie hit Dobie across the neck with her forearm and broke loose from his grip. She ran past Dobie's car and sprinted down the rough gravel road. She knew a footrace was impossible to win. She simply hoped to buy time, hoping a passerby would come and rescue her. She looked across the valley for a house, for signs of life, as she ran, but the peacefulness of the hillsides was her only companion.

Dobie soon caught her, and he placed his arms around her waist. His body pushed against hers from behind, placing his chin on her neck. "That's no way to treat an old friend." He lifted her off the road and swung her body around so that they faced her car. "Come on." He held her by the arms and pushed her toward the cars.

Callie prayed for someone to come down the road, but it was deathly quiet. The world had left her to fend for herself. Her stomach roiled with fear, knotting up as her heart began to pound. As he forced her onward, she kicked her heel up behind her, smashing his shin. She broke loose and began to run again.

She made it to her car, praying the keys were still in the ignition. He took her by the hair and again wrapped his arms around her. He carried her under his arm like a sack of grain, walked to the passenger side where the door stood open, the car seat still leaning forward. "Climb on in there. You do as I say, and you might just make it home alive." He looked east and then west one more time. He wiped his forehead. Patches of sweat under his armpits stained his white T-shirt. His black slacks smelled of oil.

"Listen," Callie pleaded. "I don't want any trouble. I just want to go home."

"I wouldn't worry about home right now. You owe me for the sorry way you treated me that night at the Dairy Bar."

"No way am I getting in the car with you."

Dobie reached in his back pocket, the loud clicking sound of the switchblade causing her to freeze. He slowly moved the blade to her chin. "I said climb on in that back seat, darlin'."

Callie lowered her head and backed in, facing him. "Please don't do this."

"Shut your mouth."

He climbed in and straddled her legs, his body hovering above hers. He rubbed the knife, sharp side up, along her neck. "How about you take off that shirt?"

"Please, Dobie. I'm begging you."

"Take it off or I'll cut it off."

Callie slowly unbuttoned her shirt and began to cry. She placed her hands across her white brassiere.

"Move your arms." He grabbed hold of her bra from underneath the bottom and cut it in two with the knife. He slid the soft material away from her breasts. "Nice. I bet that boyfriend of yours loves gettin' his hands on these."

Callie slapped him full force across the face. "Go to hell."

"You first," he said, and he slapped her, first with his forehand, then again with a backhand across her lip.

Blood began to form around the contours of her mouth. As he rubbed her breasts, she closed her eyes. Her heart pounded. She began to sweat. Tears streamed down her face and she whispered repeatedly, "Please don't."

Dobie's dry lips moved along her neck, her chest, and her stomach. Her skin tightened at every point his lips made contact. Her mind thought a thousand thoughts, the first cursing the idea of coming back to the bean pageant. She thought of Samuel and the hard times she knew he must be facing. She tried to convince herself that her ordeal would be considered minor compared to Samuel's situation.

He unbuckled her belt with one hand while holding the knife in the other. He slid his fingers along her stomach. He unzipped the jeans, exposing the top of her white panties. "That's what I want right there," he said with a grin. "Shimmy off them jeans."

Her tears flowed and her chest began to heave. Like a child taken away from her mother, she lost feeling in her extremities. She felt numb as she slid her jeans to her ankles. He moved to the side of the seat and pulled them over her canvas shoes.

He ran his sweaty hand up her inner thigh and separated her legs at the knees. As he reached further and

172

slid his fingers along her underwear, a car door slammed. When he looked out the window, his knife sliced the inner part of Callie's knee, on the underside of her kneecap. He raised his head to see above the open trunk lid as an elderly man stepped out of a dusty black truck.

"You so much as whisper and I'll slice their throat *and* yours." Dobie popped up from the seat and made his way quickly to the back of the car. "Evenin'," Dobie said as he pretended to wipe his hands.

"You need some assistance, young fella?" the stocky man said as he approached Dobie.

"That's mighty nice of you to ask, but I'm good. I just finished changin' a flat and I'm ready to go. Headin' back to Damascus."

"Damascus, huh?

"Yep. Born and raised."

A dog's bark turned Dobie's head toward the truck parked behind Dobie's car. "Quiet'n down, Slick!" the old man yelled. "Sorry about that. My dog's a little overprotective." Dobie looked at the German shepherd, his head poking out from the passenger window, teeth exposed.

"You travelin' alone?" the old man asked as he looked at the clothes on top of the car.

Dobie turned and smiled. "Yep. Just me." The elderly man rubbed his white beard, his denim overalls worn snuggly over his round belly. He tried to look over the top of the trunk and into the car.

"Who's car is that?" the old man asked, nodding his head toward Dobie's car.

"You know, sir, I don't have a clue. How peculiar was it that I had a flat almost at the spot of that there car? Don't know if it's broken down, abandoned, or what." He elbowed the old man gently. "Reckon if I hadn't had a spare, I coulda taken one of the tires off that car."

"I reckon." The man spat tobacco juice on the ground.

"Well, I guess I better get a move on. I appreciate you stoppin' and checkin' on me." Dobie started toward the car.

"Well, I guess I best head on down the road," said the old man. "Gettin' close to dinnertime, so I better go home and tell Bertha to get them pots and pans to rattlin'."

"Yes, sir. It is about dinnertime, ain't it? Enjoy your supper, and thanks again for stoppin'."

The man walked to his truck, and Callie tried to look above the trunk out the back window. Blood rolled down her calf. She thought of screaming. She thought of the consequences she might bring to the innocent man who'd stopped to help. Surely the man was no match for Dobie. Still in tears, she attempted to put her head out the window.

Dobie popped the blade open as he stood at the passenger door, his knife exposed only to her eyes. "I'll kill you and him if you so much as whisper." He spoke softly, but loud enough for her to hear as he smiled at the man in the truck. He waved once, and as the truck began to pull on the road, Dobie said, "Lower yourself down there." The shepherd barked loudly at Dobie as they passed. Dobie slipped back into the seat and as he did, he heard the squeal of brakes again. "What's the matter with this guy?"

The man got out of his truck, not bothering to pull off to the side of the road. He walked back toward Callie's car. Dobie hopped out, the knife hidden behind his back.

"Forget somethin'?" Dobie asked, walking to the front of the car.

"You said you was from Damascus, huh?

"Yes, sir."

"Do you know Eldridge Carson?"

"Sure do."

"Tell him H. Jacobs says hello."

"Yes, sir."

Dobie waved and stepped back toward the car. As the man opened the door to his truck, Dobie slipped into the back seat as the truck noisily pulled into gear. Callie had her arms crossed in front of her breasts, cowering as she shook her head for him to leave her alone.

"Now, where were we?" He rubbed the blade along Callie's thigh. "I believe we were right about here."

As Dobie began to kiss Callie's inner thigh, the sound of shells engaging in a shotgun caused Dobie to sit upright. The barrel of the old man's gun was pointed inches from Dobie's face.

"Eldridge Carson's been dead for twelve years. Get out of the car, boy."

"Now wait a minute, old-timer. Don't do anything foolish."

"Back out of the car, son. Ma'am, you grab your clothes and step on out of there. I'm going to take you out of here."

"Let's talk about this a bit," Dobie said while hiding the knife behind his back.

"Drop the knife, and get out of the car, or I'll put a hole in your gut and let Slick eat what spills out of it for dinner."

Chapter Twelve

Pete held Samuel's arm as they stepped carefully toward the house. The clouds had thickened, and the wind had picked up. Pete felt the chill against his face and wondered if Samuel felt it, too. Gabby met them at the steps, taking Samuel's left arm as Pete kept hold of the right. Together they stepped one by one until Samuel was beside the wheelchair.

Samuel looked at the chair. "No. Not today. I will not use the chair today."

Instead, Samuel slowly walked to a white rocker and shook away his daughter's offer of assistance. Blackie came running from the backside of the pond where he'd attempted to snatch a trout. Pete looked into Samuel's eyes, proud to be considered an acquaintance of the man.

"Is Caleb your son? I've heard you mention his name a few times."

"Pete," Samuel said, "I think it's time for you to head on home." Pete laughed briefly but quickly realized there was no humor in Samuel's face. Pete looked at Gabby, and she simply gave a quick shake of her head. "Besides, don't you have a family of your own? You should be spendin' time with them."

"Well, actually, Sarah took Kate to the beach for a week with her sister."

"When are you goin' down?"

"I'm not. I got too much to do here."

"If I'd a-known that, I wouldn't have been tyin' you down here. You need to be on vacation with your family."

"I can't. Don't have the time."

"Hog testicles. You should be buildin' sand castles and chasing waves with that little gal. She ain't gonna be young forever, so you best spend as much time with her as you can. If you were off fightin' in some far-off jungle, you'd be thinkin' every moment how much you missed her. Missed your wife. How you wish you were there with them. And here you are with nothin' holdin' you back and still you don't take full advantage of it."

"It's a little more complicated than that," Pete said.

"Daddy, leave Pete alone. It's not your concern."

"Not my concern? The boy's got responsibilities and priorities. Just makin' sure he knows which ones are which."

***

Pete finished the calzone he'd picked up in the drive-through at Rossini's Pizza then he decided to call Sarah. He wanted to talk to her before putting the finishing touches to the Charlie Coleman story. Once he began working on the article he didn't want any distractions, so it was best to get the phone call out of the way and strike it off his to-do list. After four rings he heard her recorded voice mail message. He told her he missed her, that he missed Kate, and that he'd be up late working in case she wanted to call back.

Pete was feeling good about his article, and to proof it one last time, he printed it to see how it read on paper. He glanced at the clock on the computer. It was almost eleven, and he thought it odd that Sarah had not called back. When he tried her again, voice mail kicked in after four rings. He expected voice mail after the first ring, assuming that meant she had shut off her phone and turned in for the night. It wasn't like her to not return his call.

Pete signed off on his article, e-mailing it to Kaitlin Tinch, the editor of *Appalachian Trail* magazine. Eleven-thirty. Pete tried Sarah again, and with still no answer, he called Peggy, Sarah's sister. Peggy picked up on the second ring.

"Hello," she said quietly.

"Hey, Peg, this is Pete."

"Hello, Pete. How's the writing coming?"

"Finishing up a story now. Haven't received any book deals, though. Say, I can't get in touch with Sarah and wanted to talk with her for a minute. Can you put her on the phone?"

In a hesitant voice, Peggy said, "She isn't here."

"Oh. Where is she? It's almost midnight."

"She went out with Tamara Stevens. You know, the Stevenses own the beach house next door."

"They went out as in dinner, or out as in on the town?"

"Both, I guess. I've got Kate with me. She's been asleep for a couple of hours. Want me to tell Sarah you called?"

"Yeah, would you? I'll be up late tonight anyway."

Sarah had not gone "out on the town" since Kate was born. Pete wondered, with the midnight hour approaching, what kind of fun she was looking for. Pete tried to focus on the recording of Samuel from earlier, and though he wrote a few paragraphs, he kept glancing at the clock. It was now after one, and Pete contemplated calling again. He began to redial Peggy, but knew she wouldn't be happy to be awakened. He dialed Sarah's phone instead.

After three rings she answered, music blaring in the background.

"Sarah?"

"Hey," she said in a voice of surprise.

"Um, where are you?"

"What? I can't hear you. Music's crazy here."

"Crazy where?"

"What?"

"Where are you?"

"Let me walk outside. Hang on." The music and background noise was so loud that Pete held his phone away from his ear. A few moments later, she said, "There, that's better. Sorry about that."

"Where are you?"

"At a place called Streamers. It's really crowded." Pete could tell immediately that she had been drinking.

"Out kind of late, aren't you?"

"We're just laughing and having a good time. I'm not doing anything wrong. Peg is at the house with Kate, and we're just not ready to go home."

"Been doing any dancing tonight?"

"Why do you want to know that?"

"Just wondering. Have you?"

"A couple of times. They play good music here."

"Who have you been dancing with?"

After a few seconds of silence, she said, "Just a couple of guys. They're harmless."

"Well, I'm glad you're having such a blast. Sounds like you're the belle of the ball."

"I'm not going to get into an argument with you now. I'll call you tomorrow."

"Are you heading back to the house now?"

"No, we're not. Talk to you tomorrow."

Pete sharply flipped his phone closed and tossed it on the vinyl chair in front of the desk that held his laptop. He reached for his recorder and began playing back the words Samuel had told him about malaria and the letter from Callie. He had only written twelve pages so far, as his original intention was to write an overview of Samuel's war experiences. The anger of knowing Sarah was at some bar in Myrtle Beach, dancing and having a grand old time, injected a shot of adrenaline throughout his body.

As Pete documented the latest interview with Samuel, the words he wrote became more expressive, and he sought to capture the smell of death on the battlefields, the fear in the hearts of the men staring at their own mortality, hunkered in foxholes clutching their weapons. He wrote to feel the sting of the river water, to see the dense jungles, and hear the bullets ripping by Samuel's head. When he finished the day's interview, he went back to the beginning, editing what he had written, dating back to the first day he interviewed Samuel.

***

The sky began to lighten, and soon the morning sun cast its light about the quiet house. Pete rolled his neck gingerly and opened his eyes. He wondered at the time, unclear as to how long he'd slept in his chair. Though his laptop was on the table, he didn't remember placing it there. His back and neck felt as stiff as the pine tree outside the Florida room window. He moved stiffly toward the shower. As he stood under the steaming water, he thought of his conversation with Sarah.

Should he call? Should he wait on her to call? After all, he wasn't the party animal last night.

After showering, he began showing signs of life. He shaved and dressed, grabbing a diet drink and a banana.

Pete drove along Cherokee Road, trying to get his bearings. He'd come to look for the building, wondering if it held any answers. He knew it was on Cherokee, but he'd been a child when his mother first pointed it out to him. He spotted two men connecting a flat-bed trailer to the back of a red tractor. Pete slowed to a stop. The men were less than thirty feet from the road in a field ready for hay to be baled.

"Excuse me," Pete said as he opened the car door. He stood with his left foot on the pavement. "Do either of you know where the old Civitan building is located? I seem to remember it being on this road."

"You ain't missed it by far," one of the men said. "Turn yourself around, drive about, oh, I'd say a half mile, and you'll see it on the left side. Look carefully, though, or you'll miss it. If you come to the herd of cattle eatin' 'round the trough by the road, you've gone too far."

"He should know," the other man said, pointing at his partner. "Them's his cows he's talkin' 'bout."

"Thank you very much. Have a great day." Pete did a quick three-point turn and sped away. What Pete found was a square cement building, with intertwining vines that made it difficult to see the faded blue writing of CARTER SPRINGS CIVITAN CLUB on the front wall. Pete guessed that the building had been empty for at least twenty years, and when he looked at it from the road, it looked smaller than he remembered. It also seemed smaller than he'd imagined it when Samuel spoke of the bean pageant.

181

A massive elm was located at the back left corner of the building, its branches covering the entire tin roof of the once-active facility. Pete's dad had once talked about attending functions of all sorts there, from boxing matches to fundraisers for the Women's Club. Carter Springs didn't have much in the way of social events, so the Civitan Club was one of the few places, outside of church, for the townspeople to dress up and entertain themselves in social gatherings.

Pete walked around the side of the building. The vines were too thick along the front door to turn the doorknob without an ax to clear the way. So he moved along the back, walking under the expansive limbs of the elm. The cool mountain wind caught him flush when he came around the back corner. A faded wood door, which seemed like it might have been a service entrance in its day, was partially open, and the wind moved it slightly. Pete pushed the door, and it creaked as it opened inward.

He opened it wider and the light of day slid across the room, illuminating a dim floor with tables and chairs set about in disarray. An old cloth blanket was tied across the front of a high window that faced the eastern sky, and Pete removed it by stepping on a chair. As he did, the sunlight brightened the building enough to where Pete could now see the front door. Trash was scattered about, including papers that looked like they weren't useful or needed anymore.

He found an old phonograph, with two-foot speakers pulled apart and leaning into each other as if to keep them from falling. He kicked around some papers and walked to what looked like an old file cabinet tipped over on its side. He slid open the top drawer of the two-drawer cabinet, and mildewed brown folders fell out. Pete lifted a few of them up one at a time toward the window, and he found flyers for a revival featuring Reverend John Perry in August of 1956. It was advertised as a week-long event. He found the minutes for a town meeting in early 1949 that looked like it discussed widening State Road 84 toward Elizabethton. Many papers were illegible, and others too mildewed to hold.

When Pete opened the bottom drawer, a folder flipped out that spilled black-and-white photos onto the floor. Pete held them up to the light. One was of men and women dressed in polyester sitting at a table, and Pete guessed it to be from the '70s. Most of the men had sideburns, and the ladies' hair was tied up in buns. As he skipped through the pictures, he came across one of a dozen or so young ladies. The girl in the center of the picture held a bouquet of roses and wore a sash that had only one legible word: BEAN.

He walked to the back door quickly, and stepped outside so he could see more clearly. He couldn't make out any more of the writing on the sash, but he noticed how beautiful the girl holding the bouquet looked. He flipped the picture over, and in the corner were the words *Bean Queen Pageant 1942*.

Pete ran to the car.

***

Shadows ran oblong along the sloping grass, connecting the trunks of two poplars standing on the east side of the pond with the kitchen window of the Gable house. The sun's light cut thin slices through the thick trees, keeping the porch in pale shadow. Pete pulled in front of the house, and the peaceful setting of the morning was not lost on his eyes. When he tapped on the door, Gabby answered, though it took a few minutes for her to answer.

"Pete," she said with surprise, still in her purple nightgown. "I didn't know Daddy called you this mornin'. I'm sorry I'm not dressed appropriately."

"He didn't call. I just think I found something he might want to see. Don't apologize for the way you're dressed. I'm the one who should apologize for dropping in without an invitation."

Gabby stood at Pete's side and cocked her head to look at the faded picture. "That old photograph sure is faded. Who are those people?"

"Let's see if your dad can tell us."

"I'll let him know you're here."

"Thanks, Gabby. Sorry again for stopping by without notice."

"It's okay. I'm sure Daddy will be glad you're here." Gabby wouldn't deny the fact *she* was glad Pete had stopped by, though she would have wanted to look more presentable.

Pete looked at the picture again. He tapped it impatiently against his palm. He'd come to feel quite at ease at the Gable house. It reminded him of his grandparents' home. Pete felt a certain kinship with it, as if it were a place that connected the past of the Appalachian way of life and the ever-changing present. There weren't many houses as old as the Gable home in the area, at least not ones where Pete knew the owners. He couldn't imagine walking up to a stranger's house and asking for a guided tour.

Within minutes Gabby returned, leading Pete to the parlor.

"Mornin', Mr. Gable."

"Pete. What brings you out this way?" Samuel lay in his bed, blue-and-white pinstriped pajamas hanging loosely on his frame, petting Blackie, who lay across Samuel's legs on the bed.

"I have something I think you might like to see. Now, I'm not sure if this is who I think it is, but take a look at it and tell me if I'm wrong." He handed the picture, bent around the edges, to Samuel.

"Gabby, bring me my readin' glasses. These folks look fuzzier than cattails by the crick." Soon his black-rimmed glasses sat low on his nose, and he began to rub his fingers across the photo, caressing the face of the young lady holding the bouquet. "My Lord. Gabby, come look."

Gabby stood in the doorway to the kitchen, fresh back from brushing her hair. "What is it, Daddy?"

"It's your Momma. The day she won the Bean Queen pageant."

The mention of her mother had Gabby quickly beside Samuel's bed. With her hand on her father's shoulder, she leaned toward him to get a closer look. Though she smiled, tears found the corners of her eyes. "Oh, my God. She looked absolutely beautiful."

"She sure did," Samuel said. "This picture don't begin to show how pretty she really looked that night. Where did you find this?"

"Inside a file cabinet in the old Civitan building. I kind of slipped in the back door to rummage around. When I looked at it I knew it had to be her. You're right. She was a stunner."

"Yes, she was," said Samuel. He studied the photo hard, his eyes squinting as if he was trying to magnify Callie to life-size. Tears welled.

"Did you and she get together soon after you got back from the war?"

For a long moment Samuel only looked at the photo. Silence filled the room. He huffed sullenly.

"I'm not ready to talk about that yet. We need to finish my time in the war." He rubbed his chin and glanced out at the pond. "You got time to sit a spell and listen?"

"Yes, sir. Let me get my recorder from the car."

***

June, 1945

The war was over, and the Battle of Luzon officially logged into the history books. Smoke carried across the sky as a reminder of the destruction that had taken place, and it cast a paleness over the rocky mountainside. Though the war was over, there was no celebration. The toll of the war had left the men weak and weary. Many had died, and for those who survived, it was a somber mood. Many soldiers wondered what they would do now that the war had come to an end. For over two years they had fought, marching forward through a savage land, merely trying to stay alive.

Samuel sat on a cot in front of a tent, alone, sipping a cup of black coffee from a gray tin cup. The wind turned from the north, and a welcome chill ran through his body. It reminded him of home, and his thoughts turned to Callie. Private Dell Rhame approached Samuel and informed him that Captain Dinkins requested his presence. Samuel walked into Dinkins' tent, an expansive tarp that resembled a circus tent. A large pole in the middle raised the canvas to a point, and there was room for ten men to sleep comfortably.

"Sergeant, we have one more task that must be carried out before we can ship off for home. The men left on that mountain deserve proper burial, proper military burial. I'm sending you and your squad out at oh-six-hundred hours to begin their retrieval. You buried many of them, and it's your job to bring them home. We only have one quartermaster left in our ranks, and frankly, I don't think he can handle the task. He will be assisting you, however."

Samuel nodded, and left the tent without speaking. It was tough enough burying his fallen comrades, and he could only imagine the condition of their bodies after weeks, and in some cases months, of lying underneath the warm soil. No matter the gruesomeness, he felt honored to be given such a duty. The Red Arrowmen were family, and family could not be left behind. Standard procedure called for all deceased soldiers to be buried at the end of the day. Some were buried in foxholes, especially if they died there during battle. Others were buried in makeshift graves whenever the bullets stopped flying. A cross was rudimentarily constructed on each grave, where dog tags and their helmet were hung.

When morning came, Samuel and thirty-two men, most of them replacement soldiers, began the task of finding the fallen soldiers. Samuel led the way, retracing the trails and paths they had carved out along the final battle. They had tried to bury the soldiers near the trails, near the paths, making the search easier when it was time to retrieve them.

And so it began. The makeshift graves began to open, and the quartermaster filled out paperwork for each soldier based on information from the dog tags. It required four men to carry each body, and to centralize matters, Samuel had the men accumulate the bodies in one location where they would be placed on trucks and carried to a predetermined permanent graveyard. With each grave unearthed, Samuel tried to focus on the body and not the dog tags. He didn't want to know whose body he was removing, in an effort to disassociate himself from the men being taken from their resting ground.

The sun bore down on the men, and the smell of death soon carried across the rugged terrain. The men grew tired, but in a way different from the daily battles they'd endured. The morbid job that lay before them took its toll emotionally. With each body retrieved, it signified in concrete terms the losses of their comrades. They came across a group of six crosses, and Samuel couldn't push from his mind the battle that cost these men their lives. They were killed along the trail by a child strapped with explosives.

The quartermaster asked Samuel's help reciting the names of the men, and for the first and only time in the war, he was overcome with grief. He knelt and wiped his eyes, reading the names of the men from their tags. In the sixth and final grave was Billy Roberts, and Samuel recalled his dying words, asking Samuel to promise he'd contact his wife to tell her he loved her. He removed Billy's dog tags from the wood cross and motioned for two men to begin digging. As the body was removed, Samuel called for another soldier to help him assist the two men who'd dug Billy from the ground. As they carefully lifted the blackened body, Billy's feet snapped off and softly fell into the putrid soil. One of the soldiers picked up the feet and Samuel's lip quivered. Private John Morrison stepped in to take over for Samuel. Morrison said no words, only placing his hand on Samuel's shoulder, letting him know he felt his pain.

Samuel turned away from the graves, looking out to the brown flatlands that lay at the base of the mountain. He fell to his knees, and two years of pent-up anguish came flowing from the depths of his soul. Quietly he cried, though his body shook. It took the other soldiers by surprise, as Samuel had been a rock every step of the way during the war. To them Samuel represented what was right and true about being a soldier. He had led them through the jungles of death and destruction. To see him with his heart and soul exposed was something that ripped at their insides.

The body count mounted, and as darkness approached, Samuel realized it would take more than one day. He sent his men back to camp, though he remained behind. He set up a foxhole, climbed inside, and held the rifle as he stared out into the darkness. He knew that Japanese soldiers were still straggling out from hiding spots, some who might not have heard that their home country had surrendered. As terrible a shape as the dead were in, Samuel would not take a chance on a Japanese soldier defacing any of the men's bodies.

And so his night was spent guarding the men, one more night, one more time. It was the least he could do.

Chapter Thirteen

Clouds clung tightly to the steep slopes of Jefferson Mountain, smoky wisps draping the treetops in abstract shapes of green and black. At the base of the mountain, white pines stood dark and powerful in front of that hazy canvas that was the mountain. A grassy meadow climbed in soft waves of green below the mountain where cattle grazed, scattered about in random formation, their bodies still and two-dimensional. A faded white barn with a dim tin roof sat empty, its only purpose a place for the cattle to find shelter. A wood fence in need of paint ran in front of the barn, parallel with the highway that carried Gabby and Samuel.

As Samuel looked out at the barn, the one Pierce Campbell's father had built back in the late '40s, his hands slowly rolled the dark cherry walking cane as he sat in the passenger seat of Gabby's car. "Has a wintry look to the day," he said, watching mist form on the window. "Dark skies. Lonely feel. I like this kind of day."

"Really?" Gabby asked. "I think it's depressing."

"Days like this test a person. Makes sure a body can live without the help of the sun and a warm breeze. In the war I went months without the first sign of a blue sky. I didn't want to see the sun. The evil of the world was all around us and we didn't deserve sunny days. Death wasn't supposed to have a cheery backdrop."

"I sure wish you hadn't gone through what you did. I couldn't imagine."

"You and me both."

"Well, let's not talk about war. Let's go home and I'll fix us lunch. You care for some collards and sweet corn?"

"That'll work."

"I'll phone in your prescription and pick it up when the nurse stops by."

"Let's just use the medicine for fish bait. We'd get better use from it that way."

"Daddy, you know the oncologist is just trying to help you feel better. She's trying to ease your pain."

"Ain't doin' no good. Makes me sicker'n a diarrheic mule anyway. If they want to make me feel better, then stop givin' me that crap. I'd rather have worm pills."

When they pulled onto Vaught's Holler, Gabby rehashed the instructions laid out by the oncologist. Samuel looked toward the creek.

"Let me out right here."

"What?"

"Let me out. I don't feel like goin' home yet. I want to see if the trout are runnin'."

"Daddy, it's cold and rainy."

"Whatsa matter? Worried I'll die of pneumonia?"

"That's not funny."

"It's just mistin'. Let me walk the creek. Come get me in an hour." Blackie whimpered from the back seat of the car. "See? Blackie wants out too."

Samuel set his cane to the dirt road when Gabby opened his door. She walked beside him as he moved slowly around the front of the car and onto the grassy bank. "You sure you want to do this?"

"Yes. Now, go home. Read a book. Take a nap. Take your mind off me."

Samuel stepped toward the creek, his body fighting to gather strength to walk the footprints of his youth. The familiar chill of the breeze blowing off the water brushed against his face.

Gabby returned to the car and turned to watch Samuel standing creekside. Blackie bolted from the back seat. Quickly he ran, strong, agile, his tail wagging high. Gabby just shook her head, started the car and headed for home.

A young man was fishing beside a weeping willow thirty yards to the right of Samuel. The long limbs of the willow brushed the stream as though it was painting the fast moving waters. Samuel stepped carefully toward the boy, who struggled with casting his bait into the creek. Blackie soon was by Samuel's side.

"How they bitin'?"

The boy looked startled, perhaps wondering if it was Samuel's land that his feet stood upon. "Uh, well, to be honest, I ain't havin' no luck." The boy kept his eyes on the plastic float bobbing quickly past a cluster of rocks. Blackie ran to the stranger's side.

"Don't worry about the pup. Your only fear would be him lickin' you to death."

The young man reached out his hand and petted Blackie briefly. "I'm tryin' to hit that pool over on the backside but can't reach it."

"Need a weight on your line. The bait can't carry that far on its own. Your bait's gonna keep slippin' into the rocks."

"Ain't got no weight. Just the pole and a few minners in the bucket."

Samuel held tight to the cane for support as he slowly went down on one knee and placed his hand in the water. He removed a smooth, nickel-sized flat rock. "Reel in your line."

The young man reeled the bait from the water and took it by the hand, warily walking to Samuel. Samuel took the line and pushed down on the top of the plastic float, releasing some slack in the line that flowed from top to bottom. He placed the stone in between the line and the float, let go his grip, and it tightened the line firmly against the float.

"Here, try that."

"Thanks." The boy checked to make sure the fishhook still penetrated the head of the minnow and drew back his rod to cast.

"Toss it as far as you can. Try to hit the bank on the far side." The boy let go of the line and it sailed past the rocks into the slow moving pool of water.

"That did the trick. Thanks, mister."

"Sure thing." Samuel eyed the young man, guessing his age to be in the late teens. "You ain't from around here, are you?"

"No, sir," he said sheepishly. "Am I trespassin' on your property?"

"Technically, no, but even if you were I wouldn't send you on your way."

Samuel watched the float bob and sink, and the boy jerked his rod skyward and began reeling furiously. After a few seconds the resistance eased and he reeled until the hook dangled in front of him. He looked at the empty hook moving about in the breeze.

"Lost him."

"You gotta watch the tip of your rod. When it starts to dip in short bursts, pop, pop, pop, then jerk that sucker skyward." The boy placed another minnow on his hook. "Ain't nothin' like fishin' these creeks. Been doin' it most of my life."

"You live up in the white house yonder?"

"That's the one." The boy cast again, his bait landing in the pool. "Where you from?"

The boy scratched above his eyebrow, as if heavy in thought. "Um, up Soda Hill way."

"That's quite a-ways down the road. How is it you ended up here?" Samuel glanced along the creek toward the road. "Where's your mode of transportation? That'd be a hard one if you walked it."

The boy continued to look out at the float on the creek. "Ain't got no car."

"How is it you came to be here?"

"To be honest with you, I been on the run a bit."

"Law after you?"

"No, sir. It ain't like that. My pa and I had it out. I graduated high school in June, and I guess I weren't showin' enough initiative to suit him. He wants me to join the service. But that kind of life ain't for me. I worked a couple of odd jobs, the last one workin' the counter at Bub's Quik Mart. I guess I ain't figgered out what I'm supposed to do. Can't see wastin' it sellin' beer and beef jerky at Bub's."

"So you took off with a rod and a bucket of minnows?"

"Not exactly. Pa kicked me out. I was thinkin' of headin' to Boone. Was hungry, had no money. I took this rod from the shed of some farmer down the road. It looked unused. Didn't think he'd miss it. I trapped a few minnows at the edge of the water into the bucket."

"When's the last time you ate?"

"I ate a couple of apples this mornin'. Found an apple tree next to a fence by the highway. Climbed it and took a few. You gonna call the law?"

Samuel shook his head and looked out at the creek. "No, son. I ain't callin' the law. Let me ask you something."

"What's that?"

"What are you plannin' on doin' if you catch a fish?"

The boy shrugged his shoulders in embarrassment. "Hadn't thought that far ahead."

"Tell you what. Any fish you catch, we'll clean 'em and have my daughter cook 'em for you."

"Much obliged, but that's askin' too much."

"Don't argue with me, or I'll beat you with my cane. In my early days I coulda whipped you, but now I couldn't whip an egg in a plastic bowl."

The kid laughed. "Well, then I best accept your offer and say thanks."

"Name's Samuel Gable. Yours?"

"Skeeter Burrows. Pleasure."

Under Samuel's guidance Skeeter caught three rainbow trout. Samuel took his pocketknife and sliced off a tender limb from a maple. He placed the limb inside the gill of each fish and then knelt and jammed it into the creek bottom. Skeeter watched in amazement at the strength in the frail man's body.

As Skeeter fished, Samuel told stories of his younger days. He talked of the fish he'd caught, and the ones that got away. Skeeter seemed to enjoy the company, enjoy the stories. At first it was hard for him to look Samuel in the eyes, partly because of the embarrassment of his situation. But the more Samuel spoke, the more Skeeter became drawn to the spark of life in the eyes of this stranger. It was as if a window to an ancient world had been uncovered, and Skeeter the only participant in the audience privy to the discovery.

As the stories continued, Samuel paused, asking, "You aim on headin' home soon? Bet your folks are worried about you."

"I'm sure Ma is. Pa, he probably ain't give it a second thought."

"Don't be too sure. Have you and your father always been at odds?"

"No, sir. We used to be real close. He taught me how to hunt, how to trap for small game. Showed me how to coon hunt at night. But since I graduated, it seems like he's lost confidence in me. It ain't like I want to just sit around and do nothin'. But I just don't see the need in doin' somethin' if it ain't helpin' me in the long run."

"Workin', no matter what capacity, helps you in the long run. It teaches you to work hard no matter what you do."

"Yes, but it ain't worth it when you have to work for jerks and dumbasses."

"The world's overflowin' with those."

"That's what Pa said."

"He's right. You know, life only gives you one shot. You need to do your best to keep the bond between family strong. How'd you feel if somethin' was to happen your pa?"

"Huh?"

"What if you found out he had gotten hurt in an accident, or worse, lookin' for your skinny tail? Wouldn't it bother you to know your last conversation with him was a bad one?"

"Sure it would." Skeeter tried to watch the end of the rod but he looked to be processing countless thoughts. "But you don't understand."

"Son, I understand more than you could ever know."

Samuel watched while Skeeter caught two more fish. Soon Gabby returned.

"Ready to come home?" she asked as she rolled down her car window.

"Yep. We're havin' company tonight. This fellow caught our dinner."

Skeeter looked puzzled for a moment and then smiled.

***

Pete walked into Lawson's Drug Store. It was a little after four, and he had come in search of printer paper. He didn't feel like driving to the superstore across town, though the way he ran through paper he should have. Lawson's was located across the street from where the Dairy Bar once stood. The '60s was the end of the line for the small drive-in, and it had been torn down, an empty lot standing in its place.

Lawson's had a small lunch counter that ran along a slender stretch connecting the drug store to a fabric shop. Pete walked to the right of the front door, passing shelves of first aid medicines, gauze, and bandages. Across from the shelf that held such items as Brylcreem and industrial strength shampoos like Prell, Pete squatted, finding one pack of printer paper amongst a stack of three-ring binders and loose-leaf notebook paper.

When he stood, he spotted Gabby walking toward the pharmacy counter. "Gabby," he said, moving down the aisle, catching up to her at the Diet Rite soft drink display. "How are you?"

"Hi." She wore a black turtleneck, and for the first time since Pete began coming to Samuel's house, she wore eyeliner. Her hair was fixed, and she wore rose-colored lipstick. Pete couldn't help but stare. "I'm picking up pain medicine for Daddy. Don't know why, though. He fights me every time I try to place them in his hand."

"I was hoping to come out and spend time with him in the next day or so. You think he's up to it?"

"Today was a pretty good day, though *good* is a relative term here. Why don't you call tomorrow morning and see how he's feeling? Mornings are still his best times, so that'd be your best bet."

"I think he's about done with the war stories, but I want to get him to talk about coming home. How it was to be reunited with your mom."

"He was crazy for Momma. You know, when she passed away, it took a lot out of him. He didn't eat, didn't sleep well. We all struggled with it, but Daddy put up a wall around himself for the longest time. He just loved Momma so much he was lost without her."

"It certainly sounds that way." Her eyes had a certain sparkle that made him a bit nervous, like back in high school on a first date. "Um, you look really…" he stammered, before saying, "…um, never mind."

"What?" She was standing close to him, and he detected that same sweet aroma as the day he'd held her on the porch.

"It's just that you look...very pretty today." She blushed. "Not that you didn't the other times I've seen you. Sound like an idiot, don't I?"

"Not at all. That's very sweet of you to say. I haven't been exactly primping up much lately. Too much other stuff to think about."

"I'm sure all this is wearing you out. Anyway, I think you look nice all the time, but today you look especially pretty." She glanced toward her feet for a moment as if to hide her blushing face. "On second thought," he said, scratching his chin, "I take that back."

"What do you mean?"

"The day I showed up and you were in the purple gown—"

"You didn't like my gown?" She popped him gently on his forearm.

"I just think it might be time for an upgrade. Do you remember the Chevy Chase movie *Vacation*?"

"Yes."

"The gown was a little too...Aunt Edna-ish."

She gasped. "I can't believe you just said that."

"Don't get me wrong. *You* still looked good, but the gown..."

"Fine. I'll burn it when I get home."

"Good idea."

He walked with her to the counter. She shook her head in mock disgust at the Aunt Edna comment. After she spoke briefly with Glenn Jordan, the pharmacist, she grabbed the bag that held the prescription.

"Are you heading home?" Pete asked.

She looked at a cardboard display. "Chocolate-covered gummy bears." She picked up a pack. "I didn't know they sold them here."

"Are they hard to find? I'm not much of a gummy guy."

"The chocolate-covered ones, yes. I haven't found them anywhere in town. Though maybe that's a good thing. I'd be big as a cow if I had a steady supplier."

"Can I ask you something?"

"Sure."

"About your brother."

Gabby's cell phone rang, and she reached into her purse. "Excuse me for a second." She turned her head away from Pete. "Daddy, you okay?" Her eyes moved about as she listened. "Yes, sir. I'm at Lawson's right now. I'll be home in just a few minutes." She folded the phone in her hand, ending the call. "Daddy's pissed at the nurse. She's trying to help him to the bathroom and he refuses. Says he's not putting on any peep show for her pleasure. Sorry, I gotta run."

***

It was Friday morning, and Sarah and Kate were due back sometime that afternoon. Pete had decided not to call Sarah after her night on the town in Myrtle Beach, instead waiting on her to make the first move. It didn't happen. No phone call, no apology. There was no let's-make-up-when-I-get-home talk. Though Pete was bothered by her apparent lack of concern, he used the quiet time to work on Samuel Gable's tales of the battlefield.

He turned down a request from the *Boone Herald* to write an article about family getaways in the

Appalachians, the first time he had ever declined any publication seeking his services. One of the articles he'd submitted to Paul Douglas at *Southern Life* magazine was picked up and set to appear in the spring edition. That bought Pete a little more time to spend on Samuel's story.

***

It was four o'clock when Kate came running through the door. "Daddy," she yelled as she ran to Pete's waiting arms.

"Hey, sweetheart. Did you have a good time?"

"Yes, sir. We built sand castles and chased sea gulls. I almost caught a crab, too."

"A crab? No way." He squeezed her once, and pulled away so he could brush her hair from her forehead. "Well, I sure missed you. Did you miss me?"

"Uh-huh. Why didn't you come?"

"Too much work to do. But it sounds like you had a great time." Pete tried to make eye contact with Sarah, but she carried the suitcase to the laundry room. Kate talked a mile a minute, telling her father about everything from the new swimmies she wore to the new friend she'd made from Texas. Soon she began playing with her dolls in her room, and Pete could hear her repeating to them the beach stories she'd told him.

He walked into the bedroom as Sarah was removing her makeup bag, toothbrush, and shampoo from her suitcase. "So, sounds like you made the most of your vacation," Pete said, taking hold of the bottle of shampoo Sarah had placed on the bed.

"What's that supposed to mean?"

"Nothing. It's just that, according to Kate, y'all had a lot of fun."

"Yes, we did. We had a great time." Pete easily detected the hint of sarcasm. "Course, Kate saw all these fathers playing with their daughters on the beach. I could tell it bothered her."

"You know I had too much going on here. Besides, it sounds like you didn't need me there to have a good time. You were the dancing queen of Myrtle Beach."

"Yep. Every night. Out till the break of dawn, living it up. I was the town skank."

"God, you're becoming a real witch."

"Well, if you don't start putting more emphasis on your family, you're going to have a lot of time to spend on your writing. That deserted island you talked about might end up being your permanent place of residence."

***

Pete drove away, gripping the steering wheel tightly with both hands. How could Sarah not understand the sacrifices he was making? The countless hours he was spending in hopes of making a career of something he loved? Did she not see that he possibly could provide financial stability and allow her to quit her job, or at least have the freedom to change jobs if she felt like it?

He couldn't concentrate on writing with her at home, so with his laptop in the passenger seat, Pete headed to Gainey's Sandwich Shop for some free Wi-Fi and a change of scenery.

There were only two people in the restaurant when he entered. One was a young teenager filling out a job application. The other was an elderly man who drank coffee and read a newspaper. Pete bought a bottle of orange juice and chose the corner table that faced the front window looking out across Campbell's Creek. He didn't have his recorder, so his writing was based on his memory of Samuel's comments from the day before.

An hour or more had passed, and Pete had written several pages on Samuel's agonizing task of removing the bodies of the soldiers. He stopped briefly to rub his wrist, and looked toward the counter. The shop had grown quite busy as the dinner crowd began filing in. Most of the patrons were teenagers, some college age kids, and a few that looked like they'd just come off the first shift at the Burlington plant.

He spotted a teenaged-looking boy dressed in faded jeans, the knees torn out, and a green T-shirt listing the concert tour schedule for 3 Doors Down. He wore a gray toboggan that fit snugly on his head, and he had tattoos on both arms. Pete overheard him say, "Dad, order me a grinder. I gotta go to the bathroom." The father nodded and smiled. He was dressed in dark pants, and a crisp white dress shirt with a red-and-blue tie. His hair was short and neatly cropped. In terms of appearance, he was the polar opposite of his son.

Pete pulled up the Internet and found several search engines that claimed to find people all over the country. Several were of the free variety, so he plugged in the name Caleb Gable. Two names were found, and they appeared to be a father and son pair in Wheaton, Illinois. One was Caleb Gable, Junior; the other William Gable III. For $19.95 one site claimed it could find public records on anyone. Pete reluctantly pulled out his credit card and paid the fee.

When he put Caleb's name in the search engine, the results showed eleven people. It had a category for associated relatives, and a frisson stole down his spine as he found the names Samuel and Gabrielle Gable. The last known address for this Caleb Gable was in Asheville.

Pete borrowed a pen from a woman at the table next to him and wrote down the address on a scrap of paper.

***

Evening came. Back at home, Pete browned a pound of ground beef in a skillet. Spaghetti sauce and noodles sat on the counter beside the stove. In thirty minutes he'd have dinner ready, and hopefully a chance to sit at the table and eat with Kate and Sarah. When he poured the noodles from the boiling water into the colander, he checked the clock. It was almost six, and the girls were not at home.

At six-thirty, Pete called Sarah. "You guys close to the house? Dinner is ready."

"Oh, we already ate. Mom fixed chicken."

"Why didn't you tell me? I fixed a big pot of spaghetti."

"I didn't know you were cooking. Just put it in some Tupperware. We can eat it for lunch tomorrow."

"So, how close are you to home?"

"We're at Lindsey's Nursery. Dad wanted some pansies for the yard."

"So are you planning on spending *any* time at home? It's like you don't live here anymore."

"Well, I know how you need peace and quiet so you can write. I'm just trying to help you out."

***

Pete stopped writing at Kate's insistence to tuck her in bed. She wanted a bedtime story, but Pete wanted to get back to the computer. So he kissed her on her forehead, tickled her under the chin, and pulled the covers up to her shoulders. "Night, sweetie. Love you."

"I love you too, Daddy." He smiled and walked out of the room.

It was quiet, and the clock read 9:44. Pete walked to the bedroom and noticed the bed was still made. He peeked into the bathroom to see if Sarah was in the shower, but the room was dark and empty. He looked in the washroom, the kitchen, and the den. Puzzled, he walked down the hall and noticed the guest bedroom door was open. Decorative throw pillows from the guest bed were on the floor. The light from the bathroom across the hall shined into the room, and as he picked up a burgundy pillow, he saw Sarah curled up under the covers, sound asleep.

Confused and hurt, he tiptoed out of the room, shut the door, and turned off the bathroom light.

Chapter Fourteen

When the phone rang, Pete had just finished sliding on his Sperrys. Sarah answered the phone in the kitchen and set the receiver on the kitchen table. "Phone's for you," she yelled while cutting into a grapefruit.

"Hello," said Pete, glancing at Sarah nonchalantly.

"Pete," said Gabby, "Daddy's in a foul mood. Wouldn't eat breakfast, wouldn't take his medicine. Says he's done with it all."

"I'm sure it's just frustration talking. I couldn't have kept as good an attitude as your father has."

"He's frustrated, all right. But I've never seen him like this. If he was in a pissy mood, I'd feel better. He looks like he's just tossed in the towel."

"Highs and lows are a part of it. It was the same way with my dad."

"Do you think you could stop by?"

"Absolutely. I'm on my way."

Pete grabbed his keys from the porcelain dish on the kitchen table. "Mr. Gable's not doing well. I'm going to go see if I can help."

"You do that," Sarah said coldly. "I'm beginning to wonder whether it's Mr. Gable or his daughter that keeps you coming back."

"What? I can't believe you'd say that."

"Well, when she calls you sure do drop everything and take off running. What's *her* story? Is she married?"

"You think Gabby and I have something going on?"

"Is she married?"

"I've never asked, but I'm guessing no."

"Don't you think it's a bit dangerous that you're over there all the time, consoling her? You don't think it's possible she's growing close to you as you ease her and her father's pain? She's fragile, she's alone. What does she look like, by the way? How old is she?"

"This is nuts. Listen, the reason I go there is for Mr. Gable, not Gabby."

"Is she pretty?"

Pete shook his head in amazement. "What is your problem? The man's dying. I promised to write his story. Get a grip."

"You know, sometimes I don't like you."

"You're breaking my heart." With that, Pete headed out the door.

***

Samuel gripped the metal bars on both sides of his bed and tried to fight the deep cough that might expel what was deep inside his throat. His hair was tousled, his face paled to that of someone anemic. Pete stood at the side of the bed, behind Gabby, in the hopes of providing assistance. Blackie sat uneasily at Gabby's feet. When Samuel coughed again, he held his closed fist to his mouth. Blackie let go a crying bark. When Samuel pulled the fist away from his mouth, a filmy ball of purple-laden blood covered most of Samuel's index finger. Gabby quickly wiped it away with a tissue.

Stoically, Gabby had assumed the dual role of nursemaid and daughter. Pete saw the frustration in her eyes. Finally the coughs began to subside, and Samuel's body slumped back against the flimsy mattress. Sweat beaded on his forehead, and his eyes told the story of a man sick and tired of the battle.

"Daddy, Pete's here." Gabby wiped Samuel's forehead with a soft, damp cloth. Pete slipped up alongside the bed.

"Mornin', Mr. Gable. Is there anything I can do for you? Get you some water or somethin'?"

Samuel simply shook his head.

"Pete, can you hold onto Daddy's arm while I dampen the rag?"

Pete placed a firm hand under Samuel's elbow, if nothing else to let Samuel know he was by his side. He placed his other hand on Samuel's shoulder, feeling the frailness of the once-broad shoulders that had led men through battles and dragged Bryson Steele from the grip of death in his foxhole. Pete looked into Samuel's eyes from the side, seeing the look of despair, the hopelessness of a dying man.

Pete fought back tears, as if he were watching the impending death of not only a man but a generation of a rare breed. Thoughts came to him of the final days of watching his dad slip into a coma, of seeing Dad's piercing blue eyes one last time before they closed forever. Pete took hold of Samuel's hand, trying to impart energy, life, into the man. The hand was cold and callused, and it was all too familiar.

When Gabby returned, she came to Samuel's side and Pete slipped out of the room. He hurried out the front door and pulled his car out of the rocky driveway and onto the dirt road. The tears fell, and Pete wiped his eyes when he got to the stop sign at State Road 84. Though his vision was blurred, he pulled out. A quarter mile he rode, and then turned off onto Spear Branch. He drove seven miles up a winding road bordered by fields of cattle and hay-strewn barns. Dogs of mixed breed gave momentary chase from Ollie Taylor's house before turning back to their yard.

He pulled his car to the edge of the dark blue gravel road, in front of the slate stone steps covered by weeds and twisty briar limbs. When he stepped from the car the familiar smell of clover carried him back to the day he'd last walked up the steps, barely six years old. He was holding his father's hand, shivering in the cold chill of the evening. The five steps were the gateway to Grandma and Papa's house, and though they died five months apart when he was seven, his mind was now filled with memories of his visits.

Pete stepped softly up the steps at the base of the yard as the briars clung to the bottom of his jeans. When he reached the top step, he stopped. The yard that was once hunter-green, soft, with plenty of room for a growing boy to wander, was now a jungle of grasses, weeds, and briars. He stepped carefully up the hilly yard, making his way to steps that once led to the front porch. The steps were the only reminder that the house had ever existed. He found a spot on the top step that was briar-free, and he sat, facing the road.

He saw the well, the rock walls of which had been caved in by a fallen tree. Beside the well, where Grandma's rose garden once was, were spindly briars. Grandma used to receive a bush each year on her birthday. Deep red, pink, yellow, and violet brought the yard to life each spring in her special garden. Now it was a lifeless, forsaken patch of land that held no regard for its past glory.

His mind conjured up memories of Dad and his brothers playing poker on the porch. He inhaled the rekindled aroma of Uncle Tommy's cigar that hung on the porch where the five brothers laughed and told lies while Papa observed stoically from his rocker. They'd discuss ghost tales and legends of the mountains, like Nicholas Wilson, the man whose spirit had supposedly haunted those venturing on Shady Mountain for fifty years. Dallas, the oldest son, always had a joke to share, sometimes told while Dad held his hands over Pete's ears. Papa, even in his older days, was a charismatic, handsome man. With eyes as blue as the morning sky, a chin strong and rock solid, he held court over his sons without saying a word. Pete remembered sitting on Papa's lap, enjoying the smell of some unknown aftershave. Papa would open his pocket watch and let Pete hold it, the chain hanging loosely from his belt.

Pete's mind rode the wind, bringing to life the kitchen where Mom and her sisters-in-law, led by Grandma's careful guidance, prepared family dinners while exchanging tips on keeping their men in line. Though all shared frustrations over the difficulties of being married to the Swift men, their laughter told the story of women who enjoyed each others' company, who thought of the kitchen not as a woman's duty but as a place that allowed them to show their love in every biscuit baked, in every slab of bacon frying in the pan.

Pete lowered his head into his hands, his elbows pushing into his kneecaps. Those days seemed like yesterday in some ways — like a lifetime ago in others. Mom and Dad, young, healthy, always close by. How he missed those days. He began to sob, and the quiet of the mountain did not console him.

***

The address he'd scrawled on the Post-it note read 281 Highland Drive, but Pete couldn't find it. He drove the busy street twice with no luck. Shops and restaurants with awnings and canopies made it hard to see the street numbers. Pete found a parking spot at a meter, dropped in a couple of quarters, and walked along the rolling avenue. He walked south toward the art district of the city.

It had been six years since he'd been to Asheville, and he was caught off guard by the eclectic feel of the town. Bluegrass music played, dimmed by the sounds of people talking and eating under canopies streetside at Anna Jane's Café. A blind man played the sax on a street corner, his hat placed upside down at his feet. Small change and a few crumpled dollars were in the bottom of the canvas hat. A pair of teenagers zipped by on skateboards, dodging those walking along the busy streets.

Pete noticed the street numbers along the street were descending. 507 was on the sign above him, a black-and-white awning for McGillicuddy's Irish Pub. Slowly the numbers made their way to the threes and then the twos. 287 was the Wild Eyes Tattoo and Piercing Parlor, and past a narrow alley, 279 hung on a piece of wood in front of an outdoor adventure store with kayaks and canoes lined against the wall.

Pete stepped back and glanced down the alley. He noticed a door on the left, a rusty doorknob barely extending past the faded red bricks. He approached, and on the solid metal door was a sign of a black electric guitar with lightning bolts shooting out from a pair of hands strumming the guitar. JG's was the name of the shop. When he entered, he noticed the tiled floors were gritty and scuffed.

"How's it goin'?" asked a slender man behind the counter, not bothering to look up as he restrung an acoustic guitar.

"Not bad," Pete said as he looked about the tiny store. On the walls were wall-to-wall guitars, electric on the left, acoustic on the right. They were held by metal prongs and angled with the necks up so that they looked as if invisible arms held them.

"What can I do for ya?" the young man asked. A cigarette hung from his lips, the ashes in need of flicking.

"I'm lookin' for Caleb Gable. Is he here?"

"Who?"

"Caleb Gable."

"Never heard of him."

"Huh. I thought maybe he worked here." It was obvious he didn't *live* there.

"Nope. Think you have the wrong shop. There's another guitar store up the hill toward campus. I think there's a guy by that name workin' there."

"Thanks. Sorry to bother you."

"Hey, man, it's cool. Say, you interested in a guitar?"

"No." Pete laughed. "I think my rockin' days are over."

The other music shop, Starz Music, was three blocks south on College Street. No one there had heard of Caleb Gable either. Pete looked again at the address on the printout from the Internet search engine. He headed back uptown. He walked along Highland again, standing in the alleyway, looking for another door or something matching the address on the paper. Across the street was the Blue Ridge Café, and Pete stepped in and ordered a turkey sandwich and a bottled water.

Biting into the sandwich, sitting near the window, he peeled back the sourdough bread. He raked off the tofu and feta cheese, and continued eating as he looked out at the busy street. Three more skateboarders slipped in and out of the crowded street, and they stopped to watch a slender man in Elvis Costello glasses play air guitar on a cardboard guitar.

Pete looked down the street to a park with hunter-green grass, cornered by long rows of orange-and-black flowers. Pete thought that was an unusual color scheme for flowers. Three benches were located at the entrance of the small park, and each bench was occupied as a woman with purple dreadlocks played a Janis Joplin tune streetside. Six kids, college age Pete guessed, sat on the grass, legs crossed, smoking cigarettes. They wore jeans, and two guys wore toboggans pulled tightly down to their eyebrows. One of them, a girl with long, straight, brown hair, sat barefoot, and Pete wondered how she kept from being cold, even though the temperature had climbed into the mid-fifties.

Pete watched as a slender man walked from the door of JG's, up the alleyway, and toward the street. He had the look of an aged rock and roller. He wore black jeans, the bottoms ruffled and torn. He had on a sleeveless T-shirt and wore a black vinyl vest. Tattoos of blacks and deep blues covered his forearms. His hair was long and braided, coming halfway down his back. Pete placed his trash in the bin and walked outside. He followed the man for two blocks, weaving in and around the lunchtime crowd. The man straddled a silver-and-black Harley-Davidson.

"Um, excuse me," Pete said in as unthreatening a voice as possible. The man revved up the hog and looked at Pete without saying a word. "Are you Caleb Gable?" The man eased up on the throttle to soften the engine.

"Who wants to know?"

"My name's Pete Swift. I'm from Carter Springs."

"Carter Springs. There's nothin' I left behind in Carter Springs." With that he looked over his shoulder and pulled out onto the road. He sped away, the bike's engine fading away long after he disappeared from sight.

Pete returned to the guitar shop. The same man he spoke to earlier was talking with a teenage-looking boy who was strumming a chrome red Fender Telecaster. A portly man in faded jeans and black T-shirt restocked guitar picks behind the counter near a gray register.

"Can I help you?" the man in black asked.

"I came in earlier looking for Caleb Gable, and your friend here said he didn't know him." The other man heard Pete's comments and looked up at Pete.

"I wasn't lyin'. I don't know the man."

"Well, he just left your store about ten minutes ago."

"Well, I don't know the name of every customer."

"I don't think he was a customer."

"Caleb Gable did just leave," the man stocking the picks said.

"Huh?" asked his coworker. "Wait, you talkin' 'bout J.G.?"

"Jonah is his first name. Gable is his last. Used to go by his middle name, Caleb."

"Well, I'll be danged," the young man said. "Goes to show you how much I know."

"Do you know when he should be back in the store?" asked Pete.

"Hard to say. He owns the place, but he only comes in a couple times a week. Let's see, today's Tuesday. I would guess Thursday, probably Friday."

"I can't wait that long. Can you tell me where he lives?"

"Sorry, I can't give out that kind of information."

"It's extremely important that I talk to him."

"I'm sorry. I just can't." The man rubbed his chin. "I can tell you this. He likes to hang out at the Double J. It's a hole in the wall out on Highway 60 toward Hendersonville. They serve wings and beer. He's in there most days."

Pete thanked the man and left the store.

The afternoon turned cold. The wind picked up from the north, and the dreary clouds moved quickly across the sky in various shades of gray as if they were in search of warmer skies. Pete sat in his car, which he'd parked backwards against a chain-link fence that separated a junkyard and the Double J. He watched as men came, some in pairs, some solo, to the bar. The men looked to be blue collar, most of them in jeans, some with work pants of blue or khaki. Pete munched on some almonds he'd bought at Cheapo's Gas Mart. He looked at his watch. He had been in his car for close to two hours.

The rumble of the bike came from the east, and Pete heard it but couldn't see it. An eighteen-wheeler rolled by, and as it passed the Harley came into view. The biker pulled his bike next to a faded picnic table. As he made his way to the glass door of the building, Pete got out and followed.

The building looked as if it was designed for something other than a bar. It looked like it might once have served as a garage, and it was dank and drab. There were a handful of tables with wooden straight-back chairs. All but one of the tables was occupied, with groups of threes and fours scattered about them. The smell of stale smoke hung heavy, and a fog drifted about the tile ceiling. The bar counter was Formica, dark green, and looked like it had been brought in from someone's kitchen. Six stools sat in front of it, and two of them were occupied.

Pete hopped on an empty one beside the biker.

"Buy you a beer?" Pete asked. The man glanced at Pete, and shook his head before letting out a muted laugh.

"Persistent little guy, ain't you?"

"I'm Batman. I appear from the shadows." He motioned to the man behind the counter. "I'll have what he's havin'." Pete placed a ten on the counter.

"So, why you followin' me? Bill collector? I pay cash for everything so I'm guessin' you cain't be that."

"I have some news about your father."

"How do you know my father? You're not even sure who I am."

"Caleb Gable, right?"

"Jonah, actually. Caleb's my middle name. It didn't bring much luck, so I decided Jonah was the name to go with."

"Well, from what I've gathered, you and your father haven't talked in years."

"You've gathered correctly. What's your point?"

"Your father's dying."

Caleb scratched his head and took a long sip of his beer. "Is that a fact?"

"He's got cancer."

"What kind?"

"Lung, originally. He's not got much time left according to the doctors. He's to the point where he's ready to throw in the towel. It didn't seem like he or your sister knew where you were, so I decided to track you down. They have no clue I'm doing this."

"What business is it of yours?"

"I'm Peter Swift. My dad grew up a few miles from your dad's home. Your home."

"Ain't my home no more."

"I'm writing something for your father. Something he wanted done before he, um, passed on. In the weeks I've got to spend with him, I've realized what an incredible man he is."

"Incredible is right."

"Look, I don't know what happened that made you sever ties with him. All I see is a look in his eyes that says he's not ready to die because there's unfinished business to tend to. I'm guessing that unfinished business is you."

Caleb took another sip, swishing the liquid in his mouth before swallowing. "It ain't that easy. I don't just show up. That won't make everything right."

"It might not make it right. But we're talkin' about your father. My father died two years ago, and what I wouldn't give to see him again."

"Good for you."

"What happened that caused you to leave? Your family is incredible, which makes it even more puzzling that you don't have anything to do with them."

"It really ain't none of your business. You know, life ain't always what it seems." Caleb took a final sip and tapped the counter. "Thanks for the beer, Al. See ya around." The man behind the counter nodded. Caleb was out the door.

Chapter Fifteen

The sun shone in such quiet brilliance it appeared as though some giant prism had been cast in the sky below it, sending light in wavy patterns too powerful for the human eye. Along Jefferson Mountain, shadows hid in small patches under trees and along thin edges of barns and farmhouses. The sky was powder blue, cloudless, bold to the point where it took some of the luster away from the deep green hills of the Appalachians. The brightness of the day gave Pete the feeling it had no choice but to be a good one.

Gabby had Samuel dressed and ready. He pressed her several times as to where he was heading, but she refused to divulge the destination. Samuel had regained a bit of color in his face, noticing it when he had looked in the bathroom mirror earlier that morning. He felt stronger, having eaten eggs and toast for breakfast. It was his first meal of substance in three days. His back hurt no matter which way he sat, but he put the pain out of his mind. The days in the war had taught him that much.

Pete showed up at the door, and when Gabby opened it, he held a bag of chocolate-covered gummy bears in front of his chest with both hands. "Hungry?"

"Oh, my God. You are too sweet." Pete smiled as though he sensed he'd brought joy to her sorely burdened heart. "Thank you so much." She hugged him, her arms reaching around his shoulders. He slipped his arms along her back and squeezed gently. Their faces touched for a moment.

219

When Pete helped Samuel into his car, Samuel noticed a look about Pete as if he were a young boy anxious to share a secret with his father. Pete's mischievous expression caused Samuel to look at him peculiarly.

"What's on your mind? You look like you hid Miss Crosswhite's pig in her china cabinet."

"Nope. No pig-stealing. I just want to take you somewhere. I want to show you something."

"Well, let's get goin' then. I could be dead by sunset for all I know."

The pair drove on, heading west toward Elizabethton. They drove along tobacco fields, slender tracts of land in a tight valley carved out of Jefferson Mountain by Sinking Creek. The waters flowed quickly along the creek, the stream wide and winding. The road ran parallel to the creek as if it tried to match the creek turn for turn. Samuel looked out at the stream, remembering days of wading it, fly rod in hand. The waters of Sinking Creek ran clear and hard, its floor a rocky carpet of brown stones, rushing to some unknown destination.

For six miles Pete drove, the sun to his back. Samuel talked of places along the hillsides known as fertile spots for groundhogs. He talked of how he'd stand creekside, looking up to the hill across the highway, waiting to blast the fat, furry creatures when they showed themselves from the grassy pockets.

Pete turned north on an unnamed lane, a soft gravelly stretch of road that headed straight for Roan Mountain. "Laurel Gap," Samuel said. "Hadn't been on this road in years. Why we headin' this way?"

"Hang on a few minutes and you'll see."

They drove on, the road at first flat and straight. On either side of the road were pastures with black Angus cows scattered about in small groups as if some sort of clique system existed amongst them. They grazed unhurriedly, some lifting their heads as Pete's car passed by. All along the fields were rickety barns and sheds a weatherbeaten gray, as pale and dull as any color had a mind to be. They were buildings constructed from another era, in a time the world had passed by, holes in tin ceilings, boards missing. Standing quietly, decaying slowly in some sort of reluctant resistance, structures more than just boards, they seemed determined not to fade away into the dark shade of the mountain behind them.

A mile or so up the road, they came to the base of Roan Mountain, a towering wall of dark timber. The rolling fields had disappeared and the pines and poplars grew tall and full. A subtle coolness eased its way into the car. They drove on through the shadows of the massive trees, passing a handful of small houses. Most were cherry-red brick, though others were a style of wood that looked like faded gray wallpaper. They passed a familiar spot beside Samson's Creek — familiar only to Samuel. The bank was overgrown with grass and weeds, a completely different look from the evening Samuel and Callie had sat by the water's edge in the dull light of the late moon.

When they pulled into Vera Patterson's driveway, Samuel's eyes began to soften, as if aches and pains within his body had completely vanished. He looked to the porch, and spotted two women sitting there. One was on the porch swing, the other in a wheelchair. The woman on the swing stood slowly, wrapping her arms around a porch column for support.

221

Pete drove across the yard, as close as he could get to the porch. He quickly walked around and opened Samuel's door, and within moments had Samuel shakily on his feet. Pete removed Samuel's cane from the back seat, and Samuel took hold of it with one hand while holding Pete's elbow with the other.

Slowly they stepped to the porch. The woman holding on to the column moved to the top of the three smooth shale steps. She smiled, and tears were forming just lightly at the base of her hazel eyes. Her graying hair was pulled tightly into a bun. She wore a patterned dress of green and light blue. Pete led Samuel up the steps slowly, and had the pair face to face.

"Sammy," she said, reaching her arms to hold him. "It's so good to see you."

"Good Lord," Samuel said, "it's nice to see somebody else as old as me still breathin'."

"Still sassy and full of yourself, I see." She placed her arms around his shoulders and he gently leaned his cheek against hers. After their embrace, Vera took Samuel by the hand and led him to the woman in the wheelchair. She had a puzzled look about her, not in the sense that she didn't have her faculties, but rather that she wasn't sure she recognized who stood in front of her. Samuel slowly bent forward, Pete holding him steady by the arm.

"Howdy, Helen. I'm Marvin Maness, and I'm here to marry your granddaughter."

Her soft laugh seemed to take every bit of energy she could muster, and her eyes sparkled with a surprised look as if she had just been told the world was hers to keep for her very own. "Sammy," she said and sighed. "Oh, dear Samuel." Samuel took hold of her hand. "It's been so long.

How in the world are you?" Her face, weathered from the years, took on a warm, rosy hue.

"Not too bad. I woke up this mornin', so I guess that right there's an accomplishment."

Pete pulled up a metal chair, one that rocked while staying flat to the floor, and guided Samuel into it. Vera took her seat on the swing, and the three looked about as if the long time span that had separated them made them unsure of what to say.

"Gabby says you live in Bristol," Samuel said.

"I do," Vera answered. "I live at the Cross Mountain Manor home. Been there, let's see, thirteen years. I'm sure they thought my room would have been freed up by now. But somehow I keep on kickin'. Arnold James is there too."

"Is that a fact?" asked Samuel. "Hadn't seen him since I threw him in Birch Tree Creek, back in '41, I believe it was. But then, I tossed so many people in the creek, they all tend to run together. How about you, Helen? Where do you live? I've asked about you for years and nobody seemed to know where you were."

Helen blinked twice, her green eyes looking across the mountainside while she collected her thoughts. "Been in Knoxville since '77. My boy Nick moved me into his house. He built a little room onto the back and he and his wife Lorraine took good care of me. Nick passed on three years ago, and Lorraine and I just try to make it as best we can."

As the old friends reminisced, Pete watched their expressions, hearing the excitement in their voices. Though they were happy, Pete could detect a hint of sadness that the years had raced by and they understood they were down to their final lap. Pete imagined them the night of the pageant, their hearts young and free, thoughts of them becoming old as distant from their minds as the furthest star.

"You gals remember the first place Callie and I lived?"

"The house down at Trader's Gap?" asked Helen.

"That's the one. We had that old bag of a landlord, Ruby Puryear. She was a mean one. Only had two teeth. Hair like a clump of dry hay. Anyway, I remember the day our sink started leaking. Water going everywhere on the floor. I called her and told her we needed a new sink, and she just snorted, 'You got dishpans, ain't you'uns?' I said, 'Yeah, we got dishpans.' And she said, 'Well then, better put 'em to use so the water don't ruin the floor.'" He laughed loudly. "So much for a new sink."

The sun stood bright and blazing, reaching the pinnacle to where shadows were short and unmoving. The shade cast by the porch was cool but comfortable. For nearly two hours they talked of the past, of family, of the changing world. Their tongues began to tire, and Helen began to nod off. Samuel looked at her frail body, a thousand years removed from the vibrant package of spunk that he loved.

"Well, I best be headin' back toward home." With Pete's help, he rose and hugged Vera one last time.

"I've always thought you hung the moon, Sammy Gable." Tears began to fill her eyes.

Samuel nodded and bit his lip gently to keep his emotions in check. He rubbed Helen's arm, and she awakened. "Helen, I'm headin' on."

Helen looked groggily up at Samuel and smiled. "Bye-bye, darlin'. I love you."

"You, too."

With that Pete helped Samuel down the porch, Samuel placing the cane gingerly to the soft grass. He stopped briefly, looked out to the crest of Jefferson Mountain as if a lifetime of thoughts were playing out in his mind. And then he slowly stepped toward the car, grimacing with each and every step. When Pete opened the passenger door, he heard Vera call from the steps.

"Sammy, wait," she said. "I have something for you."

The men walked back to the base of the porch. She reached inside a faded doily resting on her lap, fumbling with her slender, aged fingers. "I want to give you this." She lifted a necklace from her lap, looped around her index finger, and smiled.

Pete had a look of surprise. Samuel had a look of disbelief.

"Is that the necklace?" Samuel asked.

"It is. My daughter-in-law, Kathy, was helpin' me clear out some things from my dresser and my jewelry box. I wanted to pass on my heirlooms and jewelry to my family while I'm still alive to see them enjoy it. So I could see better, Kathy was pullin' out each drawer, one at a time, and settin' them on the dresser. Well, she was a-gettin' ready to set the top drawer back in, and she noticed the necklace wrapped around the back of a peg on the outside of the drawer."

"She looked for that necklace 'most every day until the day she passed," Samuel said, seemingly not convinced he was looking at the necklace he'd put around Callie's neck the night they fell in love.

"Best I can figure is she lost it when she and Gabby came to Bristol for Joan's wedding. Seems like I remember them cleaning their jewelry before the wedding. At the reception Callie realized it wasn't around her neck. She was terribly upset."

Pete steadied Samuel as he placed the cane against the metal rail, and he shakily climbed the steps. He pulled his elbow away from Pete's grip to take hold of the necklace. He held it gently, as if he was holding the world's greatest treasure. The dingy cross dangled at his wrist.

Vera began to cry, and Helen reached up and gently touched Samuel's hand. "You know, you were the love of her life. Never seen a woman so much in love as she was."

Samuel nodded, and turned back to the steps.

There were no words spoken as Pete and Samuel pulled onto the road. Samuel looked out the window, rubbing the necklace with his thumb and index finger. The hum of the engine cut through the silence along the country road, the tires leaving a dust trail behind them. At a point where the road began to straighten, at the spot where weeds grew high by the creek bank, Samuel asked Pete to pull over to the side of the narrow road.

"This is it," he said, pointing at the weeds.

"This is what?"

"This is where I sat that night with Callie after the pageant. The grass was low and soft back then. You could move down as close to the water as you wanted. Now you can't even see it." Samuel opened his door, and Pete killed the engine, not bothering to see if his car was completely off the road. He hopped from his seat and held Samuel's door. Samuel took hold of Pete's hand and steadied himself beside the car with his cane. They stepped to the waist-high weeds.

"Well, I can clear us a path if you'd like."

Samuel smiled. "Won't be necessary."

"Wait," Pete said. "I have an idea." He opened the trunk of his car and removed two chairs, folded and placed inside vinyl containers. He removed and unfolded them. "Let's sit here. We can't see the creek, but we can hear it." The men sat, the sun warming their shoulders.

"I guess it's time to tell you what you've been waiting to hear," said Samuel.

***

September, 1945

It had been so long since Samuel had driven a car, he felt nervous behind the wheel. Bert had loaned Samuel his 1941 Hudson coupe for the evening, in exchange for the use of Samuel's shotgun. Living at home, Bert was able to save enough to buy the used but sporty-looking car. Bert was off to Shady Valley to hunt coons with Jerry Weston, a high school buddy whose father owned several hunting dogs and some prime hunting land.

The car climbed steadily along the gravelly tight curves of Old Laurel Highway on its way up Iron Mountain. The sun was on the west side of the mountain, and the afternoon heat dulled the sky in a violet haze to where the sun had no sense of shape at all. Samuel eclipsed the peak of the mountain, and for a second stopped the car to look back toward Jefferson Mountain. The peacefulness of it was all the homecoming Samuel needed.

He wore black dress slacks and a white dress shirt rolled at the elbows. He'd noticed the weight loss when he put on the pants at home earlier. He felt like the clothes were swallowing him. His dark brown hair again lay thick and wavy, his forehead exposed, his eyes impossible to ignore.

***

Callie was shucking sweet corn beside the barn, sitting on a straight-back wood chair under the shading limb of a maple. The dim afternoon light made her face shimmer, giving her brown eyes a sharp, striking glow. She looked at the thin, pale wooden bushel basket bulging with ripe, firm cobs, the result of bountiful summer rains, and wondered if she'd ever finish. The silk of the corn had gathered upon her hands in thin clumps, and a few stuck to her forehead at the base of her scalp. She wore green denim jeans that stopped at the upper calf. Her blouse was white, soft to the touch, though there were small stains located along the edges of the sleeves.

She was finally getting close to the bottom of the basket when her mother stepped outside the back door. "Callie, I need you to go to the springhouse. I need a jar of buttermilk."

"Can't James do it? I'm not done with the corn." She rubbed the back of her hand against her forehead, brushing at the hair that tickled her eyebrows.

"He went fishin'. Ain't come back yet."

"Great," she mumbled. "Yes'm, I'll do it," she yelled. She slung the ear of corn she was shucking against the edge of the maple. Kernels scattered about the grass from the impact. "I'm sick of this."

Three hens in various shades of brown and red roamed the yard. As Callie walked to the springhouse, the hens wandered in her path. She kicked at one, and it flapped its wings briefly but basically paid Callie no mind. She seethed at the thought of James stepping along the banks of the creek fishing while she worked in Cinderella fashion, but without the evil stepsisters. She rubbed her hands together, shaking the thin corn silk to the ground as she stomped to the springhouse.

The springhouse was thirty yards or so behind the house, and it was carved out of the mountainside known as Baker's Mountain. Callie's home backed up to the base of the mountain, a sharply rising hill with hardwoods and thick underbrush. The one-room shanty that served as their springhouse had front and side walls of graying wood, each wall eight feet in length. A thin stream about a foot wide flowed through the middle, moving slowly under the right corner of the front wall and on down to a pond which served as a watering hole for three horses and a mule.

When Callie opened the wobbly door, she felt the cool dampness push across her face like a November breeze. She squatted beside the water and chose a Mason jar of milk from a wire basket that sat submerged in the stream. The glass felt ice-cold against Callie's tender fingers. When the door behind her suddenly shut, the room turned quickly to black. She stumbled into the cold water, her knees feeling the sting of the icy mountain creek. The jar in her hands fell on a second jar in the water and cracked, turning the stream pale white for a moment.

She began to cry, her knees still submerged in the water, in the darkness. She moved from the water and, still on her knees, dropped her elbows to the cold floor. As she cried, her body shook. For several minutes she remained on all fours, wondering why life had come to this. Day after day of not knowing, not hearing if Samuel was alive or dead. She wished she had never gone to Carter Springs, had never entered the contest, had never fallen for a boy who was to be whisked away halfway across the world. She wished even more that she had never gone back to the pageant, never had the flat tire, instilling a primitive fear that she couldn't shake. She had grown weary of passing the time while Samuel was away, waiting, worrying. Her tears pushed out the frustrations that were buried deep in her heart. No one heard her sobs.

When she finally rose from the dark, she wiped her eyes. She reached into the cold water and fumbled for another jar of buttermilk. She pushed the thick door open, and an imposing shadow stood just outside the door. Startled, she dropped the jar, and once again glass shattered and milk flowed in the spring. This time, it did not matter.

She fell into Samuel's arms, and her head pressed against his chest. She couldn't speak, and for moments all she could do was cry. Samuel didn't speak either, knowing that his arms were all she needed right then. Finally, with reddened eyes, she pulled away from his chest and searched his eyes as if she was looking to find his soul. He placed his hands behind her neck, stared into those beautiful, puffy eyes, and kissed her. Softly at first, but when she wrapped her arms around his back, he pressed his lips against hers tightly.

She began to kiss him on the chin, his forehead, and with his hands behind her head, he pulled her toward him. After a moment he lifted her off the ground, and her feet dangled as her lips moved along the contours of his face. He lowered her to where she again stood, and wiped the tears from her cheeks as they continued to kiss. She pulled away to look again into those eyes, as if making sure she wasn't in some crazy dream. She kissed him again gently, her eyes locked on his. She tried not to blink, thinking he might be gone if she closed them even for a second.

"I thought I'd never see you again," she said as her head returned to his chest. "I've thought about you every day. I've looked down the road a thousand times, imagining you running to me."

"I'm sorry it didn't happen the way you imagined, but this will have to do." He kissed her again, and the tears continued to flow down her face. "Sometimes I wondered if I'd ever make it back, but I never forgot my promise. Things got so bad over there most of us figured we were never comin' home. I got your letter when I was in the hospital."

"Which one? I sent close to a dozen letters after you left Australia. Since I never received any word back from you, I didn't know whether to keep writing."

"I only got one. It was dated October of last year. The only reason I got that one was I came down with malaria and was taken to a medical hospital for two weeks."

"I don't care that the other letters didn't make it. All I care is that you are here. Right now. Here with me." She rubbed her hands along his shoulder blades as she pressed into his chest with the side of her face. Samuel smiled and removed the strands of corn silk that were still stuck to her forehead. "Oh, I wish I'd a-known you were coming. I could have fixed myself up. I look terrible."

"You're the most beautiful thing I've ever laid eyes on. I'm the one who needs some fixin' up. I don't have much meat on my bones. Meals weren't exactly plentiful there."

"Sweetie, you look perfect to me." She rubbed her hand through his hair and kissed him softly.

Callie's mother came out and hugged Samuel after she felt the pair had had enough time to say hello. She had watched the scene unfold from the kitchen window as Samuel had already spoken with her, asking her to call Callie to the springhouse to fetch the buttermilk and allow the surprise meeting. "Come inside and let me fix you a good meal."

"Thanks for the offer, but I came to steal away your daughter for a bit. Mind if I take her to dinner?"

"You sure can. But before you do, Callie's got to finish the corn."

Callie led Samuel by the hand, as giddy as a small child on Christmas morning, to the bushel basket. He moved a wood crate that leaned against the trunk of the maple and placed it beside Callie's chair.

"What I wouldn't have given for some of this corn," he said. "I'd a-eaten it raw."

"I can't believe you are here sittin' beside me." Her smile radiated joy, her white teeth peeking from between her soft lips. "God, I missed you." She leaned forward and kissed him.

"I thought about you every day. Mostly at night when I'd try to sleep. Thinkin' of you kind of calmed me down. Kept me focused on getting back home."

"The war had to be the most frightening thing on earth."

"Let's just say it ain't anything I ever want to go through again."

"I prayed all the time that you'd be safe." She studied him. "You were wounded, weren't you? I can feel it in my bones."

"Took some shrapnel in my arm is all." She took his arm and rubbed the dark purple scars on his forearm. She kissed his hand.

"My God. It must have been horrible. How did you make it day after day for so long? Did you know that we were winning the war? How did you keep going? Keep motivated?"

"Bullets buzzin' around my ears was all the motivation I needed."

"Were you afraid?"

"I don't think I was. Worried, yes."

"Is there a difference?"

"Afraid means you question your will to do it. Worried means you know there's a good chance the outcome ain't gonna be to your likin'."

"It had to be terrible seeing people die."

Samuel lowered his head and cleared his throat. "I can't explain the feelin'. Don't want to explain it. I think that's all I care to say about it."

"I understand." She kissed his hand again. "I'll never mention it again."

It was a promise she'd keep for the rest of her life.

***

Located on Highway 421, the diner served as many travelers as it did locals. Aunt May's Place was small and quaint, serving meats and veggies to the dinner crowd, biscuits and sausage gravy to the early morning diners. Callie and Samuel sat next to the window where, on clear mornings, the purple outline of Iron Mountain carved out a piece of the eastern sky. The table was small, with four place settings, but really was designed for two. They sat face-to-face, Callie rubbing Samuel's fingers with hers. Dusk settled in, and the sharp shadows the setting sun cast across the countryside dimmed it to grays and deep greens.

They ordered food but neither of them was particularly concerned with eating. As the streetlight came to life in the parking lot, the dim yellow light chased shadows from the dirt lot. Music from a jukebox began to play, and Callie smiled.

"Be right back," Samuel said. He walked to the old Wurlitzer, placing his dime in the slot. He soon returned just as food was placed on the table. Callie took a sip of her root beer through a straw, and she couldn't help but stare into Samuel's eyes. When "You'll Never Know" began playing, Callie turned her head toward the jukebox as if making it easier for her to hear the music.

"You remembered."

"I played it through my head almost every day for the last three years. It always gave me good thoughts of you, of that first night we met."

Callie reached out and took hold of Samuel's hand. "I was with you every second you were gone."

***

Callie and Samuel married seven months later. The wedding took place at the Antioch Baptist Church in Bristol. Samuel wore a navy-blue suit with a white dress shirt and a checked tie of gray and black. On his lapel was a white rose boutonnière. His hair was trimmed, though it still contained soft waves. Porter was Samuel's best man. Vera and Helen were attendants. Bert, Anna, and Samuel's mother were there, as of course were Callie's parents and brother.

The church was small, with only eight rows of pews, an aisle splitting them in two. Not an empty seat was to be found. When Callie entered from the front of the church, arm in arm with her father, Samuel could not take his eyes off of her. Her gown of white satin was floor-length. She had sleeves of lace with a wide ruffle at her wrists. Her hair was pulled away from her face with a pearl headband. Her dark eyes and dark hair stood in perfect contrast to her gown of white. When Sally Jordan finished the "Wedding March" on the small organ which sat next to the two-row choir loft, Callie was at Samuel's side, and he took her hand — a hand that he was determined to never let go of.

The wedding reception took place at the Gable house.

When Samuel and Callie drove up, family and friends had gathered at the porch to welcome them. Marvin Maness waited at the bottom step and kissed Callie on the cheek. "You're the prettiest thing I ever saw," Marvin said. "If that old boy can't make you happy, you let me know. I'll come runnin'."

"I'll do that," Callie replied as she tried to break free from Marvin's grip.

Porter and Bert took the hats and coats of the guests, and the wedding party retreated to the living room. Still in her wedding gown, her hand never venturing far from Samuel's, Callie was careful to thank and speak with each and every person. She felt overwhelmed at how Samuel's family had extended their arms around her. Vera whispered something in Callie's ear about the honeymoon, and Callie could not hide the sudden redness in her cheeks.

Samuel went to the kitchen with Porter. "I've never liked wearin' a tie," Samuel said. "I keep thinkin' this is the way they hanged Tom Dooley."

"Take it off then, dummy. Or at least loosen it." Porter took Samuel by the collar and pulled on the tie to let some slack out. "There, now you ain't horse-collared."

Marvin walked into the kitchen, tobacco juice hanging from the corner of his mouth. "You boys get me a spittoon. I'm a-feared I'll drool on my Sunday best."

"Well, Marvin," Samuel said after taking a sip of lemonade. "You got any advice for a young man startin' out on the road of marriage?"

"I don't know. I ain't had no luck 'ceptin' when I was hitched to Pearl. Even then, that didn't last long. Had to go to Iowa to take care of her ma, she said. Horse feathers."

"So, you're sayin' it's over for you? You got no hopes? No dreams?"

"Yeah, I got a dream. I want to live to be a hun'ert and be hanged for rape."

Porter and Samuel laughed loudly and Marvin slapped Samuel on the shoulder. "Pay me no nevermind," Marvin said. "I'm just a suck-egg mule. You and that purty little filly will be just fine together."

Anna took Samuel by the hand to the porch. "I know we haven't spent much time together the last few years," she said. "When Jasper married me and took me on off to live in Wilkesboro, I felt like I was being taken away from my family. He treated me like I was his property, and he was determined to make sure that I only tended to him. I could have bucked him, put my foot down, but I didn't. I was eighteen and didn't know much about life. With you and Callie, I know your lives will be great. And I just want you to know that I love you, and Callie too. Everyone has fallen in love with her. I hope that you have the best life possible."

Samuel hugged Anna. "I've never said anything to you about the way Jasper treated you. I wanted to, but didn't out of respect. But I want you to know if you ever need Callie and me, we'll be there for you. If Jasper ever treats you bad, you let me know. I'll tear him a new one."

Anna and Jasper had two children, Perkins and Ruby. Samuel was upset that Jasper wouldn't allow Perkins and Ruby to attend the wedding. Jasper was hesitant even to let Anna come, Samuel's own sister, but in a bold and rare move, she'd told him she would not miss her brother's wedding. Though Wilkesboro was barely an hour's ride from Carter Springs, Anna rarely came home to visit. Jasper had told her on their wedding night that her priorities were Jasper, God, and any future children they might have, and in that particular order. Not an ideal marriage in Samuel's estimation, but that was Anna's business. All Samuel could do was be there for her when needed, and make sure his marriage with Callie turned out different from theirs.

For two hours the party carried on. Neighbors in the hollow stopped by to wish the couple well, bringing plates of fried chicken, casseroles, and huckleberry pie. Dusk had settled in, turning the warm spring day into a crisp, cool evening. Bert toasted Callie's family with a small glass of apricot wine, and though Eula did not approve, she kept her thoughts to herself as a show of courtesy to her firstborn.

Callie and Samuel changed into more casual clothes, took hold of their suitcases, and made their way to Samuel's car, a pale yellow 1939 DeSoto coupe. Slim Pierce, owner of the lumber company, had sold it to Samuel with the plan to deduct money from his paycheck until it was paid off.

Eula hugged Samuel tightly, crying just a little bit. "Don't cry, Momma. Remember, I'm comin' back in four days. It's not like I'm going off to war again."

"I know," she said, wiping the tears from her cheeks. "It's just knowin' that you're all grown up. I only wish your father was here to see it."

"Me too, Momma. Me too."

Bert hugged Samuel as Eula moved on to hug Callie. "You have yourself a great trip," Bert said.

"I will. Thanks for everything. I might be married, but you're still my only brother. I always want you close in my life."

"Now, you best be leavin' before you get me to cryin' like a little girl."

"We can't have that."

***

The car lights cut into the night, pulling the outlines of the tall pines alongside the road out of the depths of darkness. The rolling mountain roads were long gone, as pale strips of white line disappeared under the headlights as if being swallowed. The constant hum of tires against asphalt was monotonous. The world around them seemed fast asleep. Houses along the road lay dark, seemingly empty, as the miles rolled away. Samuel pushed on across South Carolina, finally making it across the Georgia state line.

It was almost midnight, and Callie sat snuggled up next to Samuel, her head on his shoulder. When they crossed into Savannah, Samuel spotted a motel. "Want to stay here for the night, or do you want to drive on to St. Simon's?"

"How much further is that?"

"Two hours or so."

"Let's keep driving. I want to spend our first night together at the ocean."

***

The motel was eerily quiet when the young couple pulled in. One lone streetlight shone in the lot outside the entrance to the motel office. A lamp burned in the window, and the orange neon sign hummed a noisy tune as they walked to the office. The Ocean Breeze motel, a two-wing building, had twenty-four rooms. There were nine cars in the dirt lot, scattered in distance like black keys on a piano. When they walked inside the office, an elderly man sat up on a couch behind the desk.

"Evenin', folks. You needin' accommodations?"

"Yes," Samuel said. "We need a room for three nights."

"Where you from?"

"Tennessee. We're on our honeymoon."

"That a fact? Congrats. Let me give you a key while you sign in." He fumbled around and chose a key from two rows of fishhooks. "How about room twenty-four?" It's down at the end. Should be nice and peaceful."

"Sounds good to me," Samuel said as he signed the register.

The room was decorated in coral paneling, and featured two double beds. A small radio was on the nightstand between them, along with a Bible and a lamp with an orange shade shaped like a cowbell. Samuel placed the two pieces of luggage on one of the beds while Callie took the small beige toiletries bag to the bathroom. She then walked up to Samuel from behind and pressed her body against his back.

Can you believe we're married?"

Samuel turned about and held her in his arms. He brushed her hair with his hand and placed his lips gently to hers. "It doesn't seem real, does it? How was I lucky enough to snag you?"

"What? If anybody hit the jackpot here, it's me."

"You're so full of it. I ain't nothin' more'n a simple country boy. I'll never make you rich. Don't know if I can make your dreams come true. But I can guarantee you this: I'll love you with everything I've got." He kissed her again, his hands holding her chin softly.

"Baby, you've already made my dreams come true."

The narrow road in front of the motel was a straight shot to the dunes of the Atlantic Ocean. Samuel removed a flashlight from his car, and the couple walked hand in hand down the dirt road, a blanket from the room draped across Callie's shoulders. They walked under giant oaks that formed a ceiling above them, intertwined into a tunnel of black wood and Spanish moss. They walked the quarter mile to the ocean, the flashlight cutting the darkness into wavy shadows. When they reached the dunes, they removed their shoes. Callie spread the blanket on the soft sand where the dunes met the beach.

They sat on the blanket, and when Samuel turned off the light the sand took on the look of melting snow. They looked out at the water, the waves rising up from the blackness in ghostly rolls of dull white. The stars were in every corner of the sky, sharp diamonds hanging above the horizon as though they were about to drop in the ocean. Samuel rolled his gray slacks to his knees. Callie's pleated brown skirt was just below knee-length, though it dropped to thigh-level when she rested her forearms on her kneecaps.

For long moments the young couple just smiled at each other, looking into each other's eyes as though the ocean, the stars, and the dunes had left for a new world. For all they cared, they could have. Callie smiled, the kind of smile that could steal away a man's heart to the point where he has no control over it. Samuel's eyes—those bold, dark eyes—softened as if he were sitting skin to skin with an angel.

"I know I don't have a way with words, but I'll spend the rest of my life trying to show you how much I love you."

"Baby, we're going to have a great life."

When Samuel leaned over to kiss his bride, he did so with a tenderness that caused Callie to lose her breath. Slowly, he lowered her onto the blanket, and he took her hands in his. He looked at her as though she were the greatest treasure that had ever existed. He kissed her hands and touched them to his face as if to verify her existence. He lowered himself to where his elbows touched the blanket beside her arms, and he glided his fingers through her hair where it lay across her forehead. He softly kissed her and closed his eyes as if to let his senses fully taste her sweet lips. His mouth parted, and when her tongue met his, she sighed.

They kissed as though time played no part in the order of day or night. They kissed as though the world had been brought to them, under their control, a world where they were the only inhabitants. The soft rush of the waves serenaded them as they shared their secret with the stars. On the beach, on that night long ago, hearts and bodies joined together, creating a bond more powerful than either had ever thought possible.

Chapter Sixteen

Samuel and Callie rented a small four-room house near Carter Springs in a quiet valley called Trader's Gap. Samuel took a job at the lumberyard, working ten-hour shifts Monday through Friday. Callie became a homemaker, and though their house was by no means a mansion, she kept it immaculate. She made curtains for the windows and became as proficient with a hammer as she was with a spatula.

Money was tight, as it was for most everyone in Carter Springs, and Callie kept close tabs on their budget. Mornings found the aroma of coffee and baked biscuits in the kitchen. Nights were meals made from scratch, vegetables from the garden, buttermilk from Virginia Lowe's crock, and flowers of some variety were always on the table. In the icebox there was always a pitcher of lemonade. It was Samuel's only vice—well, other than Callie. Samuel built a small oak table, setting it out back of the house on a porch that looked out over Shady Mountain, so that on warm evenings they could eat outside.

On Saturday mornings Samuel and Callie took to the creeks. Together they'd cook breakfast before dawn, playfully touching each other beside the stove as he fried the bacon and she cooked the eggs. From there it was off to the banks of the sharp, clear waters. Samuel taught Callie how to fish, and she became proficient with a fly rod. She liked to wear Samuel's Australian floppy brimmed hat he'd brought home from the war. He loved the way her eyes flashed bold and sharp underneath the bill of the hat. Saturday afternoons found them in bed most of the time, making love, sharing dreams.

***

It was in the cold of January, and winter had laid a blanket of snow across the mountains. The winds whipped, stirring up the soft powder in front of Samuel as he walked from the car to the house. The house smelled of fresh embers, as oak and maple crackled in the wood stove.

"Hey, darlin'," Callie said as she set the pan of biscuits on the stovetop. She removed her apron and tossed it on the kitchen counter. "Good gracious, how I've missed you today." She kissed him softly, and he surrounded her with his strong arms.

"Oh, yeah? I'll admit I looked at the clock a lot this afternoon. It sure feels good when the work day is over and I get to come home to a gorgeous stack of pancakes like you." Callie had a small amount of flour on her chin. Samuel rubbed it gently with his finger. "Saving this for later?"

"As a matter of fact, I am." She playfully nibbled on his lower lip, pulling it away from his gum. Letting go she said, "A bit sassy, aren't you?"

"Always. What are you going to do about it?" He placed his keys on the hook by the porch door.

"Nothing just yet." She slid the biscuits from the pan into a bowl and covered it with a soft cloth.

"Let me help you with dinner."

"No, you sit. I've got everything under control. Fixed you a meal fit for a king."

Samuel pulled out a chair, content to watch her move about the kitchen humming an unknown tune. She could almost feel him smiling at her as she poured his glass of lemonade. She handed him the glass.

"I fixed something special. You want to sample it while I get the plates ready?"

"What is it?"

"Date bars. Got the recipe from your mother. Need somebody to be a guinea pig."

"I'm your guy."

She set a blue saucer on the table, two bars on the tiny plate. Date bars were Samuel's favorite dessert, and he quickly bit into one.

"Good stuff," he said as he began to chew. "A little thick, though." His mouth moved about as if he was trying to chew a live squirrel. Callie bit her bottom lip, trying to look genuinely concerned about how much—or how little—he was enjoying it. His lips soon began to pucker, and the more he chewed the bigger the bar seemed to become in his mouth.

Callie tried to hide her smile by tucking her chin and rubbing her mouth with her hand. Samuel looked puzzled as he continued to struggle. Unable to swallow, he touched his lips and noticed they had become puffy, almost rubbery. He looked at Callie and shook his head in bewilderment, unable to speak. Finally he spat the mouthful onto the plate, crumbs hanging from his mouth and chin. When she revealed the jar of alum hidden in her hand, he shook his head and she took off down the hall. Samuel chased close behind, struggling to say, "You're gonna get it, sister."

She ran to the bedroom, as though unsure as to whether to hop across the bed or run behind it. She turned to face him, her laughter carrying across the house. She held her hands out as if that might stop him, and he took hold of them, interweaving his fingers with hers. Her face was red from laughter, and she fell back on the bed when he extended his arms by pushing her hands outward.

Samuel fell on top of her, and she laughed so hard her body shook. He noticed her looking at his puckered, fat lips, and for a moment her laughter became muted, her body shaking like someone enduring electroshock therapy. Samuel tried to speak, but his tongue had thickened.

Callie rolled Samuel on his back, tickling him. "Let me see your little pucker face," she giggled. "C'mon," she said as she continued tickling his ribs. "Let me see that chubby pud'n."

"I'm hideous," Samuel struggled to say. "Look away." He pulled her to him, rubbing his mouth against her neck. The heavy laughter appeared to have rendered her immobile, as though she could not fight him any longer.

"You *are* hideous," she managed to say, "but I still love you." She pulled away from him, looking closely at his mouth. "On second thought, maybe we should just be friends."

As he pulled her to him, she began tickling his neck with her tongue, trying to make him laugh. Feeling a bit naughty, she began to nibble on his neck with her lips, moving along the neck on both sides greedily. Her thoughts had turned to something different from laughter. Like a hot brand striking exposed skin, passion struck, and she ripped open his shirt, kissing his exposed chest.

Later that night, sitting by the wood stove, they shared dinner. Cold biscuits never tasted so good.

***

It was in the early spring, a Sunday afternoon, and Samuel and Callie decided to walk the caves of Bristol Caverns. It was not far from where Callie grew up, and Samuel had never been to the caves before. James had found a few arrowheads and some primitive pottery pieces a few weeks prior, so her curiosity was up. Flashlights in hand, they entered the edges of the dark cavern. Callie wore knee-length denim pants, a white blouse, and a wool jacket. The breezes that tended to slip through the cave were damp and cold. Samuel wore dark brown slacks and a T-shirt. He saw no need for a jacket.

"This looks like a place best suited for bats and scorpions," Samuel said, shining his light along the dark walls.

"Oh, stop being a baby," Callie said and laughed while pointing her flashlight to the rugged ceiling. "What's wrong, mister strongman, not brave if you don't have your gun to protect you?"

"I ain't never been fond of closed-in places." The ceiling above them was streaked with shades of red and blue. Many of the rock formations looked like they'd been wrung wet to dry by the hands of some giant.

"Did you know Indians used this place to hide out and navigate around? The story goes they'd ambush settlers then they'd return to the caves for protection."

"Is that a fact?" asked Samuel, his flashlight casting mutant shadows off the corridors.

"Who knows, maybe they're still here, ready to make you one on their warriors. You know, your reputation as a fighter has become widespread."

"Well, I'm retired, so best of luck to them. Now, if they want *you*, we can work up a trade. I'm in need of some new moccasins."

Callie laughed, waved her hand in the air, and stepped up on a rock to take a closer look at the expansive formations. "Hold me just a second while I steady myself," she said. Samuel took her hand and pushed upward underneath her backside as she climbed atop a vase-shaped formation five feet high. As she tried to step higher, Samuel placed his hand on her knee to steady her. "Wow, the colors are amazing," she said as her light illuminated the ceiling. "Want to come up?"

While keeping a firm grip on Callie's leg, Samuel rubbed his finger along the back of her leg, tracing the raised line. "What is that, a scar?" He shined his light against her leg.

"What?"

"This little purple line. Looks like a scar." He continued to trace the scar with his finger. "I've never noticed it before. How long have you had it?"

"Help me down." Samuel took her hands and she hopped off the rock. "Let's walk a little deeper into the cave."

"You gonna answer my question? How did you get that scar? I can't believe I've never noticed it."

"It's no big deal. Just a scar." She brushed her hair away from her eyes and stepped further into the cave, her light bouncing off the dark walls.

Samuel followed behind. "A scar from what?"

"It's nothing."

"Well, if it's nothing, then it shouldn't take long to tell me how you got it."

"I don't want to talk about it. You know, it's getting cold in here. Maybe we should just leave." She began making her way to the entrance of the cavern.

Samuel stepped up beside her. "You okay?"

She simply nodded, but Samuel easily could see she was uncomfortable.

"Callie, what is it?"

They walked outside the cave and found a flat rock to sit upon, the sun warming their backs. They looked out across a valley that held the green waters of Holston Lake. Beyond the lake, gentle waves of brown hills led to the base of the massive skyline of Iron Mountain. Amongst the tall pines, hickory trees, and poplars, on that rock looking out across the expansive Blue Ridge Mountains, Callie explained the history of her scar.

Chapter Seventeen

The world is a place where checks and balances seem to sit on the dusty desk of an otherworldly accountant, someone who is slow to bring about sweet revenge to those who choose to break the laws and commands of mankind. As if God has assigned the night watch of keeping his children safe from evil to an unmotivated distant relative, the world can be slow to right the wrongs of injustice. Evil and cowardice, free to roam the streets of decency and righteousness, lurk about as if repercussions are as far off as a fading star in a distant galaxy. It worries itself not with the here and now, and gives only a passing thought to Judgment Day, providing a world of time to prepare a compelling case to the Lord of all creation of how repentance has taken hold at the last moment.

But sometimes, revenge comes in the form of man.

***

The sun dropped behind Jefferson Mountain, the sky was soft red, the valley clothed in a sheet of serenity. Samuel drove through town and noticed only a handful of cars were parked along the streets. He pulled into the lot of Bernie's Auto Repair shop. There was a light on in the bay area, and as Samuel walked up he heard the Tommy Dorsey Band playing over a small wooden radio.

"Evenin', Bernie."

"Hey, Sammy. How's the world treatin' ya?"

"Is Dobie here?" Samuel was not usually one to pass up good conversation, so when he disregarded Bernie's question, the old man knew something was wrong. Samuel's face was blood-red, and his jaw tight and tense.

"Um, no. He left about fifteen minutes ago."

"Any clue where he went?"

Not sure. Mighta gone home. Sometimes he stops at Cape Greer's house. Cape's known to throw a party on occasion. Keeps a little moonshine on hand."

"Much obliged."

***

Samuel pulled off the road in front of Cape Greer's house. Four cars littered the driveway, and two more were parked on the front lawn. Music flowed through the flimsy screen door which led into the tiny den, and from the look of gray silhouettes through the picture window beside the door, Cape's house was apparently a popular place. The screen door rattled when Samuel tapped on it.

"Sammy Gable," Cape yelled from the den couch. "Get in here. The party's done started."

Samuel entered the room, standing just inside the doorway. A man sat near the door in a recliner covered with red terrycloth, a Pabst Blue Ribbon in his hand. Two men sat at a small table in a kitchen separated from the den only by a slender Formica counter. The men argued over the type of engine best suited for drag racing. Samuel looked about.

"Come on in, Sammy. Want a beer?"

"Is Dobie here?"

"He's around here somewheres."

"You mind tellin' him he's got a visitor?"

"Sure thing." Cape looked curiously at Samuel. "You okay?"

"Fine. Just need Dobie's all."

Dobie followed Cape from the hallway, a plastic cup of moonshine in his hand. "Yeah?"

"Evenin'."

"Evenin'. What do you want?"

"Do I look familiar?"

"Not particularly. Though you do have a certain stupid look about you. You collectin' money to put yourself through retard school?"

"I just need you to step outside. Just for a minute. It won't take long."

"You got somethin' to say," Dobie said, leaning against the living room wall, "say it to me here."

"Not here. Outside. There's somethin' I need to talk to you about. Like I said, it won't take but a minute." Samuel stared directly into Dobie's eyes, rubbing his fingers against the palms of the hands that he intended to beat Dobie with.

Dobie placed his cup on the counter, stepped out the screen door and down the steps. "Make it quick, will ya? I'm kinda wrapped up in a poker game."

"Not a problem." Out the door they went.

Dobie leaned against the brick wall on the porch. "Well, here I am." Dobie crossed his arms. "What is it that you want?"

"Don't recognize me, huh?"

"Didn't we already do this inside? No. I don't know you. Don't care to. But I'll be happy to make sure you know who I am." Dobie stepped in front of Samuel, eye to eye.

"I'll help jog your memory. The Dairy Bar. Five years ago. I was in uniform."

Dobie looked skyward briefly and smiled. "Oh, yeah. You were the GI who blindsided me. That was a lucky shot. If the old man behind the counter hadn't saved you,

I'd a-drug you up and down the street." He inched closer to Samuel's face. "You wanna try that junk on me now? How 'bout it, ace?"

"You remember the girl at the Dairy Bar? The one you were comin' on to?"

"Oh, yeah. Who wouldn't? Nice package. Uppity little broad, though."

"I hear you tried to help her a while back when she had a flat tire out on 84."

"Don't know what you're talkin' 'bout."

"Really? Memory's that bad?"

"What's it to you? She weren't nothin' but a tease."

"It's time you got a lesson on how to treat a lady."

"She weren't no lady. Just some snotty gal who didn't have the guts to ask for what she wanted. What she dreamed about at night. You know, alone, under the covers."

Samuel threw a forearm into Dobie's cheek, knocking him into the rail of the porch. Samuel grabbed him by the shirt, his fingers digging deep into Dobie's chest. Dobie took a swing at Samuel with his left hand, and Samuel caught Dobie's fist with his palm. Samuel pulled him off the porch and into the yard.

"Get your damn hands off me," Dobie shouted as he kicked Samuel in the shin. The blow loosened Samuel's grip, and Dobie lunged forward, knocking Samuel to the ground. Dobie grabbed a handful of dirt and tossed it at Samuel's eyes, but Samuel kicked Dobie away and the dirt hit Samuel's neck. Samuel jumped to his feet and grabbed Dobie by the hair. He spun him around and landed a blow to Dobie's nose and blood gushed out, spraying Samuel's shirt. Samuel punched him again in the stomach, and Dobie fell to his knees, blood now covering his mouth.

"Get up and take it like a man," Samuel said, pulling at Dobie's sleeve. Dobie drove his fist into Samuel's midsection, and Samuel laughed. "That's the best you got?"

"I'm just gettin' started," Dobie said, rising, spitting into Samuel's face. Samuel wiped his face with the back of his hand, smiled, and again landed a blow to Dobie's jaw, his knees buckling as he fell into the bushes beside the front steps.

Samuel dragged him by his pants as the others watched from the doorway. He rained blow after blow against Dobie's cheeks and eyes, each punch driven by the visual Samuel had of Dobie attacking Callie on that lonely highway, and the innocence of which he'd robbed her. Dobie staggered, swinging his fists wildly but finding no mark. Samuel steadied him once more by the shirt, and blood covered Samuel's hand.

"If you ever, *ever* come anywhere near Callie again," Samuel said as he took hold of Dobie's hair, "I swear to God I'll kill you." He pulled back his arm, made a fist, and drove it into the side of Dobie's face with all he could muster.

Dobie crumpled onto the grass like a ragdoll.

"That's for Callie, you gutless, piece of garbage."

Chapter Eighteen

Samuel's tongue was tired, and Pete saw the weary look in Samuel's eyes.

"Let's get you on home," Pete said. The afternoon sun was fading behind the purple backdrop of Roan Mountain. "Gabby's gonna send out a search party for you if we don't."

"Nope, not yet. It feels too good sittin' here. I know it will be my last trip up this holler. These mountains have been good to me. I can't imagine heaven bein' any nicer than this spot right here." Samuel rubbed his index finger with the thumb of his other hand like he was peeling a carrot. "Now, where was I?"

***

Fall, 1948

Word began spreading of communism in Korea, and the possibility that the United States could be heading for war again. Samuel heard some of the men talk about it at work, and though he tried not to think about it, he couldn't help but wonder if the military might again request his services.

Samuel rubbed the back of his neck. Sawdust was on his shirtsleeves, and he noticed the dust of yellow accumulating on the car seat. One more day of work, and then the weekend would be his and Callie's to share. It was early October, and the leaves had begun to turn, dressing the mountains in deep red and bright gold. He walked into the house, and Callie sat at the oak kitchen table, crying.

"What's wrong?" he asked, placing his black metal lunch pail on the kitchen counter. She shook her head and wiped her eyes with a tissue. Samuel sat beside her and placed his arm around her. "Baby, what is it?"

"Nita Carswell said we are going to war soon in Korea."

"I've heard talk about that. But there ain't no need in cryin' about it."

"What if they come for you? What if they send you away again?"

"Well, if I went it would be of my own choosin'." She turned away and he placed his arms around her from behind.

"Are you sure? What if they make you?"

"They can't. Besides, I've done my time. I ain't ever leavin' you again."

"Promise?" She wiped her left eye against Samuel's sleeve.

"Promise. Now, if you don't scrape up some food for us, I'll be forced to take the shotgun outside and kill a possum. Either that, or Lillie Whitmire's cat."

"Stop it." She laughed as she wiped her eyes with the inside sleeve of her blouse.

Callie sliced tomatoes and Samuel removed bread from the box. "Want me to fry up some bacon for the sandwiches?" Samuel asked.

"Let's just sprinkle some pepper and mayo on it and take it to the porch. The sunsets have been amazing the last few evenings."

Sitting side by side in rough-hewn hickory rocking chairs, facing the sunset above Jefferson Mountain, they ate, two bottles of Coca-Cola on the oak table between them.

"Sammy, I was going through some boxes this afternoon. The ones in the top of the closet in the hall. I was looking at the box that has your army uniform. It has some pictures of you and your dad."

"Is the one of us playin' baseball by the barn one of 'em?"

"Yes. Some others too. You and Bert cleaning fish out back of your house. One of Miz Eula in her Sunday dress."

"We need to get an album to keep 'em from gettin' torn up or thrown out."

"I also found your baseball glove." She took a slow sip of Coke. "When I came and stayed with Vera for the bean pageant, I remember her telling me you were a really good ballplayer."

"I forgot I still had that old glove. Dad gave it to me when I was a kid. It was the size of my head and it was hard to close with my little fingers. By the time I got to high school, though, it was a perfect fit."

"What position did you play? Pitcher, right?"

"It's not important. Want another sandwich?"

"Whatsa matter? Think you can strike me out? I was known as Crushin' Callie in my backyard. I could hit a ripe tomato into the tree tops when James pitched, so I'm sure I can handle whatever you bring."

"Playin' days are over. I got no need to spend time recollectin' on the sport."

Callie sensed an edgy tone in Samuel's voice. "Just because it's over doesn't mean you shouldn't talk about it.

Tell me about your days as the baseball hero. Were you as good as Bobby Ruth?"

"*Babe* Ruth."

"How did it feel to strike somebody out, or hit a homerun? I bet you looked good in a uniform."

"I don't want to talk about it." He took a long sip from his bottle.

Callie took hold of his hand. "Sweetie, what's wrong?"

"Nothin's wrong. Let's drop the subject."

Samuel stood and walked off the porch. He stared up into the clear, darkening sky. The North Star was just barely visible, and soon the other stars would come into view. Callie came up from behind and slid her arms around Samuel's midsection. Her head touched his shoulder. "Darlin', what's wrong?"

"Remember when you asked me about the war the first day I came to see you at your house?"

"Yes. You said you didn't want to talk about it ever again. And I made a promise not to ask you about it."

"Well, the same applies to baseball."

With that, Samuel turned and walked into the house.

***

The days were busy, and summer rains had softened the garden floor where Callie planted tomatoes, squash, and potatoes. Evenings were warm, and Callie and Samuel took to the trails along Jefferson Mountain. They would hike to Devil's Backbone, a jagged rock that jutted out from the curve of the mountain, where they'd sit, much the way they had on the bank of the creek the night of the bean pageant.

It was a Friday night and Samuel came home to a silent house. He looked about the yard, in the garden, on the tiny porch. He thought Callie had perhaps taken a walk to see Virginia Lowe across the road. He returned inside and went to the icebox for his lemonade. A small note was taped to it, and he recognized Callie's handwriting.

Summer was in its final stages, and the days were getting shorter. As Samuel walked the familiar trail, he could feel the chill in the shadows. Swallows chased each other along the treetops of the hardwoods, and the waters of Sinking Creek played a familiar tune across the rocks down in the valley one hundred yards below.

When Samuel arrived at the appointed spot, Callie had a blanket laid across the long, smooth rock, and placed on it was a wicker basket of sandwiches, grapes, and fresh blueberries she'd picked from Ms. Virginia's fields. She smiled as she saw him approach. "Thought this would be a good place for dinner. You can't beat the view."

Samuel lifted Callie to her feet. He placed his hand along her chin and softly kissed her. She was still the prettiest girl he had ever seen, and as time passed and he got to know the wonders of her heart, she became more beautiful in a way that had nothing to do with physical characteristics.

"So, did you miss me today?" Callie asked as she held a sandwich up for him.

"Never thought about you once. When that sawdust starts flyin', all I think about is two-by-fours, four-by-fours, and any other combination of fours known to man."

"Well, if you can't find time in your day to think about me, I'm thinking that there'll be no dinner tonight for you." She tucked his sandwich behind her back.

Samuel moved in front of her, reaching his hands around her slender back. "Well, I guess if I can't eat, I'll have to do somethin' to occupy my time." His lips moved softly to hers, and his strong embrace caused her to drop the sandwich. As she kissed him she placed her arms around his neck.

As he moved his lips down to her neck, she whispered, "I just dropped your dinner."

"I'll just eat yours, then."

She nuzzled his earlobe with her teeth. "What was that comment?"

"Nothin'. I meant to say that I'll just chew on some pine bark or somethin'."

"That's what I thought you said," she whispered as she released her grip on his ear.

As the sun fell, in search of new mountains to scale, an eagle, with wings curved and dark, rode the soft winds. It circled above them, crying out, its song fading lonely into the backwoods. Together they ate, sitting side by side. They spoke little, as each other's company provided a comfort neither knew could exist, but neither could ever imagine living without.

In some ways Samuel's time in the war seemed like a distant dream, as if he had never left Callie's side since that night by the creek bed.

Chapter Nineteen

Pete walked in the front door, browsing through the stack of mail. No offers, but no rejections either. The house was silent. Sarah had again taken Kate to her parents', making excuses about how Pete needed peace and quiet to write. Pete saw it as an excuse to keep her parents from knowing their marriage was in trouble.

Pete placed his tape recorder on the table beside his laptop and turned it on. Samuel's voice was becoming noticeably strained and weak as he carefully recounted his return home from the war. Each time he spoke Callie's name, however, there was an definite passion, as if the very purpose of saying her name was to profess his love for her, as if he equated *love* and *Callie* with some unbreakable bond.

Pete wrote for over six hours, not stopping to eat. The midnight hour approached, and his mind was awash in thoughts of a golden era, of a love that was cast for a lifetime, churning like a runaway train. At almost one o'clock, he lay on the couch. *Pictures*, he thought. *Need to see pictures*.

When the morning light broke, Pete looked at his watch. The house was quiet, and he was growing accustomed to the silence. After he showered, he had a banana and an English muffin. It was seven forty-five, and he picked up the cordless phone.

The phone rang twice. "Hi, Gabby, this is Pete. Sorry to call so early."

"It's okay, Pete. It's nice to hear your voice."

Pete had grown very fond of her voice, too. He liked hearing her say his name. "I was wondering if—"

"If I was wearing the purple gown?"

"As a matter of fact…" He was completely caught off guard by her quip. They shared a brief laugh, something he imagined she had not done much of since Samuel had become ill. "What I wanted to know was if you had any photo albums of your mom and dad lying around."

"Photo albums? Sure. The trunk in Daddy's bedroom is filled with them. Why?"

"I want to see some old pictures of your mom and dad, if it's okay. I'll explain later. Can I drop by and get them from you soon?"

"Tell you what. I've got to run some errands this morning. Can I meet you in town?"

"Tell me where and when."

"Ten. Sandy's Bagel Shoppe."

"Perfect."

***

Gabby spent longer than normal getting ready. She grabbed her curling iron in one hand and took some hair between her fingers with the other. She looked at herself in the mirror and replaced the iron on the counter. *He'll think I'm coming on to him*, she thought. After a few minutes of mental debate, she took hold of the iron again to finish what she'd started. Putting on the cherry-red lipstick, she wondered if he'd think she looked pretty.

When Gabby walked into Sandy's, Pete had taken the liberty of buying her a bagel and coffee. He waved to her, as if she hadn't already spotted his warm smile. She tried to hide her anxiousness.

"Mornin'," Pete said. "I took the liberty of getting you something to eat. I guessed you to be a bagel-and-cream-cheese kind of gal."

"Thanks, that was sweet of you."

She sat across from him, placing a black-and-gold photo album on the table. Her eyes sparkled, somehow even more than before, and he found himself more at ease while staring into them.

As she removed her jacket he noticed she had fixed her hair, and he liked it. She wore a black shirt, unbuttoned just enough so that Pete could see a bit of cleavage if he were so inclined. The collar of the blouse was tucked up under her hair. She wore the slightest hint of perfume. Pete thought she looked absolutely stunning, and it was only ten in the morning. How could she not be married? Surely she had a boyfriend. She was way too adorable to be unattached. When she opened the sugar packet, he glanced at her petite fingers.

"Can I ask you something?"

"No, I'm not married," she calmly said. The stunned look on his face made her laugh.

"How did you know what I was going to ask?"

"I'm a lifetime member of the Psychic Network."

Pete tore off a tiny section of his bagel and threw it at her. Her hands were at work spreading cream cheese on her bagel, so she could only flinch when it bounced off her nose.

"I'll get you for that," she said and she stuck her tongue out at him.

"I'm shaking in my shorts."

"You should be." She stirred her coffee and took a slow sip. "So, do you want the story?"

"Story?"

"Of why I'm single."

"That's up to you." *Yes, absolutely,* was what he wanted to say.

She looked about the restaurant and smiled at a woman who was saying the blessing with her small child. She took a deep breath. "Well, I guess I wanted to marry someone like my father, so I fell for a soldier. We got married, and I played the game of staying home while he was shipped overseas. First it was Germany, followed by a year of fun and sun in Syria."

"The distance got to be too much?"

"No." She stirred the straw in her coffee cup. Her beautiful eyes revealed she was thinking sad thoughts. She sighed. "His chopper went down on a reconnaissance mission over Yemen. It was three days before his twenty-ninth birthday."

"I'm so sorry." Pete pulled nervously at the label on his bottled water. There was that subject of death again that he went to great pains to avoid.

"It's okay."

"You sure you want to talk about it? We can change the subject if you'd like."

Gabby looked out at the parking lot and Pete felt terrible for asking. "You know, you go through life, and you get up each day thinking it's just one of thousands. It becomes commonplace to feel that the people you loved the night before will be there the next day. That life will be steady and comfortable. When Bobby died, I was numb for months. I knew the role of a soldier's wife, that death was always a possibility. But I never thought it would actually happen. He'd been gone for over a year, and though they brought him home in a flag-draped casket, it felt like he was still overseas somewhere, flying and doing the military games they play. And then when Momma died, I felt like a part of me died as well."

She dabbed her watery eyes with her fingers. "I know parents are supposed to die before us, but I still had trouble accepting it. As hard as it was losing her, and Bobby, it is nothing compared to watching Daddy slowly fading away. I know when he's gone, not only will I lose the man who made certain his little girl was safe and happy, but a door to my past will be shut forever. Even now when I sit with Daddy in our house or on the porch, I feel like I did when I was young. But when he passes on, that porch will never be the same. That house will become another house on the market. And then it will become just a place of memories, a place where others might wonder, if only briefly, who lived there before them. I'll be alone in the sense that Daddy will take the past with him. It'll be gone forever."

Pete took hold of her hand. By the look in her eyes she liked the way his fingers folded around hers. "But the memories can keep the past alive. That's the way I look at it with my dad. He's gone, but the memories live on."

"True, but that's all they are, memories. You can't hug a memory. You can't laugh with a memory. You can't fish Doe Creek with a memory."

Pete couldn't argue the point so he took a sip of his water. He knew the words he spoke were hollow. He missed the time he spent with his own father, yet sometimes he felt the memories were like getting a postcard from Hawaii instead of going there to see it for yourself. Postcards look nice on the refrigerator, but after a while all they do is make one sorry he wasn't the one who made the trip.

"Again, I can't thank you enough for the time you've given Daddy these last weeks. I think it's helped keep him going. It's as if he has a purpose to stay alive, to tell his story to you."

"What an incredible man he is. He is fueling my passion to be the best writer I can be."

"Your wife must be supportive of your work."

Pete looked toward the counter. "Well, I wouldn't exactly say that."

"What do you mean?"

"She and our daughter Kate moved in with her parents. They moved out two weeks ago."

"I'm sorry to hear that." Something about the way she said it was unconvincing.

"Heck, I can't help but think they are better off at her parents. My schedule has become crazy. I know I'm the one that controls that to some extent. But we talked about that before I decided to become a writer full time. And it takes an unbelievable amount of time and effort to get a novel published. So Sarah knew going into this that it might be difficult for a while."

They finished breakfast and walked outside. The sun dipped in and out of clouds that had no definable shapes, making it hard to tell where one began and one ended. The morning chill was almost gone, though Gabby put on her North Face jacket.

"Thanks for taking time to bring me the album," Pete said, flipping through the pages outside the restaurant. "Do you think Mr. Gable is doing all right alone? How would you know if he needs you?"

"The nurse is with him. She comes in three times a week. That's usually when I'll run errands, do my grocery shopping. I wouldn't leave him alone."

"Well, do you have a little more time? Would you like to go for a walk? There's something I'd like to talk to you about."

"Why don't we grab that bench?"

Across the street was a memorial for the men of Carter Springs who'd served in the two world wars. Two walls of granite listed the names and where they'd served, and honoring those who had fallen in battle. The Women's Club planted and maintained flower gardens on either side of the monument, forming a semicircle of color. The American flag flew directly between the two walls. Two park benches were located beside the flower gardens.

When they sat, they looked out toward the town that had not changed much since either of them was young. Though the town had grown, many businesses had moved to the byways. But the original look and feel of the town was virtually unchanged. Pete liked the fact that it still contained the old town feel. He scratched his chin, looked toward the sky as if he wasn't sure what to say.

"Looks like you have something weighing on your mind," Gabby said.

"Well, I do." He took a deep breath and looked out over the mountains. Finally he spoke. "I went to visit Caleb."

Gabby sat in stunned silence as she ran Pete's words through her brain again. Slowly, with a look of disbelief, she said, "Caleb? You found Caleb?" Pete fidgeted uneasily, looking toward Neely's Funeral Home across the street. "How did you find him? Where is he?"

"He lives in Asheville. Owns a music store downtown on Highland Avenue."

"How is he? What did he have to say? I mean, what did you talk to him about?"

"I told him about your dad. I thought he should know. I thought he would want to come see him before…"

"Is he coming home?"

"I don't know. He didn't have much to say."

"Did he seem okay? How did he look? Does he have family?"

"I don't know. He didn't say." Pete rubbed his hand through his hair. "He wasn't in the mood to talk, especially when I told him I knew your dad. What is the story with him? Why is he so angry? Why did he move away?"

She looked at the ground in front of her, moving her eyes about as if to gather her thoughts. She shrugged her shoulders slightly. "It happened when Caleb was eighteen. It's the day our family was turned upside down, was torn apart."

"What do you mean?"

"Caleb grew up a free spirit. He wanted Daddy's blessing, and sometimes that handcuffed his ability to be his own person. It didn't bother Daddy that Caleb had interests different from what Daddy assumed a son of his would have. Instead of sports or fishing and hunting, he was interested in hanging out and playing the guitar with his friends. They smoked and listened to bands like Led Zeppelin. Dad didn't quite know how to handle that. His years in the military and the war had made him a disciplined man with a plan. Caleb thought life was supposed to be carefree, best lived with nothing more than hope in his back pocket.

"Now, you've probably realized these last few weeks that Daddy wasn't exactly a choirboy growing up. He was the town prankster and wouldn't hesitate tipping an outhouse or tossing snakes on the bank of Birch Tree Creek just to watch fishermen scatter. But he did it more as a way to maintain levity during tough times. People were poor around here. There was nothing more than survival going on. Daddy thought what he did would help keep the folks around here from going crazy, keep *him* from going crazy. But everyone loved him. Even the sheriff was fond of him, though they tell me he never admitted it. I think Caleb tried to impress Daddy by committing pranks more daring than what Daddy did in his younger days. And the one he pulled the summer he turned eighteen, well…" Gabby lowered her head for a moment, biting her lip.

A car door slammed shut at the street. Something made Pete look up, and he was surprised at what he saw. Sarah's mother walked quickly toward Pete and Gabby, and she was visibly upset. "Pete, Sarah and Hank just took Kate to the emergency room. I was on my way there and saw your car."

Pete stood quickly and automatically removed his car keys from his jeans pocket. "What happened? Is she okay?"

"She was at the park with Hank and she jumped on a wood bench. A splinter, which Hank said looks to be several inches long, broke off and went into her thigh. Kate began screaming and Hank grabbed her and headed for the emergency room. He didn't know what else to do."

"I'm sorry, Gabby. I've got to run."

"Absolutely. Go take care of Kate."

Pete's tires screeched as he took off for the hospital.

Chapter Twenty

Kate was asleep in Pete's arms when he walked out the sliding door of the hospital. Tears had dried on her cheeks, and her hair was matted along her forehead. The splinter, over three inches long, had been successfully removed, the doctor removing it only after Pete arrived to hold Kate's hand in the ER. She cried herself to sleep after the ordeal. Her exhausted body heaved slightly as she slept.

Sarah led the way to her car as the sun beat down on the chrome and glass and the blacktop of the parking lot. She placed a cotton towel on Kate's car seat to soften it. When Pete tried to lower Kate into her car seat, she woke, clinging tightly to his shirt. "Daddy," she said.

"I'm here, sweetie. Daddy's got you." He rubbed her hair and looked at Sarah, who turned away and glanced across the parking lot. "Let her come home with me," Pete said. "Both of you. Come home." Kate tightened her grip around Pete's neck.

"That's all right," Sarah replied as she unlocked her car. "We'll just head back to Momma's."

"No, Daddy. I want to go with you."

"You go with Mommy. And if you need me, call me, and I'll come running, okay?"

Sarah started the car. "Go get your writing done."

Kate felt so good in his arms, like the nights when he rocked her to sleep listening to "Sweet Baby James." He reluctantly placed Kate in her seat and she began to cry.

"I love you, Kate. Big as the sky." Pete turned and walked toward his car, trying his best to drown out Kate's pleas to stay. He cried on the way home.

***

When Pete walked in the door the phone was ringing. He didn't check the caller ID, but he immediately recognized Gabby's voice. "Hey, Pete, I was calling to see if Kate was okay."

"She's doing fine. The splinter was close to four inches long. They used a funky-looking set of pliers to remove it. Sweet thing was so scared. She'll have a sore leg for a while."

"I'm glad she's all right." After a few seconds, she said, "Um, do you have some free time this afternoon? I could use your help."

"You're in luck. No deadlines today. What do you need?"

"Well, my friend Emma Carswell was going to help me pick apples while Porter and Miss Earline visit with Daddy. But she had to go to Knoxville for a funeral. Anyway, I wanted to bake some apples for Daddy. He loves them and it's one of the few things he can stomach. The apples are going to be too ripe to eat if they aren't picked soon."

"So basically you're searching for cheap labor."

"Exactly."

"So, what do I have to do? You gonna make me climb trees?"

"Well, you can't just set the bucket under them and expect the apples to drop in. Actually, most of the apples you can reach. But yes, there may be some climbing involved. Don't tell me you're afraid of heights."

"No, I'm not afraid of heights. I can scale trees like a ring-tail lemur."

"Well, don't forget to bring your tail."

***

Pete turned onto Vaught's Holler and followed a dirt road that bent around a tobacco field that bordered Birch Tree Creek. Gabby had told Pete to follow the road two miles, where he would then come to the end of the tobacco fields. When he passed those tobacco fields he saw her removing buckets from the back of the pickup truck. She wore faded jeans, a green and brown thermal shirt, and brown work boots. Pete liked how cute and outdoorsy she looked. He got out of his car, sporting jeans and his leather jacket.

"That's the best GQ apple-pickin' outfit I've ever seen," she said.

"This is perfect pickin' gear." He removed a pair of wool gloves from the pocket of his jacket. "And I brought gloves."

Gabby looked closely at the bulky gloves. "Well, if you're looking to build a snow man, those will work." She tossed a pair of thin cotton gloves to him. "Here, put these on."

They walked into a small orchard, the trees set out in random fashion. Gabby handed Pete a plastic bucket. "Ready to do some picking?"

"I'm psyched." He began picking apples with no regard to their ripeness. If he could reach it, he picked it.

"Easy, tiger. Make sure you pick ones that are edible."

"How do you know if they're ripe?"

"Make sure they are firm. And no holes. Don't want any bugs or worms coming home with us."

273

He began touching the apples, examining each closely.

"See," she said, holding up one she had just picked. "Like this."

"What kind of apple is that?"

"Virginia Beauty."

"A Virginia Beauty picked by a Tennessee cutie."

"Ha," she said with an air of doubt in her voice. "Aren't you the lyricist? You're not a bad-lookin' picker yourself."

As they filled their buckets, they moved about, close together, their arms touching much of the time. Pete saw a playfulness in her eyes that he had not seen before. With all that was going on in her daily life, he was glad she at least had a few moments where she could escape the grim reality taking place at home.

Pete reached for an apple that fell to the ground as soon as he touched it. "What do we do with the rotten ones? Seems a shame to let them waste away."

"The deer will eat them. Bears, too."

Pete picked the one that had just fallen, juice oozing from the peel, and it was the size of a baseball. "I bet I can throw a mean spitball with this one."

"Were you a ballplayer?"

"A pitcher. Played at UT."

"Get outta here. Daddy was a pitcher too, though I never heard him talk about it much."

"I heard he was a good one."

"I love baseball, but I suck at it."

"Well, maybe you just need some careful instruction. Let me show you a few tips. Bet I can have you knocking flies off a dead cat from fifty feet."

"I doubt that."

"Allow me to demonstrate. Pick something out, and I'll hit it."

She looked around, unsure of what to choose. "How about the empty bucket down by the truck?"

Pete studied it a few seconds and removed his jacket. He wore a tight-fitting black short-sleeve shirt that exposed his shapely triceps. "Pick a hard one, why don't you? Jeez. That's at least a hundred feet away. And downhill at that. But I think I'm up to the challenge." He removed the glove from his throwing hand. He sized up the distance, then squared his feet, shoulders, and hips toward the target. His feet shoulder-width apart, Pete rolled the sticky apple in his fingers to get a feel for its weight. He eyed his target, looked at Gabby with a smile, turned and tossed a strike. The apple struck the bucket, sending it reeling under the truck.

"Nice shot. I am impressed."

He picked up another from the ground. "Your turn."

"Sorry, bud. You've heard the term 'throws like a girl'? Well, that's me."

"I bet that's because you're not using the proper mechanics. Take off your gloves." She bit the glove on the finger and pulled it off with her teeth, smiling at him as she pulled the other one off with her bare hand. He returned the smile and placed the apple in her left hand as she held it out in front of her. "You don't look like a southpaw."

"A who?"

"Southpaw. Leftie. Left-hander."

"I'm not. Guess I'm a northpaw." She looked at the gooey apple and switched it to her right hand. "Okay, what now?"

"Stand like this." He positioned himself as though he were going to throw again. She stood beside him, laughing as she tried to imitate him. "Bend your knees a bit. Loosen up, would you? You look like a constipated statue. Get your elbows up. When you throw you want to pretend that you're waist-deep in a swimming pool and you don't want your arms to get wet."

Pete moved behind her, molding his arms around hers as if they were two action figures stuck together. He placed his right hand on her throwing hand, and his chest pushed slightly against her back. She smelled good. She sighed when his biceps touched the backs of her arms.

"Okay, before you throw you have to put your game face on." He bent his head around her to look. She frowned. "The goal is to look determined, not pissed off like somebody kicked your dog." She laughed and then shook her face as if erasing her expression like some human Etch-A-Sketch.

She lowered her eyebrows and scowled. "Like this?"

"Much better." He moved in front of her to check her stance. "Let me make sure you've got everything right." He rubbed his hands along her shoulders. "Good posture." He loosened her grip on the apple. "Don't squeeze it." Her fingers felt warm in the cool mountain air. She looked at her grip and then looked at him.

"Are we going to do this today?"

"Oh, you are such a smart ass. Okay, your target is that knotty tree twenty feet in front of us. Let her fly."

She took a deep breath, looked at her stance as though she knew what she was doing, stepped and tossed the apple. When it splattered against the tree she jumped, placing her hands over her mouth in surprise.

"Direct hit!" Pete said, and he looked into her eyes. She jumped into his arms, laughing, her head cocked back like she had tossed the last pitch of a no-hitter. She giggled for a moment, and then patted Pete's shoulders. He set her down but her body still touched his, his arm around her waist.

She sighed, and her eyes softened, letting him know she wanted him to come closer. She looked at his lips. They seemed temporarily frozen, unsure what to do next. Slowly she leaned forward, reaching toward him, toward forbidden fruit. She rubbed his face tenderly, watching her fingers glide along his cheek before touching her lips to his. She looked in his eyes, trying to gauge his willingness, and she parted her mouth slightly as he did the same. Her knees quivered when he gently touched his fingers against her face.

With careful tenderness they kissed, lips softly touching. She placed her hands around his neck, and she breathed deeply as if she was short on air. Under skies of gray, a day that looked somber and sad, they sparked the countryside to life. After a few moments, she opened her eyes, not realizing he was staring at her. She withdrew slightly, though still close enough to feel his breath on her skin.

She smiled. Again she rubbed his face with the backs of her fingers. "You have the most incredible eyes."

Pete smiled a doubtful smile. "We shouldn't be doing this." His eyes said otherwise.

"I know. I'm sorry."

"Me too."

She slowly pulled him by his shirt, their eyes locked. He took her by the hands, gently placing his fingers around hers. Their lips met again, so soft, so tenderly. When they heard the rumble of an engine in the distance, they slowly separated. A white SUV drove around the curve in the road, and Gabby looked toward the vehicle. "Here come the Coles."

Pete squinted. "Who?"

"They live across the creek." They watched as a man and two young girls stepped out of the SUV, buckets in hand. "Looks like we got apple-picking company now." Gabby handed Pete his bucket. "Guess I should be heading on back home," she said.

"Yeah, me too," Pete said reluctantly.

"You okay?" She ran her hand through his hair, above his ear.

He nodded. "I'm good."

***

When Gabby walked into the kitchen with her bucket of apples, still savoring the taste of Pete's kiss, Earline was washing plates in the sink. "Miss Earline, let me do that."

"It's okay, child. I sliced Porter and Sammy some of my angel food cake, and I don't want to leave a mess."

"Miss Earline, you should enter that cake in a contest. Nobody's is better."

"Thanks, dear. You'd be surprised to know there ain't nothin' to it."

"Thanks for coming to visit Daddy. He loves you both so much."

Earline looked out the window. "I don't know what Porter will do when he can't visit with your father anymore."

"It's going to be hard on all of us."

"Sammy's in a bit of a foul mood today."

"Oh?"

"I had told him about running into Abigail Swift at the store, and her saying that Pete's wife and daughter had moved out."

Gabby didn't know how to hide her guilt, so she began drying the plates. "I'd heard something about that." Had she said the words as though she was sad of the news? Did Earline sense something of Gabby's discomfort on the subject?

"I believe your father wants to take matters into his own hands."

Great.

***

The ringing of the phone broke the silence in the house. Pete saw the Gable name on the caller ID. "Hello?"

"Hey. You doing okay?"

"Need you ask? My spine is still tingling. You?"

"Oh, Pete. It was incredible. Part of me wants to meet you in the orchard to finish what we started. The other part of me tells me I'm playing with fire."

"I know what you mean. Those kisses were amazing. I can't stop thinking about it. About doing it again."

Brief silence. "Daddy found out that Sarah moved out. He wants to see you."

"Really? This should be fun."

***

279

When Pete arrived, Gabby was sitting in the rocker on the porch. She smiled a pensive smile, her face leaning against her knees, which she'd pulled to her chest. She wanted to rush into his arms. She wanted another kiss. When he had climbed the steps, he took her by the hand, rubbing his thumb across her fingers, smiling back.

"Hey," she said softly.

"Hi. Such a pretty girl should not look so sad." He ran his hand through her hair and squatted in front of the rocker.

She took his hand and kissed it. "Oh, Pete. What are we getting ourselves into?" She began to cry.

"Hey now. Don't do that." He brushed away a tear from her cheek.

"You should head inside. I'm sure Daddy knows you're here."

Samuel was in the parlor. In pajamas and a blue robe, he sat on top of the covers of his bed. He had a photo album beside him on the bed and pictures were scattered about like a deck of cards after a round of poker. He moved a few about with his index finger. Blackie's head lay across Samuel's leg.

"Hello, Mr. Gable."

"Pete."

"How are you today?"

"Didn't we have this conversation the first time we met?"

"Yes, sir."

"Remember what I said then?"

Pete nodded slightly. "Yes, sir."

"Okay then. Seems like you'd a-learned by now."

"It won't happen again."

"Sit down. We need to talk."

Pete sat on the cherry hardwood straight-back chair.

"We been gettin' together for almost six weeks now." Pete nodded. "You've given up a lot of your time. Time I didn't realize was cuttin' into your family time."

"Sir?"

"How are things at home?"

"Mr. Gable, you don't need to worry yourself about that. You have enough to worry about."

"You don't think I know that? Son, the last person I need to worry about is me. I know my time's short. But that ain't the case for you, the good Lord willin'. You got to fix things. Make things right. How long you been married?"

"Sir?"

"How long you been married?"

"Thirteen years."

"Do you love her?"

"Of course."

"You sure about that?"

"Yes, sir." Pete was surprised that his voice came across as a little shaky.

"Tell me about the first time you met."

"Sir?"

"You heard me. Now *I* get to do the interviewin'."

Pete took a deep breath and looked out toward the pond. As if loading a backup tape in his mind, he moved his eyes about for a moment. "Well, I was playing intramural basketball in college."

Pete paused and then continued. "Sarah worked with my older brother, and she and some of the girls she worked with came to watch the game. After the game was over, she walked up and spoke to my brother, and I was immediately drawn to her. Of course, being the slacker he was, my brother didn't introduce us and I just watched them talk. Her eyes were the most beautiful I had ever seen. Her skin was smooth as silk. Olive skin. Father was Hispanic. God, she was something right out of a magazine. Better yet, right out of a dream. My brother said something that made her laugh. She smiled."

Pete shook his head slightly, still looking at the pond. "That smile. Perfect teeth, white as snow. I asked my brother to get her number, and the next day I called her. We played racquetball, and when we took the court I had trouble focusing on the game. Each time she ran in front of me I could smell her perfume. Even while working up a sweat she looked dainty, but not in a wimpy kind of way. She was athletic, but she was one hundred percent female. Even the way her fingernails, painted the color of red wine, wrapped around her racquet handle was so alluring. The whole game I wanted to make her drop her racquet so I could wrap my fingers around hers."

As Pete spoke, Samuel watched him open up, his guard dropping bit by bit with each word. "It got to be that I wanted to be with her every day. Whether we went out to dinner or just stayed at home and sat on the porch, it was incredible. As long as I was beside her, that's all that mattered. We got married two years later."

"And you say you still love her?"

"Of course I do."

"When's the last time you told her?"

"I don't… Why are you asking me that?"

"Just answer the question."

"I'd say a while. I've been so busy I haven't really thought about it."

"You love her enough to fight for her?"

"I don't know if fighting for her is the solution. We've fought, all right."

"What if something happened to her? To Kate? How would you feel if you never got to see them again? Son, we only have so many tomorrows. I got about a month of 'em left accordin' to the doctors. I spent three years away from Callie, and it motivated me every day to make it back to her. I promised God if he'd get me home alive, I'd make up for the years I was away from her. From the day I got home, I decided to treat each day like it was the night before I was shipped off to war. Like it was my last time ever seein' her. You better start goin' about doin' the same."

"It's not that simple."

"It can't be more simple."

"You don't understand how this writing business works. It's hard work getting it off the ground. Sarah doesn't understand that."

"What would you know? Take it from a guy who was in the business of watching buddies die, of killin' men I didn't know, of goin' days with no food. What you're doin' is child's play. So you got to get your priorities straight. Either cut back on your work, or find a new career. Them gals of yours deserve that."

"But…"

"No buts."

Samuel pointed to a picture on an end table in the corner of the room. The picture was of Callie and Samuel hand in hand on a hillside. She wore an ivory-colored skirt that came to her knees and a matching jacket with a small flower print. Her left hand was held by his left hand, and his right arm pulled her close to him. He wore dark slacks and a tan sports coat, a dress white shirt, and a bold tie. They were stunning and looked like they held the world by its ear.

"I would give anything," his voice quavered and he paused briefly, "*anything* in this world to be able to hold her like that again." Tears began to form in the corners of his eyes. "Anything." He lowered his head.

Pete placed his hand on Samuel's shoulder. "Yes, sir. You're absolutely right. I don't know what I'd do if something happened to Sarah, to Kate. Like you said, life isn't going to go on forever and there are only so many tomorrows."

Pete looked out the window, the pond silent and still aside from the occasional trout skimming the surface. "Since you made me carry on about Sarah, it's your turn. Tell me more about Callie."

***

January, 1949

The ground was lifeless, cold, and hard. Patches of snow clung to the shade of the woods. Along the eastern side of the Gable house and the nearby barn was a thin line of powder hidden from the path the sun had cut that day. The sun dropped behind Jefferson Mountain, and full, gray clouds hung motionless in the sky. The wind whipped along the valley, and the treetops rattled on the hills above the house. Thin wisps of smoke trailed from

Samuel's car as he and Callie pulled up in front of the house.

"Is that cobbler?" Samuel asked. "Smells like peaches."

"Yes, it is. Our neighbor Miz Virginia fetched me a jar of canned peaches from her cellar. If you're a good boy I might let you have some."

"Good boy? I don't know how to be anything but."

"Well, you never know when you might decide to walk on the bad side of the road." Callie placed her hand on top of Samuel's hand, which clutched the steering wheel of the car. "You know, just because you're the most handsome man in the state of Tennessee doesn't mean we don't need to set up rules of a disciplinary nature."

"Are you sayin' you think I'm capable of slippin' off the straight-and-narrow path?"

"You never know. I've got to be on my toes at all times."

"Toes or no toes, I *will* be havin' a bowl of that cobbler tonight. Might even throw a little ice cream on there just for spite."

"If I didn't love you so much, I'd take you down to the auction grounds and see what I could get for you."

"You'd become a rich woman is all I can tell you."

When Samuel smiled, Callie rubbed his face. Her heart was as jumpy as that night at the Dairy Bar. As she had done a thousand times, she wondered how she could have been so lucky as to land him.

"You think your mom listened to our instructions that she not cook her own birthday dinner?"

"I think not. Ain't no way Momma is goin' to have folks in her house without openin' the oven door. She's prob'ly been cookin' all day."

"So that's where you get your stubbornness."

"No idea what you're talkin' 'bout."

The wind blew fine powder off the dirt driveway, stinging Callie's legs when she opened the car door. She wore a camel-colored dress and a brown-and-tan coat draped from her shoulders. A gray wool scarf cut the wind from her neck as she removed a baking dish covered in cloth from the back seat of the black two-door Chevrolet. Samuel wore light brown slacks, a white dress shirt, and a slim brown corduroy jacket. The pair looked Hollywood-worthy, the perfect combination of rugged handsomeness and raw beauty. They looked ready to jaunt down the red carpet, but instead walked the cold gray steps to the Gable porch.

The kitchen was filled with the aroma of casseroles and chicken and dumplings when the pair walked in. Eula came up, hands extended, lifting the dish from Callie's fingers. "How do, Callie?" She kissed Callie's cheek before placing the dish on top of the cast iron wood stove.

"Hello, Miss Eula. Happy birthday." Callie placed her arms around Eula's neck and kissed her on the cheek.

"Child, I'm older than dirt now. So *happy* and *birthday* can't be used together in the same sentence as far as I'm concerned."

Samuel kissed his mother and then wrapped his arms around her. "I love you, Momma. Happy birthday."

"Thank you, sweet young'un."

Anna walked in from the living room. After hugging both Samuel and Callie, she took Callie by the hand.

"Come say hello to the rest of the crowd." The living room was alive with conversation and laughter. Bert and Mary sat on the long gray-velvet couch. Porter sat in a cherry rocker, the pot belly stove separating the couch and the rocker.

"Well, look what the polecat drug in," said Porter.

"Well, least the polecat showed me some attention," Samuel replied. "He wouldn'ta hiked his leg to piss on you if you were burnin' to a crisp."

Callie passed out hugs as she moved about the room. Anna stood beside Vera and her husband Curtis Lee. "Jasper come?" Callie asked, keeping eye contact with Anna while she hugged Aunt Tessa, Eula's sister from Oak Ridge.

"No," Anna said, trying to hide her disappointment. "Said he has to get up early in the morning. Going fishing with Carl."

"Where's Joannie?"

"Upstairs somewhere. Jasper pissed and moaned about me bringing her, but I just put her in the car and took off."

Callie was surprised Jasper let Anna and Joannie off the compound. Surely Jasper must have sulked as he lowered the moat and uncaged the women so they could leave. Poor man, enduring the trauma of his wife and daughter leaving his side for a few hours…

Samuel sat beside Mary on the couch and looked across the room. The overhead light cast a pale yellow blanket across the shoulders and faces of those who'd come to take advantage of the chance to congregate. Vera and Helen wore light green dresses that were eerily Bobbsey Twin similar.

There was a busy buzz about the house that made Samuel smile. He heard his mother in the kitchen talking with Miss Lucy, the woman Samuel deemed too ugly to be able to capture a man, *any* man. Lucy, however, turned her loneliness into becoming the best cook in the county. Samuel reckoned she might be the only person in the world who could make rhubarb pie taste better than any fancy soufflé created in Paris. Together Lucy, Eula, and Bertie Bennett oversaw the inventory of food, sorting plates and silverware, and generally holding court in the kitchen.

"I heard Carla Jean is plannin' on coming tonight," Vera said softly to Helen.

"No way she'd be crazy enough to show up."

"You know Miss Eula has been friends with Miz Mamie since their childhood days. Miss Eula doesn't know the story about Sammy and Carla Jean. Since Miz Mamie was invited to the party, Carla Jean said to no one in particular she'd be more than happy to escort her mother, the prim and proper Mrs. Mamie Parsons, to the party."

"My dear Lord. I can only imagine the sparks that would fly if she does."

"Do you think Sammy would even let her in the house? After what she did to him?"

"She'd be a loony fool to show up here. Surely Sammy has no clue."

"Aw, Carla's probably just runnin' her mouth, talkin' big. No way she shows up."

The food line began in the kitchen, and though Eula was the birthday gal, she refused to serve herself until every guest had filled their plate. "Momma, you sit," said Samuel. "I'll fix your plate."

"No, you won't. You take care of that sweet bride of yours. She's your main responsibility now. I can fend for myself."

"If you think I'm tossin' you on the scrap pile like a jug of spoiled sweet milk, I'll get Bert to hold you while I whip your fanny." He reached over, plate in hand, and kissed her on the cheek. "You're stuck with me for the rest of your life."

Eula blushed and popped her son lightly on the shoulder. "Precious boy. You *and* Bert."

"That's because we had the finest teacher this side of the Mason-Dixon Line."

"Go on now. Stop that crazy talk and fix Callie some food."

"I can fix my own, thank you very much," Callie said as she moved up beside Eula. She placed her arm around Eula's shoulder. "I'd fix Samuel's, but he said tonight I was off the clock."

"He's got you on the clock tendin' to him? I'll take a hickory switch to his backside."

Callie kissed Samuel on the cheek. "Yes, ma'am, he's a real tyrant."

The food was picked over with the finest of spoons, forks, and fingers. Lucy brought her red-velvet cake to the living room. Eula sat in her rocker, evicting Porter from it after dinner was through. They sang "Happy Birthday" and her face glowed from the attention, though she felt it was way too unnecessary. Bert tossed four logs in the door of the pot belly stove and the house was bathed in warmth, oblivious to the bitter wind that blew along Vaught's Holler.

The murmur of voices made it hard to hear the tap, tap, tap on the glass of the front door. And when Carla Jean led Mamie by the arm into the house, the party participants didn't at first notice. The pair walked into the room, and Vera tapped Helen on the sleeve.

Callie sat beside Samuel on the couch, sideways, facing him, her legs crossed at the calves. As she spoke to him, holding his hand, lost in his dark eyes, he turned his head slightly. Callie stopped talking when she realized Samuel's attention had drifted across the room. Callie followed his eyes and saw the elderly woman speaking to Eula, and the striking girl who stood at the woman's side.

Carla Jean looked at Samuel and smiled, a short, quick smile to let him know she had spotted him. While Mamie hugged Eula, Carla Jean stepped away, as if she were trying to hide from Eula's sight. Callie noticed Vera and Helen looking Samuel's way. After a moment, Carla Jean walked to the couch.

"Sammy," she said and nodded. "Good to see you again."

Samuel squirmed in his seat. He cleared his throat. "What are you doin' here?"

"Well, Momma wanted to come, and she's got to where she can't drive anymore. So I told her I'd bring her. You're still lookin' good, by the way."

Callie stood. "Hi. I'm Callie, Samuel's wife." She extended her hand but Carla Jean ignored it.

She cut her eyes down at Samuel. "So, you got yourself hitched, did you? Us locals ain't good enough for you, I s'pose." Carla oozed confidence that she was a knockout. Her eyes looked at Samuel as if she wondered if he still thought the same.

"You sound surprised he got married," said Callie, a bit of aggravated curiosity in her voice. "Why is that?"

Carla Jean's eyes continued to look at Samuel, and she smirked briefly. Without looking in the vicinity of Callie, though they stood side by side, Carla Jean said, "Let's just say I have my reasons." She spotted Porter standing by the picture window and began walking his way.

Callie placed her hands on her hips. "Who is she? Can she be any more smug?" She folded her arms and looked at Samuel. "Who *is* she?"

"She *used* to be a family friend."

"Can you be a little more specific?"

Vera and Helen excused themselves to the kitchen with the excuse of needing a refill of iced tea.

"Samuel," Callie said, guiding his chin toward her with her fingers. "Look at me. Who is she and what does she mean to you?"

"She don't mean anything to me. Not in the least."

"But *did* she?"

Samuel looked toward the ceiling, ran his fingers through his hair, and took Callie's hand. "Callie, she's no one you need to be concerned about. She ain't worth spendin' time worryin' about."

Callie turned and watched Carla speak to Porter, and Porter looked helpless as she smiled and flirted as though it was as easy as breathing. Mary looked none too pleased with the conversation.

Anna took Callie upstairs to see Joannie. Anna must have sensed the uneasiness Carla Jean had brought, and decided it was a good time to distract Callie. Joannie lay across the bed in Samuel's old room, holding a Raggedy Ann doll while she watched her second cousin Rebecca Lynn attempt a pirouette. Rebecca was eleven and lived in Knoxville. She was the daughter of Samuel's cousin Vernon, and she'd been told she would get a dollar for playing with Joannie upstairs while the adults mingled below them.

"Hey, Joannie," Callie said, pouncing on the bed. Callie began tickling Joannie's stomach. How old are you now? Sixteen?"

"I'm *five*, silly."

"Wow, you look so grown up." Callie lay on the bed. "Okay, Rebecca. Show me how good you dance."

***

Samuel walked to the woodshed. The wind was still, as if gone to some distant world, though winter's bite was still quite strong. The clouds had given way to the full moon, and it illuminated the land in pale blue, forming shadows across the hollow as though it were high noon. The wood was stacked at the back of the shed, and Samuel disappeared into the shadows like he had stepped through a wall void of shape. The wood was cold to the touch, like rugged chunks of ice, as he placed five logs in the metal tin he carried. He took hold of the curved handle and turned toward the house.

Carla Jean stood at the edge of the shed, her hands in the pockets of her jacket. "Need any help?"

"Not from you. I've had enough help from you to last a lifetime."

Carla stood motionless, her breath escaping in short puffs of white. Her perfume briefly drove away the flat smell of dried wood, and in the cold light of the moon her eyes sparkled. Her long hair draped about her shoulders, and her petite, shapely body could not be ignored. She stepped closer, into the shadows of the shed. "I only did it because I loved you. I would have done anything to keep you. You've got to understand that." She was in front of Samuel, his arm still holding the handle of the wood tin.

"Yeah, that was a great way to demonstrate it. You took away everything. Ruined me. All that I had worked for, my dream, ruined."

Carla tenderly ran her fingers across Samuel's face. "I did it for *us*. I'll never apologize for that. Please, let me make it up to you." She leaned against him, placing her face against his chest.

"Make it up to me?" He laughed. "You spread lies to my college coach that I got you pregnant, and that I sent you away to Memphis to have an abortion? Little late for making it up to me now."

"I didn't want you to leave me. I knew if you went off to UT, that'd be the end of us. But I knew if I could keep you in Carter Springs, you'd marry me, and we'd have made an awesome couple. I would have made you the happiest man in the state of Tennessee."

"Well, in some ways, you did."

"What do you mean?"

"If I had played baseball at UT, chances are I wouldn't have met Callie. So yes, for that, you made me the happiest man in Tennessee."

"She can never make you as happy as I can."

"You're not worthy to bait her fish hook." Samuel nudged Carla Jean from his path and began walking to the house. Carla grabbed him by the hand and pulled him toward her. She placed her lips against his, putting her arm tightly around his neck.

When Callie snatched a fistful of Carla Jean's hair, it rendered her immobile. Samuel stepped away from Carla and into the moonlight.

"I'm going to tell you this once," Callie said as she tightened her grip. "If I ever, *ever* catch you within a mile of my husband, I will kick your skanky butt like a rented mule."

Carla Jean whimpered and tried to move her arms to loosen Callie's grip.

"Now, step on out of here," Callie said as she pushed Carla Jean toward the house. "Samuel, you help this sow's mother to the car while I personally escort *her* myself."

***

"Oh my God," Pete said. "Callie sounds every bit as tough as you."

"She could get riled if the situation presented itself."

Pete noticed the silence in the rest of the house, and his thoughts turned to where Gabby was. Was she on the porch with her knees pulled to her chest in that adorable pose?

"Can you tell me a bit about when Gabby was born? How long had you been married before you had her? Do you remember when Callie got pregnant? How did it feel knowing you were going to be a father?"

"Hard to put into words."

"Want to try?"

"Guess I better."

"Recorder's on."

***

May, 1951

Callie slept, lying on her stomach, her hair draped across her face in a thin veil of brown. Samuel sat on the bed next to her, watching her breathe. His fingers touched her shoulder, rubbing against her supple skin. The dim light from the lamp on the nightstand cast a yellow glow across her as morning struggled to make its first appearance.

Samuel softly brushed Callie's hair from her face, and he kissed her softly on her forehead. "Mornin', baby." Callie stirred, rubbing her hand through her hair, trying to move the hair off her face that Samuel had already moved. "I said, mornin', beautiful."

Callie opened her eyes, smiled, and closed her eyes again. "Mornin'. Is the motel on fire?"

"No." Samuel laughed, trying to keep his cup of coffee from spilling. "The motel's not on fire."

"That's nice." She turned her head on the pillow and pulled the blanket above her shoulders. "Then wake me in three hours."

"Nope. You need to get up now. I want to take you somewhere."

"Where? It's still dark. Everything's closed."

"Not where we're going." He pulled down the blanket and sheet to her waist. "Here, I fixed your coffee."

Callie rose to her elbow, looked around with foggy eyes, and looked at the coffee cup. "We can't go there after the sun's come up?"

"No. So drink this, change clothes, and let's go."

"Go where?"

"You'll see when we get there."

***

The car moved on down the flat road, its headlights slightly brightening the dusty path that cut between tall pines and Southern oaks. Spanish moss draped like specters from jagged limbs in air still and calm. The sky began to lighten, though the ceiling of stars flickered like windblown candles perched on an immeasurable window.

Callie had a blanket wrapped around her as she looked out into the heavy underbrush that held the darkness close to the earth's floor. The light aroma of salt hung in the air, and when they approached the bridge she saw the tall cord grass surrounded by the waters of the high tide. Off to her right, the creeks wound their way to Port Royal Sound.

"Are we going to the ocean?" she asked.

"No. We're going to the sound. There's a spot I want to show you."

"How do you know where it is?"

"Terry Grisham took me there when I was stationed at Fort Jackson. He was from a place near here called Frogmore. We hitched a ride one Friday night from the barracks to his house. It was the first time I had ever seen ocean water. The first time I saw a dolphin, a crab. I didn't know the difference between a dolphin and a shark. Terry thought I was a dang fool for confusin' the two."

When Samuel pulled the car on the side of the road, Callie, still wrapped in her blanket, was quick to get out. She followed Samuel across the dirt road. They saw the sound through a break in the pines and myrtles fifty yards in front of them. When they made it to the small strip of sand that bordered the sound, they removed their shoes.

The sand was cool and moist, and Callie squeezed her toes together as she stepped toward the water.

Callie had seen the ocean only twice, including her honeymoon, though this was the first time she'd ever been among the creeks and inlets. When she was nine, she'd gone with her family to New Bern, North Carolina, to visit her Uncle Ben, Aunt Tita, and cousins Laura Jane and Barry. Ben drove them to the ocean at Morehead City, and it felt strange dipping her toes in water that wasn't ice-cold or fit to drink.

Samuel placed the blanket on the soft sand, cord grass remnants lifeless and limp in the sand behind them. The water rolled to the shore in tiny waves, twelve feet from where they sat. The water was calm, the color of soft sapphire. The shoreline was straight and narrow for almost one hundred yards, curving eastward toward Port Royal Sound before bending back again. They looked across the sound at the smooth skyline of dark, arrow-straight pines. The sky was clear except in the farthest reaches to the east, where clouds of dim red and soft purple cast a veil for the sun's entrance.

A single gull cried out as it flew along the shoreline. Within minutes, two more followed its path. Samuel and Callie sat shoulder to shoulder, much like they'd done that night by Samson's Creek. Callie wore denim pants, calf-length. Samuel rolled them above her kneecaps. He wore plaid shorts and a white T-shirt. He rubbed her foot with his, the sand moist and cool between them.

"This is absolutely beautiful," she said, lowering her head to his shoulder.

"Isn't it? I've never seen anything quite so peaceful outside Jefferson Mountain."

"This is quite an anniversary present." She reached and touched his chin, so familiar, so warm, and turned him toward her. "I love you." She kissed him softly, their lips parting slightly. She looked into his eyes as she pulled away, and he rubbed her face gently with his fingertips. He took hold of her earlobe and tugged.

"I know you do," he said in all seriousness.

"That wasn't the correct response. What you were supposed to do was to go into this long drawn-out speech about how you love me too."

"You don't say." He rubbed his chin and nodded while he looked out over the sound. "Maybe you need to coach me up on what to say next time. That way there won't be any mistakes or disappointed expectations."

"I can tell you what you better not expect later tonight."

"Uh-oh. Looks like I screwed this one up."

She pinched his arm. "You're dang right, mister."

"How about I make it up to you with this beautiful setting laid out in front of you?"

"We'll see."

As they looked out on the smooth waters, a pair of dolphins rose to the top, their charcoal-gray fins sloping downward until they disappeared from sight. Fifty feet they swam before rising to the top again.

"Why don't we make this the place we come every year for our anniversary?" Callie said, brushing her hair behind her ear.

"What about when we have children? Think we could bring them too?"

"Well, technically, we just did."

Samuel pulled away slightly, looking into her eyes to make sure she wasn't playing some kind of cruel joke. "You mean…?"

"Yep. I'm almost three months pregnant. I've been dying to tell you, but I wanted to wait until we went on our anniversary trip. So, happy anniversary."

Samuel stood up suddenly and looked out across the sound. He rubbed his thick hair with his hands, and tears filled his eyes.

Callie lowered her head to her knees. "I thought you would be happy to hear the news."

Samuel knelt and took her by the hands, looking into her eyes as if he had never seen anything more beautiful.

"This…" he began, and then he rubbed the tears from his eyes, "this is the greatest gift you could ever give me." He curved his hands around her face, tears appearing as their lips met. He pressed his cheek against hers. "God, I love you."

They walked along the edge of the water, hand in hand. Plans must be made. This was the beginning of a new world for them, a unique path set upon that no one else could travel save them. They walked toward the rising sun, conscious of a new being amongst them. They stopped and kissed again as if reaching for new depths for their souls to journey.

"So, do you have a preference?" Callie asked when they returned to the blanket.

"I know I'm supposed to say it doesn't matter. As long as we created it, and it's healthy, that's all that counts. But," he smiled, "I wouldn't mind if it was a girl. Could you imagine a little girl with your eyes, with your smile?"

"She'd be spoiled rotten. Which means I'll get tossed on the back burner like a simmering pot of beans."

"Well…maybe."

"I knew you'd feel this way. I've been picturing you walking along the creek, her tiny hand in yours, watching the trout running downstream."

"So it will be okay to teach her to fish?"

"Will she have a choice?"

"Not really."

"I wouldn't have it any other way."

Chapter Twenty-One

The maple leaves clung softly to the grass, flattened and formed into a bright carpet thickened by the dew. The backyard was a sharp contrast in colors, leaves draping a blanket of gold and orange under the four maples that were planted twenty feet apart in exact distance from each other like bedposts, the deep greens of the grass that rolled from the back porch up the hill to a row of mulberry bushes and Black-eyed Susans. Sarah watched as Kate chased Windy, her grandfather's golden retriever, around the yard, trying to grab the slippery tennis ball entrenched firmly in the dog's mouth.

Pete slipped around the side of the house unnoticed. He stood by a small white pine, watching Sarah smile as she encouraged Kate to catch the spry pup. Windy soon spotted Pete and eagerly ran to him. "Daddy," Kate screamed as she realized where Windy was headed. She ran into his arms, grabbing him tight while Windy bounced off his knee.

"Hey, sweetie. Are you and Windy having a good time?"

"Yes, sir. But she won't share her ball with me."

Pete took hold of Windy's collar. "Sit." She quickly placed her haunches to the ground, her tail wagging. Pete slipped her teeth apart and removed the ball. "Don't know why you want to play with this old thing. It's got puppy spit all over it. I bet she's chewed on a rabbit or a mouse today. You're playing with mouse germs, you know."

"Yuuuuuck," Kate yelled as she took off toward Sarah. Pete stood and smiled at Sarah, raising his hand in a quick wave. Sarah smiled too, and then caught Kate in her arms. "Daddy's here."

"Yes, he is, sweetheart. Yes, he is."

Sarah's mother opened the back door. "Kate, want to help me lick the spoon from the chocolate cake I'm fixing to bake?" She noticed Pete standing in the yard. "Hello, Pete."

Pete nodded. "Hello, Mrs. Butler. Don't I get to lick the spoon?"

"Only if you get to it before this tornado does," she said as Kate flew up the three wood steps leading to the porch. She closed the door behind her and the yard was peaceful again. Pete walked up to Sarah and took her by the hands.

"Pete, there's something I need to say." Before she could speak again, he slipped his arms around her, pulling her to him. He placed his lips to hers, softly, and she moved her arms around his shoulders. They kissed as if it were their first. Pete watched Sarah, her eyes closed, so sweet and innocent. Gently, he kissed the corners of her mouth before softly kissing her cheeks. She opened her eyes, and Pete saw a tear begin to fall. He wiped it away with his finger, and he touched her face while he stared into her eyes.

"I am so sorry," he said. "I've been a terrible, selfish husband. I've neglected you and Kate and I've let my pursuit of a writing career take control of my life."

"I'm sorry too. I told you I would support you as you tried to make it as a writer, and I wasn't there when it got tough. You are such a good writer, and I believe in you. It's just a matter of time before you sign a book deal, and soon everyone will get to see how wonderful you are.

They'll see your tender heart. I don't know if I'm quite ready to share it with the world, but I'll learn to."

"You and Kate are the ones who have my heart. Now and always."

"Let's go home," she said and she kissed him softly on the lips.

***

"You gonna sleep all day?" the familiar voice asked. Samuel opened his eyes, glanced to the side of his bed, and shook his head, though he flashed a quick smile.

"Porter, no matter how old and ugly I get, you're always a little older and uglier."

"Don't I know it." Porter sat in the chair beside the bed. "I've played second fiddle to you for a lifetime. Only way I married Earline is because you'd done been hitched to Callie. I remember on our weddin' night Earline admittin' she'd tossed in the towel on you. Said you was a taken man, and she may as well accept it and move on."

"You're a liar."

"Well, she didn't exactly *say* it, but I know that's what was goin' through her mind." They looked out the window at the pond for a moment. Neither knew what to say. Strange for two lifelong friends who seemed to read each other's mind. "Can I get you anything?"

"No. Just sit a spell with me." They again looked at the pond in silence. "Where did our life go? Other than my time in the war, life seems just a blur."

"Good question. I still think of myself as a young punk, searching for trouble along the back roads."

"Look in the mirror. That'll cure you thinkin' you're a young anything. We've reached the age where it ain't safe to go to the park for fear the pigeons will light on our shoulders."

"Yep. That's what we've been reduced to, statues."

"I want to ask you somethin'."

"What is it?"

"When I'm gone, Gabby's gonna need help with sellin' the house, and there'll be bills to be paid."

"Don't worry. Earline and I will help Gabby in any way possible. She's like our own child, and we'll be there for her as long as we're alive and kickin'."

"I appreciate that. You've been as true a friend as there is in this world." Samuel nodded after he spoke those words. Tears began to form in the corners of his eyes. His lower lip quivered.

Porter placed his hand on Samuel's shoulder. "You know, I've loved you like a brother. All the memories, tucked away. Sometimes when it's quiet at home, or I'm walking along the creek, lookin' at this beautiful world God gave us, I'll think of things we did together, of the fun we had together. And I want you to know what joy our friendship still brings me."

***

Pete removed the marinated salmon from the refrigerator and wrapped sweet potatoes for the oven. Kate was not a fish lover, and had requested a hot dog with ketchup. Sarah opened the bottle of Merlot and poured it into a decanter to let it breathe. Kate played with two dolls at the kitchen table. While Pete rubbed marinade on the salmon, Sarah rubbed her fingers along his back, her head leaning against his shoulders. Pete kissed her on top of her head.

After dinner was finished, Kate put on a talent show of sorts with Miss Emily, singing made-up songs while doing pirouettes and twirling her hands above her head with Miss Emily dangling in midair. Sarah was snuggled up against Pete's shoulder, sipping wine and trying to keep from laughing when Kate lifted her skirt to bow.

"It's getting to be bedtime," Sarah said. "We better wind it down."

"No, Mommy. Let me stay up."

"How about if I tell you a bedtime story?" Pete asked. "It's big news about Goldilocks. You don't know this, but Goldilocks *hated* porridge. She puked at the thought of the stuff. She got caught recently slipping into the three bears' refrigerator, sucking down Yoo-hoos like there was no tomorrow. It made Papa Bear so mad, he went into shock. He was pulling his fur out by the fistfuls. Had to go to the animal hospital. It's an unbelievable story. But I guess you don't want to hear about that."

"Yeah, tell me about the bears!"

Pete slipped from the couch and squatted, and Kate hopped on his back, locking her arms around his neck. "Give Mommy a kiss."

Soon Pete was telling the tale of how, before she was caught with the chocolate drink, Goldilocks had wandered upstairs in the bears' house, checking the chest of drawers for Twinkies and Ho Ho's.

After Pete finished the story, and Kate was fast asleep, he stepped into his dark bedroom. As he reached for the light switch, he noticed a slender red candle burning on the nightstand beside the bed. The flame of the candle danced about in random fashion, casting soft pockets of light against the Spanish-red wall. Silhouettes moved slightly on the wall, cast by the lamp and the tall bedpost. A path of rose petals led from the doorway to the bed.

Sarah sat on the edge of the bed wearing a black teddy. Like a vision in the darkness, she waited. Her hair was shaped close to her eyes, as if playfully veiling what waited for Pete. In her hand she held a slender glass of wine. The flickering flame cast both light and shadow across Sarah's face, and her dark brown eyes caught the flame, turning them a sensual shade of red. She gazed at Pete with a look that told him she had secrets within her. Secrets she wanted to share with him. Secrets meant only for their bedroom.

She reached out and took him by the hand, gently touching his fingertips. He stepped toward her, and she placed her hand behind his neck, pulling him toward her lips.

"You look absolutely stunning," he said, and she could tell by the look in his eyes that he was pleased with what he saw. She leaned forward to kiss him, her eyes still locked on his. She wanted him to feel her love, and she wanted, needed, to feel his. She wanted him to know she was his for always.

Her lips were dark cherry, and her teeth sparkled when her lips parted, moving closer and closer to Pete's waiting mouth. She touched his lips with hers, softly, slowly, backing away for a brief second before repeating the process. She stood, kissing his cheek, her lips moving across his lips to his other cheek. Her arms circled his neck, crossing at the wrists. Her lips found his again, and she kissed him firmly, a kiss laced with unmistakable passion. She pulled him to her as she fell slowly onto the bed. He used his elbows for support, so he could kiss her about the lips and neck. They continued to kiss, and cast shadows along the wall as if two shapes were merging into one.

Sarah pushed lightly against Pete's shoulder, and he slid his body to her side. She continued until his back was flat on the bed and she was above him. She was on all fours, her knees touching the outsides of his legs. She rubbed her hands along his midsection, crisscrossing her fingers while she bit her lower lip.

Her heart rate escalated, and by the thumping of his chest, so had his. The kisses became harder and more intense, and Pete felt heat rising between them as he pulled her toward him. She grabbed him tightly behind the neck while he held a firm grip on her backside.

By candlelight they turned the angst and frustration of bitter days into a rekindling of love and commitment.

Now replete, in his arms, by his side, he pulled her tightly to him. Her tears fell on his shoulder. He squeezed, reassurance that he was there for her, forever. Within the warmth of each other's body heat, they drifted off to sleep.

Chapter Twenty-Two

Samuel tossed about in his sleep. He battled bouts of body chills that shook him to the core, followed by internal flames that left his pajamas soaked with sweat. He faded in and out of sleep so much that he had no compass point to distinguish between minutes or hours, whether night had just fallen, or if the sun was just over the horizon of Shady Mountain. Blackie struggled to sleep as well, lifting his head each time Samuel moaned, each time he moved. Though Samuel's sleep was light, he found himself caught in a vivid dream.

In the dream he found himself walking alongside someone whose face he could not see. Not that the face was covered or hidden, but that he simply chose to look at the scene unfolding before him. Together they walked along a corridor, poorly lit, where children moved about like students of some cryptic school. When the person beside him spoke, it was the voice of a female, a voice from somewhere long ago. The voice spoke with knowledge of his parents, of Bert and Anna. As if she were some otherworld broker who dealt in souls, she told him she had arranged a meeting with his family. As they walked, the children scattered in front of them into rooms that were not classrooms but long dark passages.

Soon the pair walked outdoors, and they were in a garden surrounded by sandstone walls draped with ivy. They sat on a white granite bench, and there was no breeze, no sun, and no sky above them. The air contained neither chill nor warmth, though Samuel felt at ease with the unknown sensation. As they sat, the stranger told of the ways of the world Samuel had entered. She told him his family was in close proximity, and they had been notified he had come. Like a nurse talking to someone waiting to see a patient in a hospital, she explained the proceedings. As she spoke, Samuel looked into her face. Her skin was soft and pink, and her eyes were a pale bluish color he had never seen before. As he watched her speak, he saw a screen lowering behind her. Like a projector in some ancient classroom, a reel-to-reel film began to play behind her in the air.

Samuel saw mountains, dark and cold. The slopes were jagged mountain ranges whose crests were lined with soldiers, their bodies pierced by bayonets, forming a human fence of death. He looked down, and he felt the cold rifle in his bloodstained hands. He threw the rifle to the flower-covered ground at his feet, and the flowers curled and turned to fire. In the fire he saw arms reaching up to him, and a multitude of faces with gnashing teeth, screeching in pain. Again he looked at the screen and there were more mountains. At the base of the mountains were meadows of wheat, knee-high and golden. The wind was blowing gently, and people stood around tombstones darkened by time. They began to sing, though it was music Samuel had never heard.

As they sang the headstones began to crumble. In unison, bodies began to rise from the graves that lay hidden by the stones and the wheat fields. The people began to shout, and Samuel could see tears of joy in their eyes. As the woman beside Samuel continued to speak, he saw the figures of his mother and father moving toward him on the screen. Samuel tried to speak but could not. His parents were holding hands, and soon they were standing behind the girl. She smiled at Samuel, and in an instant she was gone.

Samuel stood and reached for his mother's extended arms, but they faded to gray as he neared. He reached his hand to his father's face, but he could not feel him. And so they simply smiled at him. Their feet were bare and they hovered just off the cobblestone floor of the garden. Samuel began to cry, and his mother tried to wipe away his tears. Again she couldn't make contact, though Samuel felt a familiar warmth when her smoky hand brushed by his face. He was finally able to speak, and he told them how he had missed them. Though they said no words, they told him with their eyes that they understood him.

Within a moment Bert and Anna were by their sides, not grown but as small children. Anna held a white flower, and she tried to place it in Samuel's hand, but he could not take hold of it. He knelt to hug her, and she could only shake her head. She pointed behind her on the screen, and nodded at him. He looked to the screen and saw Callie, in a white dress, ankle-length, sitting by a small stream. Leaning on her elbow, her hair cascading around her shoulders, she flashed him a melancholy smile and beckoned him with her finger.

A small, elderly man walked up and began raising the projector screen. Samuel pleaded for him to stop, but the man would not. As the screen became smaller and smaller, Samuel saw his family return to the fields, the long wheat stalks blowing about them as they walked to the tombstones. Callie rose from beside the creek, and she floated in midair. She touched her fingers to her lips and then blew the kiss lovingly toward Samuel.

When Samuel awoke, Gabby was stroking his hair. "It's okay, Daddy. It's okay."

Chapter Twenty-Three

Signs along the hillsides around Carter Springs told of winter soon to come. The leaves were falling at a hurried pace, and pines were becoming more visible as the hardwoods turned into pale colors of gray and brown, their limbs looking barren and lonely along the hillsides. Morning greeted the sun with fields of frost. A smoky mist hovered above the fast waters of Birch Tree Creek, with unfamiliar shapes rising above the stream like ghosts from a world not seen before. Snow patches were visible on the peaks of Iron Mountain in the distance.

Gabby worked hurriedly in the kitchen, stirring a pot of grits while two eggs fried in the pan. When she slid the eggs from the pan onto a plate, she stepped away from the stove to see if Samuel had awakened. He lay in the bed in the parlor, and though asleep, he looked uncomfortable. She had noticed him sleeping more and more as the days wore on. He would wake for breakfast, but rarely before nine. For a man who had spent a lifetime of mornings waiting for the sun's appearance, sleep had become the only way to ease the pain. Breakfast had become the only meal of substance for him. He'd pick over his lunch and dinner. He was losing weight, a pound or two per week.

The phone rang and Gabby leaped for the receiver so as not to wake her father.

"Gabby?" the voice asked.

"Yes?"

"Hey, this is Pete. How are you?"

"Okay." She could not hide her sadness. She felt guilty that Pete was clouding her mind. She knew what they'd done was wrong, but she couldn't help but long to be the one he sought, the one he longed to kiss.

She had to stay strong. She knew what had happened couldn't happen again.

"How's your dad?"

"He's sleeping right now. I'm getting ready to wake him so he can eat."

"If he feels up to it, will you have him call me? Only if he's up to it."

"Sure thing." A pause of silence.

"Gabby?"

"Yes?" she said with a bit of apprehension.

"I want you to know that I feel bad about the apple orchard. Not what we shared that day. That was amazing, and I'll never forget it. But I know I should have been stronger."

Her heart sank, though she knew deep inside he was right. "It's okay, Pete. It's okay."

"You sure?"

"Yes. What happened at the orchard *was* incredible. But you have your family to think about. It's the right thing to do."

She ended the call, held the phone to her bosom, and cried softly.

***

It was just past one when Pete returned home from the grocery store. He had picked up two nice pieces of New York Strip that he planned to grill, and of course chicken for Kate. He had just placed the grocery bag on the kitchen counter when the phone rang.

"Pete," the raspy voice said. "Gabby said you wanted me to call."

"Yes, sir. How are you feeling?"

"You a doctor?"

Pete laughed. "Mr. Gable, I wanted to see if there was anything more you'd like to add to your story. I've got a lot written, but don't want to leave out anything that you might want me to know about." Pete tried to sound as if he was being completely unselfish in his motives, and he was, for the most part.

"Don't know. Think I might have said all I care to say. Besides, I don't want to keep pulling you away from your wife and daughter."

"Well, I'm glad you mentioned my wife. She wants to meet you."

"That a fact?"

"Yes, sir."

"Well, the mornin's are 'bout the only times I feel pretty decent. Want to come tomorrow? 'Bout nine-thirty?"

"Perfect. We'll see you then."

***

When Pete and Sarah stepped onto the porch, Gabby opened the door. "Come on in," she said. "Daddy's gettin' anxious."

They entered the doorway. "Gabby, this is my wife, Sarah." Gabby extended her hand, doing what Pete thought was a great job of hiding the hurt she must feel meeting the person who owned Pete's heart.

"Nice to meet you."

"It's so nice to meet you. Pete has told me so much about you and your dad. I'm glad I finally get the chance to meet you both."

In the parlor, Samuel's bed was raised to place him in a sitting position. He wore white pajamas with blue pin stripes. A robe lay draped across the blanket that covered his feet. Gabby had placed two chairs, one on either side of the bed. Blackie rotated between them both, holding his head near their knees so they would pet him.

"Daddy, Pete and his wife are here."

Sarah extended her hand. "Hello, Mr. Gable. How are you feeling?" Pete cringed.

"Call me Samuel," he said in a soft voice. "I'm doin' all right."

Pete looked at Samuel with a mock expression of surprise and disgust. How nice it would have been if Pete had received that answer from Samuel just once. Gabby smiled solemnly at Pete and excused herself from the room.

"I need to apologize for takin' up so much of Pete's time," Samuel said, taking hold of Sarah's hand.

"No need to apologize. You have made quite an impact on Pete. I can see it. He thinks you're pretty special."

"Ahh," he waved his hand into nothingness. "Let me tell you somethin', Sarah." Samuel seemed oblivious that Pete was in the room, and Pete could tell Samuel was quickly capturing Sarah's heart. "Don't ever get sick. I've tried it. Don't like it. I'm ready to give it up and lay my hook in the creek."

"Well, let's get the poles then," Sarah replied and smiled.

"Maybe tomorrow. Are you a fisherman?"

"I eat fish. Is that close enough?"

Sarah spotted the picture on the end table of Samuel and Callie. She took hold of it and held it close to her face, wiping a thin layer of dust from the glass covering the black-and-white photo. "She was beautiful. And you were a hottie. Where was this taken?"

"Out back. After church. Easter Sunday."

"How long were you married?"

"Twenty-seven years. Flew by like snowflakes in a blizzard."

"I can tell by the way you're all snuggled up, you were crazy about her." Sarah put the picture back in its place. "She must have been pretty young when she—" Sarah looked sheepishly down toward her feet. "I'm sorry."

"No need to apologize. She *was* young. Forty-nine when she died."

"Oh, my. That's so sad."

"Please sit down. Well, Pete, maybe this is the time. Got your recorder?"

Pete removed it from his jacket pocket. "Always."

"Turn it on, then."

***

July, 1973

The afternoon heat was building, chasing the coolness from the shadows of even the most remote backwoods. The thermometer had eclipsed ninety degrees for six consecutive days. Humidity hung heavy in the air, painting the sky with a haze which hid the sun, casting a dimness whereby the sun could have been moving from north to south and no one would have known the difference. Activity around Jefferson Mountain was limited. Along the pastures across from the Gable house, on the far side of Birch Tree Creek, cows knelt, knees folded under them, in patches of shade from poplars and maples that ran alongside wire fences.

Callie placed five glass bowls in front of her on the kitchen counter. Strawberries filled each bowl, and she squeezed honey from a plastic bear-shaped container. She scooped vanilla ice cream on top of the strawberries and honey before topping it off with fresh blueberries. "Gabby, how about you tell Caleb and Matthew that I have something to cool 'em down?" She wrapped one of the bowls with waxed paper and put it in the refrigerator so Samuel could eat it when he came home from work.

Gabby, who was home for the week, tried to keep her mind off the distance between her and her husband Bobby. They had only been married three months, and he'd been shipped off to Germany two months into the marriage. Other than a two-week furlough at Christmas, she wouldn't see him again until next summer when she would fly to Europe to meet up with him. She didn't want to stay alone in her small two-bedroom house and thought she'd take advantage of a chance to spend time with her family.

Caleb and Matthew, Caleb's high school friend, were trying to coax a blue carp to the surface of the pond, hoping to snag his thick skin with a treble hook. They had caught the beast, which looked to be a fifteen pounder, the previous week. It was an epic battle as the big fish parted the pond like a speedboat when it raced to the far edges of the shallow water. It had taken almost twenty minutes to land him, with Caleb fighting most of the battle. After a quick Polaroid shot to commemorate the occasion, they'd slipped the fish back into the pond. So now it was Matthew's turn to catch the large fish, and Caleb tossed crumbled cornbread onto the water to entice the carp.

Caleb glanced at the hazy blanket of pale gray above the mountaintops and scratched his itchy nose with the back of his hand. He wore cut-off blue jeans, frayed and thigh-length. His Steppenwolf T-shirt was a size too big. His black Chuck Taylors soaked in the heat like an incubator. Matthew was barefoot, wearing green denim shorts and no shirt.

"Caleb," Gabby called from the porch, "Mom fixed you boys somethin' to eat."

"Hang on. We're about to land Moby Dick."

"That fish ain't goin' anywhere. Come eat."

"Come on, Matthew. We'll catch him later."

The smell of sweat followed close behind the boys when they walked into the kitchen. "Geesh," Gabby said. "When's the last time you showered?"

"We're conserving water."

"I'll personally throw you boys in the creek if I have to," Callie said. "No call for not keeping yourself decent and presentable."

"We're presentable," Caleb argued, nudging Matthew with his elbow.

Callie had made a bowl for herself without the ice cream, and the four sat at the oak table in the kitchen.

"Mom, you want to ride into town?" asked Gabby. "I heard Miller's is going out of business. They're selling their clothes at some ridiculous discount."

"I heard they are just closing down for the fall," Callie said. "Then they're going to reopen near Elizabethton after the first of the year."

"Well, whatever the reason, let's jump on it while we have the chance."

"I don't see why not. Besides, I want to stop at Vernon Hinson's shop. He's framing a picture of the Villa Verde monument. I had it made into a painting for your father. Going to give it to him for his birthday next week."

***

Caleb and Matthew grew tired of trying to hook the carp, unable to coax it to the top. The boys were enjoying their last summer of fun together. Caleb was heading to East Tennessee State in August, and Matthew was heading to Montana with his cousin to work on a ranch for a year while he figured out what he wanted to do with his life.

Caleb became restless and felt like searching for mischief. He was known to carry out pranks around the holler, but since outhouses had become obsolete, he couldn't quite follow in his father's footsteps in that department. He had pissed off his share of folks in Carter Springs, but nothing that would keep them mad for long.

The pair walked to the barn. "C'mon," Caleb said. "Got somethin' to show you." Behind three bales of hay was what looked like a corpse.

"What the …?" Matthew said as they stepped closer to the body.

Caleb lifted the limp body by the hand. "Don't this thing look real?"

"Man, it looks like a dead man surer than shinola. Where'd you get it?"

"Harold Lowe stole it out of a truck when the carnival came to town last year. A magician used it as a prop. I borrowed it from Harold."

"What are you gonna do with it?"

"C'mon and I'll show you."

They walked down the dirt road toward the main highway. Caleb carried the dummy over his shoulder, and Matthew had a thick tan rope that was bundled tightly. They crossed State Road 84 and stood under a massive poplar with branches that stretched out over the edge of the blacktop. Caleb began climbing the tree, using a fence post to jump to a low-hanging limb. He pulled himself up and along the limb, which hung close to the road.

"Tie the rope around the neck," Caleb said while straddling the limb. "Then toss me the end of the rope."

Matthew tied a double knot, pulled on it twice to make sure it was secure, and tossed the unused end of the rope skyward. After three tries, Caleb caught Matthew's toss. He lifted the rubber body until it hung suspended from the limb, fifteen feet above the ground. The body hung limp and lifeless. It had khaki pants and a faded flannel shirt. Around its neck was a red-and-black kerchief.

After Caleb climbed down from the tree, they ran across the highway, hiding under a small bridge that allowed Birch Tree Creek to flow westward. The pair stood at the edge of the bank so they could see cars making their way from town. Caleb pulled himself up so he could briefly see the dummy. "It's amazin' how real that thing looks," he said. "Somebody's gonna freak out when they see it hangin' there in the tree."

"Most people throw water balloons at cars. You hang dead guys from the trees."

"Shhh, get down, here comes a car."

A blue Ford pickup rounded the curve, heading for the bridge. As it approached, the body twirled slightly from the tree, though there was no breeze to speak of. The tires on the truck squealed as it came to a quick halt. An elderly man in faded overalls, donning a white beard that held flakes of tobacco in it, exited the truck, not bothering to pull off the road. He left the door open and ran in hobbling fashion to the hanging corpse. As he made his way to the tree, he squinted his eyes in disbelief.

"Good Godamighty," the man said. As he spoke a spray of pebbles hit him on his boots and his pant leg.

"Get out of the road, you old fart!" came from beneath the bridge. The man jumped so that his knees nearly buckled.

He turned toward Caleb and Matthew. "You stupid boys. That ain't funny. You coulda give me a heart attack." The old man lectured them for a few moments before walking to his truck and driving off. Caleb and Matthew laughed for several minutes before resuming their spot under the bridge. The boys again positioned themselves to where they could see the highway, specifically the turn in the road.

The road was quiet, and the sound of the creek pushing fast over the rocks provided the only noise on a day where the heat seemed to put the mountain in an eerie state of deadness. The boys were getting restless, not to mention hot and sweaty. Matthew stepped out and looked across the highway.

"Oh, crap, the dummy fell," Matthew said. "It's lyin' in the road."

"We need to move it before somebody runs over it and busts it to smitherines," Caleb said as he stepped out from beneath the bridge. As they ran toward the road, a green four-door sedan rounded the curve. The vehicle approached the mangled dummy.

"Mom!" Gabby yelled from the passenger seat. "There's someone in the road!" Callie slammed on the brakes, holding tightly to the wheel as the car came to within thirty feet of the rubber body. The car had been traveling nearly fifty miles per hour, and the brakes were locking up as she tried to stop. When she realized she couldn't avoid the body, she pulled hard to the right. The car began to slide off the road and then flipped twice in a soft bank of clover before landing upside down in the creek.

Caleb and Matthew tore across the road to the vehicle. The back tires rotated in squeaky fashion, and smoke came from the underside of the engine block. The rocks were thick and scattered along the stream, and the body of the car was battered. The boys ran into the cold water and looked through the cracked glass on the passenger side. The roof of the car had collapsed and become separated from the windshield. Gabby was unconscious, upside down. She bled from her forehead, and her hair was quickly becoming thick with matted blood.

Water began filling the inside of the car, and the boys pulled hard at the door, which was bent inward at the middle. Gabby stirred a bit, and was moaning something indistinguishable. Caleb pushed his foot against the back door and strained as he pulled with all his might. Finally, the door opened. The boys took hold of her arm and shoulder and slid her out on her back. They carried her to the bank, her dark terrycloth shirt skirting the water as they carried her limp body. When they turned her over on the bank, Caleb realized it was Gabby. "My God!"

Caleb jumped back in the water, splashing and stumbling across the small pools of water as he ran to the driver's side. The bent roof had wrapped itself along the edge of the window of the driver's door, so when Caleb yanked, the door wouldn't budge.

"Mom!" he yelled. "Oh, God. Mom!" He began smacking the glass with his open palm. Through the cracked window he saw her stirring as the water reached her hairline. He began kicking at the door, and the car began to rock. He circled to the passenger door and lowered himself in. "Hold on, Mom. I'm gonna get you out. You're gonna be okay." He pulled on her shoulders, taking hold of her pastel-colored blouse. She winced in pain. Her legs were trapped by the crumpled steering wheel. Water continued to pour in. The waters that had been a friend to Caleb since he was a child were quickly becoming his enemy.

Callie opened her eyes slightly, her chest heaving as the icy water surrounded her head. Caleb saw her eyes open wide, and he could see the fear within them. Matthew had come around to the driver's door, and pounded a rock against the glass to break it. Matthew reached in and tried to help Caleb free her legs. The water was now to Callie's nose, and she raised her head up in bursts, gasping for breath.

"Hold on, Mom. I'm not gonna let anything happen to you. Move your feet. Help us. Move your legs."

She kicked frantically, her right foot still stuck behind the gas pedal.

The water was now to her upper lip, and Matthew held her head up with his hand behind her neck. "Help me, Caleb!" she screamed, water spraying from her mouth. Caleb saw her struggle to breathe as the water pushed inside her mouth and her nose, and she grabbed hold of Caleb's T-shirt. She kicked her leg and pushed downward. A gush of water poured in, and it charged into her open mouth. She gagged and coughed, and she moved her shoulders and waist about like a fish trapped in a net. Her eyes were large with the look that she had awoken from a nightmare not knowing where she was.

"Hold her head up!" Caleb cried out. "Keep her head above the water."

"I'm tryin'! The car is fillin' up too fast. Keep pulling on her legs."

"Momma!" Gabby yelled from the bank. "Oh, God. Help! Somebody help!" She tried to stand, but when she put pressure on her right foot, pain shot through her leg and she fell to the bank. She began to cry as her shouts fell unheeded on the surrounding fields and the stillness of the hot summer afternoon. Even the nearby cattle paid no mind to her screams.

The water was now to Callie's chin, and her head began thrashing furiously. Matthew looked as though he were tiring as he tried to keep his hands under Callie's head. He pushed upward above the water line as she continued to frantically move about. Bursts of air pushed from her mouth as her lungs were beginning to fill with water. As Caleb continued to pull, crying and yelling with all the might in his being, Callie's movements began to slow.

Caleb grabbed her shirt and it began to tear. Within seconds she became still, making Caleb pull even harder. Her eyes became still as if she was staring at something far off in the distance. "No!" Caleb screamed as the water was now approaching her neck. "*Momma!*"

"Caleb! The car's fillin' up. You gotta get out."

"I can't leave her. I'll get her out. Hold on, Momma." He pulled at her and she began to feel heavy and limp.

"Now, Caleb!" Matthew jumped to the passenger side and began pulling at Caleb's shirt. "It's too late. C'mon, man. C'mon!" He pulled with all his might until he pulled Caleb from the car.

"No!" Caleb cried, trying to get to the front windshield. "No!"

Gabby sobbed, her chest heaving as she lay facedown on the soft clover. Caleb began hitting the car with his fist and blood poured from his knuckles. Their sorrows, their cries carried downstream into the valley, riding along the mountain creek like fallen leaves cast by cruel winter winds.

***

The heat wave subsided. The sky was solid blue, and there was a slight breeze blowing from the north. Cars lined behind each other like metal dominoes, winding along both sides of Gunter's Road. The sun was straight up, twelve o'clock position. A single holly tree stood in isolation on the hillside at the corner of the small graveyard, providing a spot of shade for the gravedigger as he watched the ceremony begin.

Samuel led the solemn parade, Gabby holding tightly to his arm. Most of the crowd gathered under the maroon tent that covered the hole that would become Callie's final resting place. Others walked behind Samuel and Gabby, some in pairs, some as families huddled near each other as if they were worried they might lose something precious should they not cling tightly. Caleb walked, head down, his face emotionless, like a man who had just been carved from stone. The family sat in a row of folding chairs. Samuel hated the feel of the green carpet under his feet. Strangely, he wondered why the carpet was necessary. It just seemed stupid.

Reverend Jim Speagle stood in front of the casket. He held a black Bible in his hand. He read the 23rd Psalm. "The Lord is my shepherd," he began, his voice soothing yet strong, "I shall not want."

As he read aloud, Samuel gazed behind the preacher at the smoky gray backdrop of Jefferson Mountain. In the Philippines, at night when he was lying in foxholes, the smell of war all around him, he would picture the sight of Jefferson Mountain at sunrise.

"Thou preparest a table before me in the presence of mine enemies; thou anointest my head with oil; my cup runneth over."

The mountain was as much a part of Samuel as his arms, his legs, and his heart. Life began there for him; life would end there.

"Surely goodness and mercy shall follow me all the days of my life, and I will dwell in the house of the Lord forever."

There were soft sounds of women crying and sniffles in random order around the gravesite. Junior Adams stood in front of the holly tree, and the solemn strains of "Amazing Grace" poured from his mandolin. Gabby placed her head on her father's shoulder, searching for comfort in the one person who provided security like no other. Her tears flowed, wetting Samuel's dark coat. As the music played, cows grazed in a field below the holly tree. Three crows cawed in the distance as they flew toward Jefferson Mountain. Among the mourners were the graves of those who'd died as long as one hundred and twenty-five years before, marked with small tombs faded by time.

When Junior finished his song, the preacher bowed his head to pray. The mountainside grew still as she offered up her sanctified grounds for Callie Gable. Though the mountain seemed to stop in its existence of the day to accept another soul, it gave a silent reminder that many had come before. Each with a different journey, but a common bond in the destiny they shared, the final consequence the same for them all in the end. The tombstones were markers of previous generations, and a reminder that destiny waited for those yet to come.

The line of well-wishers and grievers was long, offering condolences to the family who sat in wobbly folding chairs, seven feet from Callie's casket. Samuel shook each hand offered, accepted kisses on the cheek stoically, his only response a slight nod. His eyes tried to look to Jefferson Mountain, though the steady parade of mourners hindered his view.

Family members and friends soon set off to the Gable house. Fried chicken and pork roast, vegetable casseroles of every kind, breads, and desserts — all the normal fare for feeding the sad souls of those who'd lost their loved one.

Since words could only say so much, food offered the only other way to console.

As the crowd thinned, the hearse waited with doors open to carry the family home. Caleb and Gabby stood outside the tent, talking to the few folks who remained. Samuel sat quietly, looking at the mahogany prison cell that held the love of his life.

***

Two weeks had passed since the funeral, and Gabby convinced her boss to let her take leave without pay so she could be there for Samuel and Caleb. Samuel decided the best thing to do was return to work at the lumber mill. It was all he knew to do. The men who worked with him were sympathetic, but they backed away, thinking he needed space. He quietly went about the day, doing his job, until it was time to go home.

Gabby cooked and tried to take care of the house like her mother had. The dinner table was deathly quiet each evening. Caleb began taking his food to the porch. Samuel had not spoken to him since the accident. What was there to say? How could he put into words that it was okay that he, though by accident, had killed his own mother?

It was a Saturday evening, three weeks since the funeral. Summer's heat had loosened its grip, the shadows chasing away the golden tint of the valley. Samuel worked a backhoe along a fence that ran along the south side of the pond, parallel to the road. Weeds and grasses were waist-high, and the fence was hardly visible from the road. It had not rained since the funeral, and dust kicked up high and thick as the backhoe ground up the earthen floor. Caleb returned from fishing Sinking Creek. He'd asked Matthew if he wanted to come, but Matthew excused himself. He felt as responsible for Callie's death as Caleb, and he was keeping to himself most of the time.

Caleb walked around the back of the house to a gray table. It had a small drain in the center with cutting boards around it. He placed three trout on the table and pulled his knife out from a sheath tied to his belt. He began scaling and gutting the fish, washing the remains down the drain and into a metal pail. He thought the fish would make a nice dinner for the three of them. He felt good in a way that he was doing something to contribute to the family. He scrubbed the fish inside and out until they were clean and ready for the frying pan. He walked into the kitchen, placed the fish on a platter, and began seasoning them with pepper and oregano.

Samuel walked in and took a glass from the cupboard. He filled it with water from the sink and looked out the window.

"Dad, I caught some trout. Should make for a good meal." Samuel took another sip and stared out the window. "These look like good ones. A lot of meat. I just finished seasoning it."

"You go ahead. I don't care for any."

"Oh." Caleb turned the fish with a metal spatula. "I know trout is your favorite, so I thought it'd be nice to have it tonight."

"No. Don't want any."

"Okay. I'll freeze it so you can have it later. Tomorrow, maybe?"

"Are you listening? *I don't want any damn fish.*" Samuel set the empty glass upside down in the sink.

"Yes, sir. Some other time then."

"No. No other time. I don't want the fish. I don't want to eat in this house. I don't want to be anywhere near this place. Everywhere I look, it's a memory slappin' me in the face. A constant reminder that she's never gonna walk through this house again. A reminder that we'll never hear her laugh. Never cry. Never anything."

Samuel pushed the screen door open with his foot and stepped out into the yard.

***

The car was deathly quiet as Pete and Sarah drove home from the Gable home. Sarah wiped the corners of her eyes with a tissue. Pete bit on his lower lip while he glanced about the valley. He couldn't hide the guilt he felt for having Samuel unravel the mystery of Caleb's exile. He'd assumed that Callie had passed away from an illness.

Two teenaged girls, decked in leather vests, rode horses along the side of the highway. One wore a brown cowboy hat, the other wore one of tan. They smiled and waved toward Pete's car as they passed, but he couldn't force himself to wave back.

Chapter Twenty-Four

Eight days had passed since Pete and Sarah listened to Samuel tell the story of Callie's death. Pete took on an offer from *Appalachian Trail* magazine, writing about a blind man from Abington who was preparing to hike the two-thousand-plus mile trail. Other than that, Pete continued writing the tale of Samuel Gable. He worked hard during the day, but as five o'clock approached he would step away from his computer to prepare dinner and spend time with Kate and Sarah. He was determined not to let his passion for becoming a successful writer get in the way of being the best husband and father he could be.

At bedtime Pete would entertain Kate with wacky tales of how Bert and Ernie left Sesame Street to open a windsurfing business in Miami. He spun yarns telling how Barney the Dinosaur convinced Baby Bop to start a hip-hop career. Kate's favorite was the one where the Three Little Pigs lived in a double-wide, passing on the opportunity for a brick home because of the satellite dish that came complimentary with the trailer.

Sarah read more of Pete's work, encouraging him and pointing out gently when she thought he had written something that wasn't up to his standards. Like Pete, she wanted every paragraph, every sentence, every word the best it could be.

***

One Thursday night, almost nine o'clock, Pete lay beside Kate. Miss Emily was squeezed snugly in her arms, the doll's legs and arms hanging limply across her chest. She wore a white nightgown stitched in pink along the edges of the sleeves. Her soft blond hair was bunched under her head against the pillow.

"Did you know that the Care Bears used to work at Mickey's Garage?" Pete asked, his face stone-straight and serious. His arms were folded behind his head.

"Nuh-uh," she said and laughed, "they never did."

"It's the truth."

"When? I never saw them there."

"They didn't work there long. It was right before you were born. They had trouble doing things like changing flat tires and pumping gas. You know, life is tough when you don't have thumbs. They kept dropping tools and stuff." Kate's laughter echoed down the hall. Her midsection shook like a gelatin mold. "The only things they were good at was knocking the top off of the trash can and opening oil cans with their teeth."

"You're making this up, Daddy. They never worked there."

"Cheer Bear was the slacker of the bunch. He liked to climb in the back seat of the cars on the racks. He'd take naps up there. When he would wake up he'd throw empty jars of honey at customers."

She cackled. "No way! They're pretend bears anyway."

Pete continued on, shaking his head as he related the sad saga. "Poor Cheer Bear. Who knows where life might have taken him if he hadn't dropped out of bear school. I heard he got a job with the carnival guessing people's weight until he got fired for drinking root beer while on the job."

Kate covered her mouth with her doll to mute her laughter. "You're making this up."

"And now he sits in rehab, lonely and dejected. *Cheer Bear*? I think not."

"He's not in rehab. He's not real!"

Pete began tickling Kate's stomach. "Are you callin' me a liar?" She rolled back and forth, trying to loosen her father's grip. Their laughter drowned out the ringing of the phone.

"Pete," Sarah called from the kitchen. "Phone's for you. I think it's Gabby."

"Hang on, sweetie. Be right back."

Pete left Kate's bedroom, and as he entered the kitchen he took the phone from Sarah. "Hello."

"Hi, Pete."

"Hey there. How are you?"

Pause. "It's Daddy."

***

The parking lot was dotted with cars. Visiting hours had been over for almost an hour. An ambulance's lights flashed in front of the entrance of the emergency room. Pete moved quickly through the lot, his mind unable to focus on much more than walking by the empty Visitor's Information Desk. He took the three flights of stairs, in part because he didn't want to wait on the elevator, and also because he always had the slightest fear he'd get stuck in one.

Room 316 was eerily quiet. Gabby sat alongside the edge of the bed. Samuel was asleep. A needle pushed fluids in his veins through his wrist. A tiny tube under his nose provided him with oxygen. His face was pale, noticeably thinner than when Pete and Sarah had gone to visit. Gabby's eyes were red and tired-looking. She held

Samuel's hand in a manner as if she was trying to arm wrestle with him. She looked up and tried to smile at Pete.

Pete didn't know whether to speak or just stand in respectful silence. He walked behind Gabby and simply placed his hand on her shoulder. Samuel stirred and Gabby smoothed his hair away from his forehead. He struggled to open his eyes, closing them before opening them once again. He looked at the ceiling as if he was trying to recognize where he was.

"Daddy, Pete's here." Pete stepped to Gabby's side.

"Take me home, Gabby. I will not die in a hospital."

"I had no choice but to bring you here. I got scared because you were so sick. I didn't know what else to do."

"Just take me home." Samuel pulled on the needle taped to his hand. Gabby reached across the bed and grabbed Samuel's arm.

"Don't, Daddy. You have to leave that in your hand."

Pete walked around the front of the bed, and he took hold of the IV tube. He wasn't sure why he did so. He knew Samuel could pull out the needle if he really wanted to. It was more of a gesture of support for Gabby than anything else. Gabby pushed the nurse's button on the arm of the bed. Samuel looked at Gabby. His eyes showed a man who had given up.

"Take me home so I can die in peace."

Within moments the nurse appeared. She checked the needle and retaped Samuel's hand. "Mr. Gable, we need to keep this needle secure, okay? It's only there to help you feel better."

"I don't want to feel better. I want to go home." He began coughing deep from his chest, so deep it brought him almost upright into a sitting position. Blood gathered along the corners of his mouth. Gabby wiped it with a folded tissue, tears flowing down her cheeks. Samuel looked at his daughter. His coughing subsided. "Promise me you'll take me home."

"Okay, Daddy. Okay."

***

The ambulance brought Samuel to the front porch. Blackie circled the truck, barking, his tail raised high. Porter Bennett stood next to Gabby, her head on his shoulder. Pete and Sarah stood at the top of the steps. Samuel's wheelchair was on the grass, and the two EMS workers lifted Samuel down from a gurney and carried him to his chair. Gabby draped a blanket across Samuel's lap, and Pete took hold of the handles of the wheelchair.

"Hang on, Mr. Gable," Pete said. "We'll have you in your bed in just a minute."

Samuel spoke no words, and as Pete pulled Samuel up the steps backwards, Samuel winced. Blackie moved about the wheelchair as if trying to figure out how to climb on his master's lap. They soon had Samuel in his bed in the parlor. Gabby had ice water in a pitcher, and lemonade as well. For twenty-seven years, it was a kiss from Callie and a glass of lemonade that Samuel wanted when he came home from work each day.

Gabby and Sarah stepped out on the porch, each with a cup of coffee. Pete sat by Samuel's side in the parlor, watching him struggle to breathe as he slept. Gabby sat in her rocker, and Sarah sat in the swing to Gabby's left. Gabby stared toward the creek.

"Your father is a special man," Sarah said.

"He's the most incredible man I've ever known."

"I've never seen Pete so moved by someone other than his own father. He told me your dad is the only true hero he's ever known. And not necessarily for what he did on the battlefield. He heard another elderly man describe your dad one day. 'Samuel Gable is a man's man.'"

"I truly don't know how I'm going to make it without him. I've put my life on hold for the last year, but I couldn't imagine doing it any other way. He's always been there for me."

"Can I do anything? Help you around the house?"

"No, thanks. Just having you here has been a big help." Resolved to the fact that Sarah and Pete were supposed to be together, Gabby had no thought of being anything less than supportive of their marriage. "I don't get to talk much to other girls, so thank you. I spend my time taking care of Dad, taking care of the house. You know, I'm envious of the life he and Mom had. They had almost thirty years to spend together. I think that Dad's time in the war, and being away from her for three years, made him treat every day as if it were his last with her, with us. His love for her was a great example of what true love is."

The girls talked for over an hour, and for a brief while the weight eased off Gabby's shoulders.

Samuel slept through the night and most of the next day. Porter said it was best not to wake him to feed him. Samuel was past the stage where food would do him much good. Porter had the morphine ready when that time came. Now the only thing to do was keep Samuel as comfortable as possible. Pete stayed with Samuel until dark, and told Gabby to call if anything changed or if she just needed him.

Pete tossed and turned throughout the night. He couldn't shake the thought of Samuel fading away, a man whose purpose in life seemed to be that of protector, warrior. Pete had heard, had read, about the hard life that the people of Samuel's generation had faced. He knew it from talking with his own father, and mother to a certain degree. He knew they truly were a great generation, leading simple lives based around family and hard work. Surely they were frustrated watching their children, and their grandchildren, grow up seemingly unappreciative of the easy lives they had. And here, a man who looked at death every day for two years in a world halfway around the planet, never complaining about it, treating it as if it was his right and honor to do so, was getting ready to leave this world with little fanfare. Pete thought it sad for those who had never gotten the chance to know Samuel Gable, who would read his obituary with no more than a passing glance.

Sarah stayed at home with Kate the next morning while Pete headed back to Vaught's Holler. He'd received no phone calls through the night, so he hoped it had been a quiet evening. Gabby greeted him at the door, still in her purple gown. She wore no makeup, her eyes looked tired, and her hair hung low at her eyebrows.

"How is he?" Pete asked quietly.

"He's coughing up a good bit of blood. He drank a little water, but that's all."

They stood beside the bed. Samuel's breathing was labored, and his midsection bounced when he inhaled. His bed was flat, though his head was raised by two thick pillows. Pete sat, and Gabby stroked her father's forehead. She began to cry, and when she did, she turned and left the room. Pete heard the back door open as Gabby went to the back yard. He looked at the sad eyes of Samuel's lab Blackie. He looked at Samuel's pale skin, the dark spots which had formed along his arms. He took Samuel's hand, squeezing it lightly.

Samuel began to stir and opened his eyes briefly. He winced as he tried to shift his weight. Pete stood, trying to help by placing his hands alongside Samuel's midsection. Pete sat, taking hold of Samuel's hand again. He looked out over the pond, watching two mallards fade in and out of the fog that hovered above the water like two ships on some ancient sea. He wondered if they were the same ones that had skirted across the water the first day Pete and Samuel talked in the parlor. The ducks didn't seem to have a care, even unconcerned with a brown-and-white beagle puppy that hopped along the shore. The pup scampered back and forth along the bank, looking for a way to get to the ducks without getting wet. Pete smiled for a brief second, and turned and saw Samuel's dark eyes staring at the pond.

"Morning. How are you feeling?"

Samuel looked at Pete, still able to muster up the look that asked Pete, without the use of words, how long it was going to take before Pete stopped asking him that question.

"What are you doin' here?"

"I had nothing better to do." Pete smiled.

"You don't need to spend your time lookin' after me."

"Well, Gabby promised me a free lunch if I came over. You know I'm not passing up free food." Samuel managed a smile.

"I want you to do somethin' for me."

"Name it."

"Go into my bedroom." His voice was noticeably strained. "Look at the edge of my dresser. Along the mirror. Bring me the necklace hanging there."

"Yes, sir."

Pete walked into Samuel's room, lit only by the sunshine which crept in between the curtains at the window. He looked at the dark cherrywood dresser. It had a large mirror in the middle and shelves along the side. Two small pictures in brass frames were on each of the top two shelves. In one, Samuel held Gabby. She looked to be just a few months old. Samuel was rocking her, looking down into her eyes. The other picture was Samuel standing beside what had to be Caleb. The boy looked to be about five or six, and Samuel held a fish by its gills, still attached to the hook from the boy's fishing rod.

Pete found and retrieved the necklace. It was cold to the touch. The silver chain was dark around the edges where the links connected. The cross, an inch long and about the same in width, was smooth. Its shine made Pete think it had been recently cleaned. When he returned to the parlor, Gabby was holding a glass of water to her father's lips. Pete placed the necklace in Samuel's hand.

"Thanks," Samuel said after he swallowed the cool water. He held it gently in his hand, rubbing along the cross with his thumb and forefinger.

"That necklace means a lot to you," said Pete.

Samuel nodded. "My mother gave it to me when I first joined the Army. It was my dad's. His father had given it to him. I wore it every day. It made me feel like Dad was there with me. It made me think my family was watching over me. And then I gave it to Callie that night by the creek."

Gabby dabbed the corners of Samuel's mouth with a soft damp rag. "Daddy, how about some watermelon to moisten your mouth?"

"I'll give it a try."

Gabby went to the kitchen, where she sliced the melon into bite-size chunks. When she returned, Pete watched her feed him. Samuel tried to avoid eye contact with her, almost ashamed that she was having to hand-feed him. He ate a few pieces of the melon and then said he'd had enough. As she started back to the kitchen, he took her by the hand. She held the fork and bowl with her other, trying not to drop them on the bed.

"Here," he said, placing the necklace in her hand before closing his fingers around hers. "I want you to have this."

"No, Daddy, that's yours." She tried to put the necklace in his hand, and he slid it away.

"I'm going to step out on the porch for a bit," Pete said.

"Gabby," Samuel said, "I want you to have this. Please. For me."

Gabby looked at the necklace and began to cry. "Daddy." She struggled as the tears flowed. "I know how much this necklace means to you."

"That's why I want you to take it. I'll know my two favorite girls in the world will have worn it." For the first time, Gabby witnessed her father struggle to keep his composure. "Put it on for me."

She placed the bowl and fork on the nightstand. Her hands trembled as she put the necklace on. She rubbed it reverently. "You are the best father a girl could ever have." She took his hand and kissed it. "You took such good care of me. My hero was my father."

"Your Momma was the love of my life, but you taught me what real love was all about." He gently rubbed above his eye. "Gabby?"

"Yes, Daddy?" She wanted to be able to say the word *Daddy* as many times as she could, saying it to him.

"Is Pete still here?"

"Yes, sir. He's on the porch."

"Ask him to come here. Tell him to bring his recorder. One last time."

***

Pete walked into the room. The soft yellow lamp cast a blanket of serenity across the room. If not for Samuel lying in his bed, dying, holding on to his final days, it would have looked peaceful. And it still was, to some degree. And yet the sadness of the situation limited how peaceful it was.

"Gabby said you wanted me to bring the recorder."

"I did." His voice was strained and raspy.

"The three of us have become quite a team. I never knew how valuable this recorder would turn out to be. If we had to count on my pea brain to recount your stories, we'd all be up the creek." Pete had hoped to bring a smile to Samuel's face but it was not to be.

"I have one more story for you. Might better turn up the volume. I want to make sure it picks up my voice."

Pete rubbed his thumb along the black dial. "Done. As loud as it can go." He placed the recorder on the bed beside Samuel's shoulder. "Ready when you are. Can I get you anything before you start?"

"No. Don't know how much time I've got left. I have to say this before I go."

***

December, 1952

Samuel held Callie's hand tightly as they waited for the doctor. They shared the room with a young girl who looked to be a teenager. The girl, her mother by her side, was in the early stages of labor. Callie's forehead was soaked with perspiration, her face red and round. She had gained twenty pounds, though most of her weight gain was in her stomach.

"You're lookin' good, Callie," Samuel said. "The doc's on his way."

"I can't wait much longer," she said, her breathing labored. "This baby's telling me it's time to grab the sheets and warm water."

"Hold on to my hand. I'm with you all the way. You're doin' great. You're such a trooper."

The doctor, nurse close behind, walked in and closed the curtain around them. After examining Callie, the doctor instructed the nurse to prepare the delivery room. Samuel kissed Callie on the lips as they wheeled her down the hall. "I love you. I'll be right here."

Samuel paced the floor of the Elizabethton Hospital, occasionally glancing out the narrow window that looked out toward the back side of Iron Mountain. The sun was setting in a brilliant clear sky, casting Iron Mountain in soft green. There was no one else along the halls, which pleased Samuel. He was in no mood for conversation.

Almost an hour had passed, and a nurse walked up to Samuel who was standing next to the window. "Mr. Gable?"

"Yes?"

"Please follow me. I thought you might like to hold your new baby girl."

Samuel walked into a large room where four babies lay snuggled under blankets of blue or pink. The nurse lifted the infant, her hair full and black tucked under a pink beanie, into Samuel's arms. He looked into Gabby's eyes, and in that instant realized that life had held secrets from him. The depths of love being divulged to him, showing him that it was so much more encompassing than the love he'd shared with Callie, with his mother, with his siblings. He slipped his pinky inside her delicate hand, and she took hold as he began to cry. In that moment he found the answer to the question of life. It now contained more meaning than he'd ever imagined. He knew his life had a newfound purpose. With her tiny hand wrapped around his finger, he knew his purpose was to take care of this little angel, the blessing born from the love of his life.

The jungles of the South Pacific, where the stench of death hung heavy in every breath, had shown Samuel a side of the world that made him question how God could turn his back against man. It had made him feel that Satan and God had created an arena of death, like some massive coliseum bounded by jungles instead of stone, wagering in some unknown manner on who the victors were going to be. But Gabrielle Butler Gable had come into the world carrying in her eyes a Christmas gift the likes of which neither Callie nor Samuel had ever received. She was the symbol of a good and gracious God, the representation of heaven above.

***

Samuel's cough rattled deep, his body lunging forward in his bed. "Are you okay?" asked Pete, turning off the recorder.

Samuel coughed several more times, his body limp. He tried to wipe the blood from his hand on a hand towel beside him but didn't have the strength. "Is that recorder still on?"

"No, sir." Pete gently wiped the cloth along the corners of Samuel's mouth.

"Turn it back on. I'm not done."

Pete pressed Record.

"Gabby, Caleb," his scratchy voice managed. Pete quickly placed the recorder closer to Samuel's mouth. "This is the hard part." Tears streamed down his face. "I can't put into words what you mean to me. You brought me and your momma more happiness than we deserved. You made us a family. I used to watch you sleep when you were babies. I prayed that God would always let me protect you. And now I'm getting ready to join your momma, and I won't be able to fill that role anymore. But there'll be no whining and bellyaching after I'm gone. It's part of life.

"Caleb, I don't know if you'll ever get this message. My heart's held a hollow spot since you left. I made you feel like the accident was your fault. It wasn't. You would've never done anything intentionally to hurt your momma." His voice faltered. "I hope you can forgive me. I love you, son."

He struggled to take a breath. "Gabby," he said, stopping briefly to wipe the tears from his cheeks with his pajama sleeves, "I've loved you since the moment I first laid eyes on you. You are an angel." He closed his eyes as though it would give him strength to continue. "In you God created the closest thing to perfection this side of heaven. You got your momma's eyes, her smile, and most important, her heart. And that's some kind of combination." Again he struggled to take a breath. "Thank you for takin' care of me all these months. I know it ain't been easy and I hate you had to go through it. I love you with all my heart."

The click of the recorder was the only sound in the room. Pete and Samuel sat in silence. Pete looked toward the ceiling to slow his tears, but it didn't help. Samuel looked down toward his lap. He breathed as deeply as his tired lungs would allow.

"I'm ready to go now." He breathed slowly. "I'm ready to go."

***

It was late afternoon, and a few neighbors stopped by to bring food and check on Samuel. Porter sat beside Samuel, watching him sleep, his breathing short and labored. Gabby and Pete were on the porch. The sky was china blue, trying to make the world seem as if no sadness or pain existed. The temperature hovered around fifty degrees, and the wind was still and quiet, allowing the running waters of Birch Tree Creek to sing a lonely song. Gabby sat in her rocker, taking a short break from her father's side. Pete sat in the swing facing her.

They spoke little. When Gabby heard the sharp roar of the motorcycle turn off the highway, she glanced up in mild curiosity. Bikes weren't a common sight, except maybe Sunday afternoons when tourists were out to roam the Tennessee countryside. The bike turned in the driveway and came up to the front of the house. Pete stood while Gabby watched the long-haired driver dismount.

Caleb wore no helmet. He wore black jeans, a white short-sleeved shirt, and a black leather vest. He walked toward the porch.

Gabby slowly stood and walked to the top of the steps. Pete stood too as Caleb made his way up the steps. Gabby and Caleb stood face to face. Twenty-seven years had passed, and now he was home. Their eyes met, Gabby's lined with tears, Caleb's lined with pain. Caleb just stared, not knowing what to say.

Gabby slapped his face. "You sorry excuse for a son. How could you stay away when you knew Daddy was dying?" As he tried to speak she fell into his arms, crying silently. She pounded his chest. For minutes he held her, and no words were spoken.

When Caleb finally walked up beside Samuel's bed, Gabby walked to the other side. Blackie lay on the bed, not even attempting to raise his head at the stranger come to visit. Gabby began stroking his hair.

"Daddy," she said softly, "you've got a visitor." Samuel opened his eyes briefly, and they looked cloudy and unfocused. "Daddy," she said again, and began rubbing his arm.

Samuel opened his eyes again, looking up at Gabby.

"You have a visitor, Daddy."

Samuel looked to his left. Pete and somebody else stood by the foot of his bed. He seemed to study the long, lean body standing next to Pete.

Caleb smiled when he noticed Samuel looking at him. "Hi, Pop."

"Caleb?" Samuel whispered.

Caleb nodded. "Yes, sir. It's me." Caleb took Samuel's frail hand in his. His eyes began to water. He had not envisioned his father in such a weakened state. The last time he had seen his dad, he was as strong as the tallest poplar on Jefferson Mountain.

"I'm sorry, son." Samuel's bottom lip began to quiver. "I'm sorry I...drove you away."

"You didn't drive me away. *I* drove me away."

"No, that's..."

"Yes, it is." Caleb glanced at his feet for a second before looking into his father's eyes. "That day —" He tried hard to keep his composure. "That day at the creek, two of us died. That day was the day I didn't deserve to be a son, a brother. Because of me, the family stopped being a family as far I was concerned."

"Son, that's not true."

"Let me finish. I've been rehearsin' for years what I was gonna say if I ever got the chance. I knew things could never be the same. Every time you or Gabby would look at me, you'd see the person who killed Momma."

Gabby shook her head. "Caleb, that's not true. We love you. We never got the chance to tell you that after you left. We had no idea you weren't coming back."

"How could I come back? I figured the best way to help you forget what happened that day was to take away as many reminders as possible. And I was the biggest reminder of all. But now I'm back, and I just want to say I'm so s-sorry." Caleb lowered his head as tears flowed. Samuel slowly placed his hand on Caleb's forearm.

"It's okay, son. It was an accident. We all know you would have never done anything intentionally to hurt your mother."

"Can you forgive me?"

"I've never needed to forgive you. You just need to forgive yourself."

***

Nighttime came. The clouds hung low and thick, tinted a pale orange, as if the earth was lined with hidden spotlights pointing skyward. Samuel had slept all afternoon, his head tilted to the side. His breathing was becoming more labored, and the death rattle was eerily audible. His sunken chest moved as his heart began working harder. Vital organs began shutting down. Porter had administered the morphine.

Caleb walked to the highway. The ominous sky lit up the night, not to the point where shadows were cast, as it would be on a moonlit night, but the darkness was somehow softened. Caleb stood above the tiny bridge, looking at the waters that took his mother's final breath away. He wore a leather coat, his hands slipped into the pockets. Moving to the edge of the stream, amongst the backdrop of the waters running hard across rocks centuries old, crickets called out from the meadows as he knelt. He remembered the squealing of brakes; the crashing of metal as the car overturned; the frantic pleas of his mother. The look in her eyes when she breathed her last.

As he lowered his head, he felt a hand upon his shoulder. Pete knelt beside Caleb, but spoke no words. Together they looked in silence, and Caleb had never felt such comfort from a stranger. For long moments they stayed, almost frozen beside the creek. A truck passed from the west, its exhaust pipe rattling off into nothingness.

***

The morning sun crept above the horizon of Shady Mountain, long shadows stretching across the valleys and hillsides. Sarah brought coffee and bagels, though she wasn't sure if anyone would have an appetite. Pete had slept on the couch. Caleb had slept in the guest room that once was his bedroom. Gabby spent most of the evening by her father's side, stroking his hair, talking to him about how much she loved fishing with him, and how mad it made him when boys would come to the door to take her on dates in high school.

Samuel's breathing reached a point where any breath looked like it would be his last. His chest was heaving in quick, short bursts. Hospice services from Boone sent a nurse, and she was preparing the family for what to expect. She was kind and caring as she spoke. Caleb asked how long she thought he had, and she told him it was hard to predict, but felt like it would be no more than a day or two. Gabby brought extra chairs into the parlor from the kitchen table. She and Caleb sat on either side of Samuel. Pete and Sarah sat near the foot of the bed. Porter and Earline brought food and placed it in the refrigerator and pantry. Talk was small. Most of the time they sat and watched Samuel breathing, the rattle in his throat becoming louder and more pronounced.

By late afternoon a few other families in the area had stopped by with food and to offer prayers. Sarah answered the door, to allow Gabby time to sit with her father. The wind began to pick up, and the day, though clear, was becoming brisk. Leaves blew across the yard, and the pond rippled to the point where it was no longer possible to see the bottom.

"Remember when Pop slipped possum into Momma's beef stew?" Caleb asked, holding tightly to Samuel's hand.

"She laid into him pretty good, didn't she?" Gabby said and laughed. "You know, the stew wasn't the only thing he added local livestock to."

"What? What else?"

"Well, let's see. Sometimes sausage gravy had more than sausage. It had jowls and chitterlings in it. Sometimes we had pigeon meat with our quail."

"You're kiddin' me."

"The worst was…" She paused.

"Was what?" Sarah asked.

"Meatballs."

"What about meatballs?" Caleb asked.

"He was known to toss a hog testicle in there from time to time."

"No way," said Sarah in disbelief.

"Holy crap," Caleb said as he shook his head. "Why the did he do that?"

"Daddy said everything was edible. After starvin' in the war, he was bound and determined to prove that point."

The four of them laughed quietly, though Caleb's stomach churned a bit. As Caleb talked of the time Samuel brought home a gopher to skin and eat, Gabby rose from her seat. She touched Samuel's face.

"He's gone," she whispered.

Caleb stopped laughing and joined Gabby beside the bed. There was an immediate silence in the room. Pete and Sarah stood and inched closer to Gabby and Caleb. Gabby began to cry. She leaned over and kissed him on the forehead.

"Bye, Daddy. I love you." She placed her head on his shoulder, trying to feel the warmth of his body one last time. Caleb wiped the tears from his eyes with the back of his hand, and Sarah took hold of Pete's hand. In the silence of the parlor, the hero, the man's man, passed quietly on.

Chapter Twenty-Five

The wind whipped snow across Vaught's Holler, sending flakes on an endless journey. All across the valley and along the banks of Birch Tree Creek the land had become a blanket of white. On the sharp hillsides, rising skyward in random waves as the mountains of the Appalachians were known to do, bare trees stood pale in black and gray, providing sharp contrast to the white floor below them. Gabby raised her purple scarf above her mouth as the bitter cold stung her face. The black limo slowly turned off the highway and onto the road that had not been traveled upon since the snow began falling the afternoon before.

It was Saturday morning, and the funeral was set for ten o'clock. Caleb, dressed in jeans and his leather jacket, walked down the porch steps as the limo pulled in front of the house. Two men exited the car, both wearing suits of black, and quickly opened the side doors. The portly man who sat in the passenger seat extended his hand to Caleb, and Gabby stepped down the white porch carefully while Caleb spoke to the man in hushed tones. Porter helped Earline, and Bert's widow Mary, down the steps where they'd waited in the living room. The men who'd opened the doors assisted Earline and Mary across the snowy driveway and into the limo. There were only the faint sounds of sniffling as the limo pulled back on the highway.

When the long car pulled into the parking lot of the Eternal Springs Baptist Church, Pete and Sarah waited outside the side door under a green-and-white awning. Pete hugged Gabby and shook Caleb's hand.

"Please sit with the family," Gabby said as she shook off snow from her scarf.

"Are you sure?" Pete asked.

"Absolutely. Daddy wouldn't have it any other way."

Pete helped Mary through the side door that led to the sanctuary. It had been nine years, almost to the day, since she'd buried Bert. Gabby and Caleb walked side by side, and Pete and Sarah came next with Mary. Porter and Earline brought up the rear. As they reached the front row, Pete recognized Vera and Helen standing in the second row, tissues in hand, eyes red. Every seat was taken and folks lined the back walls.

An American flag was draped over the autumn-oak casket. Gabby sat first and the others followed suit. Reverends Ed Douglas and Jim Speagle were seated near the pulpit, and silver-haired Reverend Speagle stoically watched the daughter and son of his good friend sit in front of the casket. White carnations, red roses, and pink mums were displayed on two standing sprays on either side of the casket. Reverend Douglas spoke first, and twelve-year-old Anna Spratling sang "How Great Thou Art." Reverend Speagle spoke, his voice wavering softly as he told of the man who was Samuel Gable.

When the limo made its way up Gunter's Road, Caleb stared blankly at the scene which looked so eerily familiar. The tent, the folding chairs positioned over the green carpet in front of the casket, the people gathered around the tent. His stomach churned to the point where he felt nauseous. The memories, the guilt, the anguish of feeling responsible for his mother's death surfaced like soldiers lying in wait to ambush the enemy.

Whereas Callie's burial had seemed surreal in that the serenity of the mountain stood in stark contrast to the sad occasion, on this day the mountain seemed bitter, angry. It was apropos for the passing of a man who represented the very core of the people who defined the Appalachians. It was as if the mountain was revolting, showering down the dark, desolate power which was a part of its mystery; as if the heart of the mountain had been saddened that a shining star and symbol of its own existence was no longer on display; like a mother placing her dead child into the grave, forever silent, no longer able to exhibit the power and resolve for which the child stood.

The rifles cracked loud and fast when the twenty-one-gun salute took place, the sounds quickly disappearing into the whirling wind. Afterward, two soldiers proceeded to remove the flag from the casket, where they carefully folded it with great ceremony into triangular fashion and placed it in the hands of Gabby. They saluted her, representing soldiers everywhere, past and present.

And so two souls had come to be reunited for eternity. What began on a fall night sixty-six years ago, on the soft bank of Sinking Creek, had come full circle. Their lives had been sparked by a love so strong that it endured three years of separation. And though Callie was taken away from Samuel all too soon, he treated his remaining time as he had in the jungles of the Philippines, patiently waiting, surviving, until he would be with his beloved Callie.

On that clear day up in Gunter's Hollow, he found her arms again.

Chapter Twenty-Six

Gabby barely heard the knock on her door. She sat at the kitchen table, looking at real-estate listings. A year had passed since Samuel died, and she decided she couldn't leave her home on Jefferson Mountain, her parents' home; her grandparents' home. She'd earned her real-estate license and taken a job with a company that was building home sites on Iron Mountain. Though that was her primary focus, she sold other houses in Carter Springs as well. She was dating a man from Boone named Jake McCarthy. It took several months after Samuel passed before she could even think about herself and the loneliness that engulfed the big house after he died. And then she met Jake. Sarah was the one who'd introduced them. She'd had a birthday party for Pete and introduced them to each other there.

When Gabby opened the door, Pete stood at her doorstep. His hands were behind his back. "Hello, Gabby." He stepped forward and gave her a long embrace with one arm, the other still held behind him.

"Oh, Pete. It's so good to see you."

"Can I come in for a minute?"

"Absolutely. Would you like some coffee? I have some fresh tea."

"No, thanks. I just wanted to bring you something." He took hold of her hand and placed a book in it.

She looked curiously at the hardback book, saw theT picture of a familiar house, surrounded in black so that the house jumped off the cover. She glanced at the title: *A Month of Tomorrows*.

"Thanks," she said, a bit puzzled. "A book. How sweet of you."

"It's not just *a* book. It's *his* book."

"Whose book?"

"Your father's. He wanted me to write something about his life, remember? So I wrote a novel based on him, based on the incredible man that he was."

She began crying tears of joy. "Oh my God."

Pete opened the book and turned it toward Gabby, where she read:

This book is dedicated to the memory of Samuel Gable.
Strong and brave but a man of gentle ways.
A great father and wonderful husband.
A loyal friend.
He was truly a man's man.
Rest in peace, soldier.

About the Author

Chuck Walsh is a co-author of ***Faces of Freedom*** (featured on Sean Hannity's book list), a book that recognizes the noble lives of U.S. soldiers who died while fighting in Iraq or Afghanistan. His debut novel, ***A Month of Tomorrows***, is based on the life of his uncle, WWII hero, Rubin Stout. His book about travel, ***A Passage Back***, is scheduled for release in 2015. Chuck lives with his wife in South Carolina.

Please visit Chuck's website, www.chuckwalshwriter.com, and follow him on Twitter at @ChuckWalsh

Plan Your Next Escape!
What's Your Reading Pleasure?

Whether it's brawny Highlanders, intriguing mysteries, young adult romance, illustrated children's books, or uplifting love stories, Vinspire Publishing has the adventure for you!

For a complete listing of books available, visit our website at www.vinspirepublishing.com.

Like us on Facebook at
www.facebook.com/VinspirePublishing

Follow us on Twitter at
www.twitter.com/vinspire2004

and join our newsletter for details of our upcoming releases, giveaways, and more!
http://t.co/46UoTbVaWr

We are your travel guide to your next adventure!

Made in the USA
Columbia, SC
01 September 2020

17803398R00214